Readers love
by TARA LAIN

"Don't miss this one. It will put a smile on your face. It will make your day."
—Sinfully Gay Romance Book Reviews

"This was a fun read that I would recommend to those who enjoy lighthearted romance."
—Gay Book Reviews

"The writing in *Driven Snow* is spotless, and the story unfolded beautifully! Strong characters and a solid plot made reading this story a pleasure."
—(un)Conventional Book Views

"I love how Tara Lain took this fairytale theme and turned the story into a wonderful M/M contemporary fantasy romance."
—The Novel Approach

By Tara Lain

Taylor Maid

LONG PASS CHRONICLES
Outing the Quarterback
Canning the Center
Tackling the Tight End

LOVE IN LAGUNA
Knight of Ocean Avenue
Knave of Broken Hearts
Prince of the Playhouse
Lord of a Thousand Steps

PENNYMAKER TALES
Sinders and Ash
Driven Snow
Beauty, Inc.
Sinders and Ash and Beauty, Inc. (Print Only Anthology)

TALES OF THE HARKER PACK
The Pack or the Panther
Wolf in Gucci Loafers
Winter's Wolf
The Pack or the Panther & Wolf in Gucci Loafers (Print Only Anthology)

THE ALOYSIUS TALES
Spell Cat

Published by DREAMSPINNER PRESS
www.dreamspinnerpress.com

SINDERS AND ASH AND BEAUTY, INC.

TARA LAIN

Published by
DREAMSPINNER PRESS

5032 Capital Circle SW, Suite 2, PMB# 279, Tallahassee, FL 32305-7886 USA
www.dreamspinnerpress.com

Sinders and Ash and Beauty, Inc.
© 2016 Tara Lain.

Cover Art
© 2016 Reese Dante.
http://www.reesedante.com
Cover content is for illustrative purposes only and any person depicted on the cover is a model.

ISBN: 978-1-63477-835-0
Library of Congress Control Number: 2016914704
Published November 2016
v. 1.0
Sinders and Ash (1st Edition) previously published by Amber Quill Press, 2012.
Sinders and Ash (2nd Edition) previously published by Dreamspinner Press, October 2015.
Beauty Inc. previously published by Dreamspinner Press, June 2016.

Printed in the United States of America
∞
This paper meets the requirements of
ANSI/NISO Z39.48-1992 (Permanence of Paper).

Contents

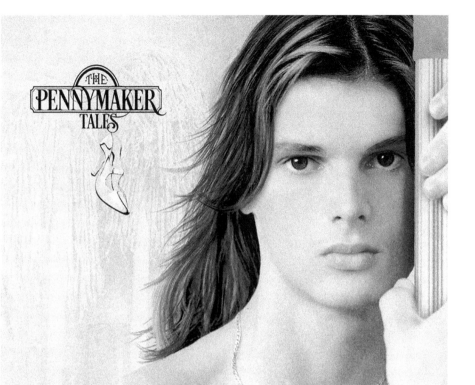

THE
PENNYMAKER
TALES

SINDERS
AND ASH

TARA LAIN

To Lynn Lorenz, a special friend,
who inspires me and has helped me so much in my career

Author's Note

FAIRY TALES are usually defined as stories of extraordinary happiness (although many original fairy tales didn't end happily). They're also sometimes described as stories that could never happen. I beg to differ. The Pennymaker Tales take popular fairy tale themes and weave them into contemporary stories that, while larger than life, could happen—and oh how we wish they would. I hope you'll enjoy these tales of heroes, wise counselors, evil queens, and wicked stepmothers; and one small elf who just may or may not be a fairy godmother. Welcome to The Pennymaker Tales.

CHAPTER 1

DAMN THE ashes! Mark pulled off his knit cap and banged it against his dirty pant leg. He could barely see for the soot. Not that you had to see well to wash fireplaces, and they had him cleaning every damned one. Everything had to be perfect for the arrival of the "handsome prince."

Mark gave his horn-rimmed glasses a quick wipe on an edge of the blue cotton jacket that housekeeping gave him to wear each day. The hotel staff washed the jacket, but the jeans were his own, and it was hell to keep them clean. He stepped away from the huge fireplace and glanced in a decorative mirror. Yep. He resembled a tall, slim raccoon. It would be funny if—

The door to the small private dining room cracked open. He yanked the cap on over his hair and quickly replaced the glasses as he stepped back into the big brick opening and began wiping the sooty walls again.

"Bernice, Bitsy, get in here. I want to check your makeup." The woman's voice accompanied a general rise in sound through the open door. When Mark came into the small dining room from the kitchen, he'd gotten a glimpse of the lobby. Packed with frantic looky-loos and hopeful contenders all intent on witnessing the arrival of the conquering hero. What the hell was their strategy? Appear casual as they hung around staring at a billionaire's son?

It got quiet again as the door closed. He kept wiping, with his eyes fixed on his task. Sponge up, down, rinse. He didn't need to look to know it was Mrs. Fanderel and her girls. Being the sister of the owner of the resort gave her all kinds of privileges—at least in her own mind.

The nasal edge to her voice grated up his spine. "Let's go over by the window. The light's better."

"Mo-ther." The lower voice was Bernice. Pretty, but with a whiny tendency that gave her face a sour look sometimes. "He's here."

Eyes crept up his back like ants. He kept wiping.

"Pay no attention, girls. Sinders won't bother us. Now let me look at you."

Mark glanced over, past the round table and chairs in the center of the room. Mrs. Fanderel had Bernice's face in her hand and was wiping at her cheeks. He looked right and found himself eye to eye with Bitsy. The little blonde gave him a smile and a slow wink. He tried not to smile back, but she really was cute. She even seemed nice, compared to the rest of the family.

Mrs. Fanderel waved a hand. "All right, Bernice. Touch up your lipstick, darling, and you're ready to go. Bitsy, your turn."

Bernice poked at her lips with a pencil. "She shu-ben't eben be going out dere." She glanced at her efforts, then looked over at her mother, who was picking at Bitsy's blonde curls. "I'm the oldest and have the first claim."

Her mother didn't pause. "We have no idea what type he likes. You don't want him in some other family, do you? If he likes Bitsy, he has her."

Bitsy tried to pull out of her mother's grasp. "She's right. She wants him; I don't. She's got way more going for her than I do. I'll go up to the room, and you guys meet him."

The mother's fingers tightened on Bitsy's arm. "This is the fifth-richest family in America. Ashton is supposed to be handsome and charming. You act as if you were being sent to your death."

"I don't want to marry anyone until I've finished school. You know that. And maybe not then."

"Dammit, his money could send you to music school on the moon if you want to go there. You'll be charming, you'll be gracious, and you will marry him if he picks you… is that understood?"

Bernice sent a glower Mark's way. He looked back at his work. "Mother, the fairy boy is taking this all in. Do you think we could discuss it elsewhere?"

Mrs. Fanderel glanced at him. "We're not going to discuss it at all. It's settled." She nodded toward him. "And I'm sure Sinders wishes both of you well, since he is a member of the staff, and therefore his future depends on my goodwill."

He just kept washing.

"Be sure you go out through the kitchen when you're finished, Sinders. It wouldn't do to have any of the guests see you looking like that."

Bitsy laughed. "Hell, even covered in soot he's prettier than either of us."

What was she thinking saying something like that?

He glanced over as Mrs. Fanderel pushed Bitsy toward the door. "Have you lost your mind? He's a strange boy in a cap, and a homosexual to boot. Who in their right mind would consider such a person pretty?"

Bernice looked back at him with an odd expression. Then they were gone the way they had come.

He dropped the sponge in the bucket with a splash. Just what his jeans needed. Wet dirt. His heart beat fast and he squatted down on the hearth. Sadly, she was right. His future did kind of depend on her. He wanted this job. Yes, it was crappy and menial, but the guests were superrich and, when they got drunk, could even be generous. The girls in housekeeping thought he was strange, but they still liked the fact he did all the really bad jobs, so they shared tips with him. They liked that he didn't hit on them too. Plus, at nights he got tips of his own when he worked overflow on room service.

He had saved a thousand dollars so far by eating only the two meals the resort provided. He could never do that in the city. Living there cost so much it was hard to even get by, much less save. And here, since he was willing to take that hole in the attic as a room, he even had a little private space to do his designs. Not much time, true, but he got by on little sleep. He just had to keep his head down and not stand out any more than he already did. Standing out was bad. Standing out got you pissed on. Yeah, standing out got you fucked.

He pulled himself up and surveyed the fireplace. One more bad spot. He rinsed the sponge in the gray water.

The door opened again. He tensed. Had the women come back? He looked up to see a tiny man in a three-piece green suit stagger in the door. *Green? Really?* "Can I help you, sir?" He stepped forward. The man looked like he might fall.

"Yes, please. May I sit down?"

Mark rushed forward, wiping his hands again before he touched the deep red upholstery. "Of course, sir." He pulled out a chair from the table and went to help the little man. Heck, he could have thrown him over his shoulder if necessary. Mark wasn't supertall. Five-eleven last he checked. But this man was just a little over five feet—gray hair, rimless glasses, a natty striped shirt with white cuffs, and a bright red flower in his buttonhole. Quite the dandy.

He helped the gentleman into the chair.

"Thank you so much. It's quite a crush out there. I got caught behind a determined mother and her trio of chicks. Thought I might be asphyxiated by the perfume."

Mark grinned. "It is quite a ravening horde, isn't it?"

The man leaned back in the chair and fanned himself with his hand. "I particularly like the subtlety with which they intend to just happen upon him. All five hundred of them. LOL, as they say."

Funny. Just what Mark had thought.

The gentleman extended the hand he'd used to fan. "I'm Carstairs Pennymaker."

Really? "Uh, Mark Sintorella. I probably shouldn't shake. I've been cleaning the fireplace and I'm really dirty."

"Nonsense, my boy, nothing gets on me." He grasped Mark's hand in his and pressed his other hand over the top of the shake. Such gestures sometimes made Mark nervous. Too creepy. But in this man it seemed natural, so he shook back.

"Can I get you something, sir? Water?"

"No, no. I'm feeling much better, thanks to your kind ministrations."

Mark stepped back. "Then I best get to work."

"But aren't you going to witness the great arrival, my boy?"

"I couldn't go out there looking like this." He waved a hand at his soot-covered jacket. Then he laughed. "In fact, I've been warned not to."

"Well now, that's easily remedied. A little face wash. Remove the jacket and, poof, you're clean. Or at least reasonably so. As for your warning, well, I am a pretty valued guest here at the resort. I require some assistance getting back to my room and"—he waved a hand in a graceful circle and ended pointing toward Mark—"I pick you."

Mark pointed behind him. "My fireplace."

"Is quite clean enough. Look." He pointed to where the afternoon sun shone in on the bricks. Damned if it didn't look remarkably clean.

"All right, sir. If you need some help, of course I'll assist you."

"You're most kind. I will sit here and catch my breath, while you go in the kitchen and clean up. Then we shall proceed."

"Actually, I could take you out through the kitchen, and then you wouldn't have to endure the crush of people."

The impish face lit up. "What? And miss all the fun?"

A few minutes later, Mark leaned over the back sink in the hotel kitchen. It was after lunch and prep for dinner was under way. He wanted to get this done and get the hell out of here before—

"This isn't your damned bathroom, Sinders."

Too late. Mark wiped his face, slipped on his glasses, and stood up, his back still to Richard the Bastard Sous Chef. Yep, that's what they called him—behind his back.

"Sorry, sir. A guest asked me to help him with something, and I needed to clean up first."

Mark felt the guy's breath on the back of his neck. *Creepy creep.* "I'm sure there are others who can help the guest. You don't need to be using my kitchen as an en suite."

"There may be others who could help, sir, but he asked me. And he's waiting."

There was a pause. Richard's sour breath warmed his neck and he tried not to shiver. "Very well. Get out of here. And don't let me catch you primping in the kitchen again."

"Yes. Thank you, chef." Shit, that man gave him the willies.

He headed full speed toward the kitchen door leading into the small dining room, ditching his dirty jacket in the hamper on the way. The short-sleeved T-shirt wasn't much, but he'd hand-painted it himself, so it had a little style. He just needed to get Mr. Pennymaker to his room in one piece.

Near the door he stopped and took a big, slow inhalation. Maybe the great arrival had already happened and he wouldn't have to deal with it at all. He had no desire to see the arrival of Ashton Armitage. Okay, that was a lie. He was fascinated. Kind of like he would be at the idea of seeing a man from outer space. That's how much Mark had in common with a person of that much wealth and privilege. Hell, he'd lived on the streets for months after his family tossed him out because he wouldn't admit that being gay was a lifestyle choice. Since then, he'd had days where he had to choose between food and buying a piece of cloth to make a new design. The material usually won.

He adjusted his hat and pushed through the swinging door. Mr. Pennymaker snored softly in the chair. Mark smiled. Maybe he'd get out of this adventure after all. "Excuse me, sir."

The gray eyes flew open. "All ready? Wonderful. I had a few winks and I'm rarin' to go."

"Perhaps Armitage has already arrived."

"Oh no, he'd never arrive without me."

"Excuse me?"

"Just joshing. But I feel certain he hasn't arrived. Come on."

The little man stood and walked toward the door to the lobby at top speed. Hadn't he just been fainting a few minutes ago? Mark hurried to keep up with him.

As they reached the door, Pennymaker looked over his shoulder. "Great shirt, by the way. Did you make it?"

"Uh, yes."

"It has that couture quality."

Mark couldn't help it. He beamed. Four hours he'd hand-painted the shirt and distressed it. It wasn't often somebody noticed him for anything he was proud of.

Through the door, the crowd hit like a warm wall. Mr. Pennymaker slithered and pushed between the bodies, dragging Mark behind him, until he emerged at the head of the pack looking straight at the front door. People stared daggers at the little man. Hiding sounded good. "Excuse me, sir. You seem much better. Why don't I leave you here and get on with my work?"

"No, dear boy. I need you to be here with me showing off your beautiful T-shirt. Besides, you want to see him too, don't you?"

"I don't really care about it, no." Why did Mr. Pennymaker care about the T-shirt?

Pennymaker cocked his head. His expression combined with his green suit made Mark think of a leprechaun. "Ah, let's not tell fibs— even to ourselves." He grinned.

No, dammit, he didn't want to see the man....

The noise of the crowd swelled. Whispers. Even a few shouts.

"He's coming."

"Car just pulled up."

"I see him!" The last was accompanied by a squeal that would have done justice to a rock star. Somebody bumped Mark from behind, and a woman smashed into Mr. Pennymaker with her purse. *Well, hell.* Mark stepped closer to protect the little elf. He maneuvered so he blocked people from the side and shielded part of Pennymaker's back with both arms spread wide. A big man smashed into him again. "Watch where you're stepping, please, sir." The man scowled but backed up a step.

"Oh my God."

"He's beautiful."

"Oh, look."

Mark tried to keep the press of bodies, mostly female, away from Mr. Pennymaker, who suddenly grinned up at him. Mark smiled back. The little man moved his gaze to the side and Mark followed. And stopped.

Some part of his mind wanted to run. He knew he shouldn't look. The sight was Medusa and—he turned to stone. He couldn't quite breathe.

Walking into the lobby behind a man who might be a bodyguard and a woman who hovered was—perfection. Tall. Not skyscraper tall so you couldn't kiss and fuck at the same time. Just the right tall. Slender but still broad shouldered. He'd say lanky, except that sounded awkward, and this guy was grace. Lithe. That was it. Like a cat. Brown hair. Totally inadequate word—brown. The light reflected off the light taupe color so it shone like a glittering silver curtain around his face. As Mark watched, Ashton Armitage took off his sunglasses and crinkled the corners of wide eyes at the man who came to greet him. Stunning.

The greeter gave a half bow. "Mr. Armitage, I'm Alan Macintosh, the manager. We're delighted to have you here."

The crinkles again. "You have a very going concern here, Mr. Macintosh."

Oh, beautiful voice. Like a song. A love song. A love song to Mark's cock.

Armitage looked around the lobby packed with people. The guy had to know they were all there to look at him, but he acted as if it were an ordinary occurrence that every guest in the resort would be in the lobby. "What a lively place. I'm sure I'll enjoy my stay."

Mrs. Fanderel pushed through the crowd. "Mr. Armitage, I'm Beatrice Fanderel, sister to Mr. Marcusi, who owns the resort. He had to be away today."

Mark knew via the grapevine that Marcusi was hiding in his suite because his sister wanted to do the greeting.

Mrs. Fanderel stuck out her hand behind her and made a fast propelling motion. Bernice stepped up. "My daughters and I… this is Bernice." The girl practically curtseyed.

Good grief.

Mrs. Fanderel looked around, stared at Bitsy hanging back, and frowned at her. The pretty little blonde looked like she controlled a sigh and stepped forward. Her mother smiled brightly at Armitage. "And this is Bitsy."

The reluctant charmer extended her hand, and Armitage took it with a smile that would have floored most women. Hell, those clean white teeth made Mark's knees weak. Bitsy stood her ground.

"I'm delighted to meet you, Bitsy." *Oh, that voice.*

She gave a little smile. "Likewise." She took her hand back.

He had to give it to the girl. Mark might have passed out at the contact.

"Thank you for the kind greeting, Mrs. Fanderel." Armitage looked at the manager. "Now, if you'll direct me to check-in."

The manager practically fainted at the thought. "Oh no, sir. All the check-in arrangements have been made." He gestured to the bellman beside him. *The lucky little sod. He'd won the lottery the bellmen conducted. Sure would have been nice to be in on that.* "Here's Ricardo, who will show you and your party to your suites."

"Thank you, Mr. Macintosh." Armitage flashed a smile at the assembled multitude, then shifted his gaze like a homing device to the left.

Blue. His eyes were blue. Did Mark imagine it? Did those wide eyes pause for a fraction of a second? Yeah, looking at the weird kid in the cap and glasses. But it still made his heart beat too fast.

Armitage turned and moved toward the elevator that would take him to a special wing of the hotel where the VIPs were kept. Of course, in this place, it was all a question of degree of VIPness.

Mr. Pennymaker was smiling up at him, gray eyes twinkling. *Cat. Canary. Yeah.* The little guy thought he was pretty smart. Of course, it didn't take a clairvoyant to see the erection pushing out the front of Mark's jeans. Jesus, he wanted to sit down. He did not want to be attracted to Ashton Armitage. No way, no how.

That little canary in his head chirped *Too late.*

MAN, IT felt good to sit down. Ash let his head fall back onto the arm of the sofa. His hand actually hurt from shaking and his cheeks from smiling. He gave one last big smile and wave to the bellman who had shown them to their rooms. "Thank you, Ricardo. I know we'll be really comfortable here."

His assistant, Veronica *call-me-Ronnie*, pushed some twenties into the guy's hand and bingo, they were alone. He let out a long, slow breath and massaged his hand.

Ronnie laughed. "How was that for a greeting? Jesus, I don't think you got that much attention when you were on the cover of *People*."

He looked up. "Which time?" He stretched out his legs on the soft cushions. "That's what a marriage rumor will do for you. Nice suite, though."

"Yeah." She looked around the huge sitting room with its elegant, traditional décor. "I thought you were crazy for choosing this place for your 'wife hunt,' but it looks like you can be comfortable while you suffer."

He sighed. "Thanks. Way to make me feel better."

She walked to the couch, shoved his feet over, and sat. Her skinny ass didn't take up much room. "You have a choice, Ash."

Shit. She was not comforting. He pulled his legs from behind her butt and sat up. "You mean I can choose not to get married and give up my inheritance."

"You're smart and talented, if you decide to exercise either one. You can live on your own. You don't need the family's money."

He grinned at her. "Why do I employ you again?"

"Because you need someone who'll tell you the truth, bucko."

"I like being rich."

"Do you? I hadn't noticed."

He stared at her. She was pretty in a boyish, coltish, touch-me-in-the-wrong-place-and-you-die sort of way. And he adored her for just the reason she gave. *Trust Ronnie for the truth. Count on it.* Right now that truthful stare hit him in the gut. Yeah, he was rich and he was miserable. "I'd probably be just as unhappy if I were poor."

Her dark eyes never wavered. "But at least you could tell the truth."

He shrugged. "Truth is overrated."

"On what planet?"

He jumped up, walked into the small, efficient kitchen, and pulled open the fridge. Champagne, chocolate-covered strawberries, iced vodka. He raised his voice. "Want a drink?"

"It's not even two o'clock yet."

"Something magic about two o'clock?" He slammed the refrigerator door and grabbed a jar of cashews from the counter. "Damned plastic." He managed to rip off the top and popped a handful of nuts into his mouth. The salt hit his tongue. Okay, this wasn't what he wanted. He wandered back into the dining area.

Ronnie patted the sofa. "Ash, sit."

She had his number. He did a slow saunter back to the couch. "Yeah."

"Quit making yourself more miserable. If you're going to go through with this travesty, then get on with it. Put on something nice, go downstairs, and meet the candidates."

"How bad can it be? I don't have anything else I want to do, right?"

"If you say so."

A half hour later, dressed in casual slacks and a summer shirt, he hit the lobby. His bodyguard hovered in the background, but Ash told him to stay out of sight. Hell, he couldn't find a wife with a handgun at his side.

Five steps off the elevator.

"Mr. Armitage, I'm Lavinda Oscular and this is my daughter Chrissy."

He smiled. *A candidate. Good.* "How do you do."

A touch on his shoulder from behind. "Hi there, Ash. I'm Anne Pulkay. I've been dying to meet you…."

"Uh, hi." *Okay, two was fine.* sep

"Hi."

"Hi." Double giggle. Two young women, so alike they probably weren't sure themselves who was which, pressed against his side.

"I'm Mimi."

"And I'm Lilli. Want to play triples?"

Holy crap.

"Can you join us for dinner?"

Who said that? He spun around.

"Ash, can we talk?" He looked over his shoulder. Two more women, who looked like they were afraid they were missing the party, hurried across the lobby toward him.

This was scary. He backed up a couple of feet and ran into another woman.

Ronnie grabbed his sleeve. Where had she come from? She pitched her voice just loud enough to be heard over the crush. "Mr. Armitage, you have a phone call in your suite."

Praise God. And thank you, Ronnie. "I'm so sorry, ladies. I'll see you all again."

He could feel Ronnie's arm guarding him as they hurried back the way they'd come. *C'mon, elevator.* It opened with a *ding*. He was on. "Press close. Quick."

Ronnie pushed the button five times. The doors *whooshed* shut. He leaned against the wall. "Holy shit, that was unreal."

"I followed you on the next elevator. I didn't think you'd make it out alive, boss. Or at least with your virtue intact." She laughed.

He took a deep breath. "Okay, here's plan B. Remember that woman and her daughters who greeted us in the lobby?"

"Yeah, the owner's sister, I think."

"The blonde was kind of cute. Let's have breakfast with them tomorrow."

"Deal."

"Meanwhile, I'm going to hide in my suite."

CHAPTER 2

DRAGGING. HAD it only been ten hours since the arrival of the handsome prince? It felt like a week—a week of solid work, and it was still the same day. At least for a few more seconds. After the big lobby scene, Mark had escorted Mr. Pennymaker to a table on the patio with some friends and then gone back to work. His being gone for a half hour had seemed to be an excuse for the housekeeping manager to start his workday over. He sighed. Finally it was done.

He really wanted to get a little more completed on the dress. Tomorrow morning he was off for a few hours, so he could sleep or sew. Sewing always won.

The bed looked good, though. He grabbed a piece of silk velvet he'd found in a scrap pile at a fabric store in the city and sank down on the bed. Too tired to undress yet.

Wonder what I can use the velvet for?

He stared at its shimmery silver taupe color and the way it caught the light. Just like his hair. Ashton Armitage. No, his hair was more beautiful. So unique.

Mark ran his fingers over the velvet. That special soft you almost couldn't feel. Would Ash's hair be like that? *Ash. Funny.* Mark spent his days in ashes. Was it a sign? *Yeah, right. A sign that he was nuts.*

He petted the fabric. *Oh, so soft.* Maybe Ash's lips would be even softer. So soft you could barely feel them and yet hot as flame.

He closed his eyes. What had Ash's lips looked like? Oh, yeah. The top lip was slender, but oh God, the bottom lip looked swollen, like he'd just been kissed. Mark's lips puckered. *Kissed. Oh, please.* Back and forth. His fingers twined in the slippery material. Slipping like Ash's cock could slip into Mark's hole and fill him with sweet liquid fire.

He squirmed. *Jeans are too tight.* Maybe that steel rod erection had something to do with it. He unfastened his button and pulled down the zipper, then scooted the scratchy denim down his hips. *Much better.*

He should get undressed anyway. A little writhing and some tricky work with his toes got the jeans all the way off. He kicked them onto the floor.

So soft. He pulled the velvet to his cheek and rubbed. It would feel good on his cock, but he didn't want to ruin it. What would Ash's hand feel like? Silky? Probably. A rich guy like that didn't clean fireplaces. Maybe he played polo. Mark chuckled. Ooh, a nice rough, hot polo hand sounded really good right now. Holding his reins.

He slid an arm down the side of the bed and grabbed a sock he'd thrown on the floor when he came in. Did it feel like a polo hand? Close enough. He slid down his boxer briefs with his thumb and slipped the sock over his throbbing dick. He giggled. Took him back to early adolescence when he used to hide all his jizzed socks in the back of the closet from his mom. When he had a mom. *Okay, don't go there.*

He tightened his hand around the sock and began to pump. Oh yeah, that's what he needed. *Do it to me, Ash. Jack me with your rough hands.* He pushed the velvet under his cheek again and shoved his other hand between his legs and stretched his ball sac. *Sweet. Yes.* Stretch. Pump. Oh God, he wished he had a cock in his ass. That would be relief from this dick that had been throbbing since he'd seen Ashton Armitage.

He pulled up his hand from his balls, wet the middle finger, rolled onto his side, and slid the slick digit into his aching hole. He pushed back, trying to get more, and wished he had a dildo. *God.* He'd get one next time he was in town. A big, thick one like Ashton's cock. *Yes, his cock must be as fat as his wallet. Oh God.*

Mark's hands pumped and pumped. He couldn't even begin to control his hips. The bed made a *thump* against the old plaster walls. Nobody to hear. *Good. Thump.* Pump. *Thump.* Pump. Pump. Pump. *Thump. Thump.* Pumppumppump. *Fuck me, Ash, fuck me. Jesus!*

His breath stopped as pictures flashed behind his eyes. Silky brown hair, soft velvet, pouty lips, sucking, sucking, blue eyes closed in ecstasy. Heat shot through every nerve, and hot cum poured into the waiting sock. He held tight and felt the heat through the sock fill his hand. Tight. Like Ashton's lips wrapped around his cockhead as he softened, softened, and sssssslept….

DAMN! MARK sucked at the drop of blood on his fingertip. His little attic room was so dark even in broad daylight that he had trouble seeing the pins in his garments. Of course, sleeping a few hours with a sock stuck to his dick hadn't exactly improved his eyesight.

What had he been thinking? Answer. He hadn't been. Just dreaming, and it was bad dreaming, baby. Dreams got you fucked, and not in a good way.

He stepped back. He needed to stay focused on what was important. That was the last pin. Done. He liked it. The red dress clung to the dress form with a businesslike sexiness. He petted the form. He'd practically had to sell his body to afford it. After sneaking it in here one night, he kept it hidden behind his clothes rack during the day so none of the nosy housekeepers would see it. Not that they cleaned his room, but they did love to spy.

The dress was just what he needed for his portfolio. He didn't have a decent camera, even on his phone, but somehow he had to get a photo. Well, he had time....

The soft rap on the door sounded like a gunshot in the quiet room. Nobody came to see him. Too many stairs. They called him when they needed him. Richard the Bastard? No, the asshole wouldn't lower himself to seek Mark out. He'd rather corner him in the pantry. "Who is it?"

"Mark, it's Carstairs. Carstairs Pennymaker."

What the hell? The little guy had climbed up here? Why? "Just a moment, Mr. Pennymaker." He scooted the dress form with the red dress behind his clothes rack and adjusted a couple of items. It didn't show too much if he wasn't looking for it. He took the few steps to the other side of the room and opened the door. Plaid! It hit him in the eye like a flying kilt. The old gentleman's sense of style was unique, but somehow it suited him—pun intended. "Mr. Pennymaker, please sit down. You shouldn't be climbing those stairs. You could've had someone in housekeeping call me."

"Nonsense, nonsense. Just a brisk climb." Instead of sitting in the straight wooden chair Mark offered, Mr. Pennymaker walked directly over to the rack and began pawing through Mark's few clothes. "I need you to do something for me."

Wish he'd get away from there. "Of course, sir. Just ask." He gestured for Mr. Pennymaker to be seated, but he didn't budge.

Pennymaker turned and looked at Mark. "What are you working on?"

"Excuse me? I, uh, have to clean some fireplaces this morning. You know they keep the rooms cool just so they can use them? Makes work for me."

"That's not what I mean, of course." Pennymaker turned back to the rack and pushed some jeans aside. "Aha!" His hand shot through the garments to the dress form. He made an opening in the clothes and stepped through to stand beside the red dress. "Perfect. Just beautiful. What a talent."

"Excuse me?"

Pennymaker beamed at him. "You have exceptional design skills."

God, it was hard to not be flattered. "Thank you, sir." But how had Mr. P. known to look for the dress? Who'd told him?

Pennymaker walked over to the chair and sat. It creaked. Hopefully the tiny man wouldn't strain the old wood too much. "I would like to show that dress to some people."

"Uh, who?"

"Let's say some potential investors."

No. He couldn't get excited. "Really, sir? You're in the clothing business?"

"I'm in many businesses, my boy."

Okay, try not to be suspicious. "How did you know I was a clothing designer?"

The little man waved a hand. "That lovely T-shirt, of course."

"No one told you?"

"Who would tell me?"

Had him there.

Pennymaker stepped back and surveyed the dress. "Now, who is your model?"

What? Mark cocked his head.

"Whom did you set the dress form to?"

"Oh, uh, myself. I, uh, don't have anyone else. I'm pretty slim, so it works."

"Perfect. Perfect. When do you have to be at work?"

This conversation was crazy. "In about an hour. This is my morning off. Unless they need me, of course."

"Good. Put on the dress."

"What? Why?"

"We're going for a little walk through the hotel. You'll be my… niece. Go on, go on." He made a shooing gesture with his hands.

Mark shook his head. "Sir, I know I fit the dress to me, but that's because I don't have anyone else. I'm not a transvestite."

"Never said you were, dear boy. But these people I want to have see the dress will be much more amenable to taking your designs seriously if they think of the idea themselves rather than me telling them. That's how we all are, now isn't it? I want them to see the clothes. We don't have another model, and we don't want anyone else in on our secret."

Secret? "What if someone recognizes me?"

Pennymaker cocked his head. "That's very unlikely. You do a good job making yourself plain and unmemorable with your cap and glasses."

Mark felt the blush. *Shoot.* The man had him dead to rights.

"Besides, people see what they expect, and they certainly don't expect to see Mark Sintorella in a dress. Now, put it on."

Mark stepped behind the rack of clothing. He stripped to his boxer briefs and stopped. What the hell was he doing? He could jeopardize his job for this crazyassed little guy with his hairbrained scheme.

The voice came from the other side of the clothes. "Do you have it on?"

"Sir, I don't mean to be rude, but are you sure about this? I really need the money I get from working here."

"Tut-tut, my boy. Hurry. I want to make one tour around the lobby and public rooms before you start your shift. Time's a wastin'."

Mark pulled the dress over his head and let it fall into place. The skirt was just full enough to swing when he walked, so no one would notice his cock under it. "Uh, I don't have any boobs."

"Let me see."

"See what? What I haven't got?"

He stepped out. Pennymaker looked at him studiously. "Gorgeous. You don't have breasts, but then neither do some women to speak of. I'm more concerned about the hairy legs. Go shave, quickly."

"What? Sir, I don't think so...."

"This won't be your only modeling assignment, I suspect, so think of it as a long-term investment. Consider that brilliant young model who used to walk the catwalks in both male and female shows. You're at least her equal in beauty."

"But—"

"No buts. This is your future. Now go!"

Three minutes later, the water ran off his back as he tried to balance on one foot and wield the razor with the other. What the hell was he doing? Fortunately he wasn't very hairy, despite being dark-haired and Italian. His chest was hairless and even his face was pretty much smooth as the proverbial baby's butt. But here he was scraping the fuzz off his legs and underarms just because that crazy leprechaun told him to. He was losing it. But the little guy was a guest, and if there was even a chance of getting investment for his designs....

No, that was beyond hope. But pleasing a guest was within his power.

Three more minutes and he had pulled on his boxer briefs, combed out his black hair, which fell to his shoulders, and walked back out to the tiny bedroom where Mr. Pennymaker sat holding the dress.

"My, my, I think you are more beautiful than that model. Your hair is astonishing. Here." He handed the dress to Mark.

This is crazy, but here goes. He slipped the dress over his head and adjusted the draped neckline so it gave the suggestion there might be a tiny something under there.

Pennymaker stared at him. Definitely appraising. "Whatever will we do for shoes?"

"Uh, I have some heels I use to get the drape of the dresses right and to check pant legs."

"Brilliant. Let me see."

Mark scooted behind the clothes rack and found the pair of precious heels. Hard to find women's shoes in size eleven. He slipped them on. Though only three-inch heels, they put him well over six feet.

"Perfect. Here." The little man held out a tube.

"What is it?"

"Clearly, a lipstick. Try it."

"You just happen to have a lipstick in your pocket?"

"I purchased it in the gift shop. Try it on. Fast!"

"Oh, good grief." He took the tube and stepped in front of the tiny mirror beside his front door. He began to apply the color. God, it took him back to childhood, when his sisters used to dress him up as a girl because he was so pretty. Now his aunt blamed them for making him gay. *Jesus.*

He stepped away and looked. *Wow.* The face staring back at him looked female. Not just female, but, well, pretty. Big eyes with heavy lashes, short, slim nose, full mouth now painted red. And all around this waterfall of black hair. His mom's hair, as he thought of it.

"My, my. That looks brilliant. Next time we'll do some eye makeup, but this will suffice for now. Let's go."

"Go?" His voice sounded like a squeak.

Pennymaker took his arm and led him out onto the small landing at the top of the creaky attic stairs. "We'll go down a flight, then cross over to the elevator and come in to the lobby from there. Your name is Mariel. You're my niece from the city."

Mark stopped and pulled back. "Jesus, I don't want to talk to anyone."

"We'll avoid it as much as possible."

His heart beat fast. "I don't think I can do this, Mr. Pennymaker. Can't you just take the dress and show it to your friends?"

"Ah, my dear, the success is all in the presentation."

He pulled back harder. "Wait. Why are you doing this? Why should you give a damn if my designs get seen?"

Mr. Pennymaker laughed. "Just think of me as your fairy godmother."

CHAPTER 3

"YOUR WORK sounds very interesting, Bernice." Ashton smiled at the dark-haired daughter while he leaned over and poured more coffee into her mother's cup, then added some cream. The woman beamed. Playboy billionaire as charming host. Always a successful persona. They knew he could have chosen any of the guests to breakfast with him in the hotel dining room and had chosen them. *Big points. Huge.*

The daughter leaned forward, flashing some plump cleavage. "Thank you. Of course, I don't want to work after I have children. I think motherhood is the most important profession for a woman, don't you?"

He started to give a glib response but stopped. "I think a woman, like a man, should be entitled to do whatever is important to her without society, Congress, or anyone else telling her how she must live her life." *Oops.* Maybe a bit more heat behind that than he'd intended. But it got him an interested glance from the little blonde daughter, who'd seemed totally unimpressed with him until now.

She cocked her head. "What do you do for a living, Mr. Armitage?"

He laughed and shrugged. "I have a degree in economics from Wharton, an MBA, and no inclinations toward work of any kind. It all adds up to me being a useless drain on the family finances. And please, call me Ash."

The mother laughed. "Delightful."

The blonde, however, frowned and returned to her serious perusal of the menu. Well, hell, that litany usually got him a point or two for charm. "What do you do, Bitsy?"

She looked up and gave him a level glance from clear blue eyes that said she did not suffer fools gladly. "I study music. The clarinet. I'm finishing my PhD."

"How wonderful. I'd love to hear you play." Oddly, it was true.

She looked back at the menu.

Man, tough crowd.

The waiter came to take their order.

Ash smiled. "What will you have, Beatrice?"

A hand tapped his arm. He looked up at Ronnie. "Sorry to bother you, Ash. There was a call from your father. I told him you were at breakfast with two, uh, three charming young ladies. He did, however, want me to let you know to please call him after your meal."

"Thank you, Ronnie. May I present Beatrice Fanderel and her daughters, Bernice and Bitsy?"

Ronnie cocked an eyebrow. "How alliterative of you."

Bitsy looked up fast and grinned, the first hint of a smile since she'd sat down. She rose from her seat and extended her hand. "Elizabeth Fanderel. Pleased to meet you."

"Ronnie Morgan, the woman he can't live without."

Bernice looked startled, but Bitsy laughed. Ronnie shook her hand. They were the proverbial study in contrasts physically. Ronnie's boy-short platinum hair, superslender body, tight jeans, and trim leather jacket were the opposite side of Bitsy's honey curls, blue doll-eyes and girly dress. Somehow, though, he guessed they were two of a kind—honest, straightforward, and hard to fool.

He looked at Bitsy again. Maybe she could be the one. Being married to a woman like that wouldn't be so bad. But what a terrible thing to do to a nice person. And the hard-to-fool part? Not good for him.

Bitsy pulled out the extra chair beside her. "Want to join us for breakfast?"

Ronnie shook her head. "Oh no, thanks. I have to get back up to the suite and do some work. You guys enjoy. Ash, I'll see you later and…. Holy shit!"

Ash looked up from his omelet and—my God. Was she real? Were they real? The couple walking through the dining room had to be from a fairy tale. A tiny man, not much more than five feet tall, wearing a wild plaid suit with a white rose in the buttonhole strutted by. He had to be an elf. On his arm was the most beautiful… no, maybe the word was astonishing, woman Ash had ever seen. Over six feet tall, wearing a red dress that clung to a body so slender and yet defined, she could have been a boy. A mane of shining black hair fell around a face of perfect contrast—carved cheekbones, soft lips, structured jawline, big doe eyes. She moved with a coltish grace, like she had just learned to walk and was trying her legs, and shit, what long legs they were. The thought of those legs wrapped around his body gave new meaning to the words *morning wood*. Not a lot of women turned Ash on at first sight, but this one… there was something about her.

The odd couple strolled through the dining room as if they were on the boulevard in Paris. No big hurry. Admiring and being admired. The little man exchanged words with a few people, but the woman seemed reserved and in her own world. She smiled a little when the man appeared to introduce her to a couple sitting near the windows, but that was as close to animation as Ash saw. She was like a goddess walking through a crowd of mere mortals. The mortals were taking notice. All around the dining room, people were staring and buzzing. *Yeah, something to talk about.*

"Who the hell is that?" He looked over to see Bernice frowning.

Beatrice stared after the man and woman as they exited the dining room out onto the terrace. "I've seen him around the hotel, but I've certainly never seen her before."

Bitsy grinned. "His name is Pennymaker, and he's as delightful a person as I've met. The woman is gorgeous."

Ronnie nodded. "I'll say. Wonder who she is?"

Beatrice stood up, looking for all the world like a mother tiger protecting her cubs. "I'll certainly find out."

Bitsy glanced at Ash and laughed. "I'll bet you will."

GOD, HE couldn't catch his breath. Mark staggered the last few steps to his attic room. He rubbed his hands up his arms to control the goose bumps. What if somebody saw him going to this room in this dress? That would be a disaster.

He opened the door, slipped inside, and slammed it behind him. He pressed his back against the inside of the door. *Breathe. Nobody saw you, idiot.* Mr. Pennymaker had taken every precaution, waltzing Mark through the whole atrium, around the gardens and the pool, in a back door, and down a little-used hall. Hell, the old guy knew more about the inner workings of the hotel than Mark did.

Mark glanced at the clock on his table. Damn, he was out of time. He pulled the dress over his head, carefully folded it, and hid it under some clothes on a shelf in his back corner. The color was so distinctive he couldn't leave it out in case someone snooped. He yanked on a pair of old jeans, a plain T-shirt, and his uniform jacket. Could not be late.

As he reached for the doorknob, he caught a glimpse of himself in the little mirror. God, his hair! It felt so comfortable just hanging around his shoulders, he'd almost forgotten. He found the hat and glasses beside the bed, where Mr. Pennymaker had put them earlier, and scrubbed the last of the lipstick off with a used tissue. The cap accommodated his hair perfectly, and it was plain black, so it wasn't too ostentatious. He'd been so emphatic about it being a religious requirement—and since he was willing to do pretty much anything else—the management had given in and let him wear it. He should really cut his hair, but his mom had loved it so much. He felt like it was all he had left of her.

Glasses on. Good to go.

He raced out of the little room, took three stairs at once, and almost fell the next ten. *Slow down. No good arriving dead.* He walked through the back hall of the basement toward the housekeeping department. This felt normal, anonymous, just like he wanted it. That walk through the hotel as Mr. Pennymaker's niece had been freaky. He might be gay, which had its own stigmas and mores, but he was still a guy. Girls were treated differently. More visible in some ways. Less in others. Kind of like the "seen, but not heard" thing they used to say to kids.

Mr. Pennymaker said the right people had seen him and the dress. That was good, he guessed, but he wasn't getting any hopes up. It was way too big a leap of faith, and he was short on that. Mr. Pennymaker was a sweet man, and Mark didn't want to disappoint him. Not many people counted themselves Mark Sintorella fans. It was flattering. But beyond that? His best hope was to save his money and try to get to school. For that, he needed this job. A quick glance at the clock broke him into a trot. One more hall.

The freakiest thing of all this morning had been seeing Ashton Armitage at his table, surrounded by doting females. "Mariel" had stopped him dead. What a look. The guy was turned to stone. Amazing. Mark didn't want to think about how badly he'd like that look to have been for the real him. Just a glimpse of Armitage had made his cock twitch—not a good idea while wearing a dress. But, Jesus, the man was beautiful. Touching that shimmering hair must be like stroking the richest silk. *Crap. Try another line of thought, idiot.*

He pushed open the swinging door into housekeeping. He had a date with toilets and fireplaces. That should put his cock in its place.

ASH PERCHED on the arm of the couch in his suite. He pulled the phone away from his ear an inch. The old man's voice rumbled.

"Yes, I know what you expect, Father."

"If I could do anything about these rules, I would. But I can't; you know that."

"You are the head of the family now. You make the rules."

"Yes, but your grandfather's trust is irrevocable. No marriage, no money. He believed in the sanctity, et cetera."

Ash barked a laugh. "Yeah, and he was sanctified four times."

"We've been over this before."

"I know. The old guy loved me."

"You don't doubt that?"

"Not for a second."

"Good. Then do what he wanted you to do."

Ash sighed. "I know. I'm doing it. I even met an interesting girl."

"That's great, son. What's her name?"

"Why? Do you want to investigate her?" The slight pause on the other end of the line told the tale. "I'll save you the trouble. She's Elizabeth Fanderel, the daughter of the sister of the owner of the resort."

"Marcusi? Nouveau riche."

"Well, nouveau is better than no riche at all, as they say. Anyway, I just met her, so don't start booking the Plaza."

"We'll have to book something. The time limit is coming up, and your mother and I are leaving for Zurich. You've had years to make this decision and you've played your time away. Two weeks. Marriage certificate in hand or the trust fund goes to charity. Personally, I'd rather have it in the family. If you ever decide you do want to grow up and take over Armitage International, I'd prefer you weren't beholden to the company for all your income. It makes you too vulnerable."

"You have money."

"Do you really think there'll be much left when your mother's done with it?"

Sixteen houses and a wardrobe the size of a small country? "Not likely."

"You have your own money, Ash. All you have to do is claim it. Or walk away and make it on your own. You're more than capable of getting by, all appearances to the contrary. Give me some news soon."

"Yes, sir." He clicked off the cell and fell onto the couch. *Shit!*

Ronnie walked in from the extra bedroom they used as an office. "Same old, same old?"

Ash blew out a breath slowly. "Pretty much. He wanted me to know that he and my mother are planning a trip to Zurich in a couple weeks, so they're prepared to get me married off before then or wash their hands of me."

"You can walk away."

"That's what he said."

"So do it."

He wiped a hand over his face. "The odd thing is that my grandfather really intended for me to have the money. He didn't know he was giving me an impossible condition. He always believed in me. I guess it didn't occur to him that I wouldn't want to marry a woman by the time I was twenty-five."

"At least talk to your parents."

"No. If I find somebody to marry, I don't want to make life any harder for her."

"Your birthday is in fifteen days." She sat on the arm of the chair opposite him. "We have to get a marriage license and set up some kind of ceremony."

"Shit, I have to find a bride first."

"I heard you mention that Fanderel chick. You like her?" Was there an edge to her voice? Maybe she didn't like Bitsy.

"Yeah, I thought she seemed to have more brains than most. Didn't you like her?"

"I liked her fine. Only met her for a couple minutes. You sure this isn't the cat syndrome?"

"What do you mean?"

"Like a cat, you just want the one who doesn't seem to want you?"

He shrugged. "Maybe. Hell, aside from my erstwhile money, there's not much reason to want me."

"Give me a break. You're smart; you're capable. You even have a disturbing streak of honesty, which you occasionally acknowledge. And I suppose some people wouldn't mind looking at you."

He grinned. "You'll give me a swelled head."

"Not a chance. It's my job to keep your balloon pricked."

"That sounds dirty."

"You wish." She picked up a glass ball from the side table and rotated it in her hands. "So, are we courting Bitsy Fanderel?"

"I guess." He stared out the window. "Who do you suppose that woman was who walked through the dining room?"

"Don't know, but she was gorgeous. Why?"

"She gave me a boner."

"No shit!"

CHAPTER 4

MARK WIPED the last of the soot off his face with the inside of his housekeeping jacket and threw it in the laundry basket at the back of the department. He'd be glad to get up to his little room tonight. Three dirty fireplaces, two restrooms, and an explosion in the kitchen later, he felt like dead housekeeping meat. He washed his hands and arms in the sink, scraping grime from under his fingernails. *Wish the gloves worked better. Okay, sleep.*

He skirted around three housekeeping carts, pushed out the swinging door, and started down the hall.

"Sinders, wait!" He turned to see Mrs. Eldridge, his boss, rushing after him.

Shoot. Almost home free.

"They have a situation in room service. Can you go over?"

Room service? Tips? Hell, yeah. "Yes, ma'am. Glad to."

She smiled. "That's my boy. Get over there now."

He took off at a trot. Didn't want someone else to get the gig.

The room service department off the kitchen proved to be a few people making a hell of a lot of noise. When he ran through the door, the assistant manager of the department grabbed his arm. "Sinders. Hell, am I glad to see you."

Nice to be wanted. "What can I do? What's going on?"

"Almost all my waiters are on that big private party in the sheik's suite."

Yeah, Mark had heard some Middle Eastern potentate was throwing a lot of money around. Would've loved to be on that assignment.

"Put on a jacket and go up to the Antoinette Suite and serve dinner for two. You can do that, right?"

Slow down, heart. "Uh, isn't that the suite Armitage is in?"

"Yes. That's why I need someone who won't fuck it up. I usually get good reports on your fill-ins, Sinders. One lady said you were"—he raised his voice in imitation—"particularly gracious and had a nice sense of style."

Wow. Nice.

"So tonight's your night."

"Thanks." His hands were shaking. He walked over to the rack and took a white jacket in his size.

"Better grab some pants too. Those jeans look like you've been rolling in ashes."

"Close."

He went into the bathroom, changed into black pants a couple of sizes too large, but not too bad, and the white jacket. Jesus, he'd get to see Armitage up close. Was that good or bad? *Both.* He just hoped the guy tipped well. *Here goes.*

Back in the department, the manager eyed his cap. "Umm…."

Mark shook his head. The manager knew his made-up story. "Sorry."

"Okay, get going. The au jus is underneath in the heating drawer. You know how to let yourself into the suite's kitchen. You'll find all the dishes and flatware you need in there."

Mark started to push the large cart out of the kitchen. Looking up, he saw creepy Richard staring at him from beside the walk-in. As he watched, the big man ran a thick tongue across his lips. *Shit. Shivers.*

The assistant manager's voice stopped him.

"Sinders."

"Yeah?"

"Don't fuck it up."

RONNIE SMILED as she let the pretty little blonde into the suite. "Hi. C'mon in. Ash will be right with you." God, she looked great in those jeans and a frilly white blouse. Nice rounded hips, small breasts. Even in pants she was supergirly.

Bitsy smiled big. "Hi. Are you going to have dinner with us?"

Interesting. The woman seemed excited about that idea. Shouldn't she be bummed? "No, I'm leaving soon. I just have a couple things to finish up in the office."

Bitsy looked around the lush, traditional room with the French provincial touches. "Office?"

Ronnie jerked her head toward the second bedroom. "We use that as an office while we're here. Ash likes to come off as a total playboy, but he actually does have quite a few business issues he needs help with. Oh, uh, please sit." Bitsy walked over to the sofa and sat. She sure smelled good.

Some really natural orange oil or something. Not that heavy stuff like most chicks wore.

"I'd love to hear more about those business issues."

"Uh, I'm sure he'll tell you." Ronnie grinned. "Of course, managing his social life is a full-time job."

The big blue eyes looked worried. *Yeah, you should be worried, dollface.*

Ronnie held up a hand. "I'm joking. He doesn't do half the stuff the newspapers report."

Bitsy sat back on the brocade couch. "Hell, if he does an eighth of the shit, it'd be a full-time job."

Ronnie threw back her head and laughed. God, she seriously liked this chick. "You have a point."

The door to the bedroom opened. Ash came in, smiling. Even she had to admit he looked delicious. This was casual Ash—jeans and a deep blue silk shirt that set off his creamy coloring and taupe brown hair. *You better get in here, babycakes, because right now your girlfriend likes me more than you.*

"Hi, Bitsy. Sorry to keep you waiting. Had one more minute's primping to do."

Ronnie smiled. *God, only Ash can get away with saying shit like that. What a charmer.* "I tried to fill in."

He gave her a quick glance. *Worried?*

"Thank you, Ronnie." He sauntered in that never-in-a-hurry Ash way over to the bar beside the windows looking out on the atrium garden. "Can I get you ladies a drink?"

Ronnie looked at Bitsy, who shrugged.

"How about I open a bottle of champagne? I know Ronnie likes that."

Ronnie shook her head. "I should go. I'll just get my stuff."

She started toward the extra bedroom. Bitsy looked up at her. "Oh, I thought you lived here. Uh, I mean were staying here."

She paused. "No. I just work in here. I have a room down the hall."

"I see."

For a second, no one said anything. *Odd.* What had the girl been thinking?

Ash popped the cork. "Too late. You better stay for a glass, or Bitsy and I will have to drink it all, which means we'll get in terrible trouble and it'll all be your fault."

For a second Bitsy looked confused. Then she smiled. "Yes, all your fault."

Ronnie shrugged. "Never let it be said I interfered with lewd and lascivious conduct, but I will have a glass, thanks." She heard dishes rattle in the kitchen. "Shall I check on the waiter?"

Ash nodded. "Sure."

Ronnie walked over to the two-way door that swung into the suite kitchen. She'd checked the little room earlier, and it was compact but well stocked. A young man in dark-rimmed glasses and a black knit cap looked startled when she pushed open the door and leaned in. She smiled. "Sorry to scare you. You can set the dining table for two. Plan on serving in about fifteen minutes. That'll keep everyone from getting too drunk. Maybe."

She laughed, and the guy returned a strained smile. *Young kid. Cute behind those glasses. Probably nervous about serving the billionaire's son.*

"Uh, yes, ma'am."

"Don't worry. I don't bite and neither does Ash. You'll do fine."

ASH WATCHED Ronnie step out of the kitchen smiling. "What's up?"

"Oh, just a cute young waiter. I about scared him witless." She lowered her voice. "I think he's new. Go easy on him." She walked over and sat in a chair across from Bitsy, who was on the couch. Ronnie picked up her champagne.

Ash leaned back in his chair and sipped. He knew Ronnie would be leaving soon and, it was stupid, but he felt kind of nervous. Bitsy was smart, nice, and damned pretty, all of which made him think he could stand being around her as his wife. It also made him afraid to be alone with her. "Tell us about your music, Bitsy."

The little blonde smiled. "Well, I told you I play the clarinet. I'm finishing up a degree."

"What are your plans? Will you make music a career?" *Brave girl.*

"In some capacity. I'd love to play in an orchestra, but those jobs are really tough to get."

"I'll bet."

"There are usually only a couple of clarinets in an orchestra, and once you've got one of those chairs, you don't give it up, so positions are scarce.

That's why I wanted the PhD. It will qualify me to teach, which I plan to do even if I'm lucky enough to get a spot in an orchestra."

"Sounds like a good plan—" The soft *clunk* of silverware hitting the table made Ash look up. The young waiter Ronnie had talked about moved quietly around the table, setting two places. Odd. He wore a cap. Not your usual waiter regalia. But he seemed efficient and not as nervous as Ash had expected from Ronnie's description.

Ash turned back to Bitsy, who had sipped very little of her wine. "You don't seem to be enjoying the champagne. Can I get you something else?"

She smiled. "I'm not much of a drinker."

"I'll bet we have something softer. Waiter?"

The young man in the cap looked up. "Yes, sir?" *Jesus, look at that face.* Under that weird cap and the big honking glasses, the kid had a delicate, almost feminine facial structure. He looked about eighteen, but Ash guessed he'd probably have to be older to serve liquor.

"Would you please see if there are some soft drinks in the refrigerator for Miss Fanderel?"

"Yes, sir." Soft, melty kind of voice.

They were still talking about music when the waiter brought a glass of something light and bubbling, complete with napkin and coaster. He carefully placed it beside Bitsy. As he withdrew, he looked up directly at Ash. *Jesus. Time warp.* Dark, dark eyes and heavy lashes. He could barely see them behind the glasses, but when he did get a look at them, those eyes mesmerized. Ash didn't want to look away. "Uh, we'll eat in about five minutes." He dragged his eyes over to Ronnie. "Why don't you join us? I ordered a lot of food. I'm sure our waiter can plate it for three."

"Yes, ma'am, I can." That voice gave Ash actual goose bumps. Who was this kid?

Ronnie drank the last inch of champagne in her glass as the waiter took a few steps back toward the kitchen. "No, thanks a lot. I'll get some work done. Great talking with you, Bitsy." She looked over her shoulder. "Dinner just for two, waiter."

The kid left the room. Black pants hung on his legs. Too big.

Jeez, wonder what that ass looks like? Oh crap, get your mind where it belongs.

Ronnie gathered a few papers she had left on a side table. "Have a great dinner, you two. By the way, does that waiter look familiar, or is it just me?"

Ash nodded. "I thought that too, but maybe we've just seen him in the halls. Or no, I think I saw him in the lobby the day we checked in. That must be it."

Bitsy nodded. "He usually works in housekeeping. He must be filling in."

Ronnie shrugged. "Guess so. Night."

MARK HELD on to the edge of the counter for a second. *Breathe, you idiot.* What about seeing Ashton Armitage had he thought was going to be a good thing? This was torture. Those women were pretty. Which one was he going to marry? The blonde who had come to talk to Armitage seemed to work for him, not like a new girlfriend. It must be Bitsy. He sighed. At least she was nice, the lucky duck. And Mrs. Fanderel would be ecstatic. Why in hell did the idea make him nauseated?

Okay, salads. *Get this dinner served and get the fuck out of here.* He arranged hearts of palm and avocado on Bibb lettuce and sprinkled on some pine nuts, then added a few dried cranberries for color and a drizzle of vinaigrette. He pulled the forks he'd set to chill from the refrigerator, placed it all on a tray, and pushed through the swinging door with his shoulder. *Heart pause.* Bitsy and Armitage were already at the table.

Mark took a deep breath and plastered on a pleasant expression. "Your salads." He placed Bitsy's salad plate on the serving charger he had set earlier. He was careful to serve from her left side and positioned the fork above her plate.

Okay, Armitage next.

Mark circled around the table. Oh God, the man smelled so good. *Focus, Mark.* He put the salad plate into position with only the slightest *clank.* He hoped Armitage didn't see his hands shaking. "Enjoy."

The damned rich guy smiled at him, all flashing white teeth and dimples so huge you could sharpen a pencil in them. "These look delicious."

Mark ducked his head a little and escaped through the swinging door. He knew delicious when he saw it, and it had nothing to do with salad.

From inside the kitchen, he heard Armitage's melodious voice say softly, "Ronnie must've been right about his being new. He seems nervous. Did a good job so far, though."

Mark's heart beat too fast. *Thank God.* If he could just survive the rest of the courses.

Bitsy's soprano added, "Bless his heart, he works really hard in housekeeping. He cleans the fireplaces a lot, so everyone calls him Sinders, which is kind of mean. Sadly, I don't actually know his real name."

Quiet. Must be chewing. Bitsy piped up. "Don't you think he's a pretty boy, though?" *Oh crap.* He held his breath. What answer did he want? He should want Armitage to say *No, I hadn't noticed such a thing*, but….

"Yeah, I was thinking that earlier. He's as pretty as a girl under those glasses."

Shit, shit, shit. He didn't want Armitage to notice him, did he?

Oh God, he just wanted to be anonymous and get the job done and make his money and—oh Jesus, his cock was a steel rod. Just thinking the damn billionaire's son thought he was pretty did it for him to the max.

Bitsy wouldn't leave it alone. "He's prettier than most girls." Quiet. "My mother hates it when I say that."

"Oh, why?" Mark couldn't believe they were still talking about him.

"Because he's a little strange with that cap and all, and he's gay, and Mother doesn't like to think there's anything good about a person like that."

That got rid of his hard-on. More quiet. "Uh, your mother doesn't like gay men?"

"Are you kidding? I think she would've joined the Tea Party if it wasn't so damned blue collar and trailer park." Pause. "Of course, there's a trailer or two in some recent generations of my family." She laughed, and Armitage joined in.

"I gather you don't agree with her?"

"About Sinders?"

"That and being gay, uh, and such."

She laughed again. "My mother and I can barely agree on whether the sun is shining." Pause. "And I have nothing against being gay. Nothing at all."

Maybe they were done with their salads and he could get them to change this fucking conversation. He ladled some tomato bisque into two porcelain bowls, put them on the tray and added the spoons and condiments, and set the whole thing on the counter.

Why did that soup make him think of licking it out of Ash's belly button? God, he had to get a grip. He bumped the door with his hip to give some warning. "Are you ready for your soup, sir?"

"Uh, yes, thank you. The salad was great." Mark could tell from the cautious look in the man's eyes that he was considering whether Mark had heard what they said. It was easy to forget servants behind closed doors.

He walked in and took away the salad plates. "I'm glad you liked it." How invisible could he seem? Trying not to show how badly he wanted out of there, he put the plates in the kitchen and served the soup, then barricaded himself behind the door, breathing hard. *Talk about hard.* Thank God for his room service jacket. It hid the boner he got just hearing Armitage's voice. This too would pass. *Breathe and don't listen.*

The soup wouldn't last long. He pulled the plates from the warmer and began to lay out garnish. Parsley. Wasn't there a legend that said parsley grew for the wicked, but not for the just? Then, man, it should grow for him right now, because his thoughts were not available on network TV. Maybe he'd chew a little parsley to disguise the smell of Ash's cum on his breath. God, that stopped him dead. *What a thought. Get to work.*

Leaning toward the door, he heard soup spoons lightly scraping the bottoms of bowls. He plated the prime rib and new potatoes, took a deep breath so he wouldn't smell Ash's aftershave, and went into the dining room to remove the soup bowls. Back in the kitchen, he added the brussels sprouts and spooned au jus over the meat. Rich aromas filled the room. Made his mouth water. He hadn't had more than ten minutes for dinner. Quietly, he slipped into the dining room and served the main course.

Armitage smiled. Oh, God save him.

"This looks delicious." Bitsy leaned back and looked up at him. "Hey, Sinders, you're really good at this. They should let you be a waiter full time and get you out of those damned fireplaces."

He wished. "Thank you, Miss Fanderel, but I think they usually have enough waiters."

"You're better than most of the waiters I've seen."

"I don't mind the fireplaces, miss. It's job security. Nobody else wants to do it." He grinned, and she laughed. "Enjoy your meal."

Back in the kitchen, he sighed. That was nice of her. Now, if he could just—

The voice penetrated beyond the door. "So I hear you're thinking of getting married."

Mark's spine turned to ice. He should leave. Go out in the hall. But his feet crept closer to the door all by themselves.

Ash's melodious voice. "Uh, yes. Yes, I am."

"People usually decide to get married after meeting someone they love. Your process seems backward."

God, he wished he could be that direct.

"I like you."

Mark's breath caught at Armitage's comment. Was he going to propose?

"That's nice, but what does it have to do with your decision to get married?"

"I'm not sure, but I really like no-bullshit people. You saw that with Ronnie."

"Yes, I saw it with Ronnie, but with you? Not so much. You seem to be mired in bullshit."

Wow. The woman knew no fear.

"Nietzsche said, 'He who cannot lie doesn't know the meaning of truth,' or something like that." He laughed.

"You're quoting Nietzsche to me? Really?" She laughed. "But, seriously, why on earth would you come to a place like this to find a woman you don't know to marry? In all your—what?—twenty-four, twenty-five years, you haven't found a single likely candidate, and suddenly you have to find someone to marry today? That is the biggest bullshit I've ever heard."

Mark agreed, but nobody had asked him. He pressed his ear closer.

"It's complicated."

Bitsy laughed. "No shit?"

"Let me say that the woman I marry stands to gain significantly from the arrangement."

"In money, I assume. Not from the pleasure of your company."

He laughed again. "I really do like you. Yes, in money. But the person will be stuck with me for an extended period of time. The provisions of the will say I can't divorce for ten years. At that point, the woman can leave with a substantial settlement."

Mark felt his hands shaking.

Her voice. "I guess it's no worse than marriage transactions through the centuries."

"Exactly."

"But don't you have a girlfriend, someone close, who can slip into this arrangement?"

"I want it to be impersonal. I have no real desire to marry, so I want the woman I choose to be entering a business arrangement and nothing more." There was a pause. Was Bitsy thinking it over? Armitage continued. "Of course, it'd be nice if I liked the woman."

Big pause. Mark held his breath.

Bitsy sounded thoughtful. "Ash, I like you too, despite your bullshit, but I don't want to get married."

"Well, that sounds perfect, then."

"No. As much as I'd love to have the money to do anything I want, the problem is there are too many strings on that money. It would give you and others a say in how I live my life, and I don't want that. I don't want that more than I want the money."

"See, even that's attractive. Won't you think about it?"

She laughed. "It's complicated."

Well, shit, for all intents and purposes, Armitage had just proposed to Bitsy. Why the hell was Mark's stomach in knots? What did he expect or hope for? Why was he obsessed with this man? He was sick. He didn't believe in hoping for breakfast in the morning, much less to have a man like Ashton Armitage.

He sighed. He had to make his hands quit shaking. Had to stop thinking about those two in the dining room.

Oh shit, he couldn't. Ash had asked her to marry him. At least she'd turned Armitage down. But for how long? Could her sterling character really stand up to all that money? Especially with the huge pressure she had to get from her mother?

He managed to get through dessert, cleared the table, and left with Armitage and Bitsy sitting on the couch together. He wanted to cry, even though he had a huge tip in his pocket. It made him understand Bitsy. He might trade the money for never having been there at all.

CHAPTER 5

CREEPY. MARK glanced over his shoulder as he pushed a cart of cleaning materials out to a mess on the patio. Richard had been staring at him all morning. What did he want? Retract that question. Mark knew what he wanted—his ass. He didn't think the guy was gay. Just a creep. It was a dominance thing. Think *Deliverance.* Seeing Mark get something good like the Armitage room service gig both attracted and repelled the weirdo. Mark shivered. He had to stay away from him. Be anonymous. Get really dirty, so Richard would think Mark was below his notice again.

The cart bumped along the concrete of the pool deck. Okay, this should meet the dirty job requirement. He looked at the splash of vomit some partier had joyfully left for him. Middle of the day.

Jeez. The guests walked around the pool in the opposite direction. Yeah, they wanted to avoid the mess and the menial who got to clean it. He pulled out the mop and bucket and went to work.

HARD TO believe that's the same guy. Ash peered over his sparkling lime squash from his spot under the corner umbrella on the far side of the pool. The young waiter from the previous night slopped a mess so disgusting it had already completely driven a few people from poolside. The guy handled it like it was all in a day's work, with not a cringe. But in the baggy blue jacket, with sunglasses over his eyes and that cap pulled low, Ash barely recognized the pretty, girly face. No hint of the sweet, sassy smile Ash had seen when the kid—what had Bitsy called him? Sinders?—when Sinders had bantered for a minute with Bitsy. *Wonder what his story is?*

The kid gathered up his mop. Then… what? He tensed and looked over his shoulder. Ash followed his line of sight. Was he looking at that mean-looking man? A big bruiser with short brown hair and a weak jaw stood in the doorway that led into the dining room from the pool terrace. The guy had no expression. Weird. He just stared. It could have been at anyone, but Ash guessed it was at the kid. His boss? Man, who'd want to work for a scary dude like that?

Sinders turned and scraped his toe on the pool deck, like maybe he was thinking of mopping it again. Then he seemed to make a decision and purposefully pushed his cart in the opposite direction from Scary Dude. The boy skirted around some bushes and disappeared into an employee entrance.

The big man stepped out the dining room french doors and skirted the patio, moving slowly and maybe sneakily in the same direction as the kid. What the hell? Ash sat up straighter on his chaise. Just watching the guy gave Ash goose bumps.

He sat back. *Okay, leave it alone, idiot. This doesn't concern you. That's just his boss who wants to… what? See if he's doing a good job? Tell him he's doing a good job? Shit!* That guy looked like he wanted to do a job on the kid. Ash pushed himself up from the chaise. If he didn't hurry, he'd lose them.

He walked straight across the patio. Forget the pussyfooting business. He went through the nondescript Employees Only door he'd seen Mr. Scary and the kid go through. A long corridor. No one in sight. *Hurry.*

He broke into a jog and started down the hall. Not a soul. Not a sound. As he passed a door along the side, it hissed. Just closed? He raced to the turn of the hall and looked down. Nobody. This felt bad. He ran back to the inconspicuous door. Where did it lead? The door scraped a little as he opened it, and he slowed his movements. He wasn't sure he wanted to announce he was there.

The hall beyond the door was dim, with only two yellow service lights. *Shoot.* Ash looked down. He wished he didn't have on flip-flops. They made a little flapping noise, but he wasn't brave enough to try this dank corridor barefoot. Still, he felt the need to hurry. Stepping softly, he rushed down the hall to where it turned. He heard sounds and stopped.

"Ummmph. Get the fuck off. Get away. Quit!"

Ash tore around the corner and saw just what he'd expected. The big asshole had the kid pushed face-first into the wall. He had Sinders's jeans halfway down his ass and his big, disgusting cock pointed right at it. The bastard. Okay, so fighting didn't come up that often in the day-to-day life of a billionaire's son. He'd smacked a couple of paparazzi, but not much more. Still… ten years of off-and-on martial arts had to be worth something. "Hey!"

Scary Dude turned, startled.

Step. Thud. Wap. His fist connected with the guy's jaw. *Shit!* He'd forgotten how much hitting hurt! But it satisfied his soul to punch that asshole with all his force.

"Ow." Scary's head snapped back, and he reeled a couple of steps away from Sinders. *Not down. Damn. Have to hit him again.* Ash took a breath and pulled back to strike. The guy raised his fists to block.

Ash saw the moment the ugly dude finally realized whom he was about to hit. His face froze.

You should be afraid.

Scary glanced at his own fists, stepped back farther, and without even tucking his cock in his drawers, turned and ran back up the hall toward the door he'd come in. Ash stepped after him. "Keep running, asshole."

Ash rested his hands on his knees. Hitting a guy for real was different than karate make-believe. It looked so easy in the movies. His hand hurt like hell, and the adrenaline made it hard to breathe.

Too quiet. He looked up. Sinders huddled against the wall, one hand holding his pants up at his hip, the other covering his eyes. From a few feet away, Ash could see him shaking.

"Are you okay, kid?"

His head nodded in some roundabout direction that could mean yes or no.

"Hey, you're okay now." Ash walked closer. "He won't be back, and when I'm done with the owner of the hotel, you won't have to worry about him ever again."

The boy's head shook, but he still huddled by the wall barely dressed. He was terrified. Hell, Ash would have sworn nothing could get that young man down. He stepped closer and put his hand on Sinders's arm. The boy tensed and started to pull away, then stopped and just crumpled like a wet sock. *Shit.* Ash caught him before he hit the floor and pulled him up into his arms. "Whoa. You don't want to be on that floor, kid. You don't know where it's been."

Sinders smiled. Just a slight turn of the lips, but it counted. He didn't stop shaking, though. Ash tightened his arms. "It's okay. I got you."

"S-sorry."

"Nothing to be sorry for. That guy was big and ugly. Don't be afraid anymore."

"N-not him. Before him. Can't talk about it." Sinders kind of burrowed into Ash's arms, making little hiccupping sounds, his body shaking like the proverbial leaf. Okay, that felt interesting. The kid was tall, but Ash was taller, so Sinders could push his face into the crook of Ash's neck like he was hiding from the bogeyman.

Not too experienced at the comfort thing, Ash rubbed a hand up Sinders's back. God, he was lean, hard, and supple. Really different from anything he'd ever felt under his hands before.

The shaking seemed to slow a little. The sounds softened. Ash just kept stroking.

Good. Seemed to be working. The boy's breath misted warm on his neck. Quieter. Quiet. Still.

Sinders's head pulled away from Ash's neck. Ash gazed down at that silly cap; then Sinders slowly looked up at him. Somewhere, those ugly glasses had been knocked askew, and all Ash saw were eyes so deep they'd swallow mastodons and preserve them for a thousand years.

He felt the kid's chest expand against his own. Sinders's arm twitched, then slowly his hand snaked up behind Ash's neck. The fingers were rough, callused, and they circled gently on Ash's skin. More goose bumps. Nice this time. For an instant Sinders froze, hand pressed but not decided. He made this little noise. "Ohhh." His fingers slipped into Ash's hair and tightened. Slow motion. It probably took a half second, but Ash felt like he saw every detail of the boy's pretty mouth—pink, pouting, trembling—getting closer until his face blocked out Ash's sight and wild heat attacked his lips. *Crap. Hot. Soft. How did this happen?*

Sinders's fingers dug into his hair, and his soft tongue pressed against Ash's startled lips. *Oh God, open.* Ash's lips parted on their own. Invasion of sweetness. Like his birthday. Sinders's tongue pressed its advantage and took possession of the field. Did that moan he heard come from his own throat?

His hands gripped Sinders's lean hips, where the unfastened jeans nearly fell down again. *Closer. Come closer.* Ash dragged him tight against his own straining erection. What was he doing? He didn't know. Too sweet, too hot to think. Sinders ate at his mouth like a starving man, making soft mewling noises. Ash pressed his body against the boy, pushing him back to the wall.

When Sinders hit that wall, it was like an alarm went off. His head flipped up, and Ash looked into wide, startled dark eyes.

"Shit, no. What am I…. I'm so sorry. Oh God, please forgive me. I'm so sorry."

Sinders grabbed his sagging jeans, made a wailing sound, and ran down the hall.

Ash gasped for breath. His cock strained against his shorts like a pole in a circus tent. What the fuck had just happened?

HAVE TO hide. Have to leave. Mark huddled on his bed. How soon before they came to fire him? He'd never called in sick before. But he'd told the truth. He was nauseated. Couldn't work. Needed the afternoon off.

What had he done? Richard the Bastard had pushed him right back into that subway station, those guys, that night. *Oh crap. Have to stop shaking.* And why had he kissed Armitage? Why? Everything had been so great until that man arrived. Mark's life had been together, predictable. Even Richard the Bastard staring at him had been a standard thing. Then Ashton Armitage arrived and all hell landed on his head. More like his cock. The guy made him crazy. Him and that elf dragging Mark around in drag!

The soft knock reminded him of a cue in a bad play. He knew who it was and knew he shouldn't answer. That insane little man gave him hope when he knew he had no hope. Only hard work. But dammit, he liked Mr. Pennymaker.

He huffed, dragged himself off the bed, cleared the couple of steps to the door, pulled it open, and headed right back to the bed and curled into a ball.

"Helloooo, my boy. How are you this lovely day?" The chirpy voice paused, and Mark peeked at him from his armadillo-like position.

Mr. Pennymaker had his hands on his knees and was gazing at Mark. Yes, he was an elf. "Hmm. I gather we are not tip-top?"

Mark shook his head. "No, sir."

"What seems to be the problem?"

"Don't really want to talk about it."

"Might as well. I want to listen."

He had a point. Mark needed another angle of vision. "I did something very bad."

The dark suit Pennymaker was wearing today would have been conservative but for the bright pink vest and the gardenia in his buttonhole. He sat on the rickety chair. "Would you like to tell me about it?"

Mark sat up. Would he? There was something about the man. Like he was on Mark's side no matter what. Mark had never had that feeling… at least not since his mom died. It made no sense. Mr. Pennymaker was a stranger, but there it was. "Well, you see, Richard the Bastard tried to force himself on me, and I was so—"

"Hold on! What happened?"

"Oh, the bastard sous chef finally quit perving on me and decided to do the deed. He didn't get to hurt me because Armitage—you know, the rich guy—came to my rescue. And now I know I'm going to get fired any minute, and I really need this job, and I don't know what I'll do if they give me a bad referral."

"Now, now, even Herman Marcusi won't fire a man for avoiding rape."

"No, you don't understand. Because I was really upset. See, I had this thing happen and I guess I went into flashbacks or something, but I was pretty messed up, and Armitage tried to help me and, shit, I kissed him."

The man grinned. "Kissed him?"

"Yeah." Mark returned to armadillohood.

Mr. Pennymaker's voice dripped with amusement. "I'm sure you were grateful."

Didn't he get it? Mark sat up. "No! I *kissed* him kissed him, like, with tongue and, you know."

The grin got bigger. "I'm sure you were *very* grateful."

Mark sighed. "Maybe. But I imagine he's reporting it to Marcusi right now and I'll be out on my ass by tomorrow."

"Maybe he enjoyed it."

Hell, he hadn't thought of that. The guy had seemed shocked, but he hadn't worked very hard to get away. After all, Mark wasn't exactly Mighty Joe Young. Still, the look on his face…. "I doubt it. Hell, you can't do anything good with Sinders and Ash."

Mr. P. chuckled. "My dear, either he enjoyed it, in which case he won't be complaining, or he didn't enjoy it, in which case he's too embarrassed to complain. Either way, you keep your job. Now, since you have a little time off, let's get you into another outfit, because my friends, whom I wish to impress with your work, are having a late luncheon. Come, come." He waggled his fingers.

Mark shook his head. This was nuts. He felt like somebody had just ripped out his guts, and this man wanted to play dress-up. "Sir, this is serious."

"Your past was serious, Mark, but your future is waiting. We can't be late for it, can we?"

"I don't know, sir. It's really risky, and I can't afford any risk right now. I don't want to be conspicuous."

"Mark, there are no successful fashion designers in the world who are inconspicuous. Your desires are contradictory. And in life, my dear, nothing ventured, nothing won. Come on… you've got balls. Use them."

Mark laughed. "Are you trying out for the coaching job with the Lakers or something?"

"Ah, what a splendid idea. All those gorgeous big men."

Funny. He hadn't thought about the fact that Mr. Pennymaker was gay. Just eccentric. But it made sense. And the man had a point. What was the saying? In order to have what you've never had, you have to be willing to do what you've never done. That applied. "Okay. I'll do it."

Pennymaker clapped his hands. "Splendid. That's my boy. Now, what shall we wow them with today?"

"I've got some full-legged pants and a really cool white shirt I could wear."

"Good. Put them on and we'll go cause a fuss."

"I'M GLAD you did it, but you have other priorities here, Ash. Stop playing rescuer of the downtrodden and get busy wooing Bitsy."

Ash played with his niçoise salad. A little tuna to the left. Three green beans on the right. He glanced at the diners at nearby tables and lowered his voice. "You should've seen him, Ronnie. The guy was big and ugly, and he'd have screwed that kid to the wall in half a second if I hadn't come along."

"The kid is gay. You sure you didn't just interrupt a little private nooner?"

He looked up. "Give me some credit, okay? He was terrified, and the bastard was about to rip him with no lube and less affection." He took a deep breath. Damn, it still made him mad. "And don't assume because the guy is gay that he loves being buggered by assholes."

"Sorry. Seriously, I didn't mean it like that."

A waiter poured him some more iced tea, and he squeezed in lemon. "Marcusi is firing the bastard today. He didn't want to, because it's not easy finding a good sous chef on short notice, but I guess I threw my weight around quite a bit, because he's doing it."

She sipped her black coffee. "You feel strongly about this."

"Hell, yeah, and so should you."

"I wasn't there. It doesn't have the sting for me. Sorry."

He finally took a bite of salad and chewed slowly.

She shifted in her chair and ran a hand through her platinum hair. "So, Bitsy?"

"Not a sure thing at all. In fact, pretty unlikely."

"Why? Shit, Ash, did you mess it up?"

"No." He pushed the plate away. "At least, I don't think so. She's too smart for me to try to convince her that it's love at first sight, so I told her the truth."

"Which is?"

"That I'm looking for a woman to marry me for my money." He laughed.

"That should've been a sure thing, you romantic, you."

"Yeah."

"And she wasn't interested?"

He shook his head. "Not much. She said she'd like to have the money but didn't want to give someone control over her life for ten years. The truth is it would be longer, really, because her money would always be doled out and overseen by Armitage lawyers and Armitage companies."

She smiled. "Smart girl."

"Like I said."

Ronnie leaned back in the upholstered chair. "But her mother has a powerful influence, and that woman wants your money bad."

"I know. That's why I haven't given up on Bitsy completely, but we need more candidates."

"There's her sister." Ronnie laughed.

He toyed with the iced tea glass. "Even I don't want my fortune that badly."

"She's pretty enough."

"Only on the outside. Ten years, Ronnie. Not ten days."

"Okay, I got it." She looked up and her eyes got wide.

He started to look over his shoulder. "What?"

She grabbed his arm. "Don't look!" Her eyes followed someone. God, he wanted to look. She leaned forward and spoke softly. "Okay, lean back in your chair nonchalantly. She's here again."

It took willpower not to jerk his head around. He leaned back, crossed his legs, and picked up his napkin, then slowly turned his head. *Jesus.* The goddess was standing at a table nearby, beside the man he'd learned was named Mr. Pennymaker. The contrast between the tiny man in the pink vest and this impossibly elegant and tall woman was so funny he wanted to giggle just looking at them. She was wearing wide-legged denim pants on her legs-for-days. Her crisp white blouse sported a high collar that covered most of her long neck and jutted out under her chin. She'd cocked a red beret on that black mane of hair.

Interesting—she didn't carry a purse. Did that mean she was staying here? He'd only seen her twice and, good Lord, he would remember.

Ronnie leaned forward. "Speaking of candidates."

Wow. His cock did a happy dance at that idea. Who would have dreamed she'd be his type? "What do we know?"

"Surprisingly little considering this place is a hellhole of gossip. I asked around. Nobody knows a lot about the man, except that he's well liked, nice to most everyone, has the money to afford this overpriced hangout in a very nice suite, and seems to have some interests in the fashion industry.

"The couple they're talking to head some kind of holding company that specializes in entertainment and fashion enterprises. They're here with a couple design groups in which they invest. Pennymaker seems to know these people, and both times I've seen them together, he's introduced her to somebody in that group. She's his niece, they say. But who knows?" She grinned.

"Maybe a model. Or an aspiring one."

"She may be a rich one, considering the clothes she wears. Of course, Sugar Uncle is probably footing the bill for them."

"I'd like to meet her."

"If she isn't his niece, but is his"—she made quotation marks in the air—"'niece,' he could be offended if I start trying to introduce her to you."

He nudged her. "Hey, you're a master at political diplomacy."

She laughed. "Right. I can arrange to have her kidnapped."

CHAPTER 6

I HAVEN'T been fired yet. I haven't been fired yet. It was like a mantra. Mark finished up the bathroom in the men's locker and hurried on to the kitchen sink backup. If he made up for lost time, maybe no one would even remember he'd been gone this afternoon.

He stuck the plunger in the sink.

"Psst. Hey, Sinders." He looked behind him at Francisco, one of the busboys. The guy grinned. "Hey, man, did you hear? The Bastard is gone!"

Mark straightened up. "Really?"

"Yeah. I hear some guest got him fired. Don't know what he done, man, but it musta been bad. Good riddance. That guy gave me the full-on creeps."

He couldn't quite catch his breath. "Me too."

"Oh, yeah. He was the worst with you, man. Always standin' around starin' and shit. I don' know how you stood it."

Mark just shook his head. The Bastard was gone. What did that mean? But he couldn't quite get words out.

"Thought you'd want to know, man. You got no worries from that dude no more."

"Th-thanks. Thanks for telling me."

"No problem, man."

Jesus, Ash had Richard fired. It must be true. He'd said it in the hall, but Mark hadn't really believed it. Hell, Richard the Bastard was a sous chef. Lots of skills. Mark was easy to replace.

He tried to control his breath. Why? Why had Ash done it? Mr. White Knight. It must have been shocking to see that in the hall, him all squashed against the wall with his ass out and Richard…. Yeah, he'd felt that ugly cock pushing against his butt. But usually straight men thought gay guys were always asking for it, so why would he care? Armitage had stood up for Mark. Jesus, he'd belted Richard the Bastard. Hard. And now he'd gotten Richard fired, and he hadn't reported Mark.

Reported. *The kiss.* Mark's mind kept glancing off that moment. He didn't want to think about it. *No.* If he did? *Oh God, those lips, that tongue.*

Ash had tasted like lime and deliciousness. Felt like packaged sin. His cock had been hard as steel. That was true. Probably just from the adrenaline, but it had felt like heaven. *Crap. Stop. There's a sink to plunge.* He pushed down with all his body weight into the muck at the bottom of the prep sink.

"Sinders." *Pop.* Water splashed, but nothing happened. *Well, hell. What now?*

He turned to see Cox, the night manager of room service. "Yes, sir."

"I need you."

Cool. "Yes, sir?"

Cox was a short man but with a big ego. "Apparently, you had a fill-in assignment the other night with Mr. Armitage." He curled his lip.

Oh God, what about Armitage? Maybe he'd complained about Mark's work instead of the kiss because he was embarrassed like Mr. Pennymaker said?

"It seems you made a good impression…" Mark almost fainted with relief. Armitage hadn't gotten him fired. *Oh, thank you.* "…and he has asked for you to serve again tonight."

What? Oh God.

Cox looked at Mark's dirty clothes with obvious disgust. "Clean up and prepare to present yourself respectably and professionally."

No, damn, he couldn't face Armitage again. And another night of watching him woo Bitsy would be torture. "Uh, sir, since I'm so dirty, maybe you should send someone else?"

A dark eyebrow rose. "Is there something about the words 'he requested you' you don't understand?"

"Uh, no, sir." *Damn.*

"I also think he's displaying questionable judgment, but you will go and you will do as good a job as your skills permit. Rise above yourself, Sinders. Rise above."

He sighed. "I'll try, sir." Sadly, the only thing rising was his cock at the thought of being anywhere near Armitage.

"Get rid of that muck." Cox flicked his fingers. "And report to me in fifteen minutes."

ASH HIT the speaker on his cell and put the phone on the end table as he paced. What was he doing? "So what did you find out?"

Ronnie sounded frustrated. "Nothing, dammit. I looked everywhere for Mr. Pennymaker. A few people said they saw him, but nada. And no sign of the woman. I left a cautious message for him at the desk."

"What did you say?"

"Just that you were looking forward to a chance to meet him and his niece very soon. I figured he might get the drift since everybody knows you're looking for a wife. If she is his niece and he's ambitious for her, he might take you up on the invite. If not, he's free to ignore it."

"I don't want him to ignore it."

"I got that, but I've done all I can for the moment. A little later I'm going to try to find Pennymaker in the bar. I'm told he often holds court in there of an evening. I'll let you know."

"Good. Thanks, Ronnie." He clicked off. He needed a drink so he could forget he had lost his flaming mind. He went to the bar, grabbed a martini glass, and poured a couple of inches of vodka and a splash of vermouth, then added two olives. The first sip burned. *Not used to the hard stuff.* He carried it into the sitting area and flopped into one of the two big, comfy chairs. He'd made a promise. True, only to himself, but that should count for more, shouldn't it? And now he was breaking it. But, damn, he hadn't expected this. He hadn't expected….

He heard soft sounds in the kitchen. *Significant heart rate increase. Deep breath in through the nose; long slow exhalation.* All that money for yoga classes should be good for something.

Should he go in? What if it was a different waiter? He waited. A couple of minutes passed. He sipped at the martini, which didn't taste very good.

The swinging door to the kitchen pushed open, and Sinders walked into the dining room with plates and silverware. His eyes cast down, he moved slowly around the table, setting it for two. He looked tense. A few seconds into the task, he seemed to realize no one was talking, no people were getting ready to party. He looked up slowly and his eyes met Ash's. His gasp was audible. "I'm sorry, sir. I didn't, uh, mean to disturb you."

Ash smiled, though it probably didn't look happy. Too conflicted. "You didn't mean to disturb me."

He hadn't said it as a question, but the kid took it as one. "No, sir. I have dinner for two. Do you want me to serve it now?"

"What did you bring?"

"Sole amandine, mashed potatoes, and broccoli, sir. As you requested."

"Do you like those foods, Sinders?" He looked up, startled, maybe, at hearing his nickname. "Sorry, I know that's not your name. What is it?"

"Uh, Mark Sintorella, sir."

"So do you like sole and mashed potatoes and broccoli, Mark?"

"Yes, sir. The chef does an excellent job."

"Good, then you'll eat it with me."

Those dark eyes seemed to consume his face. "No, sir."

"Yes, and you'll call me Ash while you're doing it."

"Sir." He looked down and then back up at Ash. "It's my job to serve the food, not to eat it."

"It's your job to make the guests happy."

His eyes returned to his shoes. "I can't imagine why eating with me would make you happy."

Ash stood and crossed the room. "Sin—uh, Mark, I don't want to play rich guest games with you. If you don't want to have dinner with me, you certainly don't have to."

"Did Miss Fanderel cancel?" He still hadn't looked up.

"No, I ordered this dinner because I wanted to see you and I wanted to eat it with you."

That got his attention. His head snapped up and the amber-brown eyes widened. "Really?"

"Yes. I thought since we have shared a, shall we say, personal moment, that we might get to know each other." He pointed to the table. "Since you're supposed to be serving my dinner, no one is going to break in and disturb us. We can relax and talk. That is, if you want to."

"I shouldn't."

"Oh, why?"

The kid wiped the top of one shoe against his pant leg in back. "I might like it."

Son of a bitch. Ash laughed. "Sometimes life is about doing stuff you do like, even for you, Sinders. C'mon. Let's eat." He took hold of Mark's white coat sleeve and pulled him toward the kitchen.

Mark pulled back. "Sir, what're you doing?"

He looked down at the pretty face hiding behind the big black glasses. "We're going to get dinner."

"That's my job."

"Hey, if I'm inviting you to have dinner with me, I can't exactly ask you to serve it. Let's see what you've got." He hauled Mark into the kitchen and stooped down to investigate the food still in the warming tray of the serving cart. "This looks so good, and I'm starving. Get the plates." It was true. He was hungry, and the idea of eating with Mark Sintorella suddenly appealed enormously. The fish smelled divine. He grabbed the serving plates and pulled them up to the counter.

"The salads…."

"Bring them along. We'll eat everything at once."

"Uh, okay."

UN-FUCKING-BELIEVABLE. MARK watched Ashton-fucking-Armitage pull plates of sole from the warmer and transport them to the table. He wanted to help, but his hands shook too hard. He pulled at the refrigerator handle and managed to get the salads as far as the counter without dropping them. Armitage grabbed them on his next flyby. This wasn't happening. Things like this didn't happen in real life.

Ash's voice called from the living room. "What kind of wine do you like?"

Mark took a deep breath and tried to get some control. "Uh, I don't drink much wine. You pick."

What in the hell was going on? What was the man up to? Mark picked up the last of the utensils and walked into the dining room just as Armitage was pouring something bubbly that looked suspiciously like champagne into two glasses. Not that Mark had ever tasted it much, but he had served it plenty. He glanced over at the bar and saw the beautiful flowered bottle he always admired when he got to open it. *Jesus.* Not just champagne, but expensive champagne. Ash had to be really rich to serve that stuff to the help.

Armitage sat in his chair. Mark stood there. Had he ever been this uncomfortable? What was he supposed to do? Ash looked up. "Sorry."

Then something happened so amazing that Mark couldn't grasp it. Ashton Armitage, boy billionaire, jumped up, walked around the table, and pulled out Mark's chair. He held it expectantly, without an obvious hint of satire or sarcasm. There was only one possible recourse. Mark sat.

Armitage picked up his flute and held it toward Mark.

Okay, he'd go along. Mark picked up the glass. Armitage clinked the edge. "To freedom from fear."

Well, hell. "To freedom from, uh, fear." He copied Armitage and brought the glass to his lips. *OMG.* He had taken a taste or two from the ten-dollar bottles of champagne he could buy in the grocery store. His mom had liked it, and he had occasionally saved his paper delivery money to buy her some. But this was a world apart. Crisp, dry, a little fruity. The bubbles exploded on his tongue and the roof of his mouth. *Oh my.* It was so good.

Armitage smiled. "Do you like it?" Mark nodded. "Good." He waved a hand toward Mark's plate. "Eat."

He was almost afraid to. The smells were so delicious it made saliva collect in the back of his mouth. A few times he'd eaten the food from the dining room when they made too much, but generally the senior employees got there first. His usual meals were things thrown together for the staff—plain and filling. This was…. Could food be divine?

He took a little of the fish on his fork. It was so tender it flaked and wouldn't stay on the tines. After a persistent shove, he managed to keep the food on it all the way to his mouth. He opened. He tasted. *Dear, blessed God.* His eyes closed in appreciation. No wonder people paid a fortune to come to this resort. They got to eat this food.

Chewing slowly, he opened his eyes and glanced up. Armitage stared at him. The expression was… odd. Like pleasure and pain at the same time.

Click. The expression changed to his usual charming smile. "I gather you like that."

"Yes, sir."

He cocked his head. "Mark, how old are you?"

"Twenty-two."

"I'm almost twenty-five. I don't think I qualify as 'sir' yet, do you?"

"No, sir." The laugh exploded from him and he sprayed a little champagne. He clapped his hand over his mouth.

Armitage laughed aloud. "That's better." He dug back into his food.

No way Mark was going to waste a bite, so he got down to some serious eating. This would never happen again. They ate in silence for a few minutes. Not exactly comfortable, but the food was so good it was an excuse not to talk.

Armitage took a sip of champagne. "Where's your home? Are you from around here?"

"Uh, New York City."

"How did you wind up here in the boonies, city boy?"

How much to say? "I heard about the job through a friend. I'm trying to save some money, and it costs too much to live in the city, so I came up here for the season. I can live cheap and save all my earnings." He finished another few bites and pushed his plate away. *Wow. That was delicious.*

Ash smiled. "Want more?"

"No. This is great, thanks. There's some dessert in there, though. You shouldn't miss it."

"I caught a glimpse. Crème brûlée?"

"Coconut."

"That sounds incredible. Let's sit for a minute and then have some with coffee."

"Okay." Mark leaned back in his chair and took another sip of the champagne. Those bubbles seemed to float in his head in the most delightful way. He had to admit, he felt more relaxed.

"So, what are you saving for that you work so hard?"

"School."

"What do you want to study?"

Mark paused. TMI for sure. "Uh, I'm not certain yet."

"Huh? Usually someone as driven as you is motivated by a big dream."

"I, uh, like the idea of school."

"Your family can't afford to send you?"

Whew. This chitchat stuff was a minefield. That's why he usually shied away. "I don't have much family."

"Really? Aren't you Italian? From New York? I thought you guys always had a million relatives."

He stared at his hands. "The relatives I used to have didn't much like that I was gay, so I don't have them anymore." *What do you make of that, rich kid?*

Armitage stared at him. "You left home?"

"Sort of. It's not something I like to talk about much." He took another sip. *Change the subject!* "What's your dream, uh, Mister—"

"Ash."

"Ash."

Armitage set his glass down. "I guess I don't have one. It's a problem of being born with a lot of money. It can kill your motivation."

"Bull." Mark gasped and slapped that hand over his mouth again.

For a second Ash looked shocked. Then he laughed so hard Mark thought he was going to throw up the food he'd just eaten. "Hell, kid, just when I think you're some shrinking violet, I get to see your true colors. That's great!"

"I'm sorry."

He took a breath and looked steadily at Mark. "No, you're not. I've watched you work your ass off around this place for what I imagine is little money and less appreciation, and yet you keep going. A dilettante rich kid like me who has never earned a dime must be beneath your contempt."

Mark shook his head, but Ash held up a hand. "The only thing I've seen slow you down is that asshole in the hall. You don't have to tell me. I know it was a flashback of some kind. But I would like to know why you kissed me."

That was direct. Mark's heart beat like a hammer. Half the truth, maybe? "I was grateful… and confused. No one had ever stood up for me like that."

"Handshakes are good."

"Like I said, I was confused."

"You kissed me. Not 'thanks a bunch for saving me,' but a 'how far down my throat can you get your tongue' kind of kiss."

Mark pushed back the chair, jumped up, and stalked into the living room area. *Okay, maybe more of the truth.* "Look, I said I'm sorry. I'm gay, for Christ's sake, and you're gorgeous. In a situation like that, it's easy to lose your bearings. You were holding me, and you smelled good, and I was scared, and adrenaline took over and—you know the rest."

Ash looked at him over steepled fingers. "Would you have kissed me under other circumstances?"

"Like what? Selling kisses for charity?" *Jesus, Sintorella, control your sarcasm before you get fired.* He took a deep breath.

"No, like if we were in a hotel suite having dinner."

"Of course not." He had to get out of here.

"Not even if you thought I wanted you to?"

Mark's heart stilled. "Why would you want me to?"

Ash got up and walked over to the bar. He splashed a little more champagne into his glass. He held the bottle out to Mark, who shook his head.

"Why don't you ask me again what my dream is?"

Stay very still. This situation is volatile. "I should go."

"No. We have crème brûlée waiting. Ask me."

"What's your dream?"

"I don't have one, because I'm too busy pretending to be someone I'm not to actually have a dream. What I really should have said to you earlier is that I'm a liar, and the person I lie to most is me. I see someone like you and it makes me ashamed to be alive."

Mark couldn't take his eyes from Ash. Maybe the man was a flame of truth, or a rattlesnake. Both were mesmerizing. "What do you lie about?"

"Almost everything. Why don't you tell me?"

"You're gay."

"Yes."

CHAPTER 7

ASH WATCHED Mark shake his head. "No, no. Hell, no." The kid backed a few steps toward the entry to the suite.

Ash frowned. "What?"

"What do you think I am? You can order the food, but you can't order me up like takeout gay boy. I'm sorry. Yes, you're very attractive—physically. But you can't buy me, no matter how poor I may be."

Ash stepped closer to him. "What in hell makes you think I take you for a whore?"

"Isn't that what this is about? Order up the rent boy for the rich guest?"

"Like you said, hell, no!"

"Then what is it?"

That was the question, wasn't it? "Truth, I'm not sure. But let me tell you this. No one knows I'm gay, except my assistant and a few select guys who've been well paid over the years to keep that secret. Even my parents don't know, or my best friends. So you're standing here holding all the cards, baby. All you have to do is pick up the phone and call the press."

The kid crossed his arms. "They'd never believe me if I told them."

"Doesn't matter if they believe you. If you say it, they'll splash it across every tabloid in the world twenty times before they question its authenticity. By then some guy is going to come forward, say he had sex with me, and try to get more money out of it. You can ruin me if you want."

Mark frowned. "Why would I want to do that?"

"I don't think you would. That's why I told you. Come on. Sit down and have some dessert." He pointed at the couch.

"I'm not one of those guys you pay to keep your secret."

Ash looked at Mark's pretty face. *That's right.* He wasn't "one of those guys." But who was he? "I agree. I just want to talk to you. It's lonely being a liar."

Mark stared at him with narrowed dark eyes framed by those ridiculous glasses. His black cap was pulled low on his forehead. Ash wanted so badly to rip it off, but no way. The kid was not inviting that kind of intrusion. Mark's chest rose and fell; then he slowly walked over and sat on the couch.

Ash felt a little giddy. He held up two hands. "Just stay there, okay?"

Coconut crème brûlée sounded like just what they needed right now. He hurried into the kitchen, grabbed the two plates out of the refrigerator, put them on the tray Mark had been using, poured two cups of coffee that Mark must have set to perc earlier, and poured in some cream. He wasn't going to ask the kid's preferences. No decisions at this time. He put his hand over his mouth. Did he really want to laugh? What was it about this guy?

When he came back with the tray, Mark was sitting on the couch with his arms crossed over his slim chest. He hadn't moved, but he wasn't radiating happiness. Ash put a plate with a small bowl of the dessert on the table in front of him, added the coffee cup and saucer, and then put an identical setup on the table by the chair. He tossed the tray onto a footstool and sat.

The crease between Mark's eyebrows deepened. "You shouldn't be serving me."

"Is that why you're frowning?"

"Among other things."

"Well, eat first and then we'll get into them. This looks good."

Ash dipped his spoon into the little ramekin and pulled out some of the creamy concoction. He licked. Tongue ecstasy. The taste of crème, coconut, and burnt sugar exploded in his mouth. He fell back against the chair, clutching his chest. "Oh God…. Delicious."

That earned him a little smile. "Told you."

"Why aren't you eating?"

Mark picked up the spoon with a hesitation suggesting suspicion.

"Hey, come on, you're the one telling me how good it is and how I shouldn't miss it."

The kid looked at the spoon. "I've never actually tasted it. Just heard people saying."

The sweet sadness of the admission made Ash's throat tighten. "Go on."

Mark looked up. "I'm afraid I'll like it."

Sweet God. Ash got up and circled the coffee table. Mark's brown eyes widened, but Ash sat beside him, took the spoon, loaded it with a heap of silky crème, and guided the spoon to Mark's pretty, pouty mouth. "Open. You deserve to have all the things you might like."

A little shininess reflected in Mark's eyes, and he slowly opened his mouth. Ash saw his tongue connect with the pudding. *Chills.* That tongue could lick him anywhere. *Okay, don't go there.* Mark actually shuddered. "Oh, yes."

"More?"

His big eyes half closed. "Yes, please."

Ash spooned more of the rich dessert into his lovely mouth.

God, he remembered how it felt. Hot and wet. Demanding too. The kid had a wonderfully confusing combination of sweet and sassy about him.

Mark's eyes closed completely as he accepted another bite. He seemed to swirl the wonderful taste across every surface before he swallowed. "Ash?"

"Yes."

"How can you stand hiding?"

Ash took another spoonful and held it in front of Mark's mouth. "I started so early I guess I got used to it. I'll bet you never hid, did you?"

Mark accepted the bite, shook his head, and swallowed. "No. I realized I was gay when I was fourteen. I told my family right away." His big eyes opened. "My mother accepted it. Everyone else hated it. She died. They threw me out."

"Wow. How old were you?"

"Sixteen."

"And you've been on your own ever since?"

"Yes."

So brave. Ash sat back on the couch, still holding the spoon. "I guess I was afraid of the very thing you're telling me. That I'd lose my family. I grew up in this, shall we say, 'structured' household. My family had big dreams and expectations for me, their only son. I couldn't bring myself to dash all their hopes in one declaration. And every year that I hid made it harder."

He sat forward and took some more dessert, holding it out to Mark. Mark shook his head, and Ash dropped the spoon into the dish. "Instead,

I've disappointed them in every other way there is. Never living up to what they expect. They aren't bad people at all. My father is capable and caring in many ways."

He took a deep breath and glanced at Mark's face. Complete attention. No judgment. "My mother spends way too much money. Sometimes I think it's to make up for all the joy she hasn't gotten from me." Heat pushed behind his eyes. *Shit.* He grabbed the bowls, stood, and carried them to the kitchen.

He tossed the dishes on the cart and propped himself against the counter, staring down into the sink. *Just breathe.* He heard footsteps.

A gentle touch on his arm. "I know she's proud of you. They both are. Who wouldn't be?"

He turned. His beautiful face under the crazy cap shone in the low light spilling in from the dining room. So close. "What should I do?"

Mark shook his head. "Your problems are much too big for me. I don't know what I'd do if I faced the loss of everything you have. I was a kid. For me, it was easy. I was who I was. It didn't occur to me not to tell people. That decision has caused me a lot of pain, but I can't imagine never having made it."

Ash reached up and touched Mark's cheek. Like satin. Barely the hint of beard. And yet his lashes were so thick and dark. What did his hair look like? "You amaze me. You have so much courage."

"Hell, no. You saw me in that hall."

"All the more proof. I know something bad must've happened to you, and yet you go on pursuing your life with energy and some vision known only to beautiful boys in caps." He touched the headgear, and Mark pulled away just an inch. Ash dropped his hand. *Decide.* "May I kiss you?"

"Yes."

"Oh… thank you." His heart hammered. He cradled Mark's face, his fingers overlapping the knit of the cap. Mark's breath smelled like coconut, and his lips looked more delicious than the crème brûlée. *Okay, be gentle. Don't scare him.* Gently he laid his lips against Mark's. One second. *Sweet.* Two seconds. Exploration. Three seconds. *Hot!* Oh God, heat crept from that soft contact up to Ash's head and straight down to his cock. *Whoa. Down, boy.* He pulled back. Needed more control.

Before he got an inch away, Mark grabbed his head and pulled him back until his tongue pressed like a hot intruder into Ash's mouth. *Oh yeah.* Ash slid his hands down Mark's round butt and tugged him close. *Hmmm. Got a nice moan on that one.* Mark ate at Ash's mouth, sucking in his lips. His tongue pressed deep. *Wow.* This guy was not kidding. Had Ash just thought he should go easy?

Mark pulled back a little and sipped at Ash's lips, then ran his tongue over the bottom one. First outside and then… oh God, he slipped his tongue inside Ash's lip and caressed that soft, sensitive skin.

Sweet Jesus, he couldn't stand up. Ash leaned back hard against the counter, but he knew his knees were crumpling. Strong hands reached around and smoothed over his ass, and then a finger pressed against the crack of his butt like Mark was tracing the seam of the denim—up and down. Jesus, Ash's cock throbbed. Too much blood in there. Too long since that cock had any exercise. He wanted to rip his pants down and let that finger do its business where it belonged.

Like Mark had read his mind, one hand moved to the front and began to unfasten the buttons on Ash's fly. Shit, he couldn't help it. His hips pushed forward, forcing his cock against that hand like a puppy looking for milk.

Mark murmured, "Yessss." He undid the last button, slipped his hand into the top of Ash's boxer briefs, and found the promised land. Hand met cock. Why had Ash ever thought this guy was shy and virginal? Dear God, he was hot!

Mark's fingers were callused, a little scratchy, but so nice. The slight abrasion on his sensitive cockhead about sent Ash into the sink in a good way. "Oh God."

There was a smile in Mark's voice. Ash couldn't quite open his eyes to see it. "You want more?"

Ash nodded. Nothing happened. "Yes. Yes, I want more." That gasping was not cool. He didn't care. This was too good.

His jeans began to move down his hips, to his thighs, and then they fell to his knees. The boxers got ripped down after.

"Hmmmm." The sound came from around his knees. Shit, what did that mean? Hmmmm bad or hmmmm good?

"Is it okay to suck without latex? Am I safe?"

Suck. God, he was going to get sucked. "Oh, uh, yes. I've been ridiculously careful. Part of my paranoia, and actually I haven't had very many partners."

"Good."

Ohhhhh God! No prelim. Just cock into hot mouth in one delicious, fantastic, mind-bending swallow. Every nerve flashed hot. He giggled. "I almost came."

Mark popped the cock from his mouth. "Wanted to be sure you were awake." His tongue reconnected and ran hot and wet from the glans down the side of Ash's shaft all the way to his hungry balls. Mark pulled his sac tight and laved his tongue over it again and again. Ash felt himself whimper.

"You okay?"

"No one's ever done that to me before."

"You like it?"

"Hell, yeah."

"Good."

Ash held the side of the sink hard to keep from falling. One, two, three more hot licks and then, oh yes, back into that hot hole of a mouth. Flashes of heat ran up his nerves. His cock was on fire and so hard it hurt.

Mark's hands held Ash's penis and shoveled it into his mouth; then he sucked like a beautiful vacuum cleaner. *Damn. Knees melting.*

Ash couldn't do it. His legs wouldn't hold him. Slowly he sank to the floor, and Mark followed him down. Lying three-quarters flat with his head against the cabinet and that funny, pretty kid in the weird cap and glasses pulling the cum from him like he was priming a hose. *Suck! God.*

"Mark!" His hips bucked once, twice, and then he froze as cum pumped from him like spurts of lava. His sight went black. His cock occupied the center of the universe, and every drop of cum slipped down the throat of the most beautiful man Ash had ever seen.

MARK STARED at the long, lean body lying on the floor. Jesus, even with his pants around his knees and his cock lying there like a limp wiener, the guy defined gorgeous. Why the hell had Mark done this? Okay, he knew why. Ash had called him brave. Plus, the guy was so achingly lonely Mark wanted to give him something. But what had he given himself but a raging hard-on and a heap of worry? He might hold some cards on Ash… cards Ash had to know it would be tough for Mark to use, even if he wanted to. However, Ash could get Mark fired and worse with a word. What if Ash thought this event entitled him to more of Mark's attention? Maybe he could have gotten away with his righteous "I can't be bought" speech before he sucked the billionaire's cock. Now? Not so much.

Why had he been this dumb? Simple. Everything about Ashton Armitage thrilled him. Especially the unexpected vulnerability. But he needed some distance. "Ash?"

"Ummm."

"I've got to go. They're going to be expecting me back with the dishes. It's been a long time."

Ash propped himself up on his forearm and reached out with his other hand to touch Mark's cheek. *God. Sweet.* "You can't go. There's at least one more blowjob on the agenda tonight."

That sounded too good. "I really better go, or they're likely to send another waiter to check on me." The likelihood of them interrupting Armitage was slim, but Ash didn't need to know that.

Ash kept caressing his cheek, and every nerve clearly connected straight to Mark's cock. "I'd love to pleasure you. I'm not as talented as you, but I can try to make up for it with enthusiasm."

Mark had to laugh. "Maybe another time." He had to keep some distance. He had to.

The blue eyes widened. "But there will be another time, right?"

Mark tried not to answer.

"Please?"

"Yes, there'll be another time."

CHAPTER 8

BITSY LOOKED around at the guests at the nearby tables. "Mother, keep your voice down."

"Don't take that tone with me, young lady. I want to know exactly what he said to you at dinner. You've been dodging me for two days, and I want answers."

Bernice smiled across the table. She seemed to be enjoying Bitsy getting the third degree. Sometimes Bitsy wanted to smack her sister. "He was charming and polite, but that's all."

"Did he kiss you?"

"Hell, no."

"What did you talk about?"

"My music, some of his charity work." That was an interesting description of his pay-for-a-bride program.

"But he never expressed interest in seeing you again?"

Bernice laughed. "I told you her sour puss was going to turn him off."

"Were you rude to Ashton, Bitsy?"

"No. We got along fine." Yep, perfect agreement. Neither of them wanted to get married.

"Then why is he not pursuing another date?"

"You'll have to ask him."

Her mother looked around the dining room. "I may just do that."

She was glad Ash wasn't in sight.

"Come along, girls, and let's see if we can stumble upon him." She got up, and Bernice stood beside her.

Bitsy shook her head. "Sorry. You can embarrass the family on your own. I've already been the sacrificial lamb."

"Bitsy…."

"No, Mother."

Her mother stared at her, gave a huge huff, and walked off toward the pool with Bernice in tow.

Bitsy sipped her coffee. *What a mess.* She would make her mother happy forever if she married Ash's money. In fact, she wouldn't mind having it herself. Music, world travel, the best teachers and instruments. What a dream. She didn't have anyone special in her life. Why the hell was she fighting so hard? The proposition wasn't exactly prostitution. No sex. From what Ash said, he wasn't going to get his money if someone didn't marry him, so he got a big reward out of it too. How bad could it be to have your millions overseen by a bunch of businessmen and CPAs? *Shit. Bad.*

"Hey, you're thinking too hard."

She looked up at Ash's assistant. *Ronnie? Right, Ronnie.* "Yeah, it's dangerous for sure. How are you?"

"Pretty good. You?"

She looked into her cup. "Pretty good."

The chair scraped on the polished marble floor, and Ronnie sat beside her. "What's going on? Anything I can help with?"

How much did Ronnie know about Ash's intentions? She had a good idea this woman knew everything. Probably Ash's best friend. Bitsy could understand that. A real no-bullshit lady. Pretty too. "I'm just struggling with my sterling character."

Ronnie laughed. A gutsy, fun sound. "That's a new one. Some temptation you're trying to avoid?"

Bitsy sat back in her chair. "No. A temptation I'm trying to succumb to."

Ronnie laughed big. "Who was it who said 'I can resist anything except temptation'?"

"Oscar Wilde, I think."

"Want to go for a walk?"

Bitsy looked at the tall, superslim woman with the platinum hair and tough edge. She liked her. A lot. "Sure."

They walked out into the sunshine by the pool and then on into the gardens beyond. The sound of tennis balls behind a high fence announced the day was about serious play for the guests.

Ronnie put on her sunglasses. "So I hear you aren't going to marry him."

Bitsy laughed. "You do get to the point. Yes, that's the temptation I'm wrestling with, of course. I don't want anyone controlling my life, at least not any more than my mother does. And I have no desire to get married. But if I was going to get married, having the money and not the man sounds like a pretty ideal way to do it."

"Yeah, I'll bet it does. Of course, Armitage Enterprises would have a say in what you do forever. You know that."

"Yeah. I suppose." She stepped off the path and sniffed at a pink rose. She loved pink. So damned girly.

"That's pretty. Looks like you."

She grinned up at Ronnie. What a sweet thing to say.

Ronnie sniffed her own rose, the lavender color they called sterling silver. "Ummm. This one's great. Do you need the money?"

"Need? That's a tricky word. My uncle is rich, but my mother isn't. She would love to have the Armitage money at her disposal, and I'd love for her to have it. She's a pain in my ass, but she's a fiercely protective mother. There're a lot worse parents around. And I wouldn't mind having some of the things that money could buy." She sighed.

They started walking again. "You'd lose your anonymity."

"I've thought of that, and it would be difficult." She looked at Ronnie. The woman's face was… neutral. "Sounds like you don't want me to marry him."

Ronnie ran a hand through her short hair. "Oh hell, I want the best for Ash, and you are the best. I just… I don't know."

"If I did marry him, I guess I'd get to see a lot of you."

Her sharply chiseled face softened with a smile. "Yeah. I've thought of that too."

MARK WIPED the mop across the marble floor. Up and down. A nice rhythm. Reminded him of stroking Ash's cock. Up and down. He knew he was crazy, but he imagined he could still taste Ash's cum in his mouth, squirting against the back of his throat. Salty, tangy, a little sweet. Would have liked more for breakfast.

Jesus, he'd clearly gotten what he wanted. Some Ashton Armitage all over him. Why wasn't he happy? Easy—because now he knew what he was missing. The man wasn't just handsome as hell. He was sweet and sensitive and strangely vulnerable. He wasn't an egotist. It seemed like the opposite. He was unsure and self-deprecating. Mark liked that.

He sighed. Being with Ash last night only underscored what Mark wouldn't have when the billionaire went away. When he married Bitsy and left the resort for good. Unless maybe he chose Mark…. *Shit! Get over it. What was he dreaming about? That Ash would want him? Like that would ever happen. Let's see. Mark Sintorella or a half billion dollars? Gee. I wonder what he'd choose?* But Ash had seemed so happy lying there on the floor.

Stroke, stroke. Up and down. Clean the floor. Stroke that beautiful man. "Psst."

Mark looked up. A few guests milled around the sunroom, but they avoided the corner he was mopping. No one looked at him. Hmm. *Stroke. Stroke.*

"Psst."

Mark looked over his shoulder. Mr. Pennymaker was standing in the archway to the sunroom. Mark started to say something, but Pennymaker put his finger to his lips and pointed to the side. Where? Oh, back in the scullery. Mark gave a little nod and went back to mopping. What did Mr. P. want now? Man, the people the little guy had been introducing Mark to were awesome. He'd looked them up on his ancient computer. Talk about connected. It was exciting and scary to think people like that were looking at his designs. He still hadn't figured out what Mr. Pennymaker got out of this whole deal. It wasn't like he was going to make a million bucks tomorrow.

Trying to look nonchalant and efficient at the same time, he stowed his mop on the cart and pushed it around the corner into the scullery closet. He opened the door and went inside. Fortunately Mr. P. was small, because the scullery was big for one person but cramped for two. Mark closed the door behind himself. "Hi. What's up?"

"I've asked a friend of mine to request you perform a room service function for him."

"Cool. Thank you."

"Except you won't be doing room service; you'll be coming with me for a very special meeting."

"Really?" *Wow, more contacts. Amazing.* "Uh, can your friend be trusted? Sorry, that came out wrong. What does he think we're doing?"

"Don't worry. He thinks you need some time to work on a gown for the big ball on Saturday."

"Ball?"

"Yes, a special event to celebrate the height of the season. But we'll talk about that later. Go get dressed in something particularly smashing and meet me in our usual place." Mark usually went out a side door and met Mr. P. in the parking lot as if "Mariel" was just arriving.

"Is this another potential investor?"

"Of a sort."

"Are you sure this is okay, Mr. P.? Aren't we pushing our luck with Mariel?"

"Nonsense, my boy. Nothing ventured…."

"Nothing gained? I know. Okay. Thank you so much for believing in me."

That twinkly smile. "You have no idea how much. Now go along."

Mark scooted out of the closet and headed for his room via the back halls. He had this blue dress he'd been working on thanks to some great material provided by his fairy godfather—uh, mother. That should qualify as "particularly smashing."

Fifteen minutes later he walked quickly to the side entrance. Damn, he wasn't really used to high heels yet. *Yet?* What did he mean, yet? He had not established his future as a cross-dresser, but he had to admit it was kind of fun. The jersey dress clung to his shaved legs. Wildly sexy. And he really loved having his hair down. Today he'd gone the whole way. Eye makeup, face powder, lipstick. Hell, he barely recognized himself in the mirror.

He spied Mr. P. and moved quickly toward him across the concrete lot. Who would he meet today?

"Ah, Mariel darling, so glad you could make it."

Mark turned his head a little to the side and saw the two busboys hanging out having a smoke.

"Hello, uncle." "Mariel" leaned down and kissed Mr. P.'s shiny cheek. Softly Mark said, "Who am I meeting?"

"You'll see. Come." He stuck out his bent arm for "her" to latch onto and they walked toward the hotel.

"Don't I need briefing?"

"No." He grinned up at Mark.

Mark smiled. "Inscrutable elf."

"You have no idea."

They walked through the front entrance of the hotel. The usual gasps and sighs barely registered. *So soon you get blasé, Sintorella.* Mr. P. led him into the dining room, which was filling up for lunch. Sun shone through the huge windows, and happy sounds floated in from the pool. Mark glanced at a couple he'd met a few days before. They were sitting with another man and woman Mark didn't know. *Maybe them?* No—Mr. P. gave a friendly nod but proceeded toward the entrance to the small private dining room at the back of the larger public space. Mark knew it well. It had its own fireplace. He clutched his free hand. No manicure time today. *Hope the hands aren't too rough.*

Mr. P. opened the door and stepped back for Mark to enter. The intimate room was dim compared to the brightness of the larger space, and of course, the air conditioning was on low and the fire was lit. The round table in the center of the room was set for four people. Two people were already seated, a woman and a man. Mark walked a few steps closer. The platinum hair of the woman he had met the other night in Ash's suite shone in the firelight. His assistant? Why would she have an interest in fashion?

And then Ash turned. His longish hair was pulled back in a short queue, which set off his beautiful bone structure. That's why Mark hadn't known him with his back turned. It made him look different but no less gorgeous.

Mark smiled. Ash smiled back, then cocked his head with a small frown. Mark stopped. He wasn't Mark. He was Mariel. He was standing here in front of Ashton Armitage dressed as a woman. Did Ash recognize him? *Shit!* Why the hell was he here? What had Mr. P. done to him?

Mark looked at Pennymaker. The man's expression was full-on inscrutable now. Mark frowned. "Does he want to invest?"

"Mr. Armitage wanted to meet you, Mariel. He said he's admired you from a distance."

Mark stared at Ash, whose mouth was slightly open. Wanted to meet him? *No.* Wanted to meet *her.* Ashton Armitage wanted to meet Mariel. And why would he want to do that when Ashton Armitage was gay as a bag of jellybeans? To propose marriage, of course. Not even a first choice. An also-ran to Bitsy.

In answer to Mark's short dream about Ash choosing him, the answer was an emphatic no. The man intended to fuck him and forget him, just like he did with those other men. And Mark wasn't even getting paid. A big, loud voice in his head screamed *What the hell did you expect, you asshole? What did you expect when you got unanonymous and tried to play in the big kids' pool?*

Tears sprang to his eyes like liquid fire. "I'm sorry. I can't do this. Won't do this." He turned, practically fell off his high heels, and ran out the door.

Behind him that lovely voice shouted, "Mark!"

WHAT THE fuck had just happened? Mark as a woman. Shit, *the* woman. He wheeled on the little man. "Pennymaker, what's the meaning of this?"

The cherubic face crinkled. "You wanted to meet Mariel."

Ronnie stepped up beside Ash and put her hand on his arm. He knew she could see how upset he was. "Hang on. I'm confused. How come you called her Mark?"

"Because her name is Mark. I mean, his name is Mark Sintorella, the guy everyone calls Sinders."

"That's a guy? Sinders?"

"Yes. Open your eyes. The same beautiful eyes and pouty lips." He took a step toward Pennymaker. "What in hell were you trying to prove with this charade?"

The elfin man leaned against a chair back. "Actually, young man, this so-called charade had nothing to do with you until you inserted yourself into it. Mark Sintorella is a magnificent clothing designer. I wanted to show his designs to some of my friends in the fashion industry, but we had no model and no one Mark would trust. He fits his clothes on himself, so we used him as a model. Obviously our disguise was eminently successful."

Ash wanted to throw the chair. "You knew I thought he was a woman and yet you brought him here to make a fool of me."

"Mr. Armitage, you have done a very fine job of that all by yourself. I only did what you asked."

"Why?"

The man's sparkling gray eyes narrowed. "I am nothing if not compliant."

"You wanted to teach me a lesson."

"And what might that lesson be, Mr. Armitage?"

He gritted his teeth. "I'll let you know when I learn it."

CHAPTER 9

HOW DID women get this fucking stuff off their faces? If he showed up to work in lipstick, he'd be fired for sure. Of course, the firing thing was pretty much a done deal. *Nothing ventured, my ass.* He poured a little more of the lotion Mr. P. had gotten him into his hand. It had to come off.

Bam. He jumped a foot at the bang against his door.

"Let me in, Mark." The voice was muffled but emphatic.

"Go fuck yourself." Jesus, had he just said that? He took the two steps required to get to the door and pulled it open, blocking it with his body, now clothed in jeans and nothing else. He stared over Ash's head so he didn't have to see him. "I don't need to talk to you, Armitage. Go back to your bride hunt and leave me the hell alone. Your secret is safe with me. Now go away." He pushed the door closed and, *wham*, it flew back in his face.

Ash shoved into the room and slammed the door behind him. "Like hell I will. We're talking about this."

Mark jumped on the bed and scooted back until he touched the wall. "About what? How you want to fuck me while you chase after all the women in the damned hotel? Forget it. I'm not that desperate."

Ash stood beside the bed. Even angry he looked delicious, damn him. "First, I haven't fucked you. I seem to recall a very impressive blowjob being delivered by, uhhhh, who was it again? Oh yes. You! As for the other, I've 'chased after,' as you say, two women. Two. One before I met you, and the other one of them *was* you, for crap sake.

"Don't you get it? I was trying to figure out why this gorgeous brunette turned me on. Gave me my first boner ever inspired by a female. Answer—because she is Mark Sintorella, the most beautiful man I have ever known."

He did say the nicest things. Mark uncrossed the arms guarding his bare chest. "But you're going to get married?"

Ash sighed noisily and sat on the edge of the bed. "Yeah. That's the plan."

Mark rested his head on his knees. "It's a lot of money, I guess."

"Yeah." Ash lay back on the bed, his shiny hair, now free from its queue, spilling out around him. "But it's kind of more than that."

"More than a lot of money?" Mark smiled, but it was hard. "A whole lot of money?"

"It's my grandfather's legacy. He believed in me and wanted me to have it."

"Doesn't seem like it."

"He didn't know I was gay. He was married four times. He really believed in marriage. I think he just wanted me to have some stability, and he figured marriage would do it. He didn't mean to make it hard." Ash blew out a breath. "But the will is the will. I can't change it."

"And like you said, it's a whole lot of money."

Ash dropped his forearm over his eyes. His voice became quiet, tentative. "I, uh, thought maybe I could do some good with that money."

"Hell, who couldn't?" Silence. Mark looked at the beautiful body spread out in front of him. Some tension; tight around the mouth too. "Hey, I'm sorry. I didn't mean it like that. I just meant it's a lot of money that could benefit a lot of people." Silence. "I'd like to know what you plan to do with it."

"It's not a plan. Just a few inquiries. Nothing much yet."

"What's the 'nothing much'?"

Ash uncovered his eyes and rolled up on one forearm, facing Mark. "Don't laugh, okay?"

"Why would I laugh? You thinking of starting comedy clubs? Laughter's the best medicine?"

Ash looked down, a crease between his eyebrows.

Mark threw up his hands. "Hell, I don't know why I'm being such an ass, except—I don't know why. Just tell me, okay?"

"I'd like to set up a worldwide adoption agency for gay kids."

Mark just stared at Ash, who smiled. His blue eyes glowed. "It would be a way to get kids out of countries where they kill them for being gay. Get young people into homes where they could be loved and safe. It's really tough. There's so much political and religious shit involved. It's going to take a lot of money to grease palms and bribe nations to get these kids out. Like ransom money, you know." He stopped, stared at

Mark, and lay back down. Like somebody had turned out the light, and that somebody was named Sintorella. "But it's just an idea."

Breathe. Just breathe. "I'm sorry."

"Because it's such a crappy idea?"

"No, because it's one of the best ideas I've ever heard."

Ash flipped back over. "Really?"

"Yes, and I'm an idiot and don't want it to be a good idea because it means you're going to marry somebody and leave and I'm never going to see you again, but it's brilliant because if I'd been fourteen or younger when my family threw me out, I could never have gotten by and would have wound up who knows where and I love this idea."

"Oh God." Ash scrambled to his knees, grabbed Mark, and consumed his mouth. Tongue to the center of the earth, caressing every nerve. Those nerves connected directly to his cock, which was instantly stiff as a block of firewood. Hell, he felt like he'd spent his whole life as kindling and this was his first flame.

Ash pulled back from the deep kiss, gasping. He pressed his mouth against Mark's ear. "I want to fuck you so bad, but I don't know if... I mean, do you do that? I would never hurt you."

Mark whispered, "Why are you asking?"

"I thought maybe... the thing in the hall with that asshole."

"God, you're sweet. It's tough to hate you."

"I hope you don't hate me." Ash's breath whispered against Mark's neck.

Mark sat back on his heels. "Here's the deal. I love fucking. So we can fuck, or I can tell you what happened."

Ash mimicked him and sat back. They looked like a couple of guys practicing yoga together. "Tell me."

"Well, damn, you called my bluff."

Ash grinned. "I know. And if I'm choosing to wait one second before fucking you, I must really want to know the story."

Deep breath. "I don't like talking about myself."

"I've noticed. I confessed my big idea to you. And I told you I'm gay. Nobody else knows. Your turn. So tell me."

Oh boy. "When I was on my own, I had to sleep in subways a lot. Sometimes I could find a spot in a shelter, but I was afraid they were going to turn me in to child services, and I really didn't want that. Anyway, one time I found a good hiding place in a station and tried to sleep. I woke up with three guys all over me. One had my pants half down, one was holding me, and the third one was peeing on my feet. Shit." He shuddered. "I can still smell their stink. And the biggest one had his cock pointed straight at me. Talk about your weapons of mass destruction." He shook his head.

"Shit, Mark, I'm sorry."

"The thing is, I got away. I barely know how. But when I woke up I reacted so fast, and I was smaller then and really slippery. The official holder asshole lost his grip on me, and I slipped out of his hands, grabbed my pants, and took off like a shot. They chased me for a while. Man, one would go one way around a garbage can and the other ones would circle the other way. I didn't think I'd make it. I even fell once, and one of the guys grabbed my hoodie, but I slipped out of it and ran like hell. I finally lost them in a park. I really missed that hoodie. It was cold." *Whew.* He was breathing hard just thinking of it.

"You must've been terrified."

"Yeah. Full-on. And I thought I'd never get their smell off me. I think that's what came back when Richard the Bastard tried his thing. Anyway, I learned real fast that it didn't pay to be noticed. I started covering my hair and wearing the glasses. It helps when people think you're weird. They leave you alone more." He grinned. "Of course, I am weird."

"What a crap way to grow up. How did you eat? How did you get any schooling?"

"I can sew really well. I worked in sweatshops with a lot of Asian ladies. When people got too curious about where my parents were, I'd move on. I was always good in school, so by the time I ran away, I'd almost finished all my high school classwork and even taken a college course or two. Then I got a job as a janitor in a night school that taught a lot of college stuff, including fashion design. I could get the work done fast and slip into the classes. It was great. I finally found a little place to live and got off the streets. But it's expensive in the city, so I came here to try to save for design school."

Ash had tears in his eyes. "You're amazing."

"I just did what I had to."

"Not many people would've survived." Ash reached out and took Mark's hand. "I want to be more like you."

No way. Mark shook his head. "You don't. It makes you hard. You're much softer, gentler, kinder."

Wide blue eyes stared at him. "Is that good?"

"Hell, yeah." They just sat there, staring at their interlocked hands. Mark ran his thumb over Ash's. "Will you fuck me now?"

The smile was huge. "Hell, yeah."

"I want the memory."

"Memory?"

"Yeah. Some of the memories that hurt the most are the ones you really value."

"Oh God, Mark." Ash reached out his hand and touched Mark's bare chest. His thumb rubbed against a taut nipple, and Mark jumped a foot. From zero-to-sixty in one second. That thumb rubbed right over his heart with a straight line to his cock. There were a thousand reasons not to, but he really wanted to fuck this man.

He rolled to the side, opened the drawer in the rickety end table, and extracted some lube. He handed it to Ash. "I only use it to jerk off. I don't have any condoms. No plans."

"I do." Ash reached into his hip pocket and pulled out a slim leather wallet. "These are a little old since I didn't have any plans either, but I think they should be good."

"Don't they say life is what happens when you're making other plans?"

"Yes. Come here, my life."

Did he really say that? Sweet God, have to kiss him. He hurled himself at Ash and was scooped up and on his back before he could breathe. That long body came down on top of him, still covered in ridiculous clothes. One deep kiss later, Mark wriggled. "Get those damned clothes off. I want to feel you naked."

"My pleasure." Ash pushed himself up and swung off the bed. He reached down and unfastened his shoes, toed them off, and then ripped off his socks. He pulled his dress shirt over his head without unbuttoning it.

OMG. Mark had never seen his chest. Carved. Hard and lean. Defined pecs, cobbled abs. "You do stay in shape."

Ash grinned as he pulled off his belt and swung it like a hoochie dancer, tossing it on the old chair. He unfastened the button of his slacks, then slowly and maddeningly slid the zipper down. He hooked his fingers in his briefs underneath and pulled them off along with the pants. *Oh, baby.*

He stood with a flourish and waggled his cock. "You like?"

Wow—a good, solid nine inches. "Oh, that old thing." He waved a hand in the direction of Ash's hard-as-stone penis. "I've had that down my throat already. What else ya got?"

Ash laughed, hopped on the bed, and grabbed the lube. "How about I push this old thing so far up your pretty ass you can give me a blowjob backwards?"

Mark had to clap a hand over his mouth to keep from spitting as he laughed.

Ash grabbed his jeans and pulled. "Let's see what you got, baby. Or should I say what I get."

He felt a little shy. He wasn't as big as Ash, and nobody had looked at him much in his checkered sexual career.

"Wow." Mark looked up at the wide blue eyes. "You're breathtaking. So lean and smooth. No wonder you look perfect in those dresses."

Mark shook his head. "I'm just a tall, skinny boy."

"A tall, skinny, beautiful boy who's about to get his ass fucked. I mean, if you like to bottom."

Mark rolled back and captured his thighs in both hands, pulling them up by his ears. A pretty daring pose for a guy who tried to be anonymous and self-protective, but there was something about Ash he trusted. At least with his body. His heart? Not so much.

"God, that is gorgeous." Ash leaned forward and—*holy crap!* Two hands spread Mark's cheeks, and a soft, wet tongue connected with his aching hole. Pleasure had a new definition. Zings of fire raced up his groin and electrified his cock. He could come just from that exquisite pleasure.

"No, uh, no one has ever done that to me before." He sounded like Marilyn Monroe. Husky and breathy.

"Then we're even." The hot tongue pressed, and an inch slipped inside him.

Jesus. "I'm already an addict." He wanted to stay still so Ash's tongue didn't have to work hard to keep doing what it was doing, but he couldn't. His hips rose, twisting and writhing.

Ash held him for a minute longer, then pulled back, opened the lube, and thrust two wet fingers into his hole. "I can't wait. Gotta get in you."

Mark watched Ash pull a condom on his big cock and then kneel into position. *Whoa.* Would it hurt? It had been a while. Forever, if you counted the size of that thing. "Go slow."

"I will." The silky, blunt head connected with the place Mark most wanted it. Ash reached between them and began a slow crank on Mark's cock. *Yes, oh God.* That was it.

He felt his hips begin to push him against Ash's dick. That's what he wanted. "In me, please."

"Ah, the go slow portion of the adventure is past?"

"Apparently. Get it the fuck in me!"

Pop. In one push, the fat head slipped inside Mark's body. *Holy crap.* Stretching, burning. "Wait." Ash seemed to hold his breath and freeze. Mark breathed out slowly. "More." Ash slid in another inch. "More. More." Two inches. "Fuck!" Ash rammed that baby home. "Holy crap!"

"Ah, a welcome from your prostate. You feel sooo good." Ash pulled his hand off Mark's cock and put his full weight on his arms, his biceps and triceps popping. It moved his hips into full fucking position and, oh God, did Ash fuck. Thrust in and pull out, in and out. In, in, in.

Every trip across Mark's tingly nerves and red-hot gland sent joy juice up his spine and bolts of pleasure to his cock. Sex had always been a rushed, clandestine affair for Mark, behind paper-thin walls with questionable partners. *Welcome to a different world.* Full-blooded, glorious sex with a man he desired more than breathing. This little room was plain and ugly, but it could have been the Taj Mahal because, man, he felt like a princess.

Ash leaned down to his ear. "You like it, baby? You like my cock in your ass? Is it good?"

"Yes. Don't stop. Do it forever." Mark pushed his hips to meet every hammering thrust. *Oh God, so good.*

"With pleasure." Ash's hips snapped and sweat dripped off his forehead onto Mark's cheek. In, in, in.

Oh God, yes, fuck yes, good. Holy—He gasped as an explosion ripped through his balls and out his cock. Spurt after spurt. "Oh God, oh, oh." A wave of perfect joy washed through him, filling him with a tingly, electric pleasure.

Ash tensed, his hips plunged to the balls into Mark's ass, and he shuddered once, twice, three times. "Unnnnnnn." He stayed suspended on his straight arms for a minute, then collapsed onto Mark's chest. A welcome weight. And a stored memory.

CHAPTER 10

DRAGGIN' AGAIN. The number of steps to Mark's room definitely had multiplied since he'd floated down them nine hours ago. And he was pretty sure his bed wasn't going to look nearly as good as it had when he slipped out of the room. He'd stood in the doorway and watched Ash sleep for minutes, just enjoying the rise and fall of that sculpted chest. *Wow.* Who would have ever thought? Who would have thought Ashton Armitage would be sleeping like a baby, naked and beautiful, in Mark's bed? Who would have thought sex could be that incredible? Who would have thought Mark would let himself get his heart broken? *What an idiot.* Who'd have thought?

He pushed the door open. *What the heck?* A huge box sat on his bed. And on his pillow lay a note. He closed the door behind him and went straight for the note.

Dear Mark—I never knew. Love, Ash

He couldn't make his eyes leave that one word. *Love.* It was a casual, idle word people threw around all the time. But they didn't throw it to Mark. *Love.* Yep, heartbreak city.

He tucked the note under his pillow. *Sweet dreams.* What about the box? He opened it and pulled back some tissue paper. *Holy crap!* Yards and yards and yards of the most exquisite white charmeuse. Like the crème brûlée he and Ash had shared at dinner had been translated into fabric. A note lay on top of the silk.

Mark, my boy, start sewing. The ball is three days away. Carstairs

The ball. Everyone had been talking about it when he went back into work this afternoon. The biggest event of the season. A true grand ball. The women were freaking out to have received such short notice. Apparently some guest had requested it and was footing a big chunk of the bill, so the hotel was knocking itself out to comply. Probably that Middle Eastern potentate. He loved to throw big parties.

Mark sat on the bed, stroking the fabric gently. Couldn't let his calluses catch on the silk. *Oh God, yes.* He could see it—a collar to the chin above a slit to the waist. Cut on the bias so it would cling in all the right places. He'd have to find a way to tuck his cock in for this one. Maybe Mr. P. would want a real woman to wear this dress? They could bring someone in from the city. Oh, but then he wouldn't get to see the ball with all the gorgeous gowns. No, he definitely wanted to go. Maybe Ash would even save a dance for him.

ASH STRETCHED his hands behind his head and wiggled his feet on the arm of the sofa. Cool. Every little movement sent happy shock waves straight to his cock. It was like Mark had plugged him into a sex faucet and juice just kept pumping through his hose. That was so damned good. He closed his eyes and remembered… that gorgeous black hair spread out on the white sheet. The pink-tinged, pouty lips opened as he cried out Ash's name and came and came.

The door to the suite opened. "Hi, Ash, just me."

He smiled at Ronnie and tried to adjust his half-hard cock without being obvious. "Hi 'just me.'"

She stopped beside the couch and stared down at him. "So did you enjoy eating the canary?"

"Excuse me?"

"Cat who ate the—Last time I saw you, you were running out of the dining room yesterday afternoon on the heels of a very gorgeous woman, who apparently isn't one. I don't think I have to ask how that turned out."

He knew his grin must look idiotic, but he just couldn't help it.

She sat across from him. "So that was really the waiter?"

"Yep."

"Man, pretty as any girl I've ever seen. And you had sex?"

"It was kind of more than that, I think."

"That's interesting. But regardless of how much the earth moved, if it even shifted a couple degrees, the fact of the matter is you're gay. It's the way you swing. You gotta come out of the freakin' closet."

"I'm thinking about it, but…."

"But what?"

"I have this idea for what I want to do with the money. I need a lot of dough to do this and—" He looked up at a sharp rap on the door. He frowned at Ronnie. "Are we expecting someone?"

She shook her head. "Shall I see?"

"Yeah."

She crossed into the entry, and he watched her open the door a few inches and peek around it. It flew out of her hands as Beatrice Fanderel, complete with Fanderel chicks, burst into the room. "I'd like to speak to Mr. Armitage, please."

He swung his feet onto the floor and stood. No shoes, but nothing he could do about that now. "Beatrice, what a surprise. I didn't know to expect you. Please excuse my informality."

"Ashton, I want to get straight to the point. May I?"

He wasn't sure he wanted to receive her point. "By all means, but why don't you and the ladies sit first." He gestured to the two chairs and the sofa. Beatrice positioned herself fully in front of him on the chair, while Bitsy took the sofa beside him and Bernice the other chair. Bitsy touched his arm lightly, and he jumped but looked at her. She shook her head and said softly, "I'm really sorry. Please tell her to go to hell."

He stared at her for a minute. *What the fuck?* Turning to Beatrice, he smiled. "What can we offer you to drink?"

Ronnie walked to the bar. "I can offer coffee, soft drinks, or most any kind of liquor you can imagine."

He nodded at Bernice. "Mimosa?"

The young woman started to answer, but Beatrice broke in. "No, thank you. We're fine. Well, at least in the drinks department. But, Ash, I want to know what intentions you might have with regard to Bitsy."

The woman he'd thought unflappable squealed, "Mother, please, I've told you."

"Nonsense. Ash is a grown-up, we're all grown-ups, and he seemed to be very interested in you, but suddenly that appears to have waned. I just wondered why."

Bitsy was beside him, so he couldn't see her expression. "Well, of course, I'm delighted by Bitsy, which is why I made the offer, but I—"

"You what? You made an offer to Bitsy? Of marriage?"

"It was more of a discussion. But the nature of the agreement was not to her liking."

"Nature?" Beatrice looked at Bitsy. "What nature?"

He looked between the women. "That's something I've asked Bitsy to keep private between us, which, of course, is why she hasn't spoken of it." *Good.* That should get the girl off the hook.

Beatrice's eyes narrowed. "How bad could it possibly be? Are you some kind of monster?"

She should only know.

Bitsy sat forward. "Good Lord, Mother, it has nothing to do with Ash. It was about the, shall we say, business factors, and as I've thought of them, they don't seem so bad, really."

Beatrice threw herself back in her chair. "So everything is fine, then."

The door to the suite opened. Ash stood. What in the bloody hell was going on?

"Thank you so much, young man. Don't worry… he won't mind."

Ash took two steps toward the door. "Mother? Dad?"

His mother looked up and smiled. "Hello, darling. Hope you don't mind. We decided to surprise you."

Some fucking surprise. All he wanted to do was lie here and think about Mark, and his suite turned into grand fucking central. "Hello, sir." He shook hands with his father.

His mother looked around the room. Perfectly dressed in expensive casual, with her short brown hair styled to the nines, she radiated gracious elegance as always. "Hello. I'm Miranda Armitage, and this is my husband Mel."

His dad appeared confused, probably by all the females surrounding Ash.

His mom waved a hand at Ronnie, who still stood by the bar. "Hi, Ronnie."

"Mrs. Armitage." Ronnie grabbed an extra chair and put it into the seating group. His mother walked around the coffee table and sat.

His father took a chair, and Ash stood. Hell, he never wanted to sit again. "Mother, Dad, may I introduce Beatrice Fanderel and her lovely daughters? This is Bernice." Bernice smiled and shook hands. "And this is Bitsy."

Bitsy stood to shake hands, and his mother sprang to her feet. "Bitsy? Ash, this is the lovely girl you've been telling us about. Charming, simply charming." She pulled her into a huge hug, then held her out at arm's length. "My dear, welcome to the family."

Fucking shit.

MARK WANTED to get some more done, but he just had a little while before he had to be at work. He moved to the front of his chair and leaned back to get out the kinks. It had been a while since he'd pulled an all-nighter. The day job was so exhausting, it was tough to sew all night and not mess stuff up. But this was a true labor of love. Just touching the silk was orgasmic. It was his best creation yet. A cross between Audrey Hepburn in *My Fair Lady* and Jean Harlow in… anything. Sexy and ladylike combined. A few more seams and he'd quit for the day.

A soft tap on his door startled him. It wasn't much like Mr. Pennymaker's knock. Who would come looking for him? He stood and about fell down, he was so stiff. Jesus, he hadn't moved out of the chair for hours. He stretched, walked to the door, and opened it. *Oh my, yes.* He beamed. He knew it was a dumb reaction. But there you have it. "Hi."

Ash smiled, but it didn't reach his eyes. Not a good sign. "May I come in?"

"Sure." Mark walked back in ahead of Ash and gathered up his sewing paraphernalia so Ash could sit on the chair.

Ash sat, accompanied by the chair's usual groaning squeak. "You making something new?"

"Yeah. For the ball."

"Uh, wow. Pretty material."

"Yes." The cold chills running up his spine were not a good sign either. "What's going on?"

Ash frowned. "My parents arrived unexpectedly."

"Oh."

"They're going to Europe soon and want me to get married before they go. Apparently someone invited them to the fucking ball, so they came here early."

"I see." He didn't see. He would never see again.

"They expect me to marry Bitsy."

Mark's hands were clammy. "I thought she said no."

"I guess she reconsidered in light of the money and how she wouldn't have to sleep with me or anything."

Mark sat on the bed. How fast could he get rid of Ash? He could stay in control for about a minute. "I can imagine that would be appealing to a lot of women."

Ash gave a half smile. "You figure I'm that tough to fuck?"

Mark tried to breathe. "No, I just imagine a woman who's marrying someone she doesn't know isn't anxious to hop into bed with him. I never got that arranged marriage shit. Just some more misogyny as far as I could tell." *I have to catch my breath.*

"Yeah, but this will be just an arrangement, you know. It doesn't mean anything—"

Mark's head snapped up, and Ash quit talking. "So you're going back to the city for the wedding?"

"Uh, no." Ash met his eyes for a second and then looked aside. "The wedding is going to be the pièce de résistance of the ball on Saturday. It happens at midnight. I wanted to tell you."

His swallow was so noisy he knew Ash could hear it. "Here at the hotel."

"Yes. I wanted to tell you before someone else did."

Mark's sight went black for a second. He shook his head. "Great. Maybe I'll get to serve and earn some tips." *Have to stop talking so fast.* "They really need all the people they can get for big events. Thanks so much for telling me. I'm sure it's going to be beautiful. I know it is."

Ash leaned forward and grabbed his wrist. "Mark…."

Mark's eyes came up and met those baby blues. He would not scream. He gritted his teeth. "Get the hell out of my room."

Approximately ten years or ten seconds after watching Ash's back retreat out his door, Mark moved ten inches to the side to keep tears from falling on the silk. He wasn't sure how to go to work when he couldn't move. *Stupid to feel this way.* He'd never had a prayer. He'd never thought he had a prayer. His heart and his cock had hope for all of them.

Have to move. He stood. His head spun, so he sat back down.

The sharp rap on the door only caused one second's leap of his blood pressure. He knew that knock, and it wasn't Ash. "Come on in, Mr. P."

His friend, the meddling elf, bustled into the room. "So how's it coming, my dear? Let me see. Let me see." Mr. P. picked up the mostly completed garment. "Well, clearly you've outdone yourself."

"Yes, I think it's good."

Mr. P. looked up at him. "A bit flat, are we?"

"Just have to get to work." He pulled on his blue jacket.

"What has occurred?"

"Nothing you don't already know, I'm sure."

"That Ashton is getting married after the ball."

"Bingo. Give that man the grand prize." He stepped toward the door. "I'm going to be late. And by the way, we need a model for the ball, because I won't be going."

Pennymaker dropped the dress and pointed at the chair. "Sit."

Mark sat. "I feel like a collie."

"No, you have a closer resemblance to an ass than a dog."

"Thanks." He shook his head and felt more hot tears pressing behind his eyes. *No way.* He was done crying.

Mr. P. planted both fists on his small hips. "Young man, you have some of the most prominent members of the fashion industry drooling over your designs and coming to this ball to see them. When we met, you told me your most fervent wish was to go to design school. Well, that goal and many beyond it are within grasp. Has that desire been supplanted by the desire for Ashton Armitage?"

There was a question. "Hell, no."

"Then how can you even think of not going to the ball?"

Mark pressed his lips together. *Answer, you stubborn ass.* "I guess I can't."

"Correct. Besides, if it was you marrying Ashton, who would support the two of you? He'd be an overeducated church mouse, and I'm sure you'd prefer not to have to clean fireplaces to put bread on your table."

"I wouldn't mind…." The words burst out in a flood of tears.

Mr. P.'s arm came around Mark's shoulders. "Ah there, young one, in love there is always hope. Don't despair. You may not always get what you want, but I'm going to help you get what you need. Now dry your eyes, go to work, and come back and finish this masterpiece. It will all sort itself out."

Mark wiped at his nose. "How?"

The gray eyes sparkled. "Trust me."

WHACK. THE tennis balls serenaded. Ronnie glanced to the side of the path, into the trees and bushes. It wasn't that she was looking for Bitsy exactly. But the woman did seem to frequent this area since they'd taken their walk here that first day.

It was a gorgeous day if you only counted the weather. Everything glistened green. As green as the Armitage money. What about the older Armitages suddenly showing up here? Poor Ash. He had enough to sort out without the arrival of the king and queen of pressure. Hell, poor Ronnie. She wasn't sure at all how *she* felt about this marriage.

A soft whimpering sound made her look toward the bushes. Was that—she pushed aside a long-leafed hedge and walked back into the shade of some bigass trees. Bitsy leaned against one of the trunks. Oh man, the chick was crying.

Ronnie walked up behind her, making just enough noise to let her know she wasn't alone. Bitsy looked over her shoulder and tried to smile, but the sobs took over. Ronnie put her hands on her shoulders and in a flash had an armful of Bitsy. *Oh yeah.* She wrapped her tight and held on.

Soft, warm, and very girly. Not usually Ronnie's style, but this woman got to every layer of her being. Bitsy was smart, independent, and ragingly honest—usually. "Having some problems with your decision?"

Bitsy nodded against Ronnie's neck. She was just the right size to cuddle in there.

"Want to talk?"

Another nod. Still holding Bitsy under one arm, Ronnie walked over to a bench tucked among the overhanging tree branches. Real lover's lane style. She sat and pulled her pretty, curvy little body down beside her. Ronnie tightened her hold, and Bitsy put her head on Ronnie's shoulder.

Ronnie smiled. "Sorry, I'm a little boney. Probably not too comfortable."

"Ummm, feels good."

Ronnie had no argument. She sighed. *Let Bitsy talk if and when she wanted to.*

Bitsy nuzzled a little against her upper chest. Goose bumps. "It's easy to have principles when they're never really tested. It's easy for me to say I want to live my own life and be my own person, but I still let my mother help put me through school, and the only thing I have to rebel against is her overprotective love. Then somebody dangles a hundred million dollars in front of me and I crack."

Ronnie laughed, and after a second Bitsy joined in. "Hey, give yourself a break. Gandhi might've had trouble with this choice. Didn't he say it took a lot of rich friends to keep him in poverty?"

"Yeah. I always loved that."

"You're being offered a whole lot of money and you don't even have to fuck the guy? Hell, I might even be tempted."

Bitsy pulled away and looked at Ronnie with a raised brow.

"Oh hell, no. Ash and I are buddies. Besides, he asked you."

"I know. I wish he hadn't. Then I wouldn't be in this pickle."

"Hey, he knows a good thing when he sees it."

Bitsy shook her head. "That's the thing, Ronnie. I don't think he believes I'm a good thing. Maybe just the best of a bunch of evils. He's in exactly the same place I am. There's an old Indian parable about how to catch a monkey. You put something good to eat in a small-mouthed jar connected to a rope. The monkey reaches in and grasps the food, but with his fist closed, he can't get his hand out. To be free, all he has to do is open his hand, but he's caught because he won't let go of the goody. Ash and I have our hands caught in a monkey jar."

"Great story."

"True story."

"So what are you going to do?"

Bitsy got up and walked a few steps into the overhanging branches. Like a wood nymph in a white cotton dress and blonde curls. "Everyone expects us to marry now, and they're all so happy."

"Fuck everyone!" Wow, that came out a bit harsher than she'd intended.

Bitsy looked at her. Her lips curved in a little smile. Mona Lisa time. Ronnie smiled back. *Who knows?*

CHAPTER 11

"I'M LOOKING forward to tonight. It promises to be quite an event." Ash's dad opened the door to the suite and stepped out into the hall.

"Yes, sir."

"You don't seem overjoyed."

"This isn't exactly a fairy tale, Father. One doesn't burst with joy over expediency."

"But she seems a fine girl. I'm proud of you, actually. I don't know what I expected, but I'm delighted you chose Bitsy."

"I like her."

"Good. That's an excellent foundation. Your grandfather would have approved."

Was there a gorilla sitting on his chest? "See you later." He closed the door and leaned against it. His grandfather wouldn't have approved of him denying who he was in order to abide by the rules of the will.

He walked over to the couch. God, that piece of furniture was like an extension of his body, he'd spent so much time lying on it trying to figure out what the hell to do. He flopped down, staring at the ceiling again.

His grandfather would have loved his idea for the adoption agency. Well, maybe not the specifics, but the old man loved big ideas and bold strokes that helped a lot of people. Did Ash have the balls to do it? If he had the balls, did he have the chops? Everything he knew about business he'd learned in a lot of fancy schools. No experience at all.

He sat up and rubbed a hand over the back of his neck. But maybe the adoption idea was just another one of his lies to himself? Hell, he liked being rich. He liked it a lot. Being famous he hated. But that would take a long time to change, even if he gave up his inheritance. Paparazzi would still follow him around, and he wouldn't have any privacy at all. It was amazing he'd been able to keep his orientation private. One or two whispers, but nothing much. Nothing much except the holes it left in his soul.

He was gay. That was true. Hiding it from people compromised every relationship he had. If someone said they loved him, he always thought they wouldn't if they knew. Only Ronnie knew him for who he really was. Ronnie… and Mark. He sighed. And there it was—Mark. A crazy boy in a cap whose existence challenged every decision Ash made about his own life. A boy he thought he could love.

Ash had never had a real relationship with a man. He might not be good at it. And at the stroke of midnight tonight, he knew he'd lose his chance to find out. At least with this man. That look Mark had given him when he floated the idea that his marriage to Bitsy was just an arrangement nailed Ash to the wall. Mark didn't have to say *expedience. Manipulator. Coward.* The words were all over his face. No, a relationship with Mark Sintorella would be a greater challenge than setting up any global charity, because it would demand that Ash be who he really was.

He dropped his head in his hands. He could think himself to death. How did he feel? Oh crap, he felt in love. Yes, he barely knew the kid, but Ash had spent twenty-five years around every kind of man. Men he could have had if he had just snapped his fingers. He'd never wanted one of them like he wanted Mark. And he could sit here like a slug and let the best thing that had ever come into his life slip away like everything else good he'd ever had, or….

He grabbed his cell and dialed. It rang a few times. A puzzled-sounding voice answered. "Ashton, is that you?"

"Yes, sir."

"What a surprise. Your father didn't tell me to expect a call. I thought you were vacationing at some resort or other."

"I am, Henry, and I apologize for calling you on Saturday. But you know how you offered me a job with your division when I got out of school?"

"Yes. The job you turned down flatter than my putting green? Besides, we always knew if you wanted to come into the firm, you'd go work with your father."

"I'd like to take you up on the offer. Come into the company as a junior executive. I can even get coffee, you know. I want to learn the business the way my dad did. From you."

Silence. *Well, shit.* He'd worn out the invitation.

"What's inspiring this now, Ash? You're about to come into more money than you'll earn in a lifetime. Why bother?"

"I have things I want to do, and I don't have time to make a lot of mistakes on my own. I want a mentor. I don't know if you'll have me, but I pick you. Besides, I need the money."

"Yeah, right." Ash didn't say anything. "You mean it?"

"About the job? Yes. I'd like to start in two weeks."

"Okay, I'm floored here."

"Does that mean no?"

"Look, I'd hire you in a minute. I see a lot of brilliance in you, Ash."

"So that means yes?"

"Yes, but don't take this job and make a big media circus out of it like Elvis going in the army."

"No, sir. I want to work. I can't guarantee the press won't pay attention, but I'm not going to tell them."

"What did your father say about this?"

"I haven't told him."

"What?"

"Why don't you tell him? I have to get ready for a ball."

MARK STARED at the dress form. It was good. His best piece so far. Mr. P. had called it brilliant. That was true. The gown seemed to glow like it was lit from the inside. He loved it. He hated it. And it was time to put it on.

A quick glance in the little mirror revealed how the makeup and hair really did a job. Huge black eyes, full pink lips, and his hair pulled up like a crown, with messy tendrils falling everywhere. Princess climbing out of bed after delicious sex. He was no princess, but the dress was.

Mr. P. had bought him a gaff to give his body a more female appearance under the slinky silk. This was going to be weird. Hell, he loved being a guy. He didn't want to be a girl. But he sure did love their clothes.

Here goes. He tucked his balls up above their sac like Mr. P. had suggested and pushed his penis back so it fit along his asscrack. The gaff came next. He looked down. Freaky. Not exactly comfortable either, but it was only for one night. This was it. After tonight, Mariel was going on a forever vacation, and Mark was going back to his fireplaces and toilets.

The fashion people had their crack at him just this once. Hell, the chances of getting somewhere in fashion were about like making it into the NBA. Or making it in the life of Ashton Armitage. *Slim, meet none.*

He pulled on panty hose that smoothed everything down. Since the dress was slit to the waist, there was simply no way to mimic breasts, and that was fine with him. Yeah, he was done. Tonight he'd give it his all, be a good little fashionista. Show off his talent, if he had any. No wedding, of course. He was heartbroken, not masochistic. He'd make his splash and leave the ball before the stroke of midnight.

He gently took the dress from the form and slipped it over his head, guarding his hair with his arms. Women sure went through a hell of a lot to be beautiful. The dress fell into place, hugging every angle with sexy perfection. Like walking inside whipped cream.

Then he looked down. There they were—the most gorgeous, crystal-encrusted high-heeled sandals he had ever seen. In his size. A gift from Mr. P.

He'd practiced half the night so he could walk without stumbling. The other half of the night he'd tried to master the intricacies of a pedicure. Right now, his size elevens were pink-tipped and beeee-utiful. But not as gorgeous as the shoes.

He felt like a close-up on a TV series as he slipped them on and stared at his feet with ecstasy. Time to go.

"DARLING, YOU look gorgeous."

"Thanks, Mother." Bitsy cocked her head. Yeah, she looked okay. Since the event was a ball first and a wedding after, they had let her wear her favorite pink rather than making her do the virginal bride routine. *Good.*

The gown hugged her bodice and flared out from a slightly dropped waist that somehow looked like it measured about eighteen inches. Her mom had loaned her a diamond necklace she'd worn as a girl that looked pretty against Bitsy's creamy skin. Not bad belle-of-the-ball material.

Her mom gave a little squeal at the tap on the door. "It's Ash. Oh, you must be so excited."

Beatrice would have been excited, so she assumed Bitsy was. This was going to be a tough night.

Her mom swung open the door. Ronnie was on the other side, dressed in a black tuxedo. *Sweet God, what a great outfit.*

"I don't understand."

"Sorry, Mrs. Fanderel. Ash asked me if I'd come and collect Bitsy. He had a last-minute call from, uh, a business associate, and he didn't want to keep Bitsy waiting."

"Well, of course I was anxious to see Ashton in his finery."

Clearly her mom thought it was weird but was doing a pretty good job of carrying it off.

Ronnie smiled at Bitsy. "You sure look beautiful."

Bitsy smiled back. "Thank you."

"Shall we go?" Ronnie offered her arm.

Hell, yes. Bitsy slipped her bare arm against the silky gabardine of the tux. Ronnie looked like a million Marlene Dietrich bucks.

Beatrice looked confused and not at all happy. "I'll see you girls later."

"See you at the ball, Mom."

Out in the hall, Ronnie looked at her again and smiled. "You really do look great."

"Thank you. So do you. I love the tux."

"I'm not much for dresses."

"I guessed."

They got on the elevator taking them to Ash's suite. Ronnie seemed nervous. That was rare. Nothing usually seemed to ruffle her feathers.

Bitsy looked at her. "You okay?"

"Yeah." The door opened on Ash's floor. Suddenly Ronnie reached out and hit the button for the top floor, a roof garden.

"What?"

"I'm not okay. I usually say what I mean, Bitsy. Lately I haven't been." The door opened to the roof, and they stepped out into a twinkle of lights and bubbling water. A few people walked with cocktails, sporting their finery for the ball.

Ronnie grabbed her hand and pulled her to the far edge of the roof, where there were no guests at the moment. She turned to Bitsy. Even with a crease between her brows, the planes of her sculpted face looked soft in the twinkle lights. Her platinum hair shone.

Ronnie gave a little huff and took Bitsy's other hand. "Look, I like you. A lot. If things were different and we were, you know, different, I might try to convert you to the girls' team."

She laughed, but it sounded nervous.

"I know you have a lot of reasons to marry Ash, and I want you to know he's a great guy. And I know you aren't expecting a real married life or anything, but the fact is, he's gay, Bitsy. Deep in the closet, but gay. I know he figures it doesn't matter since you're not going to be lovers or anything, but I thought you should know. You can tell him I told you, but please don't tell anyone else, okay?"

So there it was. "I kind of figured it was something like that. Wow. And to keep his money, he has to marry a woman." She shook her head.

"Yeah."

"Why can't the world just let people be who they are?"

"Yeah."

Bitsy looked at the tall, lean woman. She reached up a hand and threaded it through her silvery hair. Big dark eyes gazed back at her. "By the way, darling, I already play for the girls' team."

CHAPTER 12

ASH LOOKED up from the group of people who had cornered him, along with his parents. Damn, he didn't know where Bitsy was. He'd asked Ronnie to get her and bring her to his suite. When they hadn't showed up, he'd walked down to the ballroom, thinking they might have misunderstood and come here. He really wanted to talk to her. Tell her. Instead he was waylaid by well-wishers. And where was Mark? God, he ached to see the man.

A long-time friend of his family touched his arm. "I'm so anxious to meet your lovely bride, Ashton. This is all so sudden. I don't even know her name. Where will your honeymoon be?"

Hell, what should he say? Might as well continue the fiction for a little while. "Now, now, Mrs. Merson, if I told you I'd—"

"Have to kill me… I know." She laughed.

He looked around the huge outdoor patio that swept off the ballroom and the big bar with dance floor beyond. All the doors were open between the indoors and out, and the entire space was united by tiny lights suspended so they looked like fireflies in space. He had to admit it was beautiful. There were flowers floating in the pool, and they had even brought in fucking swans for the occasion. Seriously. Some other function room had been set up for the wedding. He hadn't looked and wasn't going to.

His dad was holding forth on the great future of Armitage Enterprises.

One of the other men asked, "So, you think it's a good investment for the fourth quarter, Armitage?"

Ash smiled. "Would you expect him to tell you no, Larry?"

"You've got a point there." He laughed heartily. "So where's your bride, Ash? Still primping, I'll bet. I've never seen a woman who can get ready—" The man gasped. Actually gasped.

Ash looked up. Yes, gasp-worthy. She…. He was standing at the top of the stairs leading down to the pool. Yes, he was holding the arm of an elf in a white tailcoat, but that didn't diminish the impact one whit. Mariel had finally arrived. A hush fell over the crowd by the pool. People didn't even try not to stare. His shining black hair fell in tendrils from an updo that, together with his sparkling shoes, must have made him six foot three. That lovely face, all pink lips and wide eyes, managed to look both aloof and surprised at the same time.

And the dress. The man had outdone himself. Ash didn't know fashion, but he'd seen a lot of it up close. This gown was astonishing. The high collar literally ruffled under Mark's chin, showing off his long neck—Ash smiled—and hid his Adam's apple. The shoulders were cut out, showing off the beautiful structure of his collarbones above the long, tight sleeves. From that neck, a slice in the silk slashed to his waist. Though the fabric fell in soft folds, he'd made no effort to augment his breasts, and the hard, taut skin of his chest peeked through. Ash couldn't breathe. It didn't sound like anyone else could either.

Ash's mom whispered, "Who on earth is that girl? She's gorgeous."

He turned his head from the sight with difficulty. His father was staring at him.

"Uh, her name is Mariel. She's, uh, Mr. Pennymaker's niece."

"She must be a high fashion model."

"Yes, I believe so." Ash looked back at the vision. Two men walked up and greeted Pennymaker. The little man turned to Mariel and seemed to introduce him—uh, her. The four walked away together. God, Ash had to get his eyes to stop following.

A hand touched his arm. He looked down at Bitsy, glad his tuxedo jacket covered his cock. He tried to sound normal. "Hi. I was looking all over for you. I thought you were coming to the suite. You look beautiful." She did, though the word had been redefined for him in the last five minutes.

She smiled. "Ash, dear, may I speak with you alone?"

"I CAN'T imagine a more extraordinary muse for this young designer, Mariel. You wear his clothes extraordinarily well."

"Thank you." He used the quiet voice he had adopted for Mariel. Despite how low it was, the softness seemed to convince people that he was female. Standing in the private dining room, he could be heard speaking even softly. The fireplace blazed cheerfully, pretending it was midwinter instead of midsummer.

"Of course, the clothes are quite extraordinary for such a young designer. A great gift."

Man, he could hardly believe his ears. This tall, elegant man with the slicked-back white hair was Joseph-fucking-Caliari, the head of one of New York's most innovative and elegant couture houses. Of course, they had ready-to-wear as well. With him was David somebody, his financial guy. Mark had to hand it to Mr. P. He'd produced a winner.

Caliari turned to Mark's tiny leprechaun in his blazing white tailcoat. "But, Carstairs, I thought you promised we'd meet the designer tonight."

Mark held his breath. How would they get out of this mess?

Mr. P. held up one finger. "I did, and you will. In fact, Joseph, you have."

OMG. He didn't say that.

Mr. P. gave a sweep of the hand. "This is the designer." His arm ended up pointing directly at Mark.

Caliari cocked his head. "Oh, I'm so sorry, Mariel. I thought you were the model. I had no idea… but didn't you say the designer was a man?"

Those twinkling eyes. The little guy was eating this up. "As you see, he is."

"This is a—my God, I'm used enough to androgyny, you shouldn't have been able to fool me. Brilliant, young man, brilliant." Caliari clapped his hands together.

Mark let out his breath. He smiled back at Caliari.

Mr. P. patted his back. "I should explain, gentlemen, that Mark is not a cross-dresser. Due to his limited resources, he has simply fit his clothes on himself. When I realized his extraordinary looks, I thought it best to allow him to get your attention by modeling his own creations."

Caliari laughed. "And you just happened to let us think it was your niece?"

Pennymaker gave a little nod. Caliari looked at Mark. "So you're Mark Sintorella?"

"Yes, sir."

"Have you ever walked the catwalk, Mark?"

"Oh no, sir."

"I think you should consider it."

"I love to design, sir."

"Well, obviously you're going to do that. But someone who looks like you, who could walk in male and female fashion shows, could earn some serious money… which, of course, we won't be paying you as an apprentice designer."

"Excuse me?" His heart hammered.

"You won't make much money as an apprentice designer, Mark."

"I don't care, sir. I'd do it for free."

Caliari laughed. "Hey, Carstairs, you need to represent your client better. Don't let him give away his talent."

Mr. P. swished his hand. "He's doing fine."

"All right, Mark, we'll talk about you coming aboard as an apprentice. If you'll also walk in our runway shows, we can pay you a lot more than we can for your design work. I know it's not fair, but there you have it. If you still want to go to design school, which Carstairs says is a goal of yours, then you'll have to figure out how to fit it all in. But you may decide designing for us is training enough. Assuming you want to, that is."

How could it be true? He felt his head nodding and mouth working, but nothing was coming out. "Yea… uh, yes, yes. Oh God, yes." His face couldn't smile enough. "Mr. P., thank you so much."

"All your own effort, my boy. As usual."

"Hardly. I could never have met Mr. Caliari."

Mr. P. laughed. "I know you'd have found a way. I just saved you some time."

The financial guy looked at his watch. "Time to go, Joseph."

Caliari glanced at his Rolex and pulled a card from his pocket. "Call me Monday, first thing. Can you do that?"

"You directly, sir?" Surely he meant an assistant or somebody.

Caliari glanced at Pennymaker. "Yes, please call me. I look forward to working with you."

Slow down, heart! "I can't wait until Monday."

"Good. We'll talk then." The two men left. *To hell with creases.* He collapsed into a chair. "I don't believe that just happened. It's like a dream. A fairy tale. You're amazing."

"So glad you think so."

"Wow. I can't wait to go upstairs and take off these clothes."

Mr. P. laughed. "Take them off? Of course not, my boy. Your evening has barely begun."

CHAPTER 13

BITSY CLOSED the door behind them. They'd sneaked into a small private room off the kitchen with a big fireplace blazing away, despite the mild weather outside. God, he needed to talk to her, but he felt this urgency about seeing Mark. He didn't want Mark to leave or make any decisions without him.

He turned. "Bitsy, I need—"

"Ash, I have to tell you—"

They both laughed. He shrugged. "Ladies first, I guess."

She smiled. "I'm backing out. I'm not going through with the wedding."

"Really?"

"Yes. I had myself talked into the fact that having your money in an arrangement of convenience wouldn't be compromising. But it would, Ash. Especially since—" She giggled. Not a giggler, this woman. "I've discovered I love someone else."

"Wow. That's great. I'm so happy for you. Anyone I know?"

"Give it a minute's thought."

He shrugged. "How would I—" He looked up and grinned. "Ronnie. Son of a bitch, you're in love with Ronnie."

"Yep."

His smile barely fit his face. "Well, that is great."

"We just kind of figured it out tonight when Ronnie told me you're gay."

"But that's not why… I mean, why you decided…."

"I love you, dear, but don't flatter yourself. I'm a lesbian. Women have always done it for me. I haven't had anyone special in my life since I was an undergrad, so I thought maybe it wasn't going to happen for me."

"You being so old and all."

She laughed. "Yeah. Well, I was attracted to Ronnie from the moment I met her, but I never thought she'd be interested in me. I'm sorry to leave you holding the wedding bag. However, there are still a few more days until your birthday, right? Maybe you can find another woman."

The gorilla was off his chest. "Don't worry about it, Bits. I was going to tell you I couldn't marry you anyway."

"What? You were going to leave me at the altar?" She giggled again. A trend.

"Yeah. Thanks so much for… for everything. I have to go. You find Ronnie and make her dance."

She looked startled. "That, my friend, is a good idea."

He waved and ran out into the lobby and across the space to where the ball was still in full swing. In the ballroom, dancers had flowed off the dance floor and taken over part of the seating space. The crowds at the bars were ten deep, and red ball gowns crushed against blue and black ones from wall to wall. He looked for Mark. Mariel. Hell, even in this crush he'd see him for sure. He was so tall in those shoes. *Damn. Nothing.*

He shouldered his way through the crowd. He apologized at first, but it was too packed for anyone to notice. Finally he got out into the open air. The swans had abandoned the pool and walked around the space pecking idly at tuxedos. He saw his parents and—there! Mark stood beside Pennymaker talking to an older man Ash didn't know.

How can you redefine gorgeous? It was funny to realize Mark was just as beautiful to Ash when he was wearing dirty jeans and a strange black cap. Man, he had it bad. Mark just did it for him. Ash could only hope the man felt the same way about him. He'd been damned angry the last time Ash saw him.

Ash plunged into the crowd again. After a couple of run-ins with elbows and flying evening bags, he came up behind Mark. Mariel. Pennymaker's eyes met his. Calm and appraising.

Ash touched his silk-covered arm and felt the lean muscle beneath. Giant dark eyes rimmed with kohl turned to him. The full lips started to smile and then tightened.

Ash loosened his hand. "May I talk to you?"

He got a level gaze, then a headshake. "Sorry. Just not up to it."

Okay, be calm. "Please. I have something important to tell you."

Another headshake. The wisps of hair fell in front of Mark's beautiful face. Ash saw Mr. Pennymaker's gray eyes measuring him.

And the other guy, whoever he was, seemed interested too. *Well shit, okay. You're interested; you're included.* "I'm not going to marry Bitsy."

Wide eyes. "Oh. Why?"

"She's in love with someone else."

Again the pink lips pursed. "I see."

"No, that came out wrong. I had already decided not to marry her before she told me. I'm not marrying her because I, uh, I want to be with you."

His eyes widened even farther. "With me? Why on earth?"

Okay, Ash, tell the fucking truth for once in your life. "Because I love you."

Ash heard the little gasp. *Hope that was a good reaction.* Mr. Pennymaker looked inscrutable. The other guy? Surprised.

Mark frowned. "Uh, when did you decide that?"

Ash shook his head. "I don't know. I just knew it. All along, I guess. But let's face it, all along hasn't been that long, and I've been a little distracted." He grinned, hoping the charm was working.

"What about the money?"

"I'm giving it up."

Mark's lips parted in a little *o.* "The hell you say. Just like that?"

"You know how not 'just like that' it'll be. It's not easy to give up. But I can't live like this, Mark. Not when there's a chance I could have you."

Mark looked down and spoke softly. "What about the adoption idea?"

"I'm still going to do it; it'll just take longer." He thought he'd bust with the idea. "I just took a job with my dad's mentor so I can learn the business ropes. Yeah, it's in my father's enterprise, but I won't be working for him. I'll make contacts and start a foundation. Get people to contribute. I should be able to use my family name for something besides getting a good seat in a restaurant." He laughed.

Mark grabbed his hands. "You're serious. That's so wonderful."

"Is it? Do you think so?"

"Oh yes. I love it." Mark beamed. "I have news too."

"What? Tell me."

"I think I'm going to be working for Caliari Couture. As a design apprentice. I'll be able to learn so much while I'm working. Mr. Pennymaker did it all for me."

"That's amazing. I knew you'd do it one way or another. You can do anything."

Mark's smile was huge. It slowly faded. "And what do you think this all means?"

Ash held the silken forearms. "I'm hoping maybe you and I can be together."

Mark sighed, which sent the soft silk rustling over his lean body. "Ash, I'm not going to hide in corners with you and sneak away from the press that always follows you. I love you, but I won't live like that."

Ash beamed. "You love me?"

"Of course, but hear what I'm saying."

"That you love me." Ash grinned.

Mark smirked, just the corner of his painted lips turning up. "Yes, you ass. I love you. The love is unconditional, but the being together isn't. I've been hiding from everybody for too long. I don't want to do it anymore." He looked down. "The current outfit notwithstanding."

"That's not what I'm asking. I'll come out, Mark. I'd have done it tonight, but who could get the attention of this rowdy bunch? I want to be your lover, your boyfriend, anything you'll let me be."

"Seriously?"

"All of my heart."

Mark took a deep breath, and Ash held his. "Then I think you know the answer."

Oh God! "Which is?"

"Hell, yes." One leap later, Ash was juggling a squirming mass of Mark, uh Mariel—whoever. He loved them both. In the gigantic heels, Mark was actually a little taller than Ash, which felt odd. He hugged his lithe body tight and crushed his mouth against those full lips, getting a mouthful of lipstick and delicious Mark.

He pulled back. "Sorry, didn't mean to mess up your makeup."

"Anytime."

A smattering of applause made Ash look up. *What the hell?* Crowds of partiers stood around gawking. No time like the present. Might as well spill the beans. He took a breath….

Mr. Pennymaker's voice rang out. "Ladies and gentlemen, I know you've heard that we're to cap off our grand ball tonight with a wedding.

This is the happy couple, and they have invited all of you to attend their nuptials. Please go back to your fun and we'll let you know when the ceremony is about to begin."

Mark's mouth was hanging open. "Mr. P., what are you doing?"

Ash frowned. "What the hell, Pennymaker?"

Mr. Pennymaker smiled, and it could only be described as beatific. He walked them all a little farther into the corner away from the crowds. The quiet stranger came too. "All these good folks are expecting a wedding. Don't you think we should give them one?"

Ash shook his head. "You need a license and a one-day wait—even if Mark was willing to marry me. You've lost your mind."

Mark turned to him. "You mean you'd be willing to marry me?"

Would he? He smiled. "Hell, yes."

Pennymaker extended his hand to the other man, who had been watching this whole exchange. "May I introduce you to my very good friend, Harold Langerfeld?"

Ash cocked his head. "Judge Harold Langerfeld?"

The pleasant-looking older man smiled. "The same."

Ash knew a lot about the fiery old gay judge who championed same-sex marriage in the state with the full force of his office and personality.

"I'm honored, sir. What brings you to these parts, aside from our mischievous friend here?"

"Carstairs asked me to come. He told me you two were going to need a judge in a big way, and since I owe him a great deal and we're fast friends, I couldn't say no."

Mark looked down at Mr. Pennymaker. "But how on earth did you know?"

Pennymaker chuckled. "Old queen's intuition, my boy. I knew you were meant to be together and you'd realize that on your own."

Langerfeld nodded. "And so you have. A judge has the right to do many things, one of which is waive the one-day waiting period for marriage, which I will officially do if you ask me to. And since I'm here and happen to have a license as Carstairs requested, a marriage is well within my purview."

Mark breathed out hard. "Holy shit."

Ash laughed and took both Mark's hands in his. "They've called our bluff, kid. We barely know each other in terms of time—"

Mark nodded. "But somehow we've managed to confront a lifetime of issues in a few days." He walked over to the window and looked out at the trees and night sky. "I know you're glib and charming on the outside but deeply sensitive and caring on the inside. You're smart and funny and incredible in bed." He turned back. "Not everybody has learned that much about their husband before they marry."

"And I know you're braver than I'll ever be and can leap tall buildings in a single bound. There's nothing you can't do, even make a marriage to me work."

His deep dark eyes melted into Ash's. "Hey, Mr. P., I think you have our answer."

Mr. P. smiled. "Excellent. Then why don't you celebrate your very short engagement with a dance?"

Ash looked at Mark. "Want to?"

"Our first dance."

"Come on." He took Mark's hand and led him, in his beautiful finery, a few steps to an area where people were dancing—and still watching their interaction with interest. He took his slim body into his arms. Mark leaned his head against Ash, and the wisps of black hair tickled Ash's ear. The orchestra played something about loving all the way, and they moved together like they'd been dancing for years.

Ash chuckled. "Seems funny I can't feel your cock."

"You won't believe where it's stashed. But I can sure feel yours. Man, I want it in me soon."

"Shh, or we'll give all these people more show than they bargained for." Ash nodded to the crowd that had gathered around the dance area to watch them. The music spoke of good and lean years.

"Ash."

"Hmmm?"

"Are we doing the right thing? You're giving up so much."

"You too, sweetheart. You'll be infamous overnight. The gay lover of the billionaire playboy who let down his family and went broke. Poetic justice." He laughed.

"Husband."

"What?"

"I'll be the gay husband of the billionaire playboy."

"That's right." Suddenly his heart felt too big for his chest.

"God, I love that idea." Mark beamed, his even teeth shining behind the pink lipstick.

"Me too."

"What do you say, my husband-to-be—shall we go do this thing?"

"Hell, yes."

Ash twirled Mark, captured him in his arms, and finished with a grand dip. People applauded wildly. He grabbed Mark/Mariel's hand and escorted him over to Pennymaker.

Mr. Pennymaker clapped his hands. "Excellent. Let's go find a spot where we can sign the license."

CHAPTER 14

"Bitsy, what's going on? Where's Ash? Why aren't you both getting ready for the wedding?"

Okay, the moment had arrived. *Gird your loins, woman.* A guy flew off the dance floor, bumped her, laughed an apology, and tumbled back into the press of dancers. She wished she could join them rather than face her mother. But no such luck. "There isn't going to be a wedding."

Her mother's scowl reached new face-cracking depths. "Of course there's a wedding. They're in there setting up right now. The room is beautiful."

"If they're having a wedding, it doesn't include me."

"What the fuck?"

Bitsy laughed. "Mother! I'm shocked."

"No, you're not. What's going on, young lady?"

"I decided I couldn't marry for money and surrender my independence and everything I value in a marriage of convenience. I'm sorry, Mother. It's just not me. That big a bankroll was seriously tempting, I will admit. But I can't go through with it."

"And what does Ash think about this?"

"He's happy."

"So he doesn't get the money either?"

"I guess not. He didn't tell me what his plans are. Just that he had reached the same conclusion I had."

Her mother pulled out one of the chairs from a nearby cocktail table and sat hard.

"I'm really sorry, Mom. I wanted to do it for you and Bernice. I just can't."

"I know this is hard to believe, but I only wanted it for you. All that wealth and privilege. The travel and music. Things you value. I wanted that for you."

"I do believe you. I was telling my friend what a good mother you are. But I'll get those things on my own."

Her mother smiled a little. "I know you will, dear. Or at least some of it. But Ash's money would've been so easy." She sighed.

Okay, here goes. "There's something else I want to tell you, and I guess it might as well be now."

The music from the orchestra changed. A female singer leaned into the microphone. Her sultry voice filled the space. "My love is here at last. My loneliness behind me…."

"What do you want to tell me now, dear? It'll be hard to top your last bombshell."

Bitsy smiled. Maybe not. A hand touched her shoulder. She looked up into the chiseled face and deep eyes of the woman she knew she was destined to love.

Ronnie grinned. "May I have this dance?"

"Absolutely." She glanced at her mother. "We'll talk later, okay?" She took Ronnie's hand and started toward the dance floor.

They were about to give the resort a new lesson in diversity. *Hold on to your hats.* She slipped into Ronnie's arms and felt her small breasts press against her chest. Long legs slipped between the billows of her pink gown and rubbed against her pubic bone. *Oh yes.* When she glanced back over Ronnie's shoulder, her mother didn't even look surprised.

"CARSTAIRS, WHAT in the hell is going on? Where's my son?"

Carstairs looked up from the table where, moments before, they had completed the signing. *Ah, the boys escaped in the nick of time.* "Hello, Melvin. Long time no see. You look distraught, good fellow; please sit down." He leaned over and pushed out a chair, and the tall, handsome Armitage senior practically fell into it. The sound of the party seemed distant here in the private dining room.

Armitage fixed Carstairs with his best stony gaze. "I've heard a rumor that you had something to do with this ball and with the wedding. Is that true?"

"Why would anyone think that?"

"It makes sense to me. You love to meddle, and you're a sucker for anything that smacks of romance. I remember that couple in India you got together against the express wishes of their families."

"Yes, but they were in love. Whatever should their families have to do with it?"

"Like I say, you're a sucker for romance." He leaned his chin on his bent arm. "So where is my son?"

"Getting ready for his wedding, I believe."

"I gather from all the hoopla in the ballroom that he's not marrying the woman I believed him to be marrying just a few short hours ago."

"True. He's now marrying for love."

Armitage practically broke his face with the frown. "Is that so? My son, who in twenty-five years has never had a serious relationship, is tonight marrying for love someone I have never met?"

"So it would seem."

Armitage shook his head, which was still balanced on his hand like it was too heavy to carry. "Well, at least he's getting married. I guess I don't care to whom. But I kind of liked that Bitsy girl. Good head on her shoulders."

"I think you'll find his new choice of spouse to be equally capable and levelheaded."

Armitage pushed himself up and extended his hand to Carstairs. "Glad to hear it. This is the second time today he's shocked me. Do you know he's going to work for one of my companies? He's never shown the slightest interest, and today he decides to get himself employed."

"He's a talented and capable man."

Armitage frowned. "That's one piece of news you don't have to give me. Anyway, Carstairs, sometime over drinks you can tell me how this whole marriage story unfolded."

"Ah yes. It will start 'Once upon a time.'" He laughed, and Armitage walked into the lobby shaking his head.

"MR. P., I've never been this nervous." Mark giggled. He pressed his back against the wall in the small changing area behind the large reception room the resort used for weddings and other grand affairs. "There are so many people in there. Are you sure we didn't make a mistake by not going back to the city to get married?"

"My boy, there are times when spur of the moment is the best policy. Take a deep breath."

"Oh, I stopped breathing an hour ago." Mark looked down at the silk gown. "Maybe I should've changed? This is so ostentatious."

"Remember, my dear, you're a fashion designer now, and soon to be the husband of a very well-known man. You must practice being ostentatious." Mr. Pennymaker added a few more flowers to Mark's hair, though he had to stand on a footstool to do it. "Besides, a fairy-tale wedding requires a princess, don't you think?"

"Whew. I guess so. Not everybody in there is going to be too thrilled with this princess, though."

Mr. P. took hold of his shoulders, and for once, his face was serious. "You have lived your life on your own terms. What others think does not matter to you, does it?"

Mark looked down at the beautiful sparkling shoes that peeked out from beneath his hem. "I care what you think. And what Ash thinks."

"And we both love you exactly the way you are."

Mark smiled. "Yes, that's the miracle of this whole thing."

"Ah, you understand that, do you? We are each a child of the universe, loved unconditionally. We just need to reach out with an open hand to accept the magic that is freely flowing."

"Just a couple days ago, I'd have thought that was crazy."

"And now?"

Mark waved a hand. "Here I am. Amazing."

Mr. P. stepped off the footstool and reached into the inside pocket of his tailcoat. "Here is something for you, Mark. You're going to need it very soon." He pulled out a small black box.

"What? Oh my gosh." He accepted the box. "Can I open it?"

"You better. I think they're playing your music." A lovely baroque harmony crept in under the heavy door.

Mark opened the box. The ring was simple platinum, glistening, set with tiny diamonds like stars. "I forgot I needed a ring."

"I guessed at Ash's size, but it should be close."

"It's beautiful. Beyond beautiful." Mark smiled. "And now, with my new job, I'll be able to pay you back a little at a time."

"Oh no, my boy. It's a gift. Think of it as something new."

Tears sprang to his eyes. "How can I ever repay you for everything you've done for me? No one ever believed in me before."

"Ah, but you see, you believed in yourself and made everything possible. As for repaying me, you can do that by being ridiculously happy."

"I think I already am." He threw his arms around Mr. P., though he had to lean down a foot to do it.

The little elf hugged him back. Tight. Then he pulled back and looked Mark over. "Enough of that. No wrinkles for your wedding. Now, let me carry that ring, because you have a bouquet to manage."

"I do?"

"Of course, my dear. You're the bride." He went over to a refrigerator on the far wall and pulled out a grand spray of orchids just the color of the silk charmeuse. "Are you ready?"

Mark inhaled and let it out slowly. "Yes."

Mr. P. handed him the flowers and threw open the door. The sounds of music and people hit Mark like a huge wave. Oh God, he wasn't kidding about not breathing. Mr. P. touched his hand, and he slipped his arm through that of the person who had helped make his dreams come true. His amazing mentor and friend. Mark looked down. "I'm so glad you're here giving me away. Thank you."

Tears filled Mr. P.'s eyes. "My pleasure, my boy."

They stepped forward, and the people at the back of the crowd, farthest from the actual wedding site, turned toward them. Smiles, light applause, and a few digital cameras marked their passing. Mark tried to smile back, but he found himself clutching Mr. P.'s arm. They crossed the hall to the entryway of the wedding room.

Wow. Hundreds of people were crammed into every space, sitting in all the chairs, and even lined against the walls. A long white carpet had been stretched through the room between rows of chairs leading to an archway of flowers at the front. At every row, a stand with a huge bouquet of white and yellow flowers marked the spot, and the scent filled the room. Candles burned in wall sconces. It was a fairyland.

The music swelled as they reached the back of the first row of chairs. Mark saw so many people whose faces he knew from the hotel. Funny that they thought they were watching a stranger, or at least an exotic woman they had seen only once or twice.

Mr. P. patted Mark's hand, and they proceeded down the aisle. Mark looked up and ahead of him he saw the judge, but his eyes only stopped for a second. Mark didn't know his heart could beat faster. Now it was trying to escape his chest.

Ash. Just as Mark had thought that first time he saw him walking into the hotel—perfection. Yes, he'd seen him only a short time ago, but now Ash glowed. The smile on his face would light the entire room. Candle flickers illuminated his silvery brown hair where it fell against the black of his tuxedo.

Mark just wanted to be beside him. Wanted his hand in Ash's. Wanted never to be apart again.

He took a longer step. Just that little bit, but it pulled against Mr. P.'s arm, and Mark's foot in the towering heels caught on the white runner. He stumbled forward and his shoe came off. Heat flashed to his face as he grabbed Mr. P.'s arm harder to keep from falling. All around him he heard a chorus of "Oh, dear."

"Oh no."

"Ah."

Mark felt like that deer in the headlights they always talk about. Mr. P. patted his hand. "Not a problem, my dear."

"Excuse me, my love. I think this is yours."

Mark looked down into those blue, blue eyes. Ash knelt in front of him, holding the sparkling sandal. Could eyes radiate love? *Oh yes.*

Ash held the slipper near the ground. Mr. P. grasped Mark's arm to balance him as he raised his foot, and Ash slipped the shoe back into place. He looked up and smiled. "A perfect fit."

Mark laughed. All around him, the people close enough to hear the exchange laughed too. Ash stood and took Mark's arm on the other side, and the three of them walked the short distance to where the judge stood.

Mr. P. pulled the ring from his pocket and handed it to the judge, who put it on a pillow on the small table draped with flowers beside him. Mark saw another ring much like the one Mr. P. had given him lying there as well. It had a few more diamonds. He felt his hands shaking, and the orchids started to vibrate.

Mr. P. chuckled. "Let me take those, my dear."

Mark handed him the flowers, and Mr. P. placed Mark's hand in Ash's with a flourish and went to sit in an empty chair beside Ash's parents. Oh God, Ash's parents. What were they thinking?

Mark took a deep breath and looked into the eyes of the man he loved. Yes, loved. Not "thought he could love." Not "planned to love someday." Loved now with all the depth of his soul. What a miracle. Nothing could spoil that.

Judge Langerfeld's voice rang out across the room. "Ladies and gentlemen, I know many of you are attending this wedding because you're curious and it happens to be at the end of a great party." A lot of people laughed. "But I hope you'll join me in offering your sincere wishes for the happiness of this young couple, because I believe this to be a marriage of true minds and hearts. In my position as a justice of the New York Supreme Court"—that caused a wave of whispers through the crowd—"I don't have the happy chance to marry many couples, so it is my honor today to join in matrimony Mr. Ashton Armitage and—Mr. Mark Sintorella."

Mark shivered. The place went nuts. It started as a whisper passing from person to person and then became a roar.

Ash clutched Mark's hands and leaned in. "No worries, darling. We knew to expect it. Shhh."

Langerfeld managed to quiet the crowd, but one voice stood out. Melvin Armitage stepped forward. He kept his voice soft, though the crease between his eyebrows would have challenged a load of Botox. "Ash, what's going on here? Am I to understand that this young woman is actually a man?"

Mark straightened his back. "Yes, sir, I am, but I don't usually dress this way."

Someone from the crowd, who probably was thinking about Sinders, called out, "I'll say."

Armitage frowned even deeper. "Was this costume designed to deceive us? If so, it has succeeded admirably."

"No, sir."

Mr. Pennymaker stepped up next to Armitage. "Mel, Mark is a brilliant fashion designer, soon to be in the employ of Caliari Couture. He's wearing this gown at my request to show Mr. Caliari his talent."

Armitage sighed audibly. "Carstairs, I knew you had something to do with this."

Mr. P. winked at Mark. "The wedding just happened to come up."

Ash slipped an arm around Mark's waist. It felt wonderful. "Father, I'm sorry. I wouldn't have surprised you like this, but the opportunity to marry the man I love presented itself and I had to take it. You demanded that I marry this week. That's what I'm doing. I know it's not what you expected or even what you want, but this is what I want. What I've always wanted. Mark and I both have new jobs." He smiled. "We'll work to support each other and maybe someday to make you proud."

His father stared levelly at Ash. "You're gay." It wasn't a question.

"Yes, sir."

"That explains a lot."

"Yes, sir."

Judge Langerfeld stepped in closer. "Mel, I'd like to proceed."

Armitage stared at Ash and Mark for a moment, then turned and went back to his seat. At least he was still there. Maybe that was a good sign. Mr. P. followed him.

Mark kind of heard Judge Langerfeld talking, but the words were a blur. Reality lived in the tight feel of Ash's hands holding his. Those hands. The hands he had fantasized about that night he jerked off. That made him smile.

Langerfeld's voice whispered over his skin. "It's customary for the celebrants to exchange rings as a symbol of their love. Just as the circle of this ring has no end, so your love, too, should have no end."

Mark stared at the rings. No end. He was committing himself to another human being—forever. Every person in his life had left him one way or another. But Ash would not leave.

Mark picked up the platinum circle. The diamonds winked at him. A quick glance of thanks to Mr. P., then it was just about Ash. "Will you wear this ring as a symbol of our love?"

"I will."

Mark slipped the ring onto Ash's hand. Perfect. The look. The fit. How had Mr. P. known?

Ash's smile was gentle. "Mark, will you wear this ring and be my love forever?"

Tears filled his eyes, but he still grinned. "Hell, yes."

And then they were repeating the words after Langerfeld. "I, Mark, take you, Ash, to be my lawfully wedded husband—" The words flowed like that wonderful champagne Ash had given him. Bubbles tickling his nose.

"I, Ash, take you, Mark…"

"As long as we both shall live."

"By the power vested in me by the State of New York…. You may kiss the groom." Ash brought his hand up behind Mark's head. He felt fingers thread into his hair. And then Mark's gorgeous lips touched his. It was just a gentle pressure, but it qualified as the most perfect kiss of his life.

Somewhere, hands started clapping. Mark knew a lot of people had probably left as soon as they knew he was a man, but many more were still there, and the applause swelled.

Ash pulled back from the kiss with a huge smile. "I love you, my husband."

"Double."

They turned toward the crowd. Ash whispered, "I wonder what we do now."

"I'm very interested in getting out of these clothes."

Mr. P., the mind reader, stepped in front of the group. "Friends, Ash and Mark are going to freshen up and then will be greeting people in the ballroom. A cake is being brought in and they'll be cutting it soon. Dessert is coming and there's lots more champagne. Please, let Ash and Mark exit first."

Ash offered his arm. "That's our cue, husband."

They walked down the aisle arm in arm. Ash leaned over. "I never got a chance to ask you what we should do about our names."

"What would you like?"

"We could hyphenate."

Mark shook his head. "I think Mark Armitage sounds just fine."

"You sure?"

"Yes. I have no desire to remain a Sintorella."

CHAPTER 15

WHEN THEY got to the hall outside, Mr. P. was waiting, and he ferried them into the same small room Mark had been in before the wedding. Mr. P. left and closed the door on his way out. *Alone at last.*

Ash backed Mark against the door. "Can I kiss my bride now?"

"Hell, yes."

His lips caressed, appreciated, adored, and tantalized, but with no demand. When Ash ended the kiss, he whispered against Mark's ear, "I want to fuck you so bad, and if I kiss you one more minute, the guests will have to cut their own cake."

Mark pecked Ash's lips again. "I guess I better restore my lipstick."

"Mark, look."

Mark followed Ash's pointing finger. Hanging on a rack on the other side of the room was a beautiful tuxedo. Shiny black with a shawl collar. Beside it hung a crisp white shirt. A black tie lay on a small table with a pair of socks, and polished black shoes sat waiting on the floor. He didn't have to look to know they were size eleven. "Oh." It was a breath. A sigh. He had never had a suit, much less a tuxedo.

Ash smiled. "Mr. Pennymaker?"

"Who else?"

"Can you tie your bow by yourself?"

"I'm a fashion designer, remember?"

"Then how about I leave you to change and go face the music?"

"Shouldn't I be with you?"

"I won't go far. I promise. Just come out when you're ready."

"We'll cut the cake."

"And start a new life."

HIS DAD was holding up the wall outside the door when Ash walked out. A few people still milled about, but it seemed like the offer of more champagne had done its work. The rich and famous were crowded into the ballroom area. The orchestra had switched to their interpretation of the Rolling Stones, and an odd mash-up of violins and guitars poured out of the room. He took a spot next to his father against the wall.

His dad shifted his feet. "How long have you known you're gay?"

"I knew I was different early on. At fourteen I decided I was just a late bloomer and I'd figure out what all the shouting was about sometime soon. By sixteen my attractions were clear enough I even had to admit it to myself. Didn't do much about it, though."

"You sure as hell didn't tell us."

"Let's face it, Dad; the Armitage family doesn't exactly run with the Rainbow Coalition. Every day I got messages that said it wasn't okay to be gay. You had big hopes for me. Run the company and all that. I knew as I got older that a gay son taking over any part of Armitage could affect everything. The board of directors, even the stock price."

"So you became a playboy instead."

Ash shook his head. "It wasn't exactly a conscious decision. I guess I figured I had to give you another reason to be disappointed in me besides my being gay."

"You might have given me a chance. To understand."

"I know it wasn't fair. I'm sorry. But truthfully, you guys were better at laying out ultimatums than finding reasons."

"I suppose that's true." He pushed away from the wall. "And now you're coming into the company."

Ash looked up. His dad's expression was unreadable. "Henry told you. Yes, at a low level, so I don't attract a lot of attention. I want to learn the business the way you did. I have things I want to do, and I figured he can help me get there with a minimum of mistakes. I'll tell you later. It's a big plan and—"

The door opened. *God.* The man of his dreams. Not the kid of his dreams or the beautiful woman of his dreams—the man. Mark stood outside the door of the changing room, looking a little dazed but edible. How in hell had Pennymaker found a tux to fit that tall, lean body like a second skin? Mark had pulled his silky black hair into a tight queue at his nape. *Wow.* Ash had never seen his face when it wasn't surrounded either by hair or that dumb cap. This look highlighted the masculinity of his face. Yeah, but the big eyes and soft lips still gave him a feminine edge. Ash heard his own sigh.

The female voice came from behind him. "I've been waiting a long time to see that look on your face."

He glanced over his shoulder, barely able to pull his gaze from Mark. "Hi, Mom."

She snuggled up beside him and put her arm through his. "I used to dream about you bringing home a girl and looking at her just like that. I knew on that day I'd start buying wedding invitations."

"Sorry you didn't get to."

"Nonsense." She released his arm and walked toward Mark, extending her hand. "You're Mark, I believe. I'm Miranda Armitage. Welcome to the family."

Mark looked startled but shook her hand. "Thank you, ma'am."

She took his arm. "Now, as my son's husband, you must promise me two things."

"What are those, ma'am?"

"First, that you'll never call me 'ma'am' again." Mark blushed, and Ash grinned. "You may call me Miranda, and I'll even consider Mother, only because you are so damned cute. But not ma'am."

"Yes, ma'ammMiranda." Mark laughed. "And what's the other thing?"

"You must make me a new dress immediately. I want to start promoting the new Armitage fashion line."

Mark grinned. "I'll be happy to make you a dress. In fact, I'd love to. As for the fashion line, I'll be working for Caliari Couture. I'll just be an apprentice."

She flashed her toothy smile, which had been charming heads of state for decades. "We'll see about that, won't we?" She looked back at Ash and Mel. "Shall we all go in and let them revel in the newest addition to the Armitage clan?"

Ash shook his head. "Be right there, Mom." He looked at his father. "Son of a bitch. She got used to this idea pretty quick."

His dad laughed. "In the game of sexual politics, Ash, your mother likes men best. Besides, she's a lot more addicted to Fashion Week than she is to the symphony."

Ash grinned, walking beside his father into the ballroom. At the door, Mel stopped him. "We'll talk about this more, but not tonight. Hell, son, this is your wedding night."

Yeah, and he couldn't wait. He stepped up and took Mark's hand away from his mother. "Let's go cut the cake, Mr. Armitage. Then we can take a piece or two up to our suite."

Mark leaned over near his ear. "I figured you'd be getting a piece or two tonight."

Ash looked into those deep eyes. His gorgeous man extended his tongue and licked across that full top lip, then gave the lower one a swipe. Like shiny ripe cherries. *Oh shit.* He leaned over and moaned in Mark's ear. "Do you think they have an electric knife? I want to get this damn cake cut fast."

"GOOD NIGHT. Yes, we'll see you all in the morning for breakfast. Yes, the wedding was beautiful."

Ash shoved the key card into his door, gave one last wave at the assembled multitudes, and pulled Mark into the suite, slamming the door behind them. He didn't even let go of Mark's hand, just kept pulling. Needed him now. "I thought this whole reception would never end." He pressed his mouth to the full lips that had been tantalizing him for hours, then whispered, "Jesus, it's been days since we fucked."

Mark turned and walked away from him with a sway in his hips. The effect might have been greater in his silk dress, but for Ash, that ass was irresistible in any outfit. Mark reached up and pulled the clip from his hair, letting the shiny mass fall around his shoulders, then peeked through the strands. He pointed a finger at his wiggling butt. "This old thing? Is this what you were wanting to stick that cock in?" He pulled off his silk tie and dragged it on the floor as he sashayed slowly toward the bedroom.

Massive erection! Ash took off at a run. Mark squealed and scampered toward the bed. He spun and faced Ash, arms spread like a basketball player guarding the net. Now that was funny.

"Don't you think you're just a little too pretty for that posture, cutie pie?" Ash feinted to the right. Mark shadowed him, giggling. *Okay, first the tie, then the pants, then the ass.*

He grabbed for the tie, got it, but Mark pulled back. A quick hand-over-hand and—success, he had his man. By the arm, at least. *Slippery little devil.* Mark turned quickly, leaving Ash holding the coat. He dropped it on the chair. "Let me at those pants."

Mark kicked off his formal shoes and hopped on the bed, bouncing. *Now how cute is that?*

"These pants?" The long-fingered hands undid his belt as he bounced. He pulled the belt open and unzipped his fly. He reached inside and—*hellfire*. No underwear. Just a hard-as-a-rod rod. It stuck out from the gaping fly, all shiny and sticky from precum. Mark must be turned on by danger. *Bounce. Bob. Bounce. Bob.*

Beautiful.

Mark released the trousers, and they slid down like silk all the way to his feet. He stopped bouncing, grabbed the pants, and tossed them onto the matching chair on the other side of the bed. Now this was a getup. The tails of his white formal shirt hung down so his pretty cock stuck up through the gap.

Ash shook his head. "I wish I had a camera."

"You want to take some wedding pictures, big boy?" Mark stuck out a hip and planted a fist on it, cock still bouncing. Slowly, he undid the buttons of his shirt one at a time, revealing acres of creamy white skin.

Holy crap, have to catch up. Ash hopped on one foot as he ripped off his shoe, never taking his eyes from Mark's cock. Second shoe, pants and briefs off, tie… gone. Shirt buttons next.

"My, my, we do seem to be in a hurry. Would it have something to do with this?" Mark made a huge bound, turned in midair, bent over, and spread his asscheeks. Since he hadn't quite gotten the shirt off, his shiny white butt stuck out beneath it.

Endurance ended. Ash hurled himself at Mark's waggling ass and took him down onto the bed under him. He grabbed his ribs and started to tickle.

"Ahhhh, no, no. No fair." Mark kicked and bucked like a bronc. *Oooh, speaking of broncs.* Ash rolled to the side, still applying fingers to ribcage, and reached into the drawer of the end table. He grabbed some lube and a box of condoms. *Hmm.* He stopped tickling.

"Darling, have you been tested?"

Mark caught his breath. "Yes, before I came up to the resort, and since then I've only had sex with you. I'm clean."

"Me too." He flipped the box on the floor. "But I love to hear you laugh."

He grabbed Mark's ribs again, and he squealed and gasped. "If you quit, I'll give you your surprise."

"Ummm, I love surprises." He looked over his shoulder.

"Okay, let me up."

"Maybe I don't love surprises that much." Ash pushed his cock against Mark's pert butt.

"Just for a second. The surprise is in my jacket."

Ash shook his head.

Mark grinned. Pure mischief. "Oh, you'll be happy you did. Honest."

Ash rolled off and lay on his back, hands crossed on his belly and cock sticking straight up. "Okay. Surprise me."

Mark leapt off the bed, found his jacket on the chair, and fished in the pocket. *What was he up to?* He pulled a little box from the pocket. It was one of the cake boxes the guests had been given.

"Are you hungry, sweetheart?" Ash thrust his hips up. "I'll be glad to provide a full meal."

Mark turned and opened the box. Yeah, he had to hold it high to get it above his cock. He fluttered his lashes. "My thoughts exactly." He did a slow stroll back to the bed as he finger-swiped a huge blob of the sweet cream cheese frosting that had covered the three-foot-high cake. This looked very promising.

He sat on the edge of the bed, then leaned over, circling the frosted finger. *Plop*, the frosting went right on the head of Ash's cock. Mark giggled and scooted farther over. He grabbed his decorated dick with one hand and ever so deliberately began to spread the frosting over Ash's throbbing penis with his tongue. "Ah neber got ma cake."

"Bad boy. Talking with your mouth full."

"Ah ahm ahways powite." His tongue slid up one side and down the other. Ash was shaking, both from laughing and pure pleasure. Mark added more sweet cream, and he kept decorating until his whole cock was covered with white. Then he sat back and surveyed his masterpiece. "Oh, baby, I can't tell your cream from the frosting. This is my idea of dessert."

In one gulp, Mark swallowed his creation. Down his throat.

Holy shit. "Oh yes, yes." Ash pumped up into that sweet, hot mouth. "Not too much, darling. I still want to fuck you."

Mark gave one more big suck and raised his head. "No worries. We have all night."

"No, my love. We have our whole life, but I want to fuck you now."

Mark cocked his head. His dark eyes glistened. *Tears?*

"What, darling?"

"Our whole life."

"Yes."

"This whole thing has been so much like a fairy tale, I just got that it's real life. We're married. We'll have the pain and joy and struggles that real couples have. And we have our lives to do it in."

"Are you glad? It's been a whirlwind."

Quiet. Ash held his breath.

"Hell, yes."

"I love you, Mark. I know I'm a pretty crappy bargain. Both poor and infamous."

Mark laughed. "And I'm just a crazy kid in a cap."

Ash reached up and pulled Mark down to him. He ran a hand through Mark's silken black hair. Of course, Mark got some frosting on his chest. "Not anymore. I have a feeling this mane will be your trademark when you're famous. A tribute to your mom."

"Thank you." He smiled through tears.

Ash grabbed the lube from the bed where he'd abandoned it. "Now let's see if we can get the rest of the frosting off and put this"—he grabbed his still hard cock—"where it belongs."

Mark scooted down, wiped the cream off his own skin with his hand, and licked it up. Staring at Ash with huge dark eyes, he gave two giant sucks on his cock and smiled like a satisfied cat. "Mmm. Good. Done." He flipped over and pulled his knees up by his ears. "Fuck me, husband."

Ash laughed, lubed, and pushed into Mark's perfect ass. *Hot, tight, thrilling.* Had he ever felt this free? Not even close. He threw his head back. "I am glad to know after twenty-five years I've found my purpose in life."

"I'LL MEET you at the elevator, sweetheart." Mark opened the door to Ash's suite. He stopped. His suite. *Holy shit.*

Ash's voice came from the bedroom. "Don't be long. Everyone's waiting."

"Okay." He stepped out into the hall and headed for the service elevator. He might be the new husband of Ashton Armitage, but he still had a job in housekeeping, and he was late. He at least needed to tell them why. Hell, he wanted a good reference if he could get it. Yes, he might have a new job, and Ash might have a new job, but that was all pie in the sky. Cleaning toilets was forever.

A quick ride down to the basement and a fast walk brought him to the swinging door of the housekeeping department. It felt funny to be going in there without his cap and glasses and wearing clean jeans and a good shirt. But cats were pretty much out of bags. He pushed in through the door. *Oops.* All the troops were gathered inside. The women who worked so hard to keep the hotel clean congregated in the middle of the department floor. Must be the morning attack on room cleaning. He stopped short. "Sorry."

His boss, Mrs. Eldridge, turned to him. "Good morning, Sinders. Sleeping in, are we?"

"I'm so sorry, ma'am. I didn't intend to just disappear. I honestly didn't know when I left yesterday that I was going to be married, and I didn't think I would be so late, and I...."

Everyone in the room started applauding. He heard a champagne cork. *What the hell?*

Mrs. Eldridge clapped him on the back, her white curls bouncing. "You have officially replaced every fairy tale we have ever been told. From now on we'll all tell our kids how a boy from our department worked hard and married the handsome prince. We're so happy for you, Sin—uh, Mark."

Wasn't that nice? "Thank you so much, everyone." He accepted the champagne glass thrust at him and clinked glasses with as many people as he could reach.

One cute Latina woman named Daisy laughed. "Who knew there was such a handsome boy under that cap and those glasses?"

The heat crept up his face. "I'm sorry to leave you short-handed, but we're supposed to leave soon. I could see if I can find a replacement before I go."

Mrs. Eldridge shook her head and took another swig of champagne. The rooms would be lucky if they were cleaned today.

"Don't worry about it, Mark. There are dozens of applicants every week. But none of them can replace you. I've never known anyone who worked so hard. You're an inspiration."

Someone had noticed. *Don't want to cry.* "Thank you."

Daisy poked him. "Hey, aren't you supposed to be on a honeymoon or something?"

He didn't want to explain about the money. "Actually we're putting it off for a while. But I am expected at a wedding breakfast."

Mrs. Eldridge made a shooing motion. "Go, child, go. And think of all of us as you're rubbing elbows with the rich and famous."

Daisy giggled. "Send me an autograph from Ricky Martin."

Mark laughed and handed someone his still-full glass. Mrs. Eldridge scooped him into a hug, which started a round of hugging and patting. Finally he managed to escape out the door. "Bye, everyone. I'll miss you." Oddly, it was true.

He pushed out the door and broke into a run. *Ash is waiting.* What a thrilling thought. He powered up the stairs and found his beautiful husband standing by the elevators. His usual crowd of clinging moms was missing. They must have gotten the memo. Mark sure hoped Ash was ready for how different his life would be now that the world knew he was gay. And the world undoubtedly knew. Here in the resort they were protected and isolated from screaming press and angry picketers, but Mark was pretty sure they were waiting somewhere.

Ash looked up like he'd felt a tractor beam. *Man, look at that smile.* Mark had waited a lifetime with no hope. This was all too much to believe.

Ash reached out a hand. "I thought you'd decided to clean a few fireplaces on the way to breakfast."

"No, they had champagne for me."

"That's very cool."

They walked into the dining room, and all heads turned. Many smiled. Others? Not so much. Yeah, last night people had been plied with champagne and music. This morning they had to sort out how they really felt about Ash being gay and Mark having fooled them in women's clothes. Of course, when they knew Ash had lost his fortune, they'd feel lots better. *Karma.*

Mr. P. waved from a table by the window. The gang was all there— Mr. P., Ash's parents, Ronnie, even Bitsy, Mrs. Fanderel, and Bernice. There was also a man Mark didn't recognize. His suit looked kind of too warm in the resort dining room.

They rounded the other tables and came up to their smiling group. Well, not Bernice and Mrs. Fanderel so much, but everyone else seemed happy. Ash took Mark to the man in the suit. "Mark, this is Ralph Gootmutter. He's a friend of the family. Ralph"—he got a huge shit-eating grin—"this is my husband, Mark."

The gentleman, maybe early sixties and clearly not the world's most relaxed soul, shook Mark's hand. "Glad to meet you. Yes, very glad to meet you."

Mark and Ash shook hands and hugged their way around the round table to the two chairs that had been saved for them side by side. Ash held Mark's chair and then sat himself.

The waiter poured coffee. He winked at Mark. A little insider congratulations.

Bernice leaned forward. She smiled, but her voice had a little edge. "You two sure gave everyone a shock last night. What a surprise."

Beatrice glanced at Bitsy sitting—and glowing—next to Ronnie. "Yes, there were a lot of surprises last night."

Mr. P. beamed. "And aren't surprises the whipped cream on the ice cream sundae of life?"

Beatrice and Bernice didn't quite look convinced of that wise saying.

Orange juice and pastries were passed their direction, and everyone chitchatted their way through omelets and fruit. Miranda Armitage, sitting next to Mark, put an orange scone on his plate. "I'll bet this is your favorite."

He took a little bite of one edge. *Man, orange heaven.* "Yes, it is my favorite." He didn't say, "As of this moment."

She patted his arm. "So, my dear, we must make plans for your career." She looked across the table. "Carstairs, I've already called Joseph Caliari and explained I want to put money into a line designed by my son-in-law."

Mark choked. "What? No, ma'am. I still have a great deal to learn. I don't want anyone to feel they've been forced into accepting my designs, and I certainly don't want people to see my work before it's ready. No offense, Miranda."

She gave him a level look. "Somehow I knew you'd say that. Carstairs told me what a levelheaded person you are, and I'm happy to have you in Ash's life. But I've already taken all that into account." She sipped her coffee. "That's why I told Joseph we should shoot for a collection at next year's Fashion Week, not this year's. That'll give you a chance to hone your craft but won't allow someone else to take credit for your brilliance. That I simply will not have."

Mark swallowed. "What did Mr. Caliari say?"

Mr. P. clapped his hands. "Why, of course, my dear, he said yes."

Mark fell back in his chair. This was too much. What was happening to his life? "Thank you."

Mel Armitage leaned forward and looked at both Ash and Mark. "So, gentlemen, how are you figuring you're going to live your lives?"

Bernice burst out, "What do you mean? They're rich. They can live any way they want and change their mind tomorrow."

Ash shook his head. "No, actually we're not rich." He looked at his dad. "We've talked about it a little. We need to check out really soon because"—he grinned—"we can't afford the tariff. If you wouldn't mind paying for my apartment for another month, Mark and I will find a place to live we can afford. Then I start my job, and he starts his. He'll teach me how to live the life of a working stiff." He laughed, and it sounded wild and free.

His mother frowned. "Don't be silly, darling. You have your allowance."

Ash gave her a one-armed hug. "Tempting as that is, we want to live on our own. I need the practice, but thank you so much. And thank you for helping Mark. Sounds like he'll be a superstar in no time, and he'll be keeping me in the style to which I have become accustomed." He laughed again.

His father asked, "When do you start your job?"

"I asked Henry for two weeks. That way we can find a new place and get settled. Have a moving honeymoon, so to speak." He squeezed Mark's hand.

"I'm proud of you."

Ash looked up at his father. The expression on his face said it all. He'd never expected to hear those words from the man's mouth. Ash looked like he was having trouble talking. "Thank you, sir."

"Uh, Ash?" Everyone looked at Mr. Gootmutter. He appeared to have swallowed a small animal and was having trouble getting it out. "Uh, I have some news about your grandfather's will."

Ash nodded. "Yes, Ralph. I know about the watch and the ring he left me. I'm honored to have them. He was a favorite person of mine."

"What about the other things he left you?"

"What other things?"

"The five hundred and seventy-five million, two hundred and four thousand dollars?"

Ash looked at Mark. "I didn't get married to a woman by the deadline."

"But you did."

His father held up a hand. He looked like he was going to bust a gut. "Ralph and I went through the will last night with a microscope. We are one hundred percent certain your marriage fulfills the requirements of the will. The inheritance is yours."

Miranda squealed. "Mel, why didn't you tell me?"

He laughed. "I didn't want you to think for a minute that Mark and Ash don't need your help, because I'm sure they do. Besides, you were sound asleep by the time we knew for sure."

Mark caught at his chest. Possibly he might fall off his chair.

Ash grabbed his arm. "Are you all right, dear?"

"I don't know."

Ash's arm came around his shoulders, tight and warm. He leaned near Mark's ear. "It's okay. We don't have to spend a penny of it if you don't want to. We can live exactly as we planned and just use the money for the foundation."

Bernice sounded frustrated. "What's wrong with him? Hell, he just became a multimillionaire."

Mr. P.'s voice bubbled, "Mark is a man who knows that good luck is ninety percent perspiration. He just hasn't caught up with the other ten percent."

Mark looked up into the beautiful blue eyes. "I want my job, Ash."

"And I want mine."

He grinned. "But I guess I wouldn't really mind having a nice place to live."

"Done!" Ash hugged him tight. "Do you want to stay here a few more days?"

Mr. P. leaned forward. "There are a lot of beautiful, private places. Why don't you pick one of them and have a honeymoon? I'm sure both your jobs will be waiting."

Ash grinned. "We could. Want to?"

Mark leaned his head on his husband's shoulder. "I'll go anywhere with you. Besides, I need some time to believe this fairy tale has actually happened." He sat up. His heart was going to burst. "Hey, Mr. P., you did it."

The little elf's smile lit the dining room. "What's that, my boy?"

"You proved you can make something really good out of Sinders and Ash."

His fairy godmother laughed and laughed.

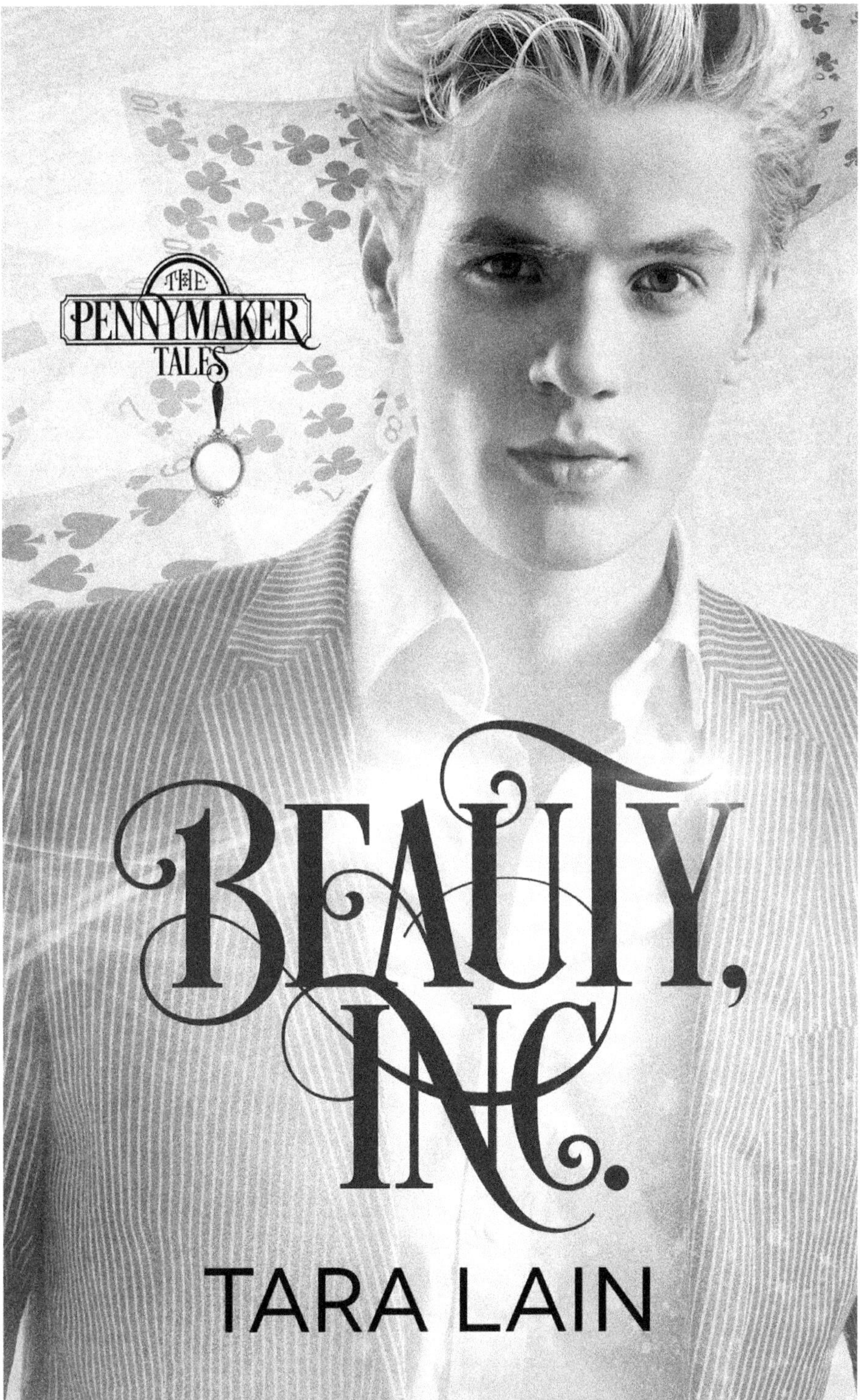
THE
PENNYMAKER
TALES
BEAUTY, INC.
TARA LAIN

To Cindy, one of the most beautiful people I know.
Thank you for being such a wonderful friend
and member of my family.

CHAPTER 1

BELLE HELD his breath and released a small amount of cream from the new container into his gloved hand. It just looked like a pretty bottle, but its airtight cap and unique double-walled design reduced oxygen impact on the contents—he hoped! His family's future depended on a hunk of plastic.

Two weeks his cream formulation had been stored in this new packaging—enough time for it to degrade and discolor like so many high-end cosmetics did, the kiss of death with discriminating buyers. He stared at the cream under the brilliant light on the laboratory table. *No change of tint. No yellowing.* His heart pounded. He sniffed. *Fresh as the day it was packaged.* Finally he dabbed a finger into the cream and slicked it between thumb and middle finger. No alteration of texture. *Silky, smooth, and rich.* The smile spread across his face like the cream itself. Rich. Just like this new product would make his father.

"Tell me it works!"

Dr. Robert Belleterre—Belle—stared up at Colin, the head of the chemistry lab at Bella Terra Cosmetics, and suppressed the urge to jump up and down. "All the tests indicate it works perfectly. You'll have samples of the formulation in the new containers by the end of the week. I want to put this under the microscope to be sure there's been no change of chemical structure, but it sure as shit looks good!" He laughed.

Colin smiled. "In time for Cosmetique?"

Belle nodded. "They can take a few samples to Las Vegas to show to select customers."

"Jesus, man, you did it!" He grabbed Belle in a tight, one-armed guy hug and held up his fingers as he ticked off the benefits. "Reduction of fine lines and wrinkles, no parabens or artificial preservatives, and the cream holds up in the packaging. This is going to set a new standard, and no other company will be able to meet it. Not even Beauty, Inc."

Belle extricated himself gently. "I wish we could afford to do the testing to prove the product claims. It would go to market faster."

Colin shrugged. "Your dad swears we can't afford it. But seriously, when women try it, they'll love it and we'll have the best evidence in the world. Right on their faces. I can't believe what you've done in less than a year."

"Thanks, Colin." He'd quit sleeping and meals had become optional, but he'd given everything to keep Bella Terra, his father's company, viable—tough duty for a small manufacturer in a field of giants. But now he had a cream so beyond just a mere cosmetic that it could change the face of the industry—literally.

"Belle."

Belle glanced over his shoulder toward the door to the lab, where his father peeked in. That was usually the only body part of his father's that ever made it into the laboratories these days. Since Belle had finished his PhD the previous summer, Ron Belleterre hadn't looked at a color or emollient. Just a lot of poker chips and booze. "Yes, Father?"

"Can I speak to you, please?"

Belle turned to Colin. "Take a look under the microscope. I'll do the same when I get back." He pulled off his lab coat, hung it on the hook by the door, and followed his father into the hall.

Tall, fair, and handsome, Rondell Belleterre radiated energy, most of it nervous. His moments of rest and peace seemed to get fewer and fewer. Hard not to worry about him. "Yes, sir?"

"Come to the office." His father took off at a good clip, and Belle fell in beside him. Ron glanced at him. "How's the new packaging?"

"It's testing well. I think we've got it this time."

"I'll be frank, Belle. You have to have it this time, because this whole project is costing me a fucking fortune. Expensive ingredients, bank-busting antioxidants, and now these damned containers that make Fort Knox look like easy access. Shit, I'm not made of money."

Belle controlled his sigh. "It will open a whole new market to us. There are a lot of women who simply won't use a cream on their face that contains parabens. With the new product, they'll flock to Bella Terra."

His father scowled. "They'd better. I'd like to see some red on the competitor's sales radar for a change." He sighed. "I doubt Beauty, Inc. is worried about us." He powered through his office door and stopped in front of Hester, the secretary he still insisted he needed. "Would you have Rusty and Rick come in, please?"

"I think they went to lunch, sir."

Ron frowned. "It's ten forty-five."

She gazed at him, but deep down her eyes said, "Duh."

"Forget it." Inside his inner office, Ron sat in his giant desk chair and pointed at one of the leather guest chairs. "Sit."

A drawing of the Bella Terra booth at the upcoming Cosmetique Conference in Las Vegas lay on his father's desk. Belle nodded toward the graphic. "Are you ready for the conference?"

"That's what I want to talk to you about."

"We can have a limited amount of demonstration units for your private showings." He had to gulp a breath to contain his excitement. "This is it, Father. We'll outstrip any single product Magnus Strong at Beauty, Inc. has got."

"If the ugly bastard even notices."

"I'm sure Strong didn't get to the top of the beauty industry by ignoring highly successful competitors. We're not going to top Beauty, Inc. They're huge. But we can replace them as the number one wrinkle cream."

His father's eyes lit up. Belle softly sighed. Ron hadn't always been so greedy. The addictions took their toll. *Poor Father.*

"I want you to come to Cosmetique."

"What?" Belle shook his head. "No, sir. You know I hate those big events. I'm needed here in the lab."

"We're unveiling your new product to our best customers. No one knows it like you do."

Belle frowned. "Rusty's in charge of marketing. It's his job to understand our products."

"He's not you. Plus you have the passion. We need you. Colin can handle the lab. It's settled." His father shoved a copy of *Forbes* across his desk, featuring a close-up photo of Magnus Strong—the face the cosmetics magnate wore like a badge of honor. A deep scar ran across his eyebrow, missed his eye, but still distorted the lid so it drooped slightly. Another dissecting slash had marred his cheek, deformed his top lip into a permanent sneer, and left a stripe across the bottom lip, while his scarred, broken nose gave him the look of a has-been prizefighter. Ugliness that created beauty. His father laughed. "If anybody can tame the beast, it's you."

Belle frowned.

TWO HOURS later Belle rocked in his glider in his backyard and soaked. That's how he thought of it. Soaking in the air so fresh and clean it vitalized his cells as it filled his lungs. Soaking in the green—green everywhere in trees and plants and moss growing on rocks that never quite got dry. People complained about the constant mist and drizzle of Oregon. Not him. Not ever. Home. He loved it. Right here he got the inspiration for his new product. His baby.

"Hey, baby."

Belle smiled. Speaking of babies. He swore to Judy that one of these days she'd wander in while he was having hot monkey sex on the dining room table, but she said she'd just whip out her phone and record it all for Instagram. Of course, he and the monkeys had very little acquaintance. "Hi, dear. Come on out."

Judy Brancoli, his best friend, stepped out of his kitchen door into the yard. Her snub nose covered in freckles pointed at the sky as she collected some mist on her tongue before she bounded toward him. "I saw your bike in the garage. Aren't you home early?"

"Yes." He leaned his head back and did his own mist collecting. "I just found out from Dad that I have to go to Las Vegas tomorrow, so I came home to pack."

She sat on the glider beside him, which required coordination of movement, but they got it going smoothly in a couple of seconds. "So this is an emergency soaking session, right?"

He laughed. Judy knew. She knew everything. "Yep. Gotta survive the desert for four fucking days."

She pushed her red curls from her face. The rain made her hair curlier and his straighter. His platinum bangs fell in front of his eyes like windshield wipers. "Why are you being subjected to this cruel and unusual punishment?"

He popped his head up and flipped his hair from his eyes. "To be honest, I'm not completely sure. Dad said something about how I know the new product better than anyone, etcetera, etcetera, bullshit, bullshit. But usually the big three don't like me getting in the way of their carousing, so I'm not sure what they really have on their agendas. I guess I'll find out."

"If I know your dad, you'll likely find out the hard way."

He ruffled her mane of hair, and mane it was—every curl a masterpiece. Judy had little vanity—she boasted that her chest could be used as a cutting board—but her hair claimed a lot of attention. Good reason too. It was gorgeous. "So how you doing, beautiful?"

A little frown flitted across her forehead. "Good. Tons of studying to do."

"How's the internship?"

She snorted. "It's okay. They work us like slaves and give us nothing in return, but I guess that's small change compared to being a big-time lawyer." That frown flashed again. "I just have to survive that long."

Belle looked at her closely. "Is that the only problem? Too much work?"

She shrugged. "Kind of. I have to go in for a doctor visit, and I don't have insurance."

"I'll give you money before I go."

"No. Thanks, luv. It's okay. The doctor said they'll do the office visit for a hundred dollar flat fee, so no worries."

But she still seemed worried somehow. "I'll give you that, okay? No need stretching your nonexistent budget."

"Hey, I haven't heard that your father's loosened the purse strings on your salary either." She nudged him. "Here we are, the working poor."

"At least I have insurance."

"Yeah."

As he handed her a hundred dollar bill, her wide brown eyes looked haunted.

BELLE STARED out the window as the plane approached its destination. Acres of barren dirt marked by the sudden uprising of fantasyland. Even the idea of Las Vegas made him sick.

"Excuse me, sir. May I take your glass?"

He looked up at the pretty brunette flight attendant. She smiled at him softly. "Oh yes, thank you." He downed a last sip of apple juice and handed it to her.

"Anything else I can get you?" Her lashes fluttered.

"No, thank you."

She looked at him over her shoulder as she walked back to the galley.

His father slapped Belle's knee. "Too bad you don't do girls, son. You could have joined the fuck-the-stewardess-in-preparation-for-landing club."

"Shhh." *Damn.* He glanced to be sure the flight attendant wasn't offended. His father had started on the champagne before they took off from Oregon and moved on to vodka at the halfway point, making him far more than halfway sauced.

"Gotta say, all that beauty sure is wasted on guys. Hell, look at that kisser." He reached out and gripped Belle's chin. *Just let him do it. He'll be done with his favorite litany soon.* "You look like her, son. Man, you got the best of the best in that face."

Funny. He usually continued his tirade with "What a waste." At least this time he left that off.

The man and woman across the aisle glanced at Belle with compassion and a hint of interest. *Jesus, why couldn't I just stay home?*

Ron yelled to Rick and Rusty in the first-class seats behind them, "You guys ready for Vegas?"

Rick, Belle's oldest brother, hooted. "Yeah, man, bring on the chorus girls." The fact that Rick had a wife and four daughters at home never seemed to stop him from indulging in alternative companionship.

Belle stared at the rapidly approaching ground. Who knew how they'd all have turned out if his mom had lived? His father hadn't acquired most of his vices until he'd lost his wife three years before. Since then he'd been making up for a lifetime of good behavior. Now he sat beside Belle, vibrating in anticipation of the buffet of debauchery soon to be spread in front of him.

His father grabbed his arm. "We all want you to have some fun here, Belle. Lots of eligible guys. Let us fix you up. It's gonna be great."

What the hell? "I'm not interested in being fixed up. I came here to work. Nothing more. I want to unveil the product and go home."

"Sure, sure, son. No problem. We'll have you unveiling plenty." He snorted, and Rusty giggled from the seat behind them.

Belle gazed out the window at the dry, dull landscape. Nothing about this trip sounded good.

As the wheels hit, they all grabbed for their phones. A quick check showed no e-mails or texts from Colin. That must mean the lab was under control.

His father frowned. "Fucking hell."

"A problem?"

Ron glanced at Belle, and his eyes took on that addict's slyness. "Oh no. Just a meeting I want to have arranged." He dialed his phone and listened, then turned away from Belle. "What do you mean I'm not in?" He paused. "I don't care what it takes. Get me in—" He glanced toward Belle over his shoulder. "Just get me in that meeting, got it?"

What's really going on?

"Well shit, look." Ron pointed out the window as the plane taxied toward the gate. Landing on another runway was a sleek executive jet marked Beauty, Inc. Ron yelled over the seat. "You guys see that?"

Rusty hollered back. "Yeah, Dad. The fucking enemy."

"Magnus fucking Strong." His father's breath hitched. "Sure would love to have that plane."

BELLE UNPACKED his suits and hung them in the hotel room closet. Nice room. Beautiful view of the Strip—to the extent that one could call any part of Vegas beautiful. Jesus, his very cells craved the green trees and tumbling water of Oregon.

He sat on the king-size bed. At least he could hole up here when he didn't have to be on the show floor. His father and brothers were housed in a two-bedroom suite on the floor below. They said they'd tried to get a bigger suite, but it had been too late when they registered him. More likely they didn't want him interfering with their idea of fun. Fine with him. The less he knew, the better. Maybe he'd go to the exhibit hall to check on the booth setup and then order room service and watch a movie.

His cell rang. He grabbed it from the nightstand. *Shoot. Rusty, not Colin.* "Hi."

"Hey, baby brother. Come get some dinner with us, then we can hit the casino."

"I need to go check on the booth setup."

"That's okay. We'll hang in the bar until you get back."

Come on. Be happy. They actually included you for once. "Sure, that'll be great. Where shall I meet you?"

Did he chuckle? "The bar off the lobby." He hung up.

Why the sudden desire to include me? He took off for the exhibit hall at speed.

Seeing his product samples in the new packaging, hidden in the small back conference room where their booth was located, totally did it for him. They might be in a twenty-foot exhibit this year, but by next year—they'd have an island. Jaime Terazzo, their West Coast sales manager, slapped his back. "I hear we've got something big. When do I get to roll it out to the sales force?"

"Soon. But we have to get some customer feedback first. Try to keep it quiet for a few more weeks."

He puffed his cheeks and blew. "Hard to do, Belle. The team hears we've got new stuff and they want it. Their commissions have been sucking wienie ever since Beauty, Inc. introduced their Breakthrough line. We need something to counter it."

"I know. But just pretend like my father didn't spill the beans to the sales force six months too soon."

He shrugged. "Your dad knows he's likely to lose his sales team if he can't compete."

"Try to be patient. If we rush and blow the launch, it's worse than not having it at all. Trust me. This will be big enough to satisfy everyone." He glanced at his smart watch. "I have to get to an appointment. Take a deep breath." He hurried out of the booth and headed back to the hotel on foot. At least he'd get in some exercise. Managing the fears of the sales team was so not his job, but with the distractions of Vegas overwhelming his father and brothers, pretty much everything became his responsibility. No wonder they'd wanted to bring him.

He pushed into the hotel lobby, cringing from the combination of air conditioning, the weird music of slot machines, and the rumbling hum of voices, voices, voices. *Where's the bar?* He looked around the big space with its garish décor until he spied the entrance to the Lobby Bar. How drunk would they be? He'd been gone an hour.

Slipping through the crowd, he entered the softer hum of the bar. He gave his name to the host, who pointed to the booths in the back. Belle took a deep breath. Okay, maybe he could have a relaxing dinner with his family.

As he approached the booth from the side, Rick looked up and waved. Belle waved back and sped up. Rusty peered around the corner of the booth and raised a glass at him. Okay, so much for sober, but it could still be fun. His brothers had never included him as a kid. Occasionally they made up for lost time.

He came up to the curved booth and stopped. Sitting beside his father was a handsome, middle-aged man with hair that might be as platinum as Belle's own—or could be doctored silver. Sharp nose, narrow, pale eyes, and a smile that might or might not be saying "All the better to eat you with." Belle shivered.

His dad half stood, which was all he could manage while squeezed in between the stranger and Rick. Rusty occupied the place beside Rick, which conspicuously left an open seat next to the stranger. "Belle, I'd like to introduce Eric Kleinschmidt. Eric's an investor in the cosmetics industry and has been very anxious to meet you."

So much for that friendly family dinner.

CHAPTER 2

BELLE NODDED and extended his hand. "Happy to meet you."

Kleinschmidt took Belle's hand in both of his, making it a caress rather than a shake. *Alrighty then.* "Ah, Rondell, you have not lied about your boy's extraordinary beauty. What is it you Americans say? Amazeballs?" Even his laugh had a German accent.

Belle eyed the available seat next to Kleinschmidt. A chair stood empty at a table behind him. He grabbed it, pulled it up to the open side of the booth, in the aisle, and sat. "There. That way I won't crowd you all."

Kleinschmidt frowned fleetingly, and Ron gave Belle a pointed look. "What would you like to drink?"

"Red wine will be fine."

Kleinschmidt leaned toward Belle. "Can't I recommend a good German white?"

How did he manage to make that sound dirty? "I prefer red, thanks."

The waitress bustled up and looked down at Belle with a plastered smile, then widened her eyes and whispered, "Oh."

Rusty snorted.

Belle gave her a smile. "May I have zinfandel, please? Whatever you have by the glass."

"Uh, white zin?"

This time Kleinschmidt snorted.

Belle flashed him a look and picked up the menu. He pointed to the reds. "The Zabaco will be fine."

"Oh yes, sir, of course."

She walked away, and his father laughed. "Eric, don't you wish you could turn women to stone like that?"

Kleinschmidt shrugged. "Perhaps it would not be so very useful in my case."

"Yes, well, the talent's wasted on Belle too."

"I'm so happy to hear it." Kleinschmidt flashed some sharp white teeth.

Belle tried to control his frown. Was this really what it appeared to be? Had his father and brothers actually brought him here for Kleinschmidt?

His father leaned in and spoke softly. "Belle, I want you to tell Eric about the new product. He's looking for good investment opportunities, and I've explained that he can't do better than your new formula."

Okay, maybe not. "I'd be glad to, but honestly, I'd like to show you the samples and the test results. I didn't know to bring those since I thought this was just family." He gave his father a look.

Ron stared at his drink. "Last-minute invitation. Eric expressed interest, and this seemed like a good time."

Kleinschmidt smiled. "I am most anxious to see these samples. Perhaps we can stop by and pick them up."

Belle shook his head. "I don't want to display them in public. Too many eyes."

"Oh, after dinner, of course. You can show me privately."

"I'll be glad to get them and bring them to my father's suite."

Ron shook his head vehemently. "No. Too many obligations tonight. You've got the samples in your suite, Belle. Take him there."

Hopefully he didn't show his shudder....

MAGNUS STRONG sipped his wine and gazed back toward the entrance to the Steuben Rose, the new "it" restaurant in Vegas. All the patrons who made it in looked like the maître d' had given them a gift instead of treating them like dirt and making them wait in the impossible line outside. He hadn't waited. Oh no, they'd fallen all over themselves for Magnus Strong, but that didn't make him like them any better. He glanced at Elliott Porter, his market evaluation consultant—euphemism for legal industrial spy. Well, mostly legal. "Let's not come back here, okay?"

"Yeah, I'm sorry, Magnus. By the time I realized what a-holes they are, I had the table."

"Not a problem, but I wouldn't want them to believe we support this kind of customer service." He took another sip. "Good wine, though. So what have you got for me?"

"This is unconfirmed."

"Never a problem." He grinned. He knew it made him look even creepier, but hell, it increased the mystique.

"You've heard the rumors that Bella Terra has a new face cream?"

"Yes. I've also heard they're getting great results in testing."

"Confirmed. But what I'm hearing now is that they've managed to take all the preservatives and most of the chemicals out of the cream, so it's going to get a huge boost in the natural cosmetic arena."

Magnus frowned. "And they're not compromising the results?"

"That's what I've heard. They're doing it with some kind of special packaging."

Magnus pushed his glass away. "Is this another breakthrough for the mysterious third son?"

"The one they call Belle. Yes. Jesus, he's just a kid. Like twenty-two or something, but since he took over that lab, shit happens. And he's not so mysterious. We know he has a PhD in chemistry from some small, obscure, but still prestigious school in Oregon. Prodigy type who finished higher ed in four years total, from entrance to PhD. They say he's devoted to the work."

"What about his personal life? He must have one."

Elliott shrugged. "Not much anyone can say. He didn't seem to date in college, and as far as I know, he's not married now. We have a couple of pictures of him from somewhere in middle school and nothing else. Very blond, like most of the family. That's all we know. Very low profile, this kid."

The waiter came, and Magnus ordered sole while Elliott got a steak. Elliott's report moved on to rumors of new introductions from major competitors in France and Italy. Magnus wiped his mouth with his napkin. "How good are the results on the new Bella Terra cream?"

Elliott laughed. "Did you hear anything I said about Londrey?"

"Every word. Tell me about Bella Terra." He glanced up as more people filed through the arch from the entry. "Wait." Rondell Belleterre walked in, looking like somebody had given him a trophy, with those two useless sons behind him. "Speak of the devil."

Elliott sat back, and they both watched the parade of Belleterres. "Great-looking family."

"If you don't count the growing signs of hard living on those handsome faces." Magnus took another swallow and glanced up. "What the hell is he doing here?" Eric Kleinschmidt, the German investor who liked dabbling in the beauty industry, followed Rick Belleterre through the archway.

"I heard he was hoping to find something big at the conference. Maybe he found Belleterre."

"Not necessarily good news for us and—who the hell is that?"

Walking behind Kleinschmidt came the most beautiful boy—man—Magnus had ever seen. Pale blond with much darker eyes, cheekbones like a lesson from Michelangelo, and a tall, slim body that filled out a gray business suit as if he were walking a runway. "Maybe a model or an actor?"

Elliott snorted. "More likely Kleinschmidt's newest boy toy."

"What a waste on that toad."

"A lot of people think Kleinschmidt's good-looking. Plus all that money." He laughed.

Magnus tried not to sigh. *Good-looking.* How often did it come to that? He tossed back the rest of his wine. Even before the car had turned over and left him mangled like he'd visited a meat grinder on holiday, he hadn't really been handsome or even attractive. "Yes, I suppose you're right." He said it lightly, but somehow thinking of that beauty at the mercy of Eric's salacious tastes made him want to puke. "Still, I'd like to know who that young man is, okay?"

Elliott gave him a smile. "Check."

BELLE ARRIVED at the table last and so had no selection of seating. They'd left him a chair conspicuously next to Kleinschmidt. It made him antsy, but it made sense. He was obviously here to persuade Eric to invest in the new product. Bella Terra didn't have the capital to really make a huge market impact with the face cream. Someone like Kleinschmidt could do that for them. Still, it made him sad to have to give up so much of his baby.

They chatted through hors d'oeuvres, covering every interesting show in Las Vegas, including the X-rated ones. His father downed another half of a vodka martini even though they'd started on their entrees. "So, Eric, I'm really anxious for our Belle to share this new development. I think it's something you'll be interested in."

Eric turned his sharp-featured face toward Belle. "I'm interested in everything your Belle has to offer."

Rick laughed—a bit too loudly. "Well, you two share more than an interest in cosmetics, that's for sure."

"I'm so happy to hear it."

Belle shifted in his chair. "Tell us what you've heard will be exciting at the conference, Eric. I'll be sure to look for the new products tomorrow."

Eric put a hand on the back of Belle's chair. "Ah well, we must never underestimate the French. I've heard some interesting talk about a new lipstick with great color and no heavy metals."

"That's hardly new. There are many lead-free lipsticks."

"I'm told the staying power of their product is extraordinary—not unlike myself." He laughed.

Shit! What an asshole. Belle stood and said softly, "Will you excuse me? I need the men's room."

His father looked up, startled, brow sweating and eyes glassy. "Belle, wait. Where are you going?"

He spoke much too loudly, his words echoing around Belle. *Jesus, announce my bladder functions much?* He could feel his face getting hot. He turned and walked away from the table, trying to ignore the interested faces craning his way.

As he got closer to the entrance to the dining room, he stopped a waiter. "Excuse me, where's the men's room?"

The man pointed toward the far wall. "Directly behind you, sir."

"Thanks." Belle turned and glanced to the side.

For a second his eyes combed the far wall for the sign. Then his gaze dropped—and his eyes met those in a face that haunted his nightmares. Magnus Strong stared directly at him, a tiny smile playing across his scarred lips. It had to be him. No one else looked even a little like that, but wow. Belle's steps slowed. Looking at Strong's face on the cover of a magazine revealed its ugliness, but in life his pure vitality and charisma leaped across the space between them and ate Belle alive. So ugly he was beautiful.

Some energy deep in Belle's belly uncoiled and oozed out into his limbs—and his balls. Holy God, he was about to get an erection standing in a restaurant staring at his company's biggest enemy.

He wanted to run out the door and not stop until he sat in his own backyard. Instead he stared directly at the restroom sign and headed toward it.

"SO THAT'S the son."

"What?" Elliott followed Magnus's gaze.

"That's the third Belleterre son, the one they call Belle. Certainly not hard to understand why. Didn't you hear them calling him?"

"No. Sorry. Are you sure? It doesn't seem likely that beautiful boy is some chemistry genius. Plus he appears to be with Kleinschmidt, doesn't he?"

Magnus raised a brow. "I'm not sure. Be right back." He slid from his banquette and crossed toward the front door, then cut through the last row of tables and made a beeline for the restroom. No use making it look like he was following Belleterre, though. Too many eyes watching. He waved at one or two friends and pulled out his phone as if he'd gotten a call. At the last minute, he slipped into the hall where the men's room sign beckoned. *Hurry. He'll be coming out.*

He pushed into the marble and glass room just as Belleterre came out of a stall. He seemed to be taking deep breaths, and his high cheekbones were flushed pink. He saw Magnus and the blush darkened, which was more than any gay man could stand.

Try to look natural. Magnus stepped up to the urinal and hauled it out—clearly a losing proposition, since the mere sight of the guy prompted a half-mast condition. *Breathe. You've gotta pee or he'll think you've lost it. In through the nose.*

Belleterre walked to the sink, pulled some paper towels from the dispenser, wet them under the water, and applied the compress to his cheeks.

Magnus managed a thin stream, shook, and zipped. He walked to the sink beside the beauty called Belle. He contained his smile since he knew it was scary. "You'd think with their prices, they could afford better air conditioning."

The guy startled, looked at Magnus with wide eyes, then burst out laughing. Clearly symphonies had less melody. "You certainly would. In fact, there's a lot about this place that could use some investment, I'd say."

"A man after my own heart." He extended his now clean hand. "I'm Magnus Strong."

The guy nodded. "Of course. I'm Robert Belleterre. I expect you know my father."

"Yes, I do. So you're Belle?"

"That's what they call me."

"A chemist."

Belle nodded.

"Honored."

"I believe you're also a chemist."

Magnus nodded. "A long time ago."

Belle's lips curved just enough to cause cardiac arrest. "Honored." He walked out the bathroom door.

Magnus leaned against the sink and took deep inhalations, then managed to get it together enough to return to his table.

Elliott stared at him anxiously. "So? Did you meet the mystery man?"

"Yes. It's Belle Belleterre, all right."

"Wow. How have they kept that under wraps all these years? Seriously, once that kid's puss hits the social sites, forget anonymity."

Magnus pushed his plate aside and leaned in. "I want every detail on their new product. I don't care who or how much you have to bribe. Just do it. Likewise on Belle Belleterre. What does he like? Hate? What drives him? Get it all for me."

Elliott nodded. "I'm on it."

Magnus stared across the restaurant, where Kleinschmidt's hand rested on the back of Belle's chair. Magnus felt his fingers clench. "And I want to know what the hell he's doing with Eric." He could still feel the tingling in his hand where they'd touched, and the tingling in his cock. He sucked a breath. *This is no time for stupid, hopeless infatuations.* "Just find out as much as you can as soon as you can."

"Will do."

"And the game you arranged for me tomorrow night?"

"Yes. All the confirmations are in. It should be great poker and hopefully some great information as well."

"You know how I said I didn't want to include Ron Belleterre?"

"Yeah, because he drinks too much."

"I changed my mind."

Elliott smiled. "May I ask why?"

Magnus grinned back. "Because he drinks too much."

They both laughed.

Magnus glanced again toward the Belleterre table. "And find out what room Belle Belleterre is in. Now."

Elliott slid out of the banquette.

CHAPTER 3

BELLE UNLOCKED his hotel room door and pushed it open. Eric walked past him into the large room with sitting area separated from the king-size bed by a combination armoire and entertainment center. He knew damned well that his father's big commitments were all with poker tables, but he still hadn't been able to talk him into meeting in Ron's suite.

Belle pointed toward the couch. "Please sit. I'll get the samples and test information."

"Do you have anything to drink?"

"There's wine and liquor in the refrigerator." Not that the man needed it. What the hell good was showing him test information when he could barely see? But Belle's father wanted the money so badly. Presumably they couldn't mass-manufacture without it. Belle had no visibility into the books, so he had to take his father and brothers' word.

Belle crossed into the sleeping area and got the samples and spreadsheets from the safe. When he rounded the armoire, Eric was sitting on the couch, jacket off, tie loosened, with a large glass of red wine in front of him on the coffee table and another beside him. Oh well, he needed to show Eric the data, so—

He walked over and sat beside Eric. "First, I'd like you to sign a confidentiality agreement."

"Oh, sure. Sure." He flicked his fingers, slurped a mouthful of wine, and then signed a scrawl on the bottom of the page Belle handed him.

Belle opened the spreadsheet. "What we have is a new resurfacing cream without harsh chemicals that still reduces lines by more than fifty percent. Not just in perception, but in actual test results. And—"

Eric grabbed Belle's head, pulled it back, and planted his lips on Belle's open, shocked mouth, spilling red wine across the spreadsheet.

Not totally surprised—the guy had been coming on like an avocado masque all night—Belle shoved Eric back. "Shit! Get off me." He sprang to his feet. "What the hell do you think you're doing?"

Eric leaned back, his erection distorting his suit pants. "Allowing you to seduce me into investing millions in the manufacture of your little cream, darling. Of course."

"Jesus. What do you think I am?" He shook his head.

"Your father and brothers made that eminently clear. I am only collecting on the goods they promised."

Belle's heart leaped into his throat. They were grasping, but surely not that bad. "You misunderstood."

"Oh? You won't do anything to have your product mass-produced?" His eyes narrowed, but his erection didn't dwindle. If anything, it got bigger.

"Not anything, no. And I don't have to. This is an amazing product, unlike anything on the market today—"

Eric waved a hand idly. "I'm sure, but without a huge investment, what good is it? You need millions in advertising alone to convince the fickle buying public that this isn't like every cream they can purchase for five dollars at the supermarket. You need me, and I want you. It's an equation that has worked in business since time immemorial."

The impact of that equation took his breath. "Sorry. No sale. Please leave."

Eric regarded him with a twisted smile. Slowly he rose from the couch, draped his jacket over his shoulder, and walked to the door.

Jesus, his father's dreams up in smoke. "I'm sorry if there was confusion about what we were offering. If you decide you're interested in the product, please let me know." He turned to open the door. An iron forearm slammed against his windpipe, knocking the breath from him. Shit! Eric stood a good three inches taller than Belle and was obviously a helluva lot stronger.

He rammed Belle's face against the door. "You little cocktease. Lead me on all night and then not deliver. We'll see, when my cock is in your ass."

A groping hand reached for Belle's fly. He twisted, but it only cut off more air. Belle pounded his foot against the door three times, then slammed backward and connected with Eric's shin.

"Ow! You little bastard!" But he didn't let go.

Belle tried it again, but he was seeing stars from lack of air, and Eric had unfastened his belt and was pulling his pants and briefs down inch by inch. *Damn.* His knees started to buckle as Eric pushed him toward the floor.

Wham. Wham!

The door vibrated with the hammering. "Belle. Belle, sorry to wake you. Let me in."

Eric leaped back, and Belle pulled himself against the wall and turned. He raised a fist at Eric, but obviously what was scaring him was the voice coming from the other side of the door.

"Belle, are you there? It's Magnus. Magnus Strong."

Holy shit.

Eric stared at Belle wildly, like he'd grown another head, slicked back his silver hair, pulled open the door, and smiled. "Hello, Magnus. How convenient. I was just leaving." The shit practically ran out the door, and Belle heard his rapid scuffs against the carpet as he retreated.

Magnus Strong stepped in the door and reached out to Belle, who shrank back. Strong was a big man, and right now Belle could do without more big men.

He snatched his hands back. "I'm sorry. That was thoughtless. I was passing by and heard the kicking on your door. It sounded like someone was in distress."

Belle half wanted to throw himself into Strong's arms—but only half. "Did you say *someone* was in distress?"

Strong nodded, with an odd expression. "Yes, I did say that."

"But you called me by name."

Strong sighed. "Yes, I suppose I did."

Belle just stared at him—and wanted to go home.

"I'm sorry, Belle. I saw you earlier with Eric. I happen to know the man's questionable proclivities, and I happened to ask what room you were staying in."

"Happened?" *Creep show.*

"I asked someone to inquire." He held up his hands. "Honestly, I only wanted to be sure you were all right."

All of a sudden, the charisma that had attracted Belle seemed more like absolute power corrupting absolutely. "So what, Mr. Strong? You figured if everything was okay with Eric, maybe you'd join in? Or perhaps you thought I'd be so grateful for your knight-in-shining-armor routine that you could take his place?"

"No. That's not what I meant." But the ugly face looked sad. Maybe sad he'd been caught with his hands in Belle's underwear.

Belle tried to pull himself together. "As it happens, I appreciate your intervention. Thank you and good night." He stared at Magnus until he backed out the door, and then Belle slammed it.

With a moan he slowly slid to the floor.

An hour later he stared at the ceiling in the dark. What had his father and brothers promised Kleinschmidt? It had to be a misunderstanding. A man like that would easily interpret something his way.

And what the hell should he think about Strong? Was the man stalking him? Dear God, why would someone so powerful turn out to be a creep?

The hammering on his door made him jump. Not Strong coming back. "Who is it?"

More hammering. He wrapped his silk robe around his body, flipped on the light, and hurried to the door. A peek through the peephole revealed exactly what he expected. He threw open the door and stepped back. "Get the hell in here before you wake all of Las Vegas."

Rusty staggered as he passed Belle. "Can't wake 'em, baby. Nobody's sleepin' but you."

He had a point.

His dad and oldest brother somehow managed to get all the way into the room and collapse into chairs. Rusty was already lying on the foot of Belle's bed.

Belle closed the door and stared at the wall.

Rick looked up blearily. "Jesus, Belle, that robe is so gay."

He raised his head and stared at them.

His father's hands trembled, and he gazed at a spot on the carpet in front of him. "What did you say to Eric Kleinschmidt?"

End. Of. Line. "What did I say? What the fuck did I say?" He stalked to the middle of the room. "What did you three promise that fucking pervert? Did you really think I'd lie down and prostitute myself to raise your fucking money?"

His father looked up with huge round eyes. "What? What do you mean?"

"That degenerate asshole tried to rape me."

"No. No. You must have misunderstood."

Belle took another step forward with his fists clenched. "Misunderstood his arm across my throat as he tried to drag down my pants? How the fuck was I supposed to misunderstand that?"

His father grasped his own chest. "I don't understand."

Rick shook his head. "We didn't mean anything, Belle. He's a good-looking guy and really rich. We just thought you might like him. You were nice to him all evening. We were just thinking of you. You never have a boyfriend, and we just wanted you to be happy."

Belle collapsed on the edge of his bed. "I was nice to him because you've told me you're desperate for the money to mass-manufacture. I wasn't going to insult the golden fucking goose."

His father let out a long, slow breath. "Well, it's sure as crap dead now. He must have gotten the idea that you wanted to fuck him. That's why he tried—you know. Some guys are into kinky. Maybe he thought if he got rough, you'd like it."

Belle wiped a hand over his head. "Maybe. He told me you three promised him I'd go along with him in exchange for money."

Rick and his dad traded glances. Rick said, "I'm sorry, Belle. It must have been a big misunderstanding all around. I'm so sorry this happened to you."

Speaking from his reclining position, Rusty said, "Me too, bro."

His father nodded, but he held his head in his hand like it was too heavy to lift.

Rusty propped up his head, seemed to think better of it, and plopped it back on the bed. "Dad won a bundle at craps and is going to buy us all a present. We came to see what you want."

Belle frowned. "The only present I need is to not be pimped out to slithering reptiles in the future."

Rick shook his head. "We didn't, Belle."

He felt relieved, but he still narrowed his eyes. "If you ever try a stunt like that again, you'll manage your own damned lab and create your own new products. Clear?" He'd never do it and they knew it, but at least it might make them think twice about crap ideas like Eric the Snake in the future.

His dad opened his eyes. God, just looking at him ripped Belle's heart. He'd always been a weak man, but his genuine love for Belle's mother had kept him sane and sober. Now? No anchor. "Sorry, son. What kind of present can I get you? Rick wants a new Lexus, and Rusty wants a Rolex. What about you?"

"There's nothing I need."

"'S not about need. Let me buy you somefin'."

"A rose, then. Buy me a rose to wear tomorrow when we introduce the new product."

"'S not much."

"You know how I love roses."

"Yeah. Just like your mom." For a second his eyes clouded. Then he shook his head and struggled to his feet.

A cell phone rang, and all three men grabbed for their pockets. His dad removed his phone, his eyes lit up, and he clicked it on. "Hullo."

He paused, his face getting more animated by the second. "Yeah, that's great. Glad to hear it. Okay, thanks." He clicked his phone off. "Sorry, guys. The presents are off. Gonna need all my capital."

Rick frowned. "Aww, Dad. You promised. I need that car for Jennifer."

"Nope. Sorry. 'S my money. I need it."

Belle crossed his arms. "What for, Dad?"

There was the sly look again. "Just a friendly game of poker with some of the other leaders in the industry." He practically shined his fingernails on his lapel, he looked so proud. "Great networking opportunity. Can't pass it up."

"Isn't it late to be issuing invitations?"

"Nah. I didn't think I got to play. I mean, you know, they didn't have an extra seat. But one came up. Great opportunity. Just great." He staggered a few steps and looked back. "I'll still get your rose, Belle."

"When is this game?"

"Tomorrow night. Wish me luck."

Belle sighed. I wish us all luck.

His dad walked to the door with new vigor, then looked back. "By the way. How the hell did you get rid of that guy?"

"I didn't. Someone knocked on my door and scared Eric away."

"Really? Room service?"

Belle shuddered. "Right. Room service."

BELLE STARED at the business card and then up at the attractive, dark-haired man standing in the Bella Terra booth. "You're an industry analyst, Mr. Porter?" He raised his voice a little to be heard over the din of eighty thousand people talking at once.

The guy smiled. "Just call me Elliott. Yes, I do reports on significant developments in beauty products, and all the whispers for weeks have been that Bella Terra has something special." He glanced around. "I don't see anything new on display."

"The new product isn't available yet. We're just completing our beta manufacturing run and anticipate a launch within, uh, a few months."

"Imminent. Perhaps you'd like to give me details?" Porter flashed his pearly whites. *Hmmm.*

Belle ran the card along his cheek. "Mr. Porter, I saw you last night sitting with Magnus Strong." *Right before I got the erection of the age.* "Just the two of you, I believe."

"Uh, yes. I'm an industry consultant. He's always interested in my take on developments."

Belle smiled. "Just the same, I think I'd prefer to wait a bit until I reveal all to Mr. Strong."

"I'll just find out from other sources." He grinned and played the game.

"I'm sure. But why make it any easier than I must for Beauty, Inc. to copy my formulas?"

Porter cocked his handsome head. "You take this competition quite seriously."

"I'm no competitor to Magnus Strong—except in my dreams. I have to protect what tiny bit of proprietary knowledge I may have."

"Bravo, Mr. Belleterre. I like your spirit. Speaking of which, I noticed you with Eric Kleinschmidt."

Belle raised his brows. "Is he a friend of yours?"

"I don't think anyone's a friend of Eric unless they're young, gay, and dumb."

"I'm only young and gay."

"I see. Didn't know."

"Most people guess."

"I wouldn't presume."

"Appreciate that."

"Have you ever met Magnus Strong, Mr. Belleterre?"

"An encounter. Not an actual meeting."

Porter smiled. "That's a meeting I hope I get to see." He extended his hand. "Good to meet you. If you'll pardon the really bad pun, whenever you're ready to spill the cream, I'm ready to lap it up." Laughing, he walked back down the aisle.

ACROSS THE hall, Magnus stared through his binoculars from the second-floor conference room in his booth. They'd designed this tower space in his exhibit just for private conversations. Right now he could use all the privacy available, and the only conversation he wanted to have was with his cock. This was the second time he'd had penis blastoff at the sight of Robert Belleterre—the beautiful Belle. Which was annoying and stupid. He prided himself on excellent self-control, for one thing. Plus he didn't usually like pretty men. Hell, why lust after someone who'd cringe from you? In this case a man who actually had cringed the night before.

Yes, his money and his power made up for his ugliness with some men, but he never pushed his luck. Watching revulsion in the eyes of a potential lover didn't turn him on. Besides, he didn't want Belle Belleterre for his beauty. Just his brain. Well, that's what he *wanted* to want him for.

His head snapped around when a hand touched his shoulder. Hell, that demonstrated how distracted he was. No one sneaked up on Magnus Strong. "Hello, Christian."

Stocky and gray-haired, his board member gave Magnus the once-over with a wry smile. "Surveying your domain?"

"Nope. Spying." He set the binoculars in the cabinet and closed it. *Hope he didn't notice the direction of my viewing.*

"How are you finding the conference this year?"

Magnus glanced down onto the show floor. "Good. I mostly came to give the keynote address tomorrow. After that I'll head back to New York."

"Can't fool me. You mostly came to play your poker game." He gave a tight smile. Christian loved to play the righteous prude, but it didn't count for much, because he'd been trying to get Magnus into bed since before Magnus took over the company from his father five years ago.

Magnus grinned. "That too."

"You do love to indulge your vices."

Magnus raised a brow. "So do we all."

Christian cleared his throat. "So what's new in the world of beauty?"

Magnus plunged into a description of new mascaras from Chanel and BB creams from Maybelline but skirted the Bella Terra rumors. He wanted to hold that close to the vest until he knew far more about the product and its inventor. Once the board got their paws in, things became too political—and too out of his control.

Christian's eyes darted around the floor below. Clearly his agenda didn't begin and end with new developments in beauty products. "Want to get a drink later?"

Ah, the lech. Magnus might be thirty, but Christian still had twenty-five years on him. *And you have eight years on that boy you're lusting after, so don't throw rocks at Christian.* "As you so rightly pointed out, I'll be playing cards."

"Good luck."

"Thanks, but it's more a fact-finding mission than an orgy of income."

"Oh really?" Christian crossed his arms.

Magnus grinned. "Yes, really."

CHAPTER 4

BELLE SIPPED his glass of champagne and tried not to freak out at his father's antsiness. Ron alternated between downing martinis and staring at his watch, the food in front of him on the restaurant table pretty much ignored. "Sorry I couldn't get you boys your presents, but I'll put this money to good use for all of us. Them that has will get, boys. Never forget that."

Belle nodded toward his father's uneaten steak. "Eat something, Dad. It's good for your concentration."

"What? Oh, right." He cut a hunk of beef, stabbed it with his fork, and then waved it as he spoke. "Don't underestimate the importance of my being invited to this poker game, boys. Only the top decision-makers in the industry get invites to Strong's big game. It's like getting your country club membership. A rite of passage."

Belle hadn't breathed in seconds. "Did you say Strong's game?"

"Of course. This is Magnus Strong's high-stakes poker game. He has it every year. I've never been invited before." He kept waving the meat. "I planted a few inquiries with friends, and bingo, I got the invite."

"Is this the invitation that came in last night?" *After I got "saved" by Magnus Strong?*

"Yes, right. I guess there'd been some mistake and I hadn't received the invite, so Strong told his people to call me right away. That's why I got it so late."

"I see." Belle pushed his plate of sole away. "Dad, be really careful in this game, okay? These are high rollers with little to lose."

"You think I don't know that?" He set down the fork, steak still uneaten. "God, I was swimming with sharks before you were a tadpole. That's why I can't use that money I won to buy presents. I need it for the buy-in. I'm a good player, and I'm on a roll. I won last night, and I'll win tonight. Can't wait. Maybe I can make up for some of the money we would have gotten from Kleinschmidt."

"You're trying to get manufacturing money at the poker table?" Belle's stomach turned.

Rick spoke with his mouth full. "You got a better idea? You chased off our one big chance at an investment." He put a hand on Ron's arm. "I think it's great, Dad. Just great."

Belle tried not to scream.

MAGNUS SIPPED a soda water and stared at the report from Elliott. Porter was worth his weight in hedge funds. The report impressed Magnus—and pissed him off. Belle Belleterre was like a magnificent new general in the army of a decadent civilization. No chance to succeed. He glanced at the clock. *Guests coming soon.* What would the night bring?

He locked the report in his room safe, pulled on his suit jacket, and ambled to the private sitting room he'd had set up for card playing just as his guests started arriving. He'd brought in a professional dealer to keep everything honest, plus he'd pay a percentage to the house. He hadn't been kidding Christian. The money mattered far less than the information. With a few drinks in them, businesspeople talked. Magnus listened—especially tonight.

Aimée Delon, one of the most prominent female CEOs, came in, giving Magnus double kisses, followed by several of the men who made women beautiful. Finally Rondell Belleterre staggered through the door, already smelling of liquor. Magnus nodded. "Evening, Ron. Glad you could come."

"Wouldn't have missed it." He rubbed his hands together. "What have you got in store, Magnus?"

"Just a friendly evening of poker. Bar's in the next room. Help yourself."

Ron chuckled. "Don't mind if I do." He walked straight into the side room.

Magnus chatted with the others as they all took their places for the game. "Aimée, what new and fabulous stuff have you seen today?"

Her thick French accent made every word a song. "Ah, some new BB creams I have seen. *C'est merveilleux.* And the combination tanner and night creams seem to be getting better." She sipped her champagne.

"I myself have a new sheer lip color you will love, Magnus." His name sounded like *Magnoose*.

Ron lurched in from the bar with a martini in his hand, but it looked like one or two might have gone down in the other room. He pulled out a chair next to Magnus and fell into it, sloshing vodka on the table. "So what're we playing?"

Magnus looked around the table. "Take your pick." Two players preferred seven-card stud, while the rest opted for no-limit Hold 'em. He nodded. "Hold 'em to start. Then we'll shift to seven-card in, shall we say, an hour?" He arched a hand at the dealer, who began the Hold 'em game.

Since it was a friendly game, the buy-in had been set at only ten thousand dollars. Hold 'em required more luck than reason—not Magnus's favorite. Ron, however, played boldly and more and more rashly. Magnus held back and watched Ron double and then triple his bets. Every winning hand got celebrated with yet another martini.

At the end of the first hour, Magnus had lost a little, while Aimée and two of the other Hold 'em fans had lost thousands—most of it to Ron Belleterre. He raked in the last Hold 'em pot with a huge smile. "Man, this is great. Thanks a lot." He added the winnings to the big pile of chips in front of him. Bill and JZ, the two fans of seven-card stud, nursed relatively small losses and smiled at Ron patiently. Yes, their game was coming up.

The dealer began to switch the table over to stud poker while the bartender took orders for drinks. Ron placed yet another drink request as he sloshed down his previous vodka.

Magnus sat back a little to keep from getting splashed as martini rolled like a tidal wave in Ron's wide-mouthed glass. "So, Ron, I keep hearing that Bella Terra is all the buzz at the show this year. You seem to have the new development everyone wants."

"'S true. Yep. We got it, all right."

"I hear your youngest boy is your secret weapon."

"Yep. My Belle." He laughed and burst into the lyrics of the old Beatles song "Michelle." "That's my Belle. He did it. Nobody could and he did. 'S 'mazing."

"Quite the beauty too, I hear. I'm surprised you don't use him in your ads."

Ron shook his head slowly and frowned. "Shy, like his mom. Smart. Too bad he's gotta be—you know." He shrugged and picked up the cards the dealer slid in front of him.

Magnus glanced at his own hole cards. "No, I don't know."

"Gay. He's a damned girlie man. Shit."

Magnus felt the edges of the cards bend in his hand.

The dealer indicated that Aimée had the low card showing. She didn't up the required one thousand dollar bring-in, and the little frown on her face suggested she didn't have much in her hand. Ron Belleterre slapped a couple thousand more on the pot and, after two others folded, managed to win. "Musht be my lucky night."

Magnus nodded. "Must be."

Ron played recklessly but well enough that he won a number of pots. Two of the players folded their cards and left the game, leaving Ron, Magnus, Aimée, and JZ Graper, another cosmetics CEO. Ron ran his fingers relentlessly through his pile of chips, which now amounted to over one hundred thousand dollars. Sweat dotted his forehead, and his eyes gleamed. Aimée put a hand on his arm. "Ron, darling, you're doing well. Don't you think you should quit while you're ahead, as they say? You've had a bit to drink, *non?*"

He pulled his arm away from her touch and frowned. "No. Hell no. Gotta respect the streak, man. I mean woman." He snorted. "Can't quit when you're hot, right, Magnus?"

"Whatever you say, Ron." Aimée gave Magnus a glance, and he shrugged. Not his job to babysit drunks. Especially not this one.

The dealer gave Aimée a four of diamonds and JZ the four of spades. She sighed. "I must do ze bring-in again. Why me?" She laughed and slapped another thousand on the table.

"Jez give it to papa, darling." Ron splashed back another mouthful and got a withering glance from Aimée.

JZ folded. Magnus raised to five thousand, and Ron called. The dealer gave Magnus a jack of clubs and Ron a king of hearts. They both checked. Ron wiped sweat from his lip.

On the next deal, Magnus got the ten of hearts, but Ron got the king of clubs, which prompted a huge smile since he now showed a pair of kings. He slid a big pile of chips into the center of the table. The dealer quickly counted. "Fifty thousand to you, Mr. Strong."

Magnus glanced at Ron, nodded, and raised twenty thousand. He didn't have enough chips, so he presented a marker.

Ron's look got sly. He saw Magnus's bid, depleting his pile as he slid the required chips to the center. The dealer gave them both a down card.

Ron glanced, and the slight widening of his eyes suggested a solid hand. He still had the bid and slid the rest of his chips to the center.

The dealer announced, "One hundred thousand to you, Mr. Strong."

Magnus laughed. "Bold move, Belleterre. Clearly you have something worth seeing." He made a show of looking at his cards and frowning slightly. "Well, what's the fun of being conservative at a time like this? I'll raise you another two hundred thousand."

Aimée clutched Ron's arm again. "You should stop."

Ron sharply shook her off. "Don' tell me what ta do." He looked at Magnus. "I'm out of chips."

"So am I. I'm good for it. Are you?"

"Uh, I don' have a lotta cash. Reinvesting in business, ya know?"

"Of course. So what's your move?"

"Uh, what can I bet? Stock? Maybe stock."

Magnus nodded. "Certainly. With all the talk of your new product, I'm sure it will be rising. Will its value cover my bet?"

"Fuck yeah."

"Then good. I'll accept his stock in Bella Terra as equivalent to my bet."

"'S worth more."

Magnus raised a brow. "Oh? How much more?"

"Twice."

"All right, then he can bet half his stock to see my bet."

"Raise!"

Magnus looked at him. "What are you saying?"

"I raise you another two hundred thou. All my stock if I lose, which I won't. So ante up, Strong."

"Very well. My marker for another two hundred thousand."

"Thash great. Magnus Strong money will fund Bella Terra. So what ya got?"

Magnus carefully laid out his ace-high straight.

Ron's face went white, then red. "No. You got nothin' showing—"

Magnus smiled. "Yes, quite remarkable. That last hole card made the straight for me. Amazing luck. What have you got, Ron?"

Ron shook his head and stared at the table like a snake had coiled on it. The dealer reached out and took his cards. "Two pair. Kings and nines."

Magnus sat back. "Oh my. It appears I have a substantial interest in your company, Ron. That should be very interesting. When is your next shareholder's meeting?"

Ron looked like he might vomit. "Can't. My boys. No. Please."

Magnus shrugged. "I won it fair and square, Ron. If you didn't want to lose the stock, why on earth did you bet it?"

"Shorry. So shorry." He shook his head.

"I'll tell you what. Why don't you and I have a talk and see what we can work out." He smiled. Yes, he knew his face must look like something on an old poster for *Jaws*.

THE HAMMERING on his door sounded damned familiar. Belle flipped on the light and grabbed his robe. Jesus, the clock said 4:00 a.m. "Okay, I'm coming." He peeked through the hole. Only his father. He opened the door.

Ron staggered into the room, grabbing the wall as he bounced off it. "Belley. I'm sho shorry, Belley."

Belley? Okay, new low in the nickname department. He slid an arm around his father's shoulders and guided him to the couch, where he carefully sat him down. "It's okay, Dad. I know Vegas's pleasures are hard to resist. But maybe when we get home, we'll get you some help for the drinking. Ya think? A short stint in rehab and you should be fine. You haven't been this bad for too long." Okay, so he was talking to himself, but it made him feel better.

His dad shook his head back and forth, back and forth, like an old cow. "Sho shorry. Shorry."

"Why don't you lie down and get a little rest? We had a great day yesterday. There's so much interest in the new product. It's going to make the company money and really put us on the map."

He smoothed his father's hair on the shaking head, but Ron didn't stop muttering, "Shorry, shorry." Usually words like "money" and "on the map" soothed him.

He pushed his father down until he was lying on the couch, his feet still dangling. With a quick yank, Belle pulled off his shoes, then covered him with a throw. "Sho shorry, Belley. Din wanna do it. Wanna keep you. Din wanna lose—" His snores filled the room.

Wonder what he means by that?

Belle grabbed his laptop and crawled back in his bed. He checked e-mail—a couple of questions from Colin, which he answered—then did a quick perusal of social media, looking for stories from the conference. Mostly he found things he'd already seen or heard. As he was about to close the computer, a tweet floated across his screen. *News said to be coming from Beauty, Inc. Watch this space.* The tweet came from Elliott Porter, the analyst Belle had spoken to on the show floor. If anyone knew about news from Beauty, Inc. it was likely Porter. *Have to watch for that.*

He set aside his laptop, curled under the covers, and turned off the light, trying to ignore his father's droning snores.

CHAPTER 5

WHAM! WHAM!

Shit, was there no other way to wake him? Once more, on with the robe. As Belle fell out of bed, he glanced at his father, who barely stirred, his snores replaced by moans and mutters. Through the peephole—sure enough, Rusty and Rick. He opened the door. "What's going on?"

Rick crossed his arms and narrowed his eyes. "That's exactly what we want to know."

Rusty pushed in front of him. "I can't believe you could do this to the family, Belle. I know Dad's not what he used to be, but come on."

Rick scowled as he walked farther into the room. "This is going to kill Dad."

Belle slammed the door and followed his brothers to the center of the big room. "As you can plainly see, nothing is killing Dad except too much booze. He's been here since 4:00 a.m., when he also woke me from a sound sleep. I, on the other hand, have been in this room since 9:00 p.m. and haven't got the slightest idea what you're talking about."

"So you don't have any idea about Beauty, Inc., right?" Rick sneered the words.

Belle planted his hands on his hips. "I suggest you tell me what in hell you're talking about. Otherwise I'm closing myself in the shower, and you can wake our father and figure out what to do with him."

Rusty finally looked confused. "You mean you don't know anything about Beauty, Inc.'s big announcement released at 6:00 a.m. this morning?"

Patience. "No. When Father woke me at four, I saw that there was to be an announcement, but I've been asleep ever since. So what is it? Has Beauty, Inc. released that they have an equivalent to our new product? Because if they have, it's a lie! I know they don't have one yet."

Rusty sounded exasperated while Rick just looked angry. Rusty ran his fingers through the only reddish hair in the family—on his own head. "Belle, the announcement is that you're going to work for Beauty, Inc."

"What?" The words didn't even compute in his head.

Rick yelled, "They say you're going to work for fucking Beauty, Inc. in their fucking laboratory!"

"I—I don't understand." Nothing made sense.

Rusty grabbed his arms. "You mean it's not true?"

"No. No, of course not!"

Their father's voice sounded old and defeated. "I'm afraid it is true."

All three of them whirled to look at Ron Belleterre.

"YOU SHOULD tell your father to go fuck himself."

Belle slowly shook his head. "Can't. It would ruin him if he has to give up his stock. If I don't carry out his promise, my dad loses the company." He released a long breath. "I can't do that to him." He folded another dress shirt into his suitcase and looked longingly at his old flannel that he wore around town sometimes, like a real Oregonian. No flannel in New York.

Judy frowned like an attack poodle. "Fuck, he's ruined you. Jesus, Belle, he's ripping you away from the places you love to drop you in the middle of New Hell City."

"Spoken like a small-town Oregon girl."

"Yes, and proud of it." She pulled her legs up to cross them yoga-style on his chaise, which sat beside his bedroom window, looking out on the trees and stream that fed his life. "And who's this dude you'll be working for?"

Belle shrugged. "Who knows who they'll assign me to? I mean, I'm small potatoes at Beauty, Inc."

"Sounds like they made an awfully big deal out of it, or do they send out press releases for everyone they hire?"

Belle sat on the edge of the bed. "No, I'm sure they don't. But my father was such an asshole to lose his stock in a card game, I expect Strong wanted to rub it in and make Dad look like an idiot in front of his peers." Shit, he didn't even want to think of other motives.

"He *is* an idiot. Who's Strong?"

"Magnus Strong, the CEO of Beauty, Inc. and its largest stockholder."

"Wasn't he on some big magazine?"

"All of them." He got up, pulled the copy of *Forbes* from his nightstand, and handed it to Judy. "Here's the most recent."

She inspected the cover. "Jesus, that's a face only a mother could love."

He went back to packing. "Yeah, I know it looks that way. I've seen him once in person, though, and weirdly, you don't think about the ugliness. He's kind of—I don't know—beautiful."

She laughed. "What were you drinking at the time?" She turned the cover in her hands. "Ironic that some giant beauty magnate should be so damned ugly. It looks like scars and a broken nose. Why didn't he get those fixed? At least he wouldn't scare small children."

"No idea. He could certainly afford it."

"Looks like he's richer than God."

Belle felt the tears behind his eyes and forced them to retreat. "He's certainly rich enough to cheat my father out of his company."

"Man, that is evil."

He wiped a hand over his hair. Should he tell her?

Judy put a hand on his shoulder. "Hey, is there something else wrong? Not that moving your whole life to a company and city you hate isn't enough."

"Yeah." He blew out a long stream of air. "It's complicated, but I wonder if maybe Strong wants—you know."

"To have sex with you?"

He barked a laugh. "You certainly didn't have to fish for that one."

"Why do you think that?"

"Like I said, it's complicated, but while I was in Vegas, I was supposed to be meeting with this investor who—well, he essentially tried to rape me. Magnus Strong stopped him."

She wrapped her arms around her legs. "Uh, sweetheart, I know you're upset, but that doesn't exactly sound like he has evil designs on you."

He sighed. "It's just that he found out my room number and purposely walked by. That's why he heard me kicking the door. It took special effort to do that."

"Yeah, creepy."

"Exactly. He said he saw me with this rapist dude and was worried, but—I don't know."

"What did you do?"

"I was pretty upset and really got up in his face."

"What did he do?"

"Looked—kind of sad, I guess."

"And that was before he traded your father back his company in exchange for your perfect ass?"

"I don't know about the perfect part, but yeah."

"Shit, Belle." She fell back on his bed. "You're going to be three thousand miles from your family and friends, sold into slavery to some beast of a billionaire."

"Thanks for the clear delineation of my situation."

She flipped on her side and stared at him. "What are you going to do when you get there? My God, you'll be working for the enemy."

"As little as damned possible. I mean, I'll work, but Strong's chemists are going to have to tell me what to do every step of the way. If that asshole thinks I'm going to come and invent new products for him, he must be smoking his money."

"But what about the—other? The 'you know'?"

"If he thinks he just bought a sex slave, he can go fuck himself."

"That's telling him, sweetie."

He dragged his eyes to Judy. Were there circles under her eyes? His mom's face flashed in his mind. "Hey, how did the doc appointment go?"

"Okay. No biggie. Thanks so much for the money."

"Least I can do."

"They just did some exams and woman crap."

"Well that's good, right? I mean, you should have that done regularly, right?"

"Yep. You haven't lived until you've been poked and prodded by a gynecologist."

"Oh, I don't know." He grinned. "Ever had a prostate exam?"

"We'll call it a draw."

Somehow, he didn't think it was.

BELLE STARED into the distance as his father hugged him good-bye. Ron smelled of alcohol. Rusty and Rick just shuffled their feet and looked like they wanted to be anywhere else.

Ron mustered up a laugh. "Just think of this as an opportunity for industrial espionage, son."

"How long do I have to stay?" He'd asked this question several times before, but his father kept sidestepping it. A seriously bad sign.

His father adjusted his shirt cuff. "Uh, we didn't exactly discuss that issue."

Rusty at least hollered, "What? You don't know?"

Belle swallowed hard. "So when you made this deal for my life, you didn't negotiate an end point?"

"I wasn't exactly operating from a position of strength. I'm sure he has a specific end in mind. Maybe a few months or something."

Belle sighed. "Or something."

"So ask him, for God's sake."

The words were out before he could haul them back. "I won't exactly be negotiating from a position of strength."

His father's cocky shoulders sagged. "The fact is, Strong wants you more than he wanted a lot of money."

"Why? He's got lots of chemists. So I came up with a new product? So what? He has fifty for my one."

"I don't know, Belle. I guess you'll find out."

That's exactly what he was afraid of. "Where am I supposed to live?"

"Stay at a hotel until you can find a place."

"Is he planning to pay me a salary, or am I some kind of indentured servant?"

"I don't know. I don't know!"

Even Rick looked shocked.

Belle grabbed his garment bag, tried to encapsulate his feelings of horror and despair in one last glance, and then walked away from all three of them, toward the boarding gate. Maybe later he'd calm down enough to wish he'd looked back. Not now.

THE PLANE'S wheels hit the ground, but Belle's heart kept racing. New York. Of course, he'd been there before—for trade shows and one meeting—but to consider living in a city this size when even Portland gave him hives? Jesus, what a nightmare. He wasn't even sure how to start. *Find a hotel, I guess, and check in.* He knew the address of Beauty, Inc. in downtown Manhattan. There had to be a hotel near there. My God, he felt alone. Of course, that wasn't new.

He moved slowly off the plane, allowing others to pass in front of him. *Let them get where they're going. I'm in no hurry.* He wasn't even sure when he was expected to report to work. In a life full of ups, downs, and uncertainty, this marked the all-time low.

As he emerged from the Jetway, he blinked up at the signs showing baggage claim. Hauling his garment bag over his shoulder, he headed toward it.

"Excuse me, sir."

Belle stepped aside and kept walking.

"Sir? Mr. Belleterre?"

He looked up at a man in a livery hat holding a sign that read Robert Belleterre. "Oh. Are you looking for me?"

The guy had a tough face, broken nose, and tattoos that climbed out of his shirt collar, but his smile cracked dimples in his craggy cheeks and flashed one preposterous gold tooth. "I figured it must be you. They said look for the angel."

"Angel? Sorry, what do you mean?"

The man grabbed his garment bag. "Here, give me that. Have you looked in the mirror lately?" He laughed good-naturedly. "Come on. Let's get your luggage, and then I'll take you to the car."

"Car?"

"Oh yes, sorry. I really am crappy at the chauffer shit, but I'm a great driver." He stuck out his hand. "I'm Leroy, and I'll be your driver, Mr. Belleterre."

Belle felt his solemn face cracking. "Uh, do I need a driver?"

"Yes, sir. Have you been in the city lately?" He laughed again. "I'll be taking you to work and home and wherever you want to go."

"Home?"

"Yeah. Come on."

After a power walk through the airport, Leroy grabbed Belle's suitcases like they were plastic bags of feathers and led him out to a reserved parking area for limos. The vehicle turned out to be a town car, so lower-key than the word limo suggested. Leroy held open the back door. "You must be tired. Help yourself to drinks and snacks. If you want privacy for conversations or sleep, just hit that button. There's a panel. Otherwise, feel free to chat."

Belle looked at Leroy. "Where am I going?"

"Your place."

"What?"

Leroy grinned. "You'll see."

Oh hell, what could he do about it? If Leroy took him to Magnus Strong's den of iniquity, he'd have to figure out how to escape when he got there. Right now he was too damned tired. He glanced at his phone. No messages from his father or brothers. *Shit.*

Belle settled into the cushy leather seat. At home he owned an old car but mostly rode to work on his bicycle.

Leroy started the quiet vehicle and maneuvered it out of the parking lot. He slid through the melee of cars trying to pick up passengers, approach curbs, and pull out into moving traffic like he was driving a motor scooter instead of an oversized town car....

Instant addict. It took exactly that long to know that being driven, especially in New York fucking City, was the best thing he could imagine. Belle rested his head against the seat and let Leroy take over.

You're being lulled by the enemy.

True. But right then he didn't give a shit.

CHAPTER 6

"MR. BELLETERRE?"

Belle flipped his head and cozied it in deeper. "Umm, call me Belle."

"Belle, we're here."

"Hmm? Where?"

"We're at your apartment. But if you want to sleep some more, I'm happy to drive you around for a while."

"Apartment?" His eyes popped open. "Oh, I'm so sorry. I didn't mean to fall asleep."

"Anytime, boss."

"I'm not your—"

"Come on, let's get you inside so you can settle in and sleep."

Belle crawled out of the car like a stranger in a strange land. "Where am I?"

"Brooklyn."

"Where?" He looked around at the old brownstones.

"It's a borough of New York."

"I know that. I mean, I thought Beauty, Inc. was in New York City."

"It is. That's where I'll drive you tomorrow."

He shook his head. At least it was humid. He liked that. But the air. Jesus, he could practically see the chunks. Dirt plus humidity made mud, and he could feel the stuff coating his lungs. Horns beeped and brakes squealed all around him. He shuddered. Still, the stores looked interesting. Almost as interesting as the people.

Leroy hefted his bags. "Come on, Belle."

The building in front of him, toward which Leroy walked, looked five or six stories high—and five or six centuries old. At least window boxes relieved the old brick façade. Oh well, what did he expect? The damned Ritz? At least he wasn't sleeping in a doorway covered with cardboard tonight, and that's where he could be for all his family knew—or cared. He'd always been the odd man out in the Belleterre family—more so since his mom died—but this was the first time he'd been ransom.

He dragged himself up the front stairs and grabbed the door before it banged closed behind the overburdened Leroy. With a sigh he stepped inside.

"Helllooo, my dear. Welcome home."

"What?" Belle tried to see where the voice was coming from, but—he couldn't. His eyes widened so hugely they strained his face. How could this be? *Impossible. Beautiful.*

He walked slowly forward through a small hall and opened a sliding glass door that led him into—fairyland. Four or five stories of soaring atrium, full, packed, alive and vibrating with tropical plants. He inhaled. Air so rich, sweet, wet, and amazing it seeped into his blood like champagne. Flowers. Flowers everywhere—red, orange, yellow, purple—so unreal now as they emerged from winter. "How is this possible?"

"It's magic."

Belle whirled to see another sight as amazing as the atrium—a tiny elf-like man wearing plaid trousers and a bright green sweater leaning against the doorjamb, smiling at him. Belle had to smile back. "I'm sorry. I didn't know I said that out loud."

"Quite all right. We pride ourselves on the amazement of new observers." He stood upright, which might have brought him to five foot two, and extended his hand. "I am assuming you're our new resident. I'm Carstairs Pennymaker."

"Belle Belleterre. Am I your new resident? I'm sorry, but I was sort of hijacked and brought here."

"Against your will?"

"Sadly, that's the case."

"Ah, my dear. Since we all have a myriad of choices in life, I trust that this choice was at least the lesser of two evils. Now, let me show you your apartment."

Belle closed his mouth. Who was this guy? "Sir, are you the landlord?"

"Something like that."

The man had to be somewhere well north of seventy, but he climbed the stairs at seventy miles an hour, talking the whole time. "We have one empty apartment on the ground floor. We call that floor G for Garden. On floor one we have Wanda Thermolopoulus. You'll love her. Wonderful cook. Then here on the second floor is Henry Kim, who is our primary gardener for the fairyland. A master, as you can see. Floor three is Ahmed and Fatima Khosropana. You'll find them quite surprising. And then—" He stopped and made a sweeping gesture toward the next closed door. "—here is your new home."

Belle's body and brain tried to catch up. "Sir, wait. Are you sure there isn't a mistake?"

Mr. Pennymaker turned with a thoughtful crease between his reddish brows. "Does this seem the sort of place you would like to live?"

"Well yes, of course. Who wouldn't?"

"Many people, I'm sure. But if this is your place, then there's no mistake." He threw open the door to the apartment.

Okay, the little guy must be batshit crazy, but Belle had to look inside.

He stared, then followed his eyes and his nose into—heaven.

The apartment wasn't large, but then he didn't like large. He walked into the living room, where a big sectional couch just made for snuggling into sat in front of a brick fireplace. And, most wondrous of all, on either side of the fireplace were windows that looked out into the atrium—and they opened. Belle walked over and peered into the mystifying, magnificent array of plants. There were no apartments on the other side of the atrium, which meant each apartment on this side must have its own unimpeded view of beauty. His breath escaped, long and slow.

Mr. Pennymaker clapped his hands. "Excellent. You like it. But there's more."

Belle tore himself away from the view and looked back. Small, open, modern kitchen—just his size—and a sliding glass door. Mr. Pennymaker led him to that door, which he opened.

"Ta-da!"

It was a solarium porch. In the daylight it would be brilliant and sunny, unlike the tropical atrium that enjoyed more filtered light, and in every corner and cranny—roses. Everywhere. Pots and planters full of roses of every color. Tears pooled in his eyes. It was hard to grow roses in his part of Oregon—too wet. And he loved them so very, very much.

"Ah, I see you're pleased."

"I don't understand."

"What, my dear?"

"Any of this." He looked around the place that must have been built from his dreams. "How do I get to live here?"

"It's my understanding that all executives of Beauty, Inc. are given a residence, but I'm not certain."

Belle frowned. "Who chose it?"

"I'm sure I don't know. I just received a phone call and a deposit."

"Are all the residents here Beauty, Inc. employees?"

"No. Only you."

Belle heard rustling and turned to see Leroy walk in with his bags. "Hey, man, quite a place you got here."

Belle's frown got deeper. "Leroy, who chose this place for me?"

He shrugged as he set down the bags. "No idea. I just got the address."

"From whom?"

"HR."

"Excuse me?"

"Human Resources—at Beauty, Inc. They give all the drivers our new assignments."

Mr. Pennymaker crossed his arms, increasing his resemblance to someone at the end of the rainbow. "Perhaps we should stop looking gift horses in the mouth, unpack our bags, and come down to the first floor and join some of us for dinner."

Exactly what choice did he have? "All right. Thank you."

Leroy smiled. "Cool. You need me to help unpack?"

"No. Thanks."

"Okay then, I'll see you tomorrow morning at 8:00 a.m. sharp. But here's my number." He set a card on the table inside the door. "If you need me, just holler. I don't live far away, and I'm your guy. I know the neighborhood like my own face. Have a good night in your new place."

As Leroy left, Mr. Pennymaker bustled to the door. "So when you're ready, come down to the first floor and walk through the open door. See you in a few." He waved and closed the front door of the apartment behind him.

Belle stared at the closed door, the pile of suitcases, and the view of flowers and plants in every direction. This must be exactly how Dorothy felt when she woke up in Oz.

The feeling had barely dissipated an hour later when he walked tentatively down the stairs that flanked the atrium. He'd left his door unlocked, since he didn't have a key and, besides his laptop, had very little for anyone to steal. He'd left the laptop in the bathroom cabinet, just in case.

As he passed the door of the apartment one floor down, a young couple came barging out, the guy backing up. The beautiful dark-haired woman, who wore a headscarf and a tank top, revealing full sleeves of elaborate flower tattoos, was gesticulating wildly. "I don't care if she's your frigging cousin. I'm not covering my tats to impress her."

"It's just one day, my love." The handsome guy sported a full beard, which looked a little incongruous with his black jeans, tight T-shirt, and Doc Martens.

"I don't care if it's a full minute."

Belle stopped, but the guy still banged into him, whirled, grabbed Belle's arm, and held him steady. "I'm so sorry. I was totally not watching where I was going. I'm not used to having anyone come from upstairs."

Belle smiled. "It's okay. I didn't stop fast enough."

The woman put a hand on her curvy hip and cocked her head. "You must be the new guy. You're gonna love it here."

The guy laughed. "Right. Because we're such damned cool neighbors."

Belle wasn't quite sure what to say, so he stuck out his hand. "I'm Belle."

The girl grabbed it first. "Fatima. Yep, that one." She made a little dancing move. "This is my hubby, Ahmed."

"I'm happy to meet you both."

"We'll give you five minutes to settle into the party before we involve you in our argument."

"Okay," he laughed. "Deal."

Ahmed took his arm and ushered him down the stairs. "You're not going to believe Wanda's food. Seriously, this is like the reason to live here."

Fatima laughed. "Or the reason to live."

"They had me at the atrium." Belle smiled. He couldn't help it.

"Oh yeah. Isn't it great? It's like heaven to us desert dwellers."

Belle looked over his shoulder. "Really? Are you both from the Middle East? You sound so—"

Fatima laughed. "We're from the middle of Manhattan, but Ahmed loves to dream of his desert ancestors."

Ahmed pointed into the atrium. "I think of it as the hanging gardens of Babylon."

"Don't let Henry hear you say that. You know he's recreating Jamaica in there."

Belle tried to look between them and walk at the same time. "Isn't his name Kim?"

Fatima laughed. "Yep. Some distant and nearly forgotten ancestor. Henry is all Jamaica, mon."

Belle felt mountains of stereotypes crashing under his feet.

On the first floor, Ahmed let Fatima and then Belle go into the apartment before him. The place smelled like some heavenly cathedral to food. Mr. Pennymaker, in plaid, green, and an apron, came out of what must be the kitchen in the apartment. "Ah, welcome, my dears. Wanda is putting the final touches on a splendid feast. We'll welcome our new friend Belle."

Ahmed flopped on the serviceable brown couch like he owned the place. "So how come you're called Belle? Your mom was bitten by a Disney princess?"

"My last name's Belleterre. I was the last one in line, so I got the nickname."

Ahmed laughed. "Plus you're so damned pretty."

He shrugged and blushed.

Fatima hooted at her husband. "Now you've embarrassed him, which means I can't stare at him without tipping my hand." She chortled, then pulled Belle down on the couch between her and Ahmed. "Okay, so here's the question." She looked up. "This is for you too, Mr. P. Ahmed's cousin is this serious-ass Muslim, and she's coming to visit next week. Now, we're Shiite, and there's nothing proscribed about tats in the Shia brand of Islam. His sister's just a fanatic. So I'll be damned if I'm covering my arms because she's here."

Mr. P, as she called him, scratched his chin. "Ahmed, tell me why you feel strongly about this."

"I don't know. I guess I just hate making my cousin uncomfortable."

"What about making your wife uncomfortable, my dear?"

"No, of course I don't want to do that, but it's kind of a hospitality thing. Azia will be the guest, you know?"

"Yes, I do. Fatima, what do you say about that?"

She sighed. "I guess he has a point. I mean, hospitality is like the whole deal in Islam, you know?"

"Yes, I do." He smiled. "So what if you were to say that you won't go out of your way to reveal your body art, but if she happens to see it, you'll all remain calm and not act as if you've been trying to hide it?"

"Yeah, that works for me." Ahmed looked at Belle. "What do you think?"

"The tats are beautiful. All flowers. I think they're not proscribed images, right?"

Fatima slapped his arm. "Exactly. Okay, so I can do that. I mean, it's not prickly heat out there, so I'm fine with wearing long sleeves. But if she sees, she sees, and I don't want any mad signals from you telling me to hide my arms or something, deal?"

Ahmed leaned around Belle. "Deal."

A tall woman of indeterminate age, with a great flurry of dark hair and eyes rimmed with kohl, came bursting in from the kitchen. "Dinner's almost ready. Carstairs, come help me get it on the table." She stuck out a hand holding a wooden spoon toward Belle, laughed, grabbed the spoon with her other hand, and continued to offer the handshake. "Hi, I'm Wanda. You must be Belle."

"I am." He shook her hand. "Thank you for inviting me."

"Always welcome."

"How can I help?"

"Just come on in and I'll put you to work."

An hour later he was propping his eyes open, but his stomach was one seriously happy organ. Wanda had stuffed him full of shish kebab, grape leaves, a huge pile of Greek salad with wonderful tangy dressing and piles of feta cheese, tomatoes that tasted like the real thing, cucumbers so fresh they snapped, and honey-dripping baklava for dessert. He held his stomach. "I feel like someone wheeled a Trojan horse full of food into my stomach. But I'd eat it all again, it was so delicious. Thank you, Wanda."

"My pleasure, dear."

They'd talked about everything from trees to tattoos to tabouli at dinner, but very little about Belle—which suited him fine. Still, the trend was too good to last. As he sipped a cup of peppermint tea, Ahmed asked, "So what's this big job you start tomorrow?"

"I don't exactly know. Something for Beauty, Inc."

"Cool. Good company."

Belle frowned. "Why do you say that?"

"They do a boatload of charity work. Anyone in New York will tell you. Especially in the LGBT community. How come you're working for them and you aren't aware of that?"

"I didn't exactly choose to work for them."

"What? I'm confused."

Belle looked up. Mr. P. had a small smile on his lips. "As Mr. Pennymaker would say, I made the best of two bad choices. Magnus Strong won me in a poker game."

Fatima fell back against her chair. "What the hell?"

Wanda said, "How could something like that happen?"

"My father drank too much and lost all his company stock in a game with Magnus Strong. It would have ruined him and essentially given control of our family business to Strong. He agreed to return the stock if I came to work for him for some indeterminate time. Here I am."

Ahmed shook his head. "That is one wildass story."

"Yeah. My life story at the moment."

Fatima rounded her dark eyes. "I think it's amazing."

"What part?"

"He gave up control of a competitive company for you? Magnus Strong must want you to work for him one helluva lot."

Mr. Pennymaker laughed.

Belle didn't.

CHAPTER 7

"GOOD MORNING, boss. Ready for your first day?"

Belle stepped out of his apartment door dressed in a suit and tie, his pale hair slicked back except for the floppy bangs, which expressed themselves at all times. "Good morning, Leroy, and don't call me boss."

Leroy gazed around the hall where he was standing. "See anyone else round here that I'll take a bullet for?"

Belle folded his arms and tried not to laugh. "You think it may come to that?"

"I don't know. You chemists are some badassed dudes."

"And you, for someone whose boss I supposedly am, are a smartass."

He grinned, flashing brilliant white and gold teeth. "The nature of the beast, boss, the nature of the beast."

Belle finally gave up and laughed, which helped quell the space-shuttle-sized Lepidoptera in his stomach. As they walked down the stairs, Wanda peeked out of her apartment, still dressed in her robe. "Just wanted to wish you a happy day, Belle."

"Thanks, Wanda. Nice of you." This really was a friendly place.

Outside, Leroy held the car door, and even though Belle felt idiotic, he didn't make a face at him. *Let the man do his job in peace.* As they drove, the brownstone neighborhoods of Brooklyn began to give way to the skyscrapers of Manhattan, and Belle's stomach tightened into an iron band of panic. Okay, so he lived in the best of all possible places in New York—but he couldn't stay home all the time.

His phone buzzed, and he grabbed at it. "Hello."

"So, are you ever going to call me?" *Judy.*

He sighed. "Hi, dear. Sorry."

"Hey, I don't get up at this hour for just anyone. How are you? Is it just awful? Did you sleep on a park bench last night?"

Compared to that description, he felt pretty idiotic for complaining. "No. I'm in a cushy town car, being driven from my beautiful apartment full of flowers and trees to my first day on the job."

"Are you kidding me?"

"Nope. I have this place in Brooklyn with a huge tropical garden in the atrium. I started to call and tell you last night, but I fell asleep."

"Did you find it, or—"

"No. It was waiting for me. Along with the car and chauffer."

"Have you seen Strong yet?"

"Not yet."

"Just be really careful, Belle. They're getting you fattened up. You know what comes next."

Leroy pulled onto Park Avenue, and in front of Belle rose the glistening silver tower of Beauty, Inc. Belle couldn't keep his voice from shaking. "Yeah. The slaughter."

MAGNUS STRAIGHTENED the paperweight on his desk for the third time. He pushed his intercom. "Sherry, has Mr. Belleterre arrived?"

"Yes, sir. I got a call from Dr. Hauser about five minutes ago to say he was going out to meet him in the lobby."

"Thank you. Excellent."

"Shall I set up a time for you to meet with him?"

"Uh, no. That's not necessary now. I just want to be sure he settles in comfortably. Have Eugene give me a call after they meet."

"I will."

"Thanks."

He hung up. Stupid to be so nervous. Just another chemist. Just another chemist. Just another chemist.

"AND THIS is your office, Dr. Belleterre. We thought you'd prefer to be close to the lab, but if not, just say so and we can move you to the administration floor."

"No. This is fine, thank you." Belle looked around the pristine office. A big desk equipped with the latest computer equipment, and his favorite—a huge whiteboard on which he could scribble ideas and work out formulas. Not that he'd be doing any of that. He turned to Dr.

Hauser. "Do I report to you, sir?" He wished he could dislike this man, but Hauser appeared as kind and genial as Belle knew he was brilliant.

Hauser cleared his throat. "Well, we'd rather you work on your own, but technically I do head the research department, so I guess you technically do report to me. Still, think of me as a collaborator and colleague. We want you to undertake any line of research you think may forward the industry and help make skincare more beneficial to more people."

The war in Belle's chest actually hurt. To work with Eugene Hauser, the inventor of the most advanced botanical skincare products in the world, would ordinarily have thrilled him. This wasn't ordinarily. "I'd prefer if you'd give me assignments, sir."

Hauser adjusted his glasses. "May I ask why?"

He didn't want to be rude to this man. It wasn't his fault. "I've worked very hard for two years to set my father's company apart from the rest of the industry. I can't compromise that effort."

Hauser nodded. "I see. So the rumors about how you came to Beauty, Inc. aren't exaggerated."

"I don't know what you've heard, but I imagine the stories are all at least partly true."

"I see. Well—let's move on. Let me show you our experimental programs."

Belle frowned. "Sir, are you sure you want to do that?"

"Oh yes. I was instructed specifically to acquaint you in detail with what we're working on."

Belle couldn't catch his breath. For an hour he followed after Hauser in ecstasy through lab after lab where every kind of exotic ingredient was being formulated into new types of solutions, emulsions, pastes, sticks, and suspensions. Formulation techniques he'd barely seen were laid out before him. The smells filled Belle's head until he wanted to simply stop and breathe.

Hauser pointed to a group of chemists crowded around a microscope. "We're trying some new botanicals from South America to increase the line-softening effect of our new cream."

If only he could leap into the group and guide them. He held back. "You have so much to be proud of in this work, Dr. Hauser. And of course, I'll sign a confidentiality agreement to ensure my discretion."

Hauser patted his arm. "No worries, Dr. Belleterre. Your reputation for integrity precedes you."

Something about the whole situation made him want to cry. Especially when he looked at his phone and saw no messages from his family.

MAGNUS STARED at his computer screen and tried to look like he was interested in it. "So he's settled in his new office."

Eugene leaned back in the guest chair. "Yes. He seems so taken with his whiteboard. The moment I left him, he made a beeline to it and started working out something in his head. Quite charming. Startlingly beautiful. But he seems very sad."

Magnus looked up sharply. "He does?"

"Yes. I noticed he stared at his phone several times like he was willing it to ring. He's a long way from family and friends. I'd say he's lonely."

"Oh." He tried to control his expression.

Eugene frowned. "I should also let you know that Belleterre seems very wary. He's obviously still thinking of Beauty, Inc. as a competitor rather than an employer. He asked me to give him instructions on what tasks we want him to carry out, so it's clearly his intention to do exactly what we request and nothing else."

"I see."

"The sad thing is I saw him get very caught up in the new projects. He looked like he wanted to dig in and give advice, but he held back. If you're thinking you traded all that stock for a brilliant researcher, you may be sadly disappointed." He raised an eyebrow and gave Magnus a fatherly scolding with his eyes.

Magnus sighed. "Belle—eterre can do anything he wants. Sometimes people don't know what's in their own self-interest."

"Are we operating in his best interest, Magnus?" Eugene gave him that level look Magnus had been respecting since his father was still alive.

"Yes, I believe so. At the very least, he'll learn a lot and see how a really first-class research facility operates."

Eugene gave him an appreciative head nod.

"Ron Belleterre was a good enough man in his day, but that day is past. He's no model for a brilliant son."

"And you are?"

"Certainly not. But you are." He wasn't ready to fully explain himself to Eugene or anyone. His motives were still too murky. He sat back. "Tomorrow, take him over to meet the staff at the Foundation…. Maybe Belleterre will get inspired if he's working on charitable programs."

"Actually, that's a pretty great idea."

Magnus sucked in a deep breath and then swallowed hard.

Eugene didn't miss a detail.

"HOW WAS your first day, boss?"

Belle leaned back into the soft leather. He wanted to say *confusing*. "Good, thanks."

"I really admire the work you guys do."

"How's that?"

"My cousin got out of a really crappy marriage—abusive, you know? And she went to a safe house with her kid to get herself back together. Beauty, Inc. gave all the women in the house these great face creams and makeup and shit. I think she felt pretty and, you know, like a person for the first time in years. She went out and got a good job and is taking care of herself and her son, no problem. I think having somebody do something nice for her gave her a boost."

"That's great." He'd tried to get his father to set up a charity program since he'd gotten out of school. Ron always swore he couldn't afford it.

Belle closed his eyes and drifted for a minute. Everything seemed out of focus. A snippet of an old musical drifted through his head. Something about being confused by conclusions he concluded a long time ago. Was that the case?

Don't be sucked in.

Yeah.

His phone rang and he grabbed it without looking. "Hello?"

"Uh, hi, son. How's it going?"

Jesus. He'd been dying to hear his father's voice, but now it made his breath stop. "Hi, Dad. Okay."

"All settled? Did you find a good hotel?"

Suddenly he wanted to scream. He tightened his hand on the phone and took two deep breaths. "Beauty, Inc. got me an apartment. They had it waiting for me when I arrived."

"Oh, buttering you up, are they?" He said it with a smile, but his voice sounded edgy and strained.

"I think they might have realized I'd be pretty disoriented coming to a strange city all alone."

"Hey, you're a big boy."

Belle winced. "Actually, Dad, that was twenty-four hours ago. Someone from the family might have checked to be sure I wasn't sleeping on the fucking sidewalk." *Take another breath.*

"Sorry. It's been crazy."

Belle blew out his breath slowly. "What's going on?"

"The lab says the packaging for the day cream isn't working."

Belle straightened. "How not working?"

"I don't know. You've got to talk to Colin."

He started to speak—and stopped. "Dad, I can't. I don't work for you anymore. You can't expect that you give me away to Beauty, Inc. and I'm still going to run your lab? That's a conflict of interest."

"But it's *your* packaging." His father sounded desperate.

"Do you want me to give the packaging design to Magnus Strong?"

"Hell no, you can't—"

"Because I'm on his clock and his payroll. You better encourage me to keep things compartmentalized."

"But I need you."

"You should have thought of that before you traded me for your fucking stock. Sorry, Father. I love you, but you don't get to have it both ways. I'll give nothing to Beauty, Inc. they don't ask for, but I can't be working against them behind their backs. They actually trust me. Sleep well." He hung up, and heat pressed behind his eyes. How the hell could this have happened?

Leroy glanced in the rearview mirror. "Did I hear that or not?"

Belle snorted. "Sorry. I didn't mean to make you a part of it."

"Hey, man, I'm your guy. I hear nothing you don't want me to hear and say nothing to anyone ever unless you tell me to."

Belle cocked his head. "Leroy, obviously I don't pay your salary. Your loyalty must lie with your employer."

"No, sir. Those are my instructions, and I've been told that no one can rescind them, including Mr. Strong himself. Think of me as Las Vegas. What happens here stays here."

Amazing. Belle shook his head. "My father actually expected me to work for him while I'm working for his biggest competitor."

"I gathered that. He's probably desperate."

"Yes, I guess." It felt like the blood ran out of his heart. "The sad thing is that the product is my baby. I worked my ass off to develop a new formulation and a new packaging technique, and now I can't do anything about it. I can't even see it through to success."

"Man, that's shitty. Maybe Beauty, Inc. will buy it? Your baby, I mean."

"That's the odd thing. Magnus Strong beat my father at cards and won his company stock. It's not all the stock. My brothers own some, and I own a small number of shares, and there are external shareholders, but Strong would have had a powerful position and could have seriously influenced the future of the product and the company itself. He gave my father back the stock in return for my working for him."

"He must figure you can do even better things for him." Leroy turned onto the street where the apartment building occupied one corner.

"But I can't do that, Leroy." It came out like a cry. "I can't devote my life to my father's company and then turn around and help his biggest competitor beat him out."

"Maybe true. But it doesn't sound like it's really his company much anymore, does it?" He pulled to the curb and parked. "Do you need anything? Food? Liquor?"

"No. The apartment is so well stocked, I don't know how I'll ever eat it all. I mostly want to go to bed." He felt like he could sleep for a year.

"How about I get you a little earlier tomorrow and take you to a terrific coffee shop on the way?"

Belle forced a smile. "That sounds great."

Leroy hopped out and opened the car door. "So I'll see you in the morning."

"Thank you. Good night."

He dragged himself up the front steps and opened the door. The sweet, moist air of the atrium enfolded him like a welcoming blanket, and he found himself smiling. He started up the stairs, but on the first floor, the door flew open and Wanda reached out an arm and grabbed him as he went by. "Hey, Belle, perfect timing. Go get out of that monkey suit and have some dinner with us."

"Oh, thank you, but I have all this food in my refrigerator."

"Do you feel like cooking it?" She grinned, her wild black hair still moving even though she'd stopped.

He had to smile back. "Gotta admit, I don't."

"So grab some of that food and bring it on down. I'll cook it later. You don't have to stay late. I know you must be tired."

He looked at her. At home, except for Judy's unexpected arrivals, he spent a lot of time alone. He liked it. Didn't he? Still— "Thank you, Wanda. That's really great of you. I'll see you in a few."

He bounded up the first few stairs toward his floor, then stopped. Whoever had picked this apartment for him knew him better than he knew himself. He sighed. And that scared the shit out of him.

CHAPTER 8

WITH HIS medium chai latte clutched in his hand, Belle walked into the lab and headed toward his office. He felt like a traitor, but he loved this lab—all clean, shining, and packed with the latest equipment, along with enough old standard materials to feel comfortable. A couple of the scientists looked up and nodded with a smile. He nodded back and pulled his ID card from his pocket to let himself into his private space. Inside, the whiteboard already boasted lines and rows of his scribbled ideas. *Restrain yourself.*

He sipped the chai—a product of Leroy's favorite coffeehouse and totally living up to his praise—and flipped on his computer. Yes, he'd said he wouldn't do anything he wasn't instructed to do, but that didn't stop him from hoping they wanted him to do something fun and challenging.

Flipping through his e-mails, he found a message from his father.

Son. I apologize for asking you to act dishonorably. I was stressed and not thinking clearly. It's only your unflagging integrity that lets me know I was safe making such a ridiculous request. Love you. Dad.

Well, son of a bitch. He wiped a hand across his eyes.

A tap on his doorframe made him look up. *Oh.* Everything in him turned to ice—and then it quietly melted. Magnus Strong occupied his door—and dominated the room. Power. Force. And a sexual magnetism that defied his ugly face.

Magnus smiled, which exaggerated his disfigured nose, his scarred lips and cheek. He stuck out a hand and crossed the room vigorously. "Dr. Belleterre, welcome. I wanted to come and personally express our admiration for your talent. We're delighted to have you at Beauty, Inc."

Warring emotions flashed through Belle's chest—the lingering amazement from his father's praise, admiration for Strong, guilt over that admiration, and embarrassment that his cock stood at half-mast just from the impact of Strong's presence. He wanted to smile and hated that he wanted to. If he stood up, would his erection show?

Strong's smile slipped just a little. Belle panicked. *Don't be an ass.* He half rose. "Thank you. And thank you for the apartment and the driver. I appreciate both very much."

Strong had started to pull his hand back, but now he stuck it forward again. Belle had to shake it. His hand was swallowed by Strong's big paw—interestingly rough and disturbingly hot. *Sweet Jesus, why does he turn me on?* He looked everywhere except at the man who so confused him.

Strong said, "Well, I just wanted to say welcome. Let me know if there's anything you need."

Belle nodded, dragging his eyes up from the desk. "Thank you. I will."

Just that fast, Strong was gone.

Belle collapsed in the desk chair. Why didn't I ask him who picked the apartment?

Because you're afraid to know the answer.

MAGNUS HURRIED back to his office and sank down on his desk chair. *He didn't even want to look at me.*

Good Lord, what did I expect? I dragged him three thousand miles from his home to work for somebody he hates. Not exactly hugs-engendering.

Jesus, it was hard to describe how—what? Disappointed? Upset? Unsettled?—he felt. He wiped a hand over his own ugliness. Eugene's words echoed in his brain. *He's lonely.* Who wasn't? Still, it was funny that someone that beautiful would ever be lonely.

Suddenly he sat up in the chair, grabbed the phone, and dialed. "Eugene, did you take Belleterre over to check out the Foundation work?"

"Not yet."

"When you do, make sure you introduce him to Owen Cleese. I expect they'll click."

Silence. "Uh, are you sure you want to do that?"

Shit no. "Sure. Why? Do you think they won't get along?"

"No. Owen's a delightful guy. It's just that—well, he's not the only gay man around here."

"And your point is?"

Eugene sighed audibly. "Nothing, Magnus. I'll introduce them. But one of these days, how about you do something for yourself?"

Magnus hung up.

BELLE FOLLOWED Dr. Hauser through a passcoded door into another set of inner offices. He pointed to the labs and assembly areas. "This is where we do all the work of the Strong Foundation. We have many different programs and projects, which include the distribution of products to people all over the world, contribution of funds to worthwhile programs that aid women and girls particularly, and also our special research into new formulations to aid in the healing of burn wounds and reduction of scar tissue for people in war zones."

Belle's heart beat fast. "Really? What a wonderful program."

"Yes, Mr. Strong thought you might enjoy working on it."

"He-he did?"

"Yes. I want you to meet Owen Cleese, who heads that research project." They walked down a long hall. Hauser glanced at Belle. "So how are you settling in?"

Belle nodded but couldn't quite hide the little smile.

Hauser grinned. "That seems a good response."

"It's just that the company found me an apartment with all these beautiful plants and all these great people in it. I mean, if someone reached into my head for a place I'd like, they probably wouldn't have found anything so perfect." He shrugged. "So I guess I'm settling in better than I might have expected. I genuinely love Oregon, but this apartment makes it not quite so foreign to be here."

"Well, that's excellent. Yes, Magnus does have a way of judging people's wants and needs."

"Magnus?" It came out more sharply than he planned.

"Oh yes. I'm assuming he may have given HR the specs on what kind of place you might enjoy. I mean, none of us knew you, did we?"

Belle frowned. "No, no one from Beauty, Inc. knows me."

"Ah, perhaps that's true." Hauser glanced at him and then away.

They threaded their way through a busy lab to a group of men and women gathered around a big table, apparently sharing ideas. It seemed very informal, but a really handsome guy with brown hair and gleaming blue eyes, all set off by a British accent, appeared to be vaguely in charge. He looked up as Dr. Hauser approached, and several of the other people glanced at Belle with interest. The Brit rose. "Dr. Hauser, come to join the melee?" He smiled, and dimples the size of moon craters popped out in his cheeks.

Hauser laughed. "No, but I brought a candidate for your brainstorming. Owen, this is Robert Belleterre." He turned to Belle. "Dr. Belleterre. Dr. Owen Cleese."

Cleese extended a hand with a smile and a look of interest. Maybe even a sparkle. "I've been hearing rumors of a new chemist in our midst. Delighted to meet you, Dr. Belleterre."

"Just Belle." He shook Cleese's hand, and the grip seemed to linger a moment or two longer than absolutely needed.

"Would you care to join our discussion group, Belle?"

One of the women grinned. "Riotous arguing horde, more like."

Cleese gave her an arched brow. "Ignore the peanut gallery, as I believe you Yanks call it. We're actually coming up with ideas for new products and services the Foundation can provide."

"I'm afraid I wouldn't be a lot of help."

"No worries. It will give you a feel for the work of the company." He gestured toward an empty chair.

Belle didn't say that's what he was afraid of. The more he heard about the "work of the company," the more he liked it—and the more he felt like a backstabbing turncoat. Still, he couldn't resist. "Thank you. I'd enjoy it."

He sat, and Dr. Hauser nodded. "I'll leave you to it, then." He walked off, and Cleese began to introduce Belle to the six people sitting around the table.

An hour later Belle fought being impressed to the marrow of his bones with the brilliance and caring exhibited by the scientists working for the Foundation. He'd tried to stay mute but hadn't been able to fight sharing some ideas he'd had for keeping aloe fresh and active for the treatment of burns. It had turned into a lively discussion, and Belle had agreed to work on a possible formulation for the Foundation to use in its worldwide charities. *I may be a turncoat rat, but at least I can help some people.*

All the participants shook his hand as they scattered back to their desks. Cleese approached Belle. "Thank you for your participation. I'm excited that I might get you on our team."

"Dr. Hauser mentioned such a possibility. I'd like that, I think."

Cleese smiled that sparkling grin. "Come with me."

Belle followed him back to his office, where he closed the door. "Please sit for a moment."

Belle sat, and Cleese walked around to his chair.

"We can find you a desk among us right away if you'd like. Then you can interact with my team on the aloe research."

Belle swallowed. He'd said he'd only do what he was told, but this position would clearly require creativity and original thought. Still, it was for such a worthy cause, and not really competitive to Bella Terra. "Okay. That would be great."

"Then starting tomorrow." Cleese adjusted a paperweight in the shape of a globe. "Perhaps I could persuade you to accompany me to dinner this evening?"

"Oh."

The dimples flashed. "The latter is in no way a command performance. All you have to do is say no. But in introducing us, I suspect some attention might have been given to the fact that I'm a gay, single man who might find you attractive."

Belle smoothed the frown that popped out. "Oh. Whose attention?"

Cleese shrugged. "Dr. Hauser, perhaps. Magnus Strong? I'm not sure. The company has no antifraternization policy, since they recognize that people who work hard are likely to meet each other while working."

Why did the "attention" part make him both a little angry and a little sad? Fuck it. Cleese was gorgeous. Belle smiled. "And do you find me attractive?"

"Are you kidding? Look at you."

He wanted to say beauty wasn't everything, but he didn't. "Yes, I'd be delighted to have dinner."

"Wonderful. Shall I pick you up?"

"Actually, I live in Brooklyn. But I have a great driver who can bring me anywhere you want to meet."

He laughed. "In that case, you come and get me."

BELLE PATTED his stomach and leaned back in his chair, eyeing the third of a slice of salmon still on his plate. "I can't believe I ate so much. That salmon is wonderful. I feel like a traitor to the Great Northwest for saying so." His treasons mounted up.

"I hoped you'd like this place. They fly the fish in from your region, but the preparation is uniquely delicious, I think."

"Yes. I may never eat again." He laughed. Of course, there was Wanda.

Owen sipped some of the merlot he'd ordered for the two of them. "Can I tempt you with dessert? They make a delicious hot fudge sundae."

"Maybe another time. I really am full."

"Ah, so exercise is required. How about some dancing?"

Belle grinned. "I do love to dance." He picked up his wineglass. "Maybe another few sips and I'll be ready to test my skills."

"Then drink up, my lovely. There's quite a nice queer club within walking distance. They have a bar where you can grab a quiet drink as well as a flashier club with live music and dancing."

"Sounds like a good place for a new man in town to know about."

Owen cocked his head. "I hope to keep you so engaged you have little time for being a new man in town."

He laughed and Belle joined in, but oddly the idea of having all his time monopolized by Owen, while pleasant, didn't totally excite him.

Owen insisted on paying the bill, after which they walked a few blocks in the cold night air to a building with a low-key façade. Just a small gold plaque said Bae.

Belle raised a brow. "Baby?"

Owen rang a bell. "It harkens back to what I'm told was the original meaning of the word. 'Before anyone else.'"

A tall man with black hair and an elegant face opened the door. "Good evening, Dr. Cleese. Delighted to see you."

"Good evening, Weldon. This is Dr. Belleterre."

"Delighted." He held the door open, and Belle walked into a small reception room that defined elegance—marble floors further decorated with one Persian carpet, soft impressionist paintings on the walls, flowers, and the delicious scent of vanilla and tangerine. Altogether sensual, while still being subtle enough to suggest the effect might be accidental.

Owen gave their coats to Weldon and took Belle's arm, guiding him past the arched entry that led into what must be the bar he'd described, to a silver door. He grabbed the handle and pulled. Belle caught his breath. The sound, scent, gleaming lights, and blatant nudity of the men in golden cages blasted Belle in the chest. "Wow. We're not in Kansas anymore."

Owen laughed. "Welcome to Bae."

A host took them to a booth against the back wall, where Belle ordered a glass of champagne and Owen a beer. The room wasn't too large. The crowd probably didn't exceed a hundred, but the gleaming mirrors on the walls multiplied them to infinity. The men on the dance floor sported every kind of dress, from business suits to leather and lace. Interestingly, the music wasn't raucous. When they'd walked in, the band had been playing something from the fifties that was more than energetic, but now they oozed out a slow ballad originally sung by some 1940s chanteuse, Belle was pretty sure. "Interesting choice of music."

"Yes. They do themes. Tonight must be midcentury modern." He chuckled. "Ready to dance?"

"Okay."

Owen held him close but not tight enough to rub cocks, which was good, since Belle's dick didn't seem into it—yet. Maybe he'd been so long between guys, his penis had given up in despair. Still, he let himself relax and enjoyed the brushing of thighs and occasional bumping of hips. A chorus of whispers behind him made him glance over his shoulder, but he couldn't see what the fuss was.

Owen murmured, "Oh my. The great man himself."

"Who?"

Owen danced in a circle so Belle could look toward the entrance. He froze and stumbled a step. Magnus Strong was just slipping into a booth with a tall man, oddly plain, beside him. Some wild, weird heat rose up Belle's spine until his chest tightened and his head got hot.

Owen took another step and Belle stumbled again. Hell, he'd forgotten to dance. "Sorry." He tried to move—and breathe—normally.

Owen chuckled. "So the rumors are true?"

"What?" He tried to drag his eyes from Strong.

"Did Magnus Strong really win you in a poker game?"

Belle ground his teeth. "Magnus Strong defeated my idiot father in a poker game, won a big chunk of his company stock, and for some inexplicable reason, exchanged that stock for my employment. If that's winning me in a poker game, I suppose it's true." He pulled away. "I think I'd like to leave."

Owen grasped his arms. "No. I'm so sorry. I didn't mean to offend you. Come on, let's go in the bar. It's quiet and pleasant."

Belle nodded and tried not to look toward Magnus Strong as he walked out of the club with Owen. What the hell? So Magnus set him up with Owen and then somehow knew Owen would come to the club he belonged to, so he followed him? *Don't get paranoid. You don't matter that much to Magnus Strong.*

CHAPTER 9

OWEN LED them through the archway to the bar part of the club and to a quiet booth in the back. The big bar was dimly lit and attractive in a moderately too-masculine way. How many ducks and hunting dogs did a New Yorker see in a week? The waiter came, and Owen ordered Belle champagne and himself another beer.

When the drinks arrived, Owen took a sip and placed a warm palm on Belle's arm. "I apologize again. I heard a few words about the story and didn't understand the true implications. What in hell was your father thinking?"

The champagne didn't taste so bubbly. "He wasn't thinking. He got drunk, as he's too fond of doing since my mother died, and gave in to his biggest addiction, which is gambling. Alcohol and cards don't mix. He lost his stock to Strong."

"I heard that your father's company has a new product that's very competitive."

Belle sighed. "Yes."

Owen glanced over the top of his glass. "Did you invent it?"

"Yes."

"So Magnus got compassion and decided to let your father keep his company."

"I don't know about the compassion, but he said he'd return the stock if I went to work for Beauty, Inc." He pushed his glass a couple of inches away.

Owen chuckled.

"What?"

"Simple. Magnus is one of the smartest people I know. He figured, why buy the milk when he can have the cow."

Belle frowned. "But he owned the cow and the milk and most of the milking machines. Why did he give them back?"

"Hard to say. Magnus seldom acquires companies. He has a particular way of doing things. Perhaps he thought it would be easier to integrate you into his company than to try to bring your whole staff over to the Beauty, Inc. way."

Belle gripped the stem of his glass. "What is the Beauty, Inc. way?"

"You've been here a couple of days. What do you think?" Owen dimpled.

Belle shrugged. "He seems to, I don't know, value his employees a lot." Jesus, he hated to admit that.

"Quite true. He loves to quote an old advertising man who said, 'The assets of this company go out the door each night.'"

"He gives a lot to charity."

"Yes. And it's not an act or a tax dodge. He's deeply committed to our Foundation. Come up with an idea to help people—especially women—and he'll back you one hundred percent."

"Why doesn't that sound like the same man who'd win his competitor's stock in a card game, then trade it for his son like so much human trafficking?"

Owen held up a hand. "Oooh, harsh. In truth, I can't say. He's a hard man, and a complicated one."

"Why has he never had plastic surgery on his face?"

Owen drank the last of his beer. "There's the million-dollar question. To my knowledge, he's never told anyone."

YOU'RE A crazy man.

Magnus sat in his dark sedan and stared across the street at Owen Cleese's apartment. Right after Belle left the club, Magnus had taken Carl home and come here. Stupid. But he'd practically forced Belle and Owen together. What did he really know about Owen? Yes, he was a brilliant scientist and businessman. Magnus planned to promote him into general administration for the Foundation, but what about his personal life? Hell, he could be an axe murderer for all Magnus knew.

Overreacting much?

He scrunched down behind the steering wheel and waited. Might as well accept that he was a fool when it came to Belle Belleterre. Had been since the first glimpse of that angel face. Belle was brilliant but also very innocent, and Magnus wasn't letting the world tarnish his luster if he could help it. Belle had been dealt an idiot for a father and buffoons for brothers. Somebody had to take care of him.

Who appointed you?

The limo pulled up in front of the building.

Magnus tensed.

Nothing happened.

Finally Leroy climbed out of the driver's seat and opened the back door. Owen stepped out in all his British beauty. He leaned down and looked into the car, smiling, said something, and then, with a wave, he walked up the front steps to his brownstone—alone. Belle hadn't gone in.

Magnus couldn't catch his breath. Relief coursed through him like too much alcohol. The limo pulled away. Belle hadn't gone in.

Of course, that car had a privacy panel. Maybe they'd fucked like rabbits all the way home? Still, Magnus started his car with a smile on his face.

BELLE WALKED into the entry of his building and felt the wonder and peace seep into his veins.

"Hello, Belle. How are you this evening?" Mr. P. was in full gardening mode, with plastic clogs on his feet, a huge apron over his clothes, and large gloves.

Belle smiled. "Better now, Mr. P. Thanks. Doing some late-night gardening?"

"Ah yes. Some of these little devils respond best to water at night. Care to join me? I have wine."

What the hell? "Sure. Give me a second to change." He ran up the four flights, tossed his suit and tie on the bed, pulled on some old jeans, sneakers, and a sweatshirt, and headed back down. Mr. P. was digging in the dirt. Two glasses of white wine sat on a bench nearby. Belle looked around at the lush greenery. "So how can I help?"

Mr. P. pointed at some gloves sitting on the bench. "Put those on, grab that trowel, and loosen the dirt around the base of the bushes. They like airy soil." Mr. P. picked up the wineglass with his dirty glove. "Maybe a nice swallow first."

Belle smiled and accepted the wine. For the first time all evening, it tasted good going down. He sighed, put down the glass and started digging in the dirt. Man, he loved dirt.

"How was your evening?"

"Very nice, thank you."

Quiet.

Belle cleared his throat. "Well, I guess it was more like fine." All he heard was the scratching of Mr. P's trowel as he dug. "Actually, it was kind of weird."

Mr. P. looked up and grinned like he only responded to the truth. "Oh? In what way weird?"

Belle shrugged. "I went out with the guy who's the head of the lab that works for Beauty, Inc.'s Foundation. He's really nice. Interesting too. But I guess I feel like we were set up."

Mr. P. grabbed a spritzer and sprayed the lower leaves of a small bush. "Is that a bad thing? Don't people fix other people up all the time?"

"Yes, I guess."

Quiet.

Mr. P. seemed perfectly happy without talking. Belle? Not so much. "But it's kind of strange that Magnus Strong worked to get me to New York, and now he's fixing me up with some member of his staff."

Mr. P.'s voice came from behind a large hibiscus plant. "Oh? Would you rather he'd asked you to dinner himself?"

"No!"

Mr. P. just kept digging and snipping.

"I mean, it all just seems kind of intrusive."

"Umm. But then, you are a stranger here. Perhaps he's just trying to make you feel welcome and doesn't quite know how to breach your defenses."

Belle frowned. "I don't want my defenses breached."

"Ah, my dear, don't we all rather enjoy having someone care about us?"

Belle tried to breathe. "Why, uh, why should he care about me?"

Mr. P. handed him the wineglass again. "An important question, don't you think?"

Belle took a sip.

"Perhaps you should ask your friend?"

"Friend?"

"Your best friend."

"Judy?"

Mr. P. just smiled and kept digging.

He should call Judy. He hadn't spoken to her since his first morning on the way to work. "That's a great idea. Thanks." He pulled his phone from his pocket, grabbed the wineglass, and sauntered out into the entry to the building, kicking his sneakers to be sure he didn't track dirt. It wasn't too late in Oregon. He dialed and sipped.

"He-hello?"

"Judy?" Sweet Jesus, was she crying? "What's wrong? Are you okay? Tell me."

"So-sorry, Belle. Just being silly."

"How silly? Why silly?"

"Just worried about stuff."

"What stuff?"

"It's not important. Honest."

"Is everything okay with your folks?"

"Yeah. Fine." Her family just barely squeaked by—her dad as a supermarket stocker and her mom as a babysitter. They'd helped Judy get to law school as much as they could, but mostly she did it on her own with scholarships and loans, plus she tried to have two cents left over to supplement the family income.

"You worried about the student loans?"

"Some."

He took a breath. "How did the doctor's appointment go?"

The pause was almost imperceptible, except he knew her so well. "Okay. The tests aren't back yet or anything."

"But you're worried about them, right? Come on, sweetie, tell me."

She took a deep breath. "I have a lump in my breast. They did a biopsy."

"Oh man, Judy."

"Yeah. I mean, what if it's cancer, Belle? I don't have insurance or any money." A hysterical edge crept into her voice before she controlled it. "But it won't be cancer, right? I've had fibrocystic breasts forever. It's just that again. Tell me it is."

Fuck, what did he know about breasts? "Yes, I'm sure that's what it is." He inhaled slowly. "But if there's any issue, we do it together, okay? We'll find the money. We'll make it work."

"But you're there and I'm h-here." The last came out as a whimper.

"Doesn't matter. If I have to go AWOL, I will. You're top priority to me, darling. You know that."

"I love you."

"Love you back. When will you know?"

"Maybe tomorrow or the next day."

"Call me right away."

"I will."

"Promise? No holding back."

"I promise." Her voice lightened a little. "So how's it going? The job and—everything?"

He leaned against the wall. All his troubles felt stupid at this moment. Still, it might distract her. "Actually, Beauty, Inc. is weirdly great. If Strong wasn't such an asshole, I might even enjoy working there."

She giggled. "What's the beast done now?"

"I think he tried to fix me up with one of his scientists, and when I went out with the guy, Strong shows up at the same club."

"Maybe a coincidence?"

"Could be."

"Except for his stalker track record."

"Exactly."

"So how was the date?"

"Nice enough."

"Oooh, that sounds thrilling—not."

He cracked a smile. "I'm not sure why. The guy's handsome, smart, a good dancer, a chemist like me. Hell, he's even British."

"What's not to like?"

He couldn't bring himself to say that beside Magnus Strong, everyone seemed a little dull. "Maybe I'm just too upset over the move and stuff."

"And here I am adding to your worries."

"Hey, the rest of the crap seems like small potatoes. A guy only has one best friend."

She sniffled. "Thank you."

"So text me tomorrow if you don't hear, or call me if you do, okay?"

"Okay." She blew out a long exhale. "Cancer just has to wait until I'm a big lawyer and can afford all this shit."

"Absolutely. Love you."

"Love you more."

He hung up and stared at the phone. Sadly, the universe almost never waited until anyone was fucking ready.

He stood and took his now empty wineglass back into the atrium. Mr. P. was stripping off his gloves. "Have a nice chat?"

Belle frowned. "My friend—my best friend—may have cancer."

"Ah."

Belle looked up at Mr. Pennymaker. "Did you know that?"

"How could I know?"

Obviously true. "Sorry. I just feel a little nutty. I don't know what to do if my friend is sick."

"The same as all people who are faced with trials. You rise to the occasion and cope."

"Yes. Yes, you're right."

"Did your friend answer your question?"

"What?"

"Did she tell you why someone would care about you?"

Weird thing to bring up. "I forgot to ask her."

Mr. P. smiled, picked up the wineglasses, and headed toward what must be his ground-floor apartment. "Did you?"

CHAPTER 10

BELLE STARED at the aloe formula he was working on, then glanced at his phone, then back to the formula. Jesus, he'd been doing this since before he started work. No word. He didn't want Judy to think he was so concerned he had to call her—but, shit, he was.

A warm hand touched his back, and he tensed.

Owen pulled his hand away. "Sorry. You just seem upset."

Belle ran his fingers through the floppy hair that consistently fell over his forehead. "I am. I have a friend who's waiting for results of a biopsy. I'm going nuts because I haven't heard, but I don't want to scare her worse than she is."

"I'm so sorry. Want to grab a bite to eat and worry together?"

"I'm not sure I'll be good company."

"Eating requires no charm. Besides, getting a ride with your wonderful Leroy is a treat."

Belle tried to smile. "You just love me for my driver."

Owen gave him a sideways look. "Something like that."

An hour later they sat in a casual-dining place, side by side in a booth. Belle pushed his chopped salad around and stared at his phone. "Maybe I better call her."

"I'd give it until tomorrow, after nine her time. She told you she'd have results in the next couple of days."

"I know, but I said to text me if she didn't know anything."

"She's probably just caught up."

"More likely she's hiding how upset she is."

"You're expecting the worst?"

"Kind of. Trying not to." He took a sip of iced tea. "If the diagnosis is cancer, I'm going to need to go back and help her."

"Yes. Just talk to HR. The company's very generous with time for family emergencies."

"She's like family." He tried to breathe, but his chest hurt. "And she doesn't have anyone to help her."

"Does she have a job?"

"She's a fucking slave intern for a law firm. No pay and no benefits."

"Maybe it won't come to that."

"Right. I'm not helping anything by freaking the hell out. I think I should get home." He stopped. Funny that home had somehow become the atrium in his Brooklyn apartment.

"Certainly. I understand."

Belle threw some money on the table and powered toward the door. Leroy had said he'd stay nearby. Sure enough, outside, the big town car waited by the curb with its engine running—like maybe he knew Belle needed a quick getaway.

They didn't say much on the way to Owen's apartment. Belle tried not to be maudlin and laughed at Owen's story about an explosion in the chem lab that day. When they got to his townhome, Owen leaned over and pushed the button that raised the privacy panel. He grinned. "Just thought I might take your mind off things a bit."

Belle felt himself stiffen. *Come on. Since when did you decide romance was boring?* He made himself smile and lean in as Owen did the same. When their lips touched, a little jolt zinged through Belle. Yes, it had been a long time. Too much chemistry—not enough chemistry.

Owen pressed his advantage and let his lips explore Belle's. *Warm, soft, pleasant.* Tongue got added to the equation, and Owen caressed Belle's mouth back and forth until his lips parted. Tongue inside. *Hmm. No goose bumps or firecrackers. Nice enough.*

Suddenly Owen sat back. Not the happiest face on the planet but somehow resigned. "Would I be correct in assuming that I simply don't do it for you, chappie?"

Belle stared at the crease in his trousers. "I'm really distracted."

Owen slipped a finger under Belle's chin and raised his eyes. "Yes, but before you were distracted, I didn't do it for you either, did I?"

Belle sighed. "Maybe I'm so out of practice, I've lost my libido?"

Owen laughed, and it sounded genuine, if a bit disappointed. "How old are you, dear? Twenty-three? Twenty-four?"

"Twenty-two."

"Ah, and have you been with men who, shall we say, did it for you?"

"Yes. In college. Then I went to work for my father and gave up everything except the job."

"All the more reason your cock should have given me at least a tiny howdy-do."

Belle snorted. "I'm truly sorry. Maybe it's worth trying again when things are—better."

"Ah, I shall never say die until you tell me there's no hope. Deal?" He stuck out his hand.

Belle shook it with a smile. "Deal."

"See you tomorrow." He leaned over and kissed Belle's cheek, then climbed out of the car.

Belle waved, Leroy closed the door, and Belle opened the privacy panel. "Sorry about that, Leroy."

"That's what it's for, boss." He glanced in the mirror as he drove. "But you guys didn't test my powers of discretion much."

"I'm really worried about a friend."

"Got it. Still, Dr. Cleese is a nice guy, but I think you might be looking for something—not quite so vanilla." He laughed.

"I'll tell you the truth. I've got so little experience, I barely know who I like." That was kind of true. But JP Engstrom, his senior class president in undergrad, who'd stayed in the closet but loved dragging Belle to the forest and fucking him against tree trunks and in freezing streams a few times a week, had sure revved his engine. The memory even made him twitch.

The phone rang in Belle's pocket, and he grabbed for it. Judy! He clicked. "Hi, sweetie. What's happening?"

Her voice broke. "B-bad news. I mean, not awful. First stage, but oh God, Belle. What am I going to do?"

"Don't worry. I'll be there to help you. What did they say is next?"

"The doctor recommended a surgeon." She sobbed. "A surgeon. They cost moneeeeey."

"Breathe."

For the next twenty minutes, he soothed Judy while his knee bounced. Somebody had to be there. "Baby, take a half a Benadryl and let it knock you out, okay? Sleep. I'll talk to you first thing tomorrow about what we're going to do next."

"Belle, you just got there. You can't be turning everything upside down for me."

"Watch me."

"Oh God. Thank you. I'll do what you say."

"Good. Take the pill and crash. You need lots of sleep to heal."

"I love you."

"I love you too." He hung up and let his head fall down onto his knees. Leroy spoke softly. "It's gonna be okay, boss."

"Yes. Yes, it is." He dialed the phone. It rang once, twice. *Come on. It's still early in Oregon.*

"Belle, is that you? Thank God. Oh man, we need you so badly."

"Hi, Dad. I'm not calling to help. I actually need help from you."

"What? No, Belle, the new product formulation won't hold in the packaging. We need you to look at it and reengineer it."

"I've explained to you I can't do that. It's a conflict of interest." Still, the fate of his product made his stomach sick.

"Shit on your conflict. We need you."

"Dad, listen for a minute. You know Judy, my best friend? She's been diagnosed with cancer, and she doesn't have any money. Can you contact her and make sure she has enough for her operation? And for good aftercare? I'll try to get out there to help her as soon as I can, but meanwhile—"

"Money? Have you heard a fucking word I said? I don't have any money. I'm going to lose the business and everything that goes with it if we can't get this problem fixed."

"That's not true. You have your ongoing product lines. Okay, so you may not get the growth we hoped for this year, but you won't go out of business."

Silence.

"Dad? What's happened? What have you done?"

"I—I counted on the new product, Belle. I took out some loans. You know, against future earnings." He sighed deeply. "If I can't pay them back, they'll take the company."

"Shit."

"Tell me about it."

"What did you do with the money?" He didn't have to ask.

"I, uh, wanted to increase it."

"You gambled with it."

More silence.

"Okay. I need to find some help for Judy."

"What about me?"

"I'm sorry. I don't know what I can do." He hung up, dropped the phone into his pocket, and flopped his head back on the seat. The phone buzzed again. He glanced at it and pushed Ignore.

Okay, so he still had himself. "Leroy, I need to go back to Beauty, Inc."

"You bet, boss." Without a moment's hesitation, Leroy swung the car in a U-turn on the Brooklyn street and pointed it back toward the city.

Belle glanced at the time. It was only 8:00 p.m. Somebody might still be in HR. People around there seemed to make their own schedules. Maybe he'd get lucky. He stared out the window, clenching and unclenching his fists. "Do you think anyone will be in HR at this hour?"

He'd mostly asked himself, but Leroy answered. "Stranger things have happened."

It took twenty minutes of hard driving, but finally Leroy pulled the car to the curb in front of the building. "I'll wait as close as I can get. Don't worry."

Leroy jumped out and held the door for Belle. The nighttime, big-city traffic swam all around him. He barely noticed. He stared up at the huge skyscraper like he could see through its walls. *Be there. Be there.* Leroy squeezed his shoulder before Belle took off toward the building. Half running, he approached the door and buzzed. The night guard clicked the intercom. "This is Dr. Robert Belleterre."

Brief pause.

The buzzer sounded and the door clicked. Belle walked in, waved at the guard, and ran to the elevator. Part of HR was located on the forty-fifth floor, but the executives were in the C-suite on the sixty-second. That's where he needed to go. He pushed and leaned against the wall.

He could just go to the airport and call them from Oregon in the morning. But what if they didn't believe him? Would Strong take back Belle's father's stock? Hell, not that the stock had any value now. What if Beauty, Inc. fired him? He actually made a decent salary—one that might help Judy. *Jesus, I'll think about that later.*

His ears popped, the elevator car slowed, and the doors opened. Low illumination gave the floor a ghostly look, but from a couple of offices, Belle saw bright lights. He jogged toward them. In one office the janitor ran the vacuum. *Damn.* Farther down the hall, two women he didn't know appeared deep in conversation. They looked up as he slid into the doorway. One of them, an older, silver-haired woman, smiled. "Can I help you?"

"I'm looking for someone in HR. It's an emergency."

"Oh dear."

The other woman shook her head. "Sorry. We're both marketing. No help at all. I haven't seen anyone in HR this evening. They often get in early, though."

He nodded. "Thank you. I just took a chance."

"Worth doing. You can find unexpected people around this place at all hours."

"Thanks again."

Slowly he walked down the hall toward the elevator. His throat felt clogged, and his heart beat too fast. He wanted to have something firm decided before he called Judy in the morning. Of course, he had three hours on her, so maybe he could get ahold of HR first thing and get on a plane. *Shit!* He stopped and leaned against the paneled wall. Maybe he'd just go to the airport now and take his chances. If they fired him, so what?

Oh man, they'd been so nice to him; he couldn't just walk out. They'd won him fair and square.

"Belle? Uh, Dr. Belleterre?"

He turned slowly. Just what I don't need tonight. A face-to-face encounter with Magnus Strong. "Good evening, sir."

Strong's scarred lips stretched upward slightly. "Sir? I seem to recall some far less deferential appellations being used in the past."

"You weren't my employer at the time." He didn't feel like sparring. Belle glanced up, then back at his feet. He always thought of Strong as a big man. Standing here, he could tell Strong was no more than six foot one or two, and actually very well built, but his big head and ugly face made him more formidable.

Strong cocked his head. "Are you all right? You seem upset."

"I'm okay."

"Were you looking for someone?"

"Uh, I was hoping someone would be in HR."

Strong's powerful gaze bored into him, and he squirmed. Suddenly a hard hand took his arm and he was half walking, half being dragged down the dimly lit hall by Magnus Strong. Before he could scream—although who the hell would intervene?—he was inside Strong's office with the door closed behind him. Strong pointed to a guest chair as he walked behind his large and very clean desk. "Sit."

The room surprised Belle. Smallish, modest, not much fancier than Belle's office or Dr. Hauser's. He sat.

Strong leaned forward. "Tell me what's wrong."

Okay, hell, maybe if Strong knew he'd be more likely to give him the time off. "I just discovered that my best friend has cancer."

Strong sat back with a frown that, on his face, would scare old women. "I'm very sorry to hear that."

"It's just that she has no one to look after her, so I was hoping to get some time to go back to Oregon and help her."

"Her?"

"Yes, a woman. She has breast cancer."

"I see. What's her name?"

"What? Oh. Judy. Judy Brancoli."

"What does Judy do?"

"She's studying for her bar exam and working as an intern for a law firm, but that's the problem. They don't pay her or give her any benefits at all. Her parents are dirt-poor, so she's got no insurance or money. I need to help her."

"That's probably going to take big bucks."

Belle blew out a stream of air. "I know. I'm hoping I can get people to chip in."

"Does she have a good cancer center in her area?"

"She lives near me, and it's very rural. She'll probably have to go to Portland. But she's so stuck over not having any money, I'm afraid she won't pay attention to what she really needs to get well." The last part came out more pleading than he'd planned.

"I see. Well, I'll tell HR to contact you in your office tomorrow morning. Meanwhile, why don't you get a good night's sleep?"

Belle frowned. "I was kind of hoping to get on a plane tonight."

"No, tomorrow is plenty of time. Hospitals get disturbingly less anxious to perform treatment when they think they won't get paid."

"Crap. I know."

"I'm sure it will work out."

Shit, what did he know? *Rich bastard.* "Thanks. So HR will call me?"

He leaned back in his chair. "Yes."

"First thing?"

"As soon as they can."

"Thanks." Belle rose and walked out the door of Strong's office. *Thanks for nothing.*

SHIT! BELLE stared at the clock on his desk. His eyes drooped. It had been one long and crappy night, but now the big hand was on six and the little one on eleven. Damn! He'd tried to call HR three times since he came into the office that morning at eight and had been put off each time. He'd said that Strong told him to call and still nothing. What the fuck had the fucker told them? Keep the guy here? Don't let him leave?

He stalked out into the hall and blazed into Owen's glass-enclosed office. "I need you to help me. I have to get back to Oregon, and I can't seem to get HR to pay any attention."

Owen looked up from some engrossing problem. "Really? They're usually so responsive."

"Not to me!" He fell into Owen's guest chair and buried his head in his hands. "I need to help Judy."

"Belle?"

His head came up at the sound of the familiar voice. Like he was sitting in his garden at home and Judy had come out the back door. He sprang up and whirled. "Judy!" He raced across the small space and grabbed her up in his arms. "How the hell did you get here? I mean, I'm so happy to see you."

She smiled tentatively. "I barely know. I got a call last night saying I had a ticket on the red-eye to come to New York, and that someone named Leroy would meet me and bring me here." She spread her arms. "Here I am."

Owen laughed. "I'd say HR proved to be responsive yet again." He walked forward. "Hello, Judy. My name is Owen Cleese. Glad you're here. Now, Belle, why don't you take Judy to your office and figure out the details of this arrival—while I get back to work."

Belle tightened his arm around Judy's shoulders. "Right. Okay, come on, sweetie. Thanks, Owen." He led her back down the hall and closed the door behind her, then turned and stared at her. She looked tired and confused but pretty happy. "How the hell did this happen?"

"I got this call last night about 7:00 p.m. He said I should pack and go to the airport."

"He?"

"Yes, it was a man. Lovely voice. He just said he was with HR for Beauty, Inc. I told him I had to be at work, and he said if I wasn't being paid, it wasn't a real job. Don't know how he knew." She laughed. "Anyway, he said they have better cancer care in New York. Don't know how he knew that either, but I figured, what the hell? I left a message for the law firm, shoved shit in a bag, and got on the plane. Leroy met me at the gate, and here I am."

Belle just stared. He didn't want to think what he was thinking. A tap on the door brought his head up. "Come in."

A woman he remembered from when he'd filled out some papers in HR bustled into his office. "Hello, Dr. Belleterre. I'm Amy Landers. I'm assuming this is Ms. Brancoli?"

Judy stood and nodded, looking even more like the Jabberwocky might show up at any time. "Yes."

"Lovely. Welcome to Beauty, Inc. I need you to fill out a few papers. May I sit?"

Belle could barely get his mouth to close enough to answer. "Uh, of course."

Ms. Landers sat close to Judy and laid papers out on Belle's desk. "Now, these will contract your employment. You'll be on minimal hours while you complete your bar exam for the state of New York. At that time you'll join our legal department. Meanwhile, these documents will enroll you in the health insurance program. There's no waiting period, and we do not exclude preexisting conditions." She smiled. "I believe there's already an appointment made with a surgeon for you. Of course, you have complete veto power if you don't like her. But I assure you, she's one of the finest."

Belle glanced at Judy. She stared at Ms. Landers without a movement except for the tears pouring down her face. She opened her mouth, closed it, then tried again. "I—I don't understand."

Ms. Landers placed a hand over Judy's where she clutched them in her lap. "This company helps people—particularly women. When we heard of your situation, it represented so many of the ways that companies and individuals take advantage of women, making them work twice as hard to achieve less than they give to men. We know if you're a friend of Dr. Belleterre, you're a friend of this company. It's our honor to be able to assist you at this critical time." She stood. "Look over these papers, sign them if they seem in order, and return them to me tomorrow. Meanwhile, Leroy will take you to your residence, where you can move in and get some sleep. I hope it's a worry-free rest." She walked to the door. "See you tomorrow."

They both just stared at the door. Judy turned. "How on earth did you do this?"

"I didn't. Believe me, I'm as flabbergasted as you are." *Maybe not quite.* His heart flipped in his chest.

"How did they even know about me?"

"I, uh, told them. I was trying to get time off to come to Oregon. They took things into their own hands."

"I'll say. When did you tell them? Hell, we didn't even talk until last evening."

"Yeah, I came right back here and, uh, tried to find someone in HR."

"Oh, baby, you're amazing." She fell back in her chair. "I feel like I wandered into some fantasyland, and I'm hoping I don't wake up."

He hoped so too. "Why don't you let Leroy take you home? He's my driver, so he'll get you installed in my place."

"Oh, I don't want to horn in on you. You need some privacy."

"Since when?" He grinned. "Hey, I can't think of a better roommate. I'm so excited to have you here. It's like this just became home." He got up and hugged her. "Move your stuff right in, and we'll sort things later. Crawl into bed and sleep until tomorrow."

"I actually think I can sleep." She hugged him tighter. "This is so far beyond amazing. A job with benefits and living near my best friend. It's like a dream." She shook her head.

"Hey there, Ms. Brancoli, ready to boogey?" Leroy leaned in the door.

She smiled and tossed her mane of red curls. "I may not be in full boogey mode, but I can probably manage a small twerk."

Leroy's laugh filled the room. "Where you been hiding this lady, boss? She's aces."

Yeah. She is. He watched as Leroy led a very tired Judy out the door. He flashed a wink as they headed down the hall. Belle got up and stared out his window at the skyscrapers beyond, then paced back to his desk. *Keep busy.*

He grabbed a sandwich from a street vendor and returned to his computer, where he started researching cancer treatments and tests. After only a few minutes, he got absorbed and began making long lists of the most important factors—genetic testing, individualized chemotherapy, antiangiogenesis postcare to help prevent recurrence. After hours of research, he wandered into Owen's office. "Hey, does Beauty, Inc. do anything to support cancer research?"

"Some contributions. Nothing more. It's such a mishmash, it's hard to know where to throw one's support. So how is your friend? I gather her arrival was a surprise?"

"Yes. A complete surprise."

"So your anxiety has decreased?" He flashed that perfect smile.

"Yes. Thank you." *In some ways.* With his head still in the "mishmash," as Owen called it, he wandered back to his office for some more exploration. Finally, at almost 5:00 p.m., he raised his head. Was there a chance he could catch him?

CHAPTER 11

THE THERAPEUTIC effects of aloe are far higher when the actual plant is used versus a cream or gel formulation. But the properties of the leaves' outer coatings might hold an answer for maintaining the effectiveness of the gel's salicylic acids and amino acids. Belle plowed a hand through his hair as he played with possible formulations on his whiteboard.

"Night, Belle."

"See you tomorrow."

Belle looked up from the computer. "Good night."

The two scientists walked past, and quiet settled over the lab outside Belle's door. Belle set down the marker. *I wonder if it's quiet upstairs?*

He took a breath. Do I want to do this?

Hell yes, I need to know.

He stepped to the door, peered out, then left the lab and took the elevator to the C-suite he'd visited the previous night. The doors opened on a softly lighted scene. Belle stepped out and let the doors close behind him. He listened. No voices. Just some music. *Adele?* He walked down the hall, trying not to sneak, since that would look very weird if someone saw him.

MAGNUS STARED at the photo he kept in the top drawer. *Quit being sappy.* Still, helping Judy Brancoli brought it all back. He sighed. A good reason to stick with other philanthropies.

Is someone here?

He looked up just as Belle stepped into his doorway. His heart skipped. What did Belle's expression mean? Confusion? Anger? Hope? "Hello."

Belle swallowed hard. "Are you the one who called Judy last night?"

Okay, what had he done now? "Uh, yes. I—I thought—it was so late, and no one else was here."

"You had a ticket waiting for her at the airport and got Leroy to meet her?"

"Yes."

"And gave her a job and insurance?"

"I talked to HR, yes."

Some huge storm battled behind Belle's midnight blue eyes. He didn't seem to be able to catch his breath. He just gasped and clutched his chest. Magnus stood. "Are you okay? Can I get you water?"

Suddenly Belle took off like a gazelle that had spotted a lion—except he ran *to* the lion. In three bounding steps, he crossed the office and hurled himself at Magnus. Before Magnus could prepare, a tall, slim body hit him full force, arms wrapping around his neck. "Thank you. Thank you. Oh my God, how can I ever thank you?"

Magnus lost his balance and staggered, arms coming around Belle, falling until his butt hit the office chair, which rolled back. They smacked the wall with Belle sprawled on his lap. He gasped for breath, and the exhale came out as a laugh. It was like having the world's cutest Dalmatian on his lap—a dalmatian he'd like to kiss and embrace and otherwise manhandle. *Dream on.*

Belle kept hugging and muttering, "Thank you. Thank you."

Magnus adjusted Belle a little so he was actually sitting on Magnus's lap but didn't make a big enough thing out of it to scare him off. Hell, this was a moment to savor and prolong.

Finally Belle stopped wiggling, which was good, since the vibration was getting to Magnus's cock. Belle stilled and seemed to hesitate. Reluctance or embarrassment? He sat back and looked into Magnus's face. "Hi."

"Hi." Magnus couldn't help smiling, even though the effect wasn't really friendly. "I'm very glad you're happy."

"No one's ever done such a wonderful thing for me before."

Magnus tried to be corporate and fatherly—very challenging in his current position. "It's the mission of this company to help women."

"Yes, but this was very personal. I'll be grateful all my life."

"I'm glad." His heart beat so hard they both should have been able to hear it.

Belle looked down at where he was firmly planted on Magnus's lap. "I guess I was a bit more enthusiastic than I planned."

"You don't hear me complaining."

Belle slowly looked up at Magnus, which made Magnus want to cringe or hide. *Too close.* Belle cocked his head and inspected every inch of Magnus's ruined landscape of a face. Slowly, he leaned forward and kissed the scar across the bridge of Magnus's nose. He whispered, "In for a penny—" and his mouth moved south until he kissed the distorted corner of Magnus's mouth.

No breathing. No movement. Don't frighten him.

Belle closed his mouth over Magnus's lips and gently caressed the seam—back and forth—until Magnus opened. In. Went. The. Tongue.

Whatever control Magnus had maintained over his dick dissolved as Belle pressed his tongue deeper into the soft folds of Magnus's mouth. Magnus loved sex but contented himself with having it with people who only moderately attracted him. He used fantasy and pure horniness to make up for what his partners didn't inspire. To be sitting here being kissed by a man who so turned him on that looking at him across a crowded room could practically make Magnus come had to be some fucking dream. His whole body burst into white-hot fire. He wrapped his arms around Belle and twisted him so his legs surrounded Magnus's ass and slid out the back of the chair. Their dicks pressed close. Sweet Jesus, Belle was as hard as he was. *Dream. Pure dream.*

Belle rocked forward, and the pressure on Magnus's cock about blasted him into outer space. Belle started riding hard against Magnus's erection as he plundered his mouth, making little mewling sounds.

How could this be happening? Jesus, he was about to come in his pants.

Wait, why is this happening? An ugly worm burrowed into Magnus's brain. He's grateful. He wants to show me how thankful he is. Sweet Jesus, he'd never do this for any other reason. Am I going to let him prostitute himself just because I gave his girlfriend a job and some insurance?

But his dick is as hard as yours.

Shit, he's twenty-two. He gets hard in a stiff wind.

Belle was still kissing him, but obviously he'd felt Magnus stiffen and stop moving. Slowly he stopped kissing and pulled back.

Magnus smiled at him. "Got a little carried away there, didn't we?"

Belle's beautiful face turned pale and then a pink so bright Magnus could even make it out in the low lights. Belle pushed against Magnus's chest and stumbled to his feet. "Oh, I'm so sorry. I guess I did get—I'm so very sorry."

"Think nothing of it, Belle. Probably both of us are a little too busy for much companionship. I'm happy you're happy."

"Yes, I am. Thank you. Thank you again." He backed up, turned, and walked quickly out Magnus's office door without so much as a glance back.

A second later, faster footsteps suggested he'd broken into a run. *Yes, escape, little deer.* Magnus sighed. Good thing he'd come to his senses, or Belle might have found himself in a very compromising position. Magnus touched his twisted lips. *How could someone that beautiful have stood to even touch this mouth? There are limits to gratitude.*

He opened his desk drawer and looked at the picture again.

BELLE BARGED in the front door of his apartment building. He'd barely spoken to Leroy the whole way home, but he didn't want to start talking in case he broke into a scream.

He ran through the lobby and up two flights without a breath. *Wait. Judy's up there asleep.* He slowed his steps and took some deep inhales. *Don't let her see you're upset.* When he got to four he opened the door quietly. The kitchen light he'd probably left on that morning still shone, but nothing else had changed. He walked to the bedroom and peered in. No suitcases, no body in his bed—no Judy. What the hell?

He spun around like maybe she was hiding from him. *Come on, the place isn't that big.*

When he made a full circle back to the door, there was Mr. P, hand poised to knock on the doorframe. "Looking for someone?"

"Yes. Judy. My friend. I thought she was coming here."

"Oh yes. She has her apartment on the ground floor. Mr. Strong thought it would be best if she didn't have to climb too many stairs while she's being treated."

Belle just stared. He felt the tears welling in his eyes but couldn't stop them. Limb by limb, he collapsed to the floor like an old plastic bag.

His own father hadn't even paid attention, and Magnus Strong put Judy on the ground floor to keep her from having to climb stairs.

Mr. P. closed the door and flopped down beside him. "So, my dear, what seems to be the trouble?"

Belle shook his head and snuffled.

"Try again."

"I did a really bad thing."

"What might that have been, my dear?"

He sniffed. "I humped my boss."

"Hmm. Humped. I'm failing to get a mental image."

Belle sighed. "It's probably just as well. I got overzealous and threw myself on Magnus Strong. That might have been okay, but then I—" He dropped his face in his hand. "Oh God."

"I'm starting to get an image. Continue."

He popped his head up. "I kissed him, okay? And then, as if that wasn't the stupidest thing ever done since W said 'mission accomplished,' I managed to get my penis in contact with his and—humped. Now do you get the picture?"

Mr. P. clapped his hands. "Perfect."

"Oh, so far from perfect." He fell back against the large Asian throw rug. "Why did I do it? Why?"

"Excellent question. Why did you do it?"

"He turns me on."

"What?"

Belle sat up, in his best Frankenstein's monster imitation. "He turns me on like a large neon light."

"Because he helped your friend?"

"Way before he helped Judy. Before he helped me, in fact."

Mr. P. smiled. "So you acknowledge that he's helped you?"

"Oh hell, Mr. P, I'm so confused. I mean, getting won in a poker game doesn't exactly kick a relationship off on a sterling foot. Plus, that was after he seemed to be stalking me. I assumed he was trying to get me here to—you know—screw me instead of my father."

"Ah, I see. And now you've thrown at him the very thing you assumed he wanted—and he refused it."

"In a word—yes. I don't know what to think."

"There's only one answer, my dear. Outside the box."

Belle gave him a look. "Thanks so much, I think, but I may walk in there tomorrow and get fired."

"He didn't fire you for your disdain. I expect he's unlikely to do so for your gratitude." He sprang to his feet like he was a gymnast masquerading as a little old man. "Besides, if he does, you can return to the life you imagined you wanted."

Belle swiped at the nearly white bangs that flipped in his eyes. "But—but I'm not so sure that's what I want anymore."

"Then we've learned something important, haven't we?" He patted Belle's head. "Get some sleep, and in the morning you'll see your friend and embark on your journey."

"Journey?"

"Of course. To your new life."

HE HADN'T slept much, but thankfully Judy had. He sat on the edge of her rumpled queen-size bed and watched her put on the last of her makeup in the mirror above her cool little dressing table. In fact, the whole apartment was cool. Which managed to make him feel even worse.

She glanced at Belle as she slicked on her mascara, mouth open as seemed to be *de rigueur* for this feminine operation. "Ah oo okay?"

"What? Oh, yes. I'm fine. Much better now that you're here."

She lowered the mascara wand. "You seem distracted."

Judy knew him too well. "Sorry. For one thing, it seems the whole manufacturing operation for my new product is going to hell, and there's nothing I can do about it."

"Well, that's the shits. You put your soul into that product."

"Yes." He scratched his ear. "But now it's a competitor, so I guess I should be happy that they're having problems."

"Wow. That is tough. Of course, from what I've seen of Beauty, Inc., there's not much chance one product is going to rock its foundations."

He forced a smile. "Shouldn't you be apprising me of my legal responsibilities?"

"Not until I pass the New York bar." She glanced at him. "So the packaging is the problem?"

"Yes. I know it will work. I tested it. Dammit. This is crazy-making."

"I'll bet." She drew on some lipstick. "I'm very impressed with Beauty, Inc., Belle. Imagine doing something like this for a stranger." She pressed her lips together. "They really must want to make you happy."

He leaned back on his elbows. "You know, I might have agreed with you a week ago, but now I honestly think they're just that caring." Heat pressed behind his eyes, and he sat up and looked at his phone so she wouldn't notice.

She did. "Want to tell me what's going on in your heart of hearts?"

"I'm not completely sure. But I do know I asked my family for help and got nothing. I asked Magnus Strong for help and got far more than I dreamed of handed to me with nothing asked in return."

"Nothing?"

"They haven't even asked me to sign a nondisclosure. Jesus, they trust me."

"Who wouldn't?"

He looked up at her crinkly, smiling eyes and halo of red curls. "Usually not a competitor."

"But that's the point, isn't it? They don't treat you like a competitor, so you don't act like one. They're giving me a place to live, a job that has an actual salary, and my medical care. Crap, I'll work for this company until my brain bleeds. They're going to have to tell me to go home, because otherwise, I'm there. Everything I know I'll give to them. They know what makes people tick, Belle."

Belle nodded. But what the hell makes Magnus Strong tick?

MAGNUS SMILED at the redheaded young woman across his desk.

"Sir, I just want you to know that I'll work for you until I'm old and gray. I'll do whatever it takes to pay you back for your amazing generosity."

He laughed. "Miss Brancoli, I have no doubt you'll more than compensate Beauty, Inc. for our investment. I've looked into your background and I'm impressed. But I want you to focus on getting well, and that means good sleep, good nutrition, and good friends."

She swiped a tear off her cheek. "You've made it possible for me to have all three."

"Good." Easy to see why she was Belle's best friend.

"Sir, there's something you should know."

"Yes?"

"The new product Belle developed for his father's company is in trouble due to some kind of packaging issues."

Magnus sat back. "I'd heard rumors." Straight from Elliott Porter.

"I thought you might have." She smiled. "As I understand it, this product deserves to see the light of day. It's a significant improvement in skin care."

"Yes." He gave her a small smile.

"Since I don't know how dire the financial circumstances are at Bella Terra, I can't advise you on a course of action. I just know it would be a shame to waste this development. Belle—Dr. Belleterre—is between the proverbial rock and hard place. He can't give you the formula, and he can't help his father make it work."

"Yes, I understand that. Would he object to your telling me?"

"Oh no. He can't tell you himself. He was told by his father, and I'm sure he considers that sacrosanct. I think that's why he told me. I don't like his father at all." She stood and gave him a sassy redheaded smile. "You, however, I do like." She leaned over and shook his hand firmly. "So do something." She grinned and walked out of his office. If she'd had a tail, she would have swished it.

CHAPTER 12

BELLE KNOCKED on Owen's open door and got a welcoming smile. "Hello, my friend. What's up?"

Belle crossed and sat in front of Owen's desk. "Remember we talked about cancer research and the mishmash of information?"

Owen nodded. "Yes. It's a jungle out there."

"The fact is, people make a hell of a lot of money from cancer treatment, and patients aren't always the winners. What if we set up special support centers for women with cancer, where they could meet and mingle, get beauty and makeup advice, and at the same time, we give them access to the best thinking in the field? We'd have no axe to grind; no money to make except maybe on a lipstick or two, so they could trust us." He pulled up a stack of printouts. "I've been looking through some of the jumble of information and misinformation. There are things every patient deserves to know."

"Such as?"

Belle pointed at one of the pages. "There are a lot of different kinds of cancer and different kinds of chemo that treat them, but there are actually tests that can match the right chemo to the right cancer. Hell, many surgeons don't know this. But it can prevent the trial and error they put people through trying to find a chemo that doesn't kill them while it's killing the cancer." He sat back. "I'm going to be sure Judy has a surgeon who knows how to use the test."

"This is a hell of an idea, but it's above my pay grade."

"Who should I talk to? The chairman of the Foundation?"

Owen shook his head. "I'd say you need to discuss it with Strong. He's the one who's guided most of the big decisions regarding the Foundation."

Belle tried not to frown. "You said he doesn't go for cancer research."

"But this isn't research. It's more in our wheelhouse. Plus if he doesn't go for it, it won't happen. You know that."

"Yeah. I know that." He stood.

Owen cocked his head. "You look tired."

"Thanks."

He grinned. "I should have mentioned beautiful and tired."

"Okay. You're forgiven. I just have a few things on my mind."

"Let me know any time you need a distraction."

Belle smiled. "Thanks." He really should take Owen up on his offer. He was nice, handsome, eligible—not Magnus Strong. "Talk to you later." He walked slowly back to his office. Sadly, every time he tried to think of another man, the fire that shot through him at the touch of Strong's lips that night flashed in his mind—and his balls. Tough to buy vanilla when jalapeño was on the menu next door. But then, jalapeño wasn't interested.

He sat at his computer, but his fingers didn't touch the keys. *Do it! Call him. The world needs this idea.* He grabbed the company phone and dialed Magnus Strong's office. Ring. *Okay, just explain to his secretary that you want to present an idea—*

"Strong."

Belle's breath rushed out of his chest. *Shit. Of course Strong would answer his own damn phone.* His hand twitched, he wanted to hang up so badly.

"Hello?"

"Hello. I'm so sorry. I expected someone—uh, this is Belle."

"Hello, Belle." What did the smile in his voice mean? Was he thinking of the same thing Belle was thinking of? If so, the phone line might be raided by the FBI.

"Uh, sir, I have an idea for the Foundation I'd like to present to you. I wonder if I could, uh—" The words rushed out on a long breath. "—take you to lunch."

"Today?"

Holy shit! Belle glanced at the clock on his desk. It was quarter to eleven. Where could he take Magnus Strong on an hour's notice? "Yes. If you're free."

"Where shall I meet you?"

"Uh, I'll ask Leroy to meet us at eleven thirty outside."

"I'll be there."

Oh. My. God.

He grabbed for his cell. "Leroy!"

Thirty minutes later, Belle paced outside the Beauty, Inc. building. He liked Leroy's suggestion, but it meant he had to ride in the back of the car with Magnus Strong for at least twenty interminable minutes. What would they talk about?

Would you like me to hump you again?

Oh no. This is my favorite suit. Maybe later.

Leroy pulled the car up in front and hopped out. "So we're carrying the big boss, huh?"

"Yes." It sounded more like "Eep."

"A tad nervous, are we?"

At that moment Magnus Strong swept out of the building. *Why didn't I ever notice how beautifully he moves?* His overcoat even flew out behind him like a scene in a John Woo movie. Badass.

Leroy held the door. Strong smiled. "Morning, Leroy. How's your mom?"

"She's doing well, sir. Her hair's grown back in, and she's sporting a survivor T-shirt."

"Glad to hear it." He slid into the car.

Belle just stood there. *Fuck me.*

Leroy nodded toward the door. "Hop in, boss."

He hopped.

Leroy had already raised the privacy screen—a move Belle wished he could undo gracefully, but no go. He stared at the back of the seat in front of him. The car started moving.

Silence.

Magnus said, "Is everything all right, Belle?"

Belle took a breath. Without planning it, he whirled on Strong. "How do you do it? How? I've been in this car for over a week with Leroy, who is one of the most terrific men I've ever met. I didn't know that he has a mother, much less that she has fucking cancer. But you! You must see the man once a month, and yet you know every detail. How can you do it? How can you be so—nice?"

Magnus gazed at him. "I've got to admit, that's one of the best backhanded compliments I ever got."

Belle wiped a hand over his face. "I'm sorry."

"I'm not. The fact is, when you look like me, you can't stand too much self-absorption, so you focus more on others."

"Come on. You're not—" Okay, he couldn't exactly say that. "You're—"

Magnus grinned, which looked kind of sad and scary. "What? I'm not ugly, I'm interesting-looking?" He barked a laugh. "How many times have I heard that? I'm only interesting if you're seriously into horror movies."

"That's not so! You're—"

"Hey, boss, we're at the restaurant." Leroy's voice sounded tinny and disembodied.

Belle clicked the switch. "I thought you said twenty minutes?"

"No traffic. Want me to drive around?"

Belle glanced at Magnus and sighed. "No. I can't keep Mr. Strong longer than necessary."

Leroy stopped the car and in seconds opened the back door for Magnus, whose expression looked—neutral. A few moments of self-control later, the door opened for Belle. They were someplace in the closest part of Brooklyn Belle hadn't been before, and he knew nothing about this restaurant, but Leroy assured him the food was delicious. Italian. And Brooklynites knew Italian. He looked up in time to see Magnus slap Leroy on the shoulder. "Good choice. I haven't been here in ages."

Leroy beamed. "Thank you, Mr. Strong."

Well, so much for being the cool restaurant selector.

They went in, and Belle gave his name for the reservation. Of course, that was before the chef/owner came out of the kitchen to greet Magnus personally. He led them to a booth in the back with a view through the glass-enclosed kitchen but still lots of privacy. It wasn't a big place, and most of the tables were filled with an eclectic group of diners, from white-haired grandmas to three-piece-suited businessmen. Several people looked up as they passed, then whispered behind their hands.

When they were seated and the chef assured Magnus he'd take good care of him, so no menus required, they finally faced each other alone. Man, talk about awkward. Belle wanted to continue the conversation from the car, but that seemed like false pretenses. He'd asked Magnus to hear his proposal, and he should get on with it. He cleared his throat and Magnus looked up, meeting Belle's eyes in that direct way of his. Belle swallowed. "Sir, I have an idea I'd like to propose for the Foundation." It felt odd calling Magnus "sir" after humping him. Plus the man was no more than five or ten years older than Belle.

"Yes, I'm anxious to hear it."

"Since I discovered that Judy has cancer, I've done a lot of research. I'm pretty shocked to discover what a mishmash of information, as Ow—uh, Dr. Cleese calls it, is out there. It appears there are claims and counterclaims and every drug company yelling louder than the next. I can't imagine doctors can sort it all out, much less patients."

A crease popped between Magnus's eyebrows. "Yes, that's why we only donate to very carefully considered areas of cancer care."

"It seems to me some important information isn't getting to patients. I've made a list of a few examples." He placed that in front of Magnus. "I believe we should open a center here in New York for women with cancer. We could provide an opportunity for them to socialize, share experiences, get makeovers, plus we'd provide a steady stream of vetted information to help them make informed decisions. We'd be the only sponsor—although people could donate—since we have nothing to gain from the information we share. If the center works, we could open more."

Magnus stared at his hands.

Belle chewed his lip. What had he said? "Uh, is this something you've tried and it didn't work?"

"No."

"Maybe it's too far from our core business?"

"No." He looked up. "My mother had cancer when she died."

"Oh, I'm sorry. I didn't realize she died of cancer. My mom did too. Maybe this is all too painful for you?"

Magnus's face looked haunted. Belle wanted to touch him—but didn't. Magnus exhaled. "She didn't die of cancer." He slid to the end of the booth and stood.

What?

"I think it's a worthy idea. Tell Owen I said so. You head it. Thank you for your presentation." He walked directly to the entrance before Belle could even get up—and was gone.

Holy bloody hell. What had he done?

The chef ran out of the kitchen.

Belle stood there with no idea what to do. "I'm sorry. Mr. Strong had an emergency. He had to leave suddenly."

"Oh, I'm so sorry."

Shit. Me too.

The front door opened, and Leroy walked in. He glanced around, saw Belle, and hurried to him. "Mr. Strong says you should eat lunch." He looked down. "Actually, he said I should come and eat lunch with you. I guess he paid for the food in some magical way."

Belle nodded at the chef. "I guess it's two for lunch after all." He waved at the table. "Sit, Leroy, and help me figure out what kind of loony bin I'm living in."

They sent back the wine, since Leroy didn't want to drink and drive, and Belle figured if he started, he'd never stop. The food they didn't send back.

"He just got up and left." Belle ran a hand through his floppy hair and took another bite of steamed artichoke with heavenly, never-want-to-stop-eating-it sauce.

"You gotta be pretty upset to walk out on this food." Leroy was basking in some kind of beef dish while Belle dug into chicken scallopini to die for.

"The weird thing is, he said he liked my idea and we should do it, but he walked out like some hounds were chasing him."

"What's your idea?"

"Kind of like gathering places for women with cancer to get the latest information—"

Leroy had stopped eating. "Cancer. His mom—"

Belle nodded. "I know. She had cancer. But he said she didn't die from it."

"No. She died in an auto accident."

"Well, hell. That's hard."

"Yeah. The same accident where Mr. Strong got scarred."

Shit.

"YES, THANK you. I'll have someone from my office call to discuss the terms of the lease. It will be a nonprofit operation."

"Do you plan to conduct medical practice in the building?"

"No. Nothing of that kind. Think of it as a support and education center. We won't do heavy cooking but will need sinks and garbage disposals—much like an office."

"It sounds like an ideal building for your needs."

"I'll want to have it inspected before we sign any lease."

"Of course."

"Thanks again." Belle hung up and checked off the line item on his list. He glanced at the clock. Dammit, this was the night. Three days since his lunch—or not lunch—with Magnus Strong. Strong's sudden defection haunted Belle, but not as much as the unfinished conversation. Over and over, he played that dialogue in his mind. *You're not— You're—* He needed to fill in those blanks or he'd go nuts.

"Hey, baby." Judy leaned in his door. "You going home soon?"

"Uh, no. I've got more to do. Tell Leroy I'll catch a cab or take the train."

She wandered in. "You're totally into this new project."

"It's exciting."

"Man, I agree. I can't wait to go to this center."

He got up and went over to give her a hug. "You're my inspiration, love."

She was such a great hugger. She looked up at him. "What are you going to call the place?"

He smiled. "I think I know, but I have to get permission first, so I'll keep it secret for now."

"Aww, you can tell *moi*."

"Don't tempt me, devil." He held her out at arm's length. "Go home and get some good rest. Only two days to go."

She nodded with a smile, but he saw the fear flickering in her eyes.

"I'll be there watching every step. We'll have the tissue test standing by so they can get the samples to the lab in California. If you need chemo, we'll know what kind." He gave her another hug. "And the plastic surgeon too, if we need her."

Judy looked down at her nearly flat chest. "Anything she does will be an improvement." She glanced back and forth at her boobs. "Man, that must be one small tumor."

Belle laughed and swatted her butt. "Go rest."

"Okay, but you too. I need my wingman to be ready to go."

"I'll keep that in mind. I take my responsibilities seriously."

"Speaking of seriously—thank you. For everything."

He gazed at her sweet face. "My pleasure."

"See you tomorrow." She walked out into the rapidly quieting office.

He took a deep breath. This was it. For three damned days, he'd tried to convince himself he didn't care if Magnus wasn't interested in him. He'd pounded into his own head that Magnus's erection was merely an automatic response and had nothing to do with Belle personally. He'd tried. No go, baby. His cock cared not one tiny shit's worth. It knew what it wanted. He'd had a taste. His balls demanded the whole meal. Time to eat.

CHAPTER 13

BELLE WALKED out his office door. Hell, he almost didn't care who was on the C-suite floor right now. He needed to talk to Magnus. "Talk" was definitely a euphemism.

When the elevator door swung open on the sixty-second floor, he stalked down the hall, noticing things were pretty quiet. His step tripped. *What if Magnus isn't there? Only one way to find out.*

At the end of the hall, he almost lost his nerve when he saw Magnus's admin gathering her stuff. The desire to dive into a cubicle and hide swept over him. *No, dammit.*

She looked up and smiled. "Oh, hi. Dr. Belleterre, right?"

"Yes." He smiled back. "Is he in?"

She glanced toward the closed door and made a long-suffering face. "Of course. Just try to outwork that man. Not gonna happen." Belle kept his smile plastered on and watched while she slung her purse over her shoulder. "Want me to tell him you're here?"

"No, that's okay."

"Have a good night." She walked toward the elevator.

Do not pass out. Just do it! He walked to the door, knocked twice, and opened it before he lost his nerve. He peered into the dimly lit office in time to catch Magnus looking up with his mouth open—probably to say, "Come in." Instead he said, "Hello."

"Amazing."

"What?"

"Amazing!" Belle took two steps forward. "That's what I was going to say you are. Remember, in the car? I wasn't going to say you're interesting or any shit like that—even though you are the most interesting person I've ever known. But I think you're amazing." He let out the breath that was about to choke him. "That's it. I just wanted you to know."

Magnus cocked his big head. "Is amazing good or bad?"

Belle threw his hands in the air. "Good, of course. You're brilliant and hardworking and kind and generous—and observant. Oh God, so observant. And a great businessman, and—oh, I don't know."

Magnus kind of chuckled, like maybe he was embarrassed. "Uh, thank you."

"I don't want you to thank me."

"No?"

"No." Belle took two more steps. "I want you to kiss me."

Magnus's face went very still. "That's not an invitation I'm strong enough to resist, Dr. Belleterre."

Another step. "Good."

Magnus rose. Belle gazed at him—tall and strong and ugly. As fast as that man made decisions, he could be out the door before Belle saw him move.

Not gonna happen.

Belle leaped across the few remaining steps between them and grasped Magnus's head in his hands. "I'm going to kiss how amazing you are into your head." Promise—delivered. He closed his mouth over Magnus's scarred lips. Though he was prepared to breach any resistance, he got none. Magnus wrapped his arms around Belle.

Wow. Just wow. Belle's mother, when she wasn't sick, had embraced him often, his father seldom; his lovers—a euphemism for fucks of convenience—had provided peremptory cuddles. This one hug blew them all out of the water. Belle felt—safe.

He pressed his tongue deep inside Magnus's mouth. The warmth spread from his lips to his dick in a direct, fiery line. Just in time, Magnus grabbed Belle's butt and allowed both his legs to wrap around Magnus, bringing cock to cock in a mash-up of lavalike heat. Belle monkey-clung to Magnus's neck while his hips slid over Magnus's torso like a fire pole, every jolt of up and down friction frying his brain. "Oh God, oh man."

"Skin. Need skin."

Not a request he had to hear twice. Belle stopped his frantic humping enough to pull his own dick out of his suit pants, then reached toward Magnus's crotch.

Magnus balanced Belle's butt on his strong arm while he insinuated his hand between them to free himself. He must have reached the goal, because he popped his other arm under Belle and dropped him down enough to allow Magnus's cock to stand like a soldier in front of Belle's. "Wow." Thick, long, and veiny, nested in a bush of brown hair. "Beautiful." Belle grabbed for it and tried to wrap his hand around their two cocks together. *Too much of a handful.* Relying on Magnus's arms to hold him up, he pulled his other hand from behind Magnus's neck and closed it around their mutual bundle. *Two-handed, baby.*

First he squeezed. Magnus gasped and closed his eyes.

Belle whispered, "Oooh, don't stop looking. It's so pretty."

Magnus opened up and gazed into Belle's eyes. "You're a naughty, naughty boy."

"I think I could be." He started pumping as if maybe there was oil to be discovered at the end of the process. "Oh God, you feel so good."

Magnus staggered toward his desk and managed to prop Belle's butt on it without disturbing the mutual masturbation at all. Not holding all of Belle's weight seemed to allow him to go nuts, because he did, pumping his hips, head flailing, and all kinds of delicious sounds pouring from his lips.

Belle gritted his teeth. *So close. Oh crap, so close.* But not going alone.

Magnus's moans changed to whimpers, then little shrieks of "Oh God, oh God, yes." Vaguely Belle considered that if anyone was working late that night in the C-suite, they might be getting an extra dose of inspiration, but he didn't give a damn. *Closer. Closer.*

"Ooooh!" Magnus's head slammed backward into space as hot spunk filled Belle's palm and squeezed out between his fingers. Just the feel of it threw him so far over the edge his brain exploded and his own cum spurted out in jets to form their own eau de Big O. One blast. Two. Three!

Belle wanted to scream but sucked it in until his eyeballs threatened to vacate his head. How could a simple hand job that he'd administered himself be so fucking fantastic?

It took practice to get his breathing to calm. Magnus let his head drop forward until it rested on Belle's shoulder, a position so much better than nice Belle couldn't contain his sappy grin.

Magnus chuckled. "Whoa. I gotta say, for once I'm really grateful for gratitude."

Belle started to laugh with him, then stopped. *What did he say?* "Gratitude?"

Magnus nodded against Belle's shoulder. "Um-hm."

"You mean—my gratitude?"

His voice must have been strained, because Magnus tensed. "I, uh—"

Belle pushed against Magnus, slid from the desk, and tucked in his softening cock. "You think I'd have sex of any kind with you because I'm grateful?"

Magnus's expression looked—resigned. "I didn't exactly mean it like that."

Belle adjusted his clothes and stood in front of Magnus. Nobody tried to touch anybody. "When I arrived here, I felt I'd been purchased for who knew what purpose, but regardless, you had assumed I was for sale and my father confirmed the status. Over the last couple of weeks, I've been lulled into thinking otherwise. Obviously my instincts barely covered the situation. Give the little whore enough to feel grateful for and he'll surely come across, right?"

"No. No, I don't feel that way." But Magnus stared at his hands.

"What's the old joke? What I am has already been established. Now we're just haggling over price." Belle walked to the door. "Since you own me, Mr. Strong, you can tell me what to do. And if you want anything more from me, you'd better be prepared to issue some orders."

He walked out the door with some weird, betraying, self-abusing part of his brain hoping Magnus would follow him.

No footsteps. No hand stopping the elevator. No orders to turn around. No reprieve.

BELLE FLIPPED through his e-mails on his phone again—and again. He didn't see them; it just kept his hands busy. The doctor said she was out of surgery, and they'd been able to perform a lumpectomy. That had to be good. He said they'd have a pathology report soon—or part of one. They'd done the tissue test to determine chemo effectiveness in case she needed it.

He glanced at the time again. Damn, he wanted in there. Worrying about Judy was the only thing holding him together—self-centered but true. He couldn't take too much thinking about himself right now. A nurse came out. Belle stood. "Excuse me. Can I go in to see Judy Brancoli yet?"

"Oh yes, sir. She's awake. Room 168."

He frowned just enough to show some pique for the delay and then rushed back toward the room. *Hmm. One sixty-four, one sixty-six, there.* He skidded around the corner with a big smile—and froze in the doorway. Magnus Strong sat beside Judy's bed, holding her hand and laughing. *Well, son of a bloody two-headed bitch!* He wished he could glower five times more ferociously than he was. And he wished his cock didn't perk up at the mere sight of that ugly face. "I suppose rank has its privileges."

Judy glanced up with a slightly pale smile, but Magnus looked like his hand had been caught in the whole cookie factory. "Uh, my family endowed this hospital."

"Of course they did."

He stood slowly, smiled at Judy, and leaned way down to kiss her cheek, since she was lying flat. "Hang in there with the nausea. Chances are it won't last long, but if it does, be sure to tell the nurse."

"Thank you, Magnus. I will."

"And call if you need me." He patted her cell phone sitting on the table beside her bed.

"Thank you."

He nodded at Belle as he passed. "Dr. Belleterre."

Belle wanted to chew nails and spit them all over Magnus Strong. *Call if you need me, my ass.* He slid into the chair Magnus had vacated and took Judy's hand, being careful not to bump her IV. "Hi, baby. I hear from the doc you did great. But you aren't feeling well?"

She frowned. "It's just the effects of the anesthesia. Normal, I'm told, but I can't make any sudden moves. So will you tell me what the hell that whole performance with Magnus was about?"

He felt his lips flatten into a tight line. "Nothing."

She sighed, and it sounded weary. "Right. And I'm not lying in this bed about to barf on your shoes."

He dropped his forehead to the back of her hand. "I'm sorry for acting like a spoiled kid."

"You never had time to be a spoiled kid. Now tell me what's going on. Clearly Magnus Strong isn't any of the things we were so afraid of before you came here."

"That's what I thought too."

"What? You mean all this kindness and generosity is an act? Sorry to be skeptical, darling, but I doubt it."

Belle blew out his breath. "I don't want to get into the TMI range, but I'm attracted to him."

"Who wouldn't be?"

"So you see it too?"

"Powerful, brilliant, kind, generous almost past believing. Yes, I'm not blind."

"But I—well, let's say we got a bit hot and heavy, and then he suggested I was doing it out of gratitude. Because of what he was doing for you."

"Were you?"

"Judy! Hell, I'm not some whore who'd sell myself for my best friend's health insurance."

She grinned. "You wouldn't? Now you tell me."

His lips turned up.

"Belle, how easy do you think it is for Magnus Strong to believe anyone can see past his scars?"

He shifted in his seat. "I don't know."

"We probably can't imagine how many times he's been rejected for his face. It might be easier for him to think you're grateful than to believe you really care about him." Her eyelids drooped and then popped open.

Belle stared at her. Son of a bitch—truth from the lips of friends. He squeezed her hand. "Hey, my wise friend, you need to sleep. I'm going to go home, but I'll check in with the doctor first. Then I'll be here first thing in the morning."

"You gotta work." The words sounded muffled, and her eyes closed fully.

"Tomorrow's Saturday, goose." He leaned over and kissed her, listened to her deep breathing and the beeping of the machines around her, then left the room quietly.

He leaned against the wall outside her room. Was she right? In the midst of all Magnus's intelligence and sensitivity, could he be that blind to his own appeal? *Got to find out.*

Since it was the weekend, another sneak attack on Magnus's office might get him nowhere. *What about his club? Would he go there? Maybe.*

But how the hell do I get in?

OWEN SWIRLED his martini and took the olive in his mouth. Probably designed to be a sexy move. Belle smiled. *Too distracted.*

Owen put a hand on his arm. "So are you going to tell me why I'm really here?"

Belle nodded. "Sorry I'm such crappy company."

"Not crappy. After all, I got a wonderful dinner at my favorite bistro and a good ten percent of your attention, which is actually more engaging than one hundred percent from many men."

Belle snorted. It would be so much easier if he could just settle down and be attracted to Owen. "Actually, I had an argument with Strong, and it was officially too late to find him in his office when I came to my senses and wanted to apologize." He shrugged. "I thought he might come here. I'm so sorry to have used you."

"You didn't exactly. After all, you asked if you could take me to dinner in exchange for my taking you to my club, so I rather thought this was something other than a purely social interaction."

Belle sipped his champagne. "But I seem to have struck out. I guess it was a long shot."

"Not at all. He comes here frequently on the weekend with that man he sees. Name's Carl, I think."

"Yes, what's his story?"

"No idea, really. I've seen them together here and at one or two Beauty, Inc. functions. Seems a pleasant enough chap. Perhaps not the brain or wit you might expect in a partner of Magnus Strong."

Belle smoothed the little frown that crept across his forehead. "Do you think that's because Magnus sells himself short? Doesn't think he's worth the kind of guy we'd assume he'd hook up with?"

"Hmm. You do seem to have given this some serious thought."

Belle glanced up. "Actually, a friend of mine suggested the idea. I thought it made sense."

"Interesting. But I think you can now observe the interaction for yourself, because, don't turn around, but Magnus Strong just walked in with his dubious boy toy." Owen chuckled, and Belle swallowed hard.

CHAPTER 14

HE DIDN'T have to walk five steps into the club before Magnus knew he was there—Belle. *It's like my body is some giant homing beacon that points toward Belle. And he's with Cleese.* It took him no time to move right on. He clenched his fists. *Shit, it's your own fault. Why did you say those stupid things? You pushed them together, idiot.*

Carl peered at him. "Everything okay, honey?"

"Fine, thanks, Carl." *And why are you with Carl? You said you were done with playacting!*

The maître d' showed them to Magnus's favorite booth, and they slid in. *Wish I could just leave.* He sighed. *But that would look weird, even to Carl.*

The waiter came and he ordered a red wine. Carl asked for a Dubonnet on the rocks, which Magnus hated to admit was just one of the reasons he shouldn't be with Carl. *If you want soda pop, drink it. Don't pretend it's a liqueur. Of course, if Belle did it you'd think it was cute.*

"Want to dance?"

Carl loved to dance, and he did it well. Occasionally Magnus joined him. Mostly Carl danced his way onto the floor, where there were always miscellaneous guys who appreciated his moves. "No, you go ahead."

Carl slid out of the booth and was dancing before his feet hit the floor. Magnus smiled. Aside from the fact that they had nothing in common, Carl was a nice enough guy. His eyes crept toward Belle of their own accord. He was leaning in toward Owen and smiling. Maybe this was a good time to go to the men's room.

He slipped out of the seat and headed toward the lobby where the restrooms were located.

"Magnus!"

He turned. "Hello, Christian. Surprised to see you here." Though Christian was as gay as Chinese New Year, he seldom advertised the fact publicly for fear of it interfering with his board positions. Those seats made him a lot of money, gave him insider information, and didn't tax his work ethic.

"Uh, yes. An executive from one of the companies I'm a board member for, uh, likes this club."

"Great." His point was—?

"I saw your date dancing with someone else."

Magnus shrugged. "He likes to dance. I don't feel like it. He finds other partners."

Christian raised an eyebrow. "No jealousy? Must not be a love match. With that in mind, perhaps you'd like to have a drink with me—later?"

He doesn't give up. "Thanks, but I'll be taking Carl home and then heading for bed."

"Alone?"

"None of your business." He smiled to soften the rebuke. "Thanks for the invitation, though."

Christian stepped closer, crowding Magnus's space. The smell of alcohol on his breath explained why he'd push his luck with the CEO of one of his cash cows. At least he kept his voice down. "I know you think I'm too old, but I can still get it up at the smell of a lube bottle, and I know right what to do with it once it's arrived."

"Thanks, Christian. Glad to hear it." He stepped back. "See you next week."

Christian frowned briefly, then gave a forced smile. "Absolutely, I'll be there. I never miss a board meeting."

Magnus hurried down the hall, glancing back once to be sure Christian wasn't following. He pushed into the men's room, stepped into a stall, and sat on the toilet lid. He didn't have to go. He just wanted a minute.

Why had he come out tonight? Something in his brain said he needed to get on with his life and stop dwelling on Belle Belleterre, but what a crappy evening this had turned into. Seeing Belle clearly moving on without a backward glance, and then Magnus getting hit on by someone he could barely stomach—together they just reminded him of how hopeless his personal life really was.

The door to the stall next to him opened and closed, and he heard shuffling feet. Probably better flush for effect and get out of there.

A slim foot in a black loafer slid under the partition. What the hell? No one would be soliciting gay sex in a gay club, would they?

"Magnus?"

His breath caught. *Belle.* "Yes."

The foot waggled—kind of like it was saying hello. Magnus snorted, then listened to be sure no one else was in the men's room. Didn't sound like it. "Uh, what do you want?"

"Why did you suggest that I wanted to have sex with you out of gratitude?"

Magnus frowned. Why did they have to do this again? "Because I know how much you love Judy."

"Why can't I love Judy and want to have sex with you because you're sexy?"

The words flew out of his mouth. "Because I'm not." The sound of the men's room door opening froze any more words. Somebody must be using the urinal. Peeing sounds. The guy hummed "Wrecking Ball" to himself. Wrecking *balls*, more like it.

Belle's foot waggled again, then crept across the floor until he bumped into Magnus's shoe. What the hell did he have in mind?

The foot vanished. A second later it reappeared, shoeless. A burgundy sock clung to the slim foot as Belle searched the premises until his foot again came in contact with Magnus's leg. The foot slid down until it hooked the bottom of Magnus's pant leg, then insinuated itself up inside the pants until the stockinged foot made it to Magnus's bare calf. What kind of gymnastics was Belle having to do to get his foot this far into Magnus's stall?

This should be silly, not sexy. So why had his cock just sprung to attention like someone played "Hail to the Chief"? The guy outside the stall had turned on the electronic hand dryer and raised his Miley Cyrus cover to full voice. Magnus wanted to laugh, but mostly he wanted to crawl under the stall and fuck Belle Belleterre until the guy couldn't think up any more ways to drive him crazy.

The toes tickled his calf. The devil must be stretched out like an otter to get his toes so far up Magnus's leg. Enough! He grabbed Belle's foot and apparently about knocked him off his toilet seat, because an "eep" sounded through the bathroom.

The singer quit instantly. Silence.

Suddenly the bathroom door opened again.

The singer said, "Hey, man. I was just coming back."

"No problem. Gotta pee. See you at the table."

More peeing sounds.

Belle's toes wiggled. Damn!

Magnus grabbed Belle's foot, slid forward, and pressed the sock against his cock, which was hard as the marble on the walls. *Oh yeah.* He shoved the foot right into his crotch, and Belle's toes began to gyrate, sending shocks of electricity through Magnus's groin. He ripped off the sock, leaned down and kissed Belle's bare toes one at a time, then opened his fly, scooted farther forward, and pressed the bare, moist digits against his aching rod. Holy crap, had he ever done anything this sexy in his life? Belle must have thought so too, because a soft whimper came from the next stall as Belle wrapped his toes around Magnus's dick.

Peeing man chuckled, washed his hands, and then the men's room door opened and closed. All quiet on the bathroom front.

Belle's foot yanked from Magnus's hands, all kinds of scuffling sounds ensued, and then there was hammering on Magnus's stall door. Standing, he opened it and Belle scooted in, then closed the door behind him.

Belle glanced down at Magnus's still rampant cock sticking out of his fly. His eyes danced, but he didn't laugh. Staring directly at Magnus's penis, Belle said, "I'd like to have a serious conversation with you about desirability. You should be aware that you're one seriously hunky piece of man flesh, and so far as I can tell, all your other parts are equally sexy, so assuming the only reason I would want you in here—" He bobbed his cute butt to the side and pointed at it. "—is because I'm grateful for your extraordinary generosity is actually kind of insulting. That's why I got so mad. But our wise mutual friend, Judy, suggested that you weren't trying to insult me—you were insulting you." He flashed his big blue eyes directly at Magnus. "Is that true?"

Magnus tried to reply, but some lump the size of Australia stuck in his throat. Finally he said, "I-I can't really imagine why you'd be interested in me."

"You've got more magnetism and charisma in your upper lip than most men have in their whole body."

Magnus touched the scar on his lip.

Belle grabbed Magnus's hand and touched the scar with his own finger. "I've made my move and said my piece. Last I checked we were both here with other men who likely think we fell in. So I'm going back to my table, and very shortly thereafter I'm going home. Ball's in your court, bucko." He reached down and tweaked Magnus's balls, leaned up and kissed his mouth, then exited the stall just as the door opened to the restroom.

"Jesus, Belle. I thought you'd been accosted in the bathroom."

"Sorry, Owen. I got into a discussion with a friend and just got in here."

The conversation went silent for a moment, someone snorted, then the bathroom door opened and closed.

Magnus stared down at his cock, still amazingly erect. *It's in your court, buddy.*

"WHAT DO you think Magnus will do?"

Belle looked over at Owen and then beyond him to the brownstone where Owen lived. "I honestly don't know. He's a complex man."

"Yes. And if anyone deserves happiness, it's Magnus. You're not incorrect in saying he gives everything to others and keeps little for himself."

"I don't know if I could make him happy, but I'm sure willing to give it a shot."

Owen dropped a warm hand over Belle's. "Good luck. Seriously, I'd be raging jealous if it was any other man, but I get the attraction. If you have the eyes to see how special Magnus is, I can't begrudge you happiness together."

"Keep your fingers crossed."

Owen held up both hands with crossed fingers. "See you Monday." He climbed out of the car as Leroy held the door.

Belle waved to Owen, then powered down the privacy panel.

Leroy smiled back at him, all white teeth and mischievous eyes. "Where to, boss?"

"Home, Leroy!"

He laughed and started the car.

It took forty minutes to get home, New York weekend time, and Belle was swearing at drivers through the windows by the time they pulled onto his street. *What if Magnus already came? What if he didn't come at all?*

When Leroy guided the car to the curb, Belle was out before Leroy had set the brake. "Thanks, Leroy. Have a great night. See you Monday."

Leroy laughed. "I hope it's a great night! Call me tomorrow if you need me."

"Will do." Belle was already running up the front steps. He hadn't told Leroy what he was doing. Maybe he could hear more through the privacy panel than Belle knew—or maybe he was just a good guesser.

Belle threw open the door—and stopped. Sitting in the atrium, sipping champagne, were Mr. P, Wanda, Fatima, Ahmed—and Magnus. Uh, maybe they could have invited the mayor or the governor?

"Good evening, my dear." Mr. P. stood and held out a champagne flute. "Come, we've been waiting for you."

"Uh, hello."

Magnus grinned. "I stopped by to see you, Belle, and all these lovely people made me feel at home." His eyes danced.

Belle walked into the atrium, and Mr. P. conspicuously sauntered away from his seat next to Magnus and shoved in beside Wanda on a large rattan chair. *Okay, I'm not arguing.* He took the champagne glass from Mr. P. and sat by Magnus. With a smile, he clinked his glass with Magnus's. "Cheers."

"Indeed."

Mr. P. sipped. "So, Belle, Magnus was just telling us about your wonderful project. The gathering and information centers for women with cancer."

Fatima raised her glass of iced tea—no liquor for these unique Muslims. "Helluv'an idea, Belle. But you can't call it 'gathering and information centers,' right? So do you have a name?"

Belle glanced at Magnus. "Uh, yes. I have an idea. But I haven't cleared it yet, so I haven't told anyone."

Wanda laughed. "Hey, we're all family here."

"No. I better wait."

Magnus glanced at him but didn't insist he share.

Wanda asked, "So how's our Judy?"

"She's doing well."

Magnus nodded. "The doctor says they'll have the pathology reports back tomorrow, but they tested the margins as they operated, and they got it all. She may not even have to have chemo or radiation."

Belle loved his interest. What an amazing man. "We'll need to get her on a good program of herbs and minerals to help prevent recurrence."

Fatima said, "Is that what you're going to teach women at your center, Belle?"

"It's not my center, it's Magnus's. But yes, we'll make all the newest and best research available so women can make informed decisions."

"Right on, my brother!"

Mr. P. stood and stretched elaborately. "Well, I'm thinking we should all turn in. Why don't we give the rest of the champagne to Belle and Magnus and call it a night?"

Mr. P. was not setting records in subtlety, but Belle wasn't going to object.

Wanda smiled. "I hope we'll see you again, Magnus." She stepped out of the atrium.

Fatima and Ahmed followed. Fatima glanced back and winked. "Yeah, like tomorrow morning. Sleep well." Her husky laugh bounced off the walls of atrium glass.

Mr. Pennymaker extended his hand to Magnus. "Don't mind us. We're just fond family."

Magnus shook his hand. "Thank you for taking such good care of two members of our Beauty, Inc. family."

Mr. P. gave him that level gaze. "My pleasure."

"This really is an extraordinary place."

"Made just for extraordinary people. I hope you'll visit us often."

"Thank you." Funny. It looked like Magnus blushed.

CHAPTER 15

MR. P. left and Magnus cleared his throat. "What an amazing man. Magical."

Belle smiled. "You see that? A lot of people would call him eccentric, but I agree with you. Magical." He turned to Magnus. "And you gave him to me. How is it you've never met him?"

"I was told that you loved plants and flowers."

"Oh? By whom?"

"Uh, a consultant of mine."

"Elliott Porter?"

Magnus cracked a half smile. "How did you know that?"

"He asked me so many questions. And I saw him with you at that restaurant in Las Vegas. I figured there was a connection. I don't remember him asking me about flowers, however." He gave Magnus a level gaze.

"He might have done a little digging on his own." He grinned but looked at his shoes, which made his battered face almost childlike. "Anyway, the day he told me that, HR called me about being contacted by a man in Brooklyn who said he had a few apartments in a building with a tropical atrium. It sounded so perfect, I told them to jump on it."

"Amazing coincidence."

"Yes. But I've learned that the universe does enjoy synchronicity on occasion, so I didn't look this gift garden in the mouth."

"Thank you. I've never really felt quite so at home anywhere—except home, I guess. And when Judy arrived here, it was like better than home."

"I'm so glad." He glanced at Belle and then away.

"So, I actually am very, very grateful to you." He took a breath. "But that has no bearing on my desire to hop on your cock and go for a very long ride."

"Belle!" Magnus grabbed his dick through his suit pants. "You say the damnedest things!"

"We have a half bottle of champagne, two glasses, and the rest of the night. What would you like to do with it?"

"I—I guess we could go upstairs to your place and see what comes up."

"Excellent plan." Belle grabbed the champagne bottle and took off at a run up the stairs, laughing at the frantic sound of Magnus's footsteps behind him. Since no one in the building locked their apartments, he threw open the door and raced across the living room to the bedroom, at which point the champagne had bubbled to the top of the bottle.

Magnus caught up with him just in time to catch the foamy liquid in the two flutes he carried. "Gotcha."

Belle set the bottle on the end table, and Magnus handed him a glass. They clinked and stared in each other's eyes as they drank. He'd never noticed how Magnus's chocolate brown eyes had gold flecks that sparkled when he laughed.

Magnus smiled. "You done running?"

"More to the point, are you?"

The smile faded. "It's hard for me, Belle."

"I'm not asking you to drop your suit of armor—at least for now. But I need you to open the chest plate a little. Oh, and you'll probably have to remove the pants, don't you think?"

Magnus raised his eyes slowly. Since Belle was tall, Magnus only had a couple of inches on him, though probably twenty or thirty pounds of what appeared to be solid muscle. Still, he looked like Belle could knock him over with a breath. "You sure you want to do this?"

Belle pointed at the pushed-out front of his tight black jeans. "Uh, do you want to negotiate with him?"

Magnus cracked a half smile. That was something.

"Want to see?"

"Hell yes." His deep voice roughened even more.

Belle sipped his champagne as he slowly drew down the zipper of his jeans, then unsnapped the waist. The pants gaped open, revealing the tiny tiger-striped bikinis he'd worn underneath with more than a modest helping of wishful thinking.

Magnus swallowed hard. "Oh my, Dr. Belleterre, if I'd only known what was under your lab coat."

"See what you've been missing?" He set down the champagne. Magnus collapsed on the end of the bed, his eyes glued to Belle's crotch.

Belle wiggled until the jeans slid down his narrow hips by themselves, but they stopped on the very prominent bulge in the tiger pants. "Oh dear. We seem to have a hang-up." Hooking his thumbs in his jeans, he slid them to the floor and kicked off his loafers. He stepped out and snagged the pants with his foot—the one with no sock—and sent them flying onto the bedroom chair.

"You do have very talented feet." Magnus stared at the one sock on and one off. He reached in his pocket and pulled out the other sock.

"Oh look. You made a match. You win!" Belle grabbed his bikinis and dragged them down his legs, waggling his hips so his erection stuck out through the gap in his shirttail.

"Is-is that my prize?"

"You get your pick of prizes. You can have him." Belle wagged again. "Or him." He leaped in the air and landed with his butt facing Magnus. Flipping up his shirttail, he mooned disgracefully, then peered through his legs upside down. "Take your pick."

"Uh, you may have heard that I'm a big-time businessman, right?"

"The biggest." He stretched his hole a little farther for Magnus's edification.

"Well, obviously that means I choose—both." Magnus dove forward, grabbed Belle by the butt, sank to his knees, and began rimming Belle's hole.

"Holy hell, when you decide to get unreticent, you don't mess around! Oh, oh God."

Magnus's tongue slid far, farther into Belle's more than willing channel. Okay, Belle had done one-night stands with the best of them, but not often did his wham-bam-thank-you-sir evenings get to anything this intimate. In fact, he'd always been so protected he practically wore a plastic bubble. This was way more than his poor nervous system could take. His knees softened, and he slowly sank to the Middle Eastern carpet on the floor.

Magnus never left him. He followed every move, his tongue doing things that were clearly illegal in many states and most countries. Belle's hips and groin turned into a cauldron of fire, flames zinging in every direction. He pushed back wantonly with each deep exploration.

Magnus's fingers slid across his taint and fondled his balls gently. *Yeah, he must know he's playing with molten lava in there.* Magnus's tongue pulled back, and he gasped, "Where? Condoms and lube?"

Belle pressed his cheek into the carpet while his ass flailed in the air. "Bedside. Hurry."

Without the strength to open his eyes, he only heard Magnus stomp to the bedside table, the drawer open, a box fall on the floor near him, then rustling and grunting he hoped represented a lot of undressing.

Not nearly soon enough, he felt Magnus's heat near his ass. The cardboard ripping and unpackaging sounds fell like music on his ears, and then there was a heavenly squirt. He waved his ass like a flag. "Come on. Hurry."

"Jesus, you're a bossy little bottom."

A cold, wet finger slid into his ass, and Belle moaned. "Yes. More."

Magnus slid that finger in deep, then pulled out and added a second. By the time he got three in there, Belle was wailing. "Come on, I need the burn."

Magnus's rough voice murmured, "You're going to get it."

A big object, soft and hard at the same time, pressed against his hole. Magnus gripped Belle's shoulder hard and—wham. He drove his cock through the ring of muscle into Neverland. "Oh. My. Goooood."

"This what you want, sweetheart? Is this it?" Whatever reticence Magnus might have displayed in courting was long gone. This was the white-hot tycoon taking what he wanted and the devil take the rest. Magnus's hips thrust again and again, big heavy balls slapping and leg hair chafing against Belle's thighs, ramming himself as far into Belle's hole as physics allowed.

Belle loved it. Loved it beyond reason. Never ever had anything come close. How could he feel so out-of-control and so safe at the same time? "More. Yes, yes. Oh God, Magnus, yes. Don't ever stop. Ever."

For a second Magnus's hips paused; then he turned into a giant piston, thrusting and ramming, his hand jerking Belle's cock until everything in Belle's brain fried to white light and the fire lit the blood in his veins. *Amazement. Awe. Blastoff.*

The cells of his being tried to squeeze out through his cock. One shot of jism hit the wall in front of him, and two more were swallowed by Magnus's big hand. Belle wailed as the pleasure in his groin spread like a flow through him and blacked out his sight.

From far off he felt Magnus freeze, his hips stuttered in their hammering, and suddenly a roar like a great ocean filled the room. "Oh, Belle. Ohhhhhh."

Can't hold up anymore. Slowly all of Belle's body dissolved into the carpet, with Magnus following him down. Fuzzy on his front. Hot, sticky, and heavenly heavy on his back. He giggled.

Magnus's heart beat so hard it vibrated through to Belle's chest. He muttered, "I'll quit squashing you as soon as it's humanly possible to move."

"Don't hurry on my account. Feels wonderful."

"You're kidding?"

"When will you learn to take what I say as gospel, Mr. Strong?"

He had the good grace to laugh, which tickled Belle and made him giggle harder.

Belle sighed. "This was one of the great events of my life, you know? The earth moved." He said it lightly and felt Magnus tense. "Magnus."

"Yes?"

"I'm serious."

Magnus's tension shifted, like it relaxed, but something new took its place. "It was wonderful."

"Can you spend the night with me?"

"You want me to?"

"I wouldn't have asked if I didn't."

"Thank you. I'd love to."

Belle chuckled.

"What?"

"You're so beautifully formal—when you're not hammering my ass."

More tension. "I hope I didn't hurt you."

Belle looked over his shoulder. "Raise up a little."

Magnus lifted the bulk of his weight from Belle's back. Belle flipped over. When Magnus started to slide off him, Belle grabbed his back. "No. Don't go anywhere. I love this."

Magnus looked skeptical, but he lowered his body back to Belle's and gradually gave him his weight. He kept his forearms planted so he could look down at Belle. That close, the scars were like art—both smooth and rough.

Belle smiled softly. "How come you're so generous to everyone else and so hard on yourself?"

A frown flittered across Magnus's face. "I'm not."

"I just told you this was one of the best experiences of my life— and you asked if you hurt me. These don't compute. I'm not a masochist and I'm not a liar."

"I didn't mean that."

"I know. But I want to make my point. I'm here because I want to be, and so far it's proved to be better than I could even have imagined."

Magnus looked down. "Me too."

"Good. Want to get some sleep? Or do you want to move a little and see if we can get additional action out of these used and abused cocks?" He laughed.

"Whoa. Don't tempt me with sex, then ask me to sleep."

Belle maneuvered a hand up to touch Magnus's face. "But I'm also not going anywhere, so if you'd like some shut-eye now, I can guarantee later I'll be a sure thing."

"Sounds perfect."

After some acrobatic maneuvering, they managed to move their operation from the floor to the bathroom to the bed. A few seconds after tucking the two of them in and curling up on his side so Magnus could spoon him, Belle heard the soft, deep breathing of sleep and felt Magnus's powerful abdomen rising and falling against his back.

He's exhausted. Who knows when he slept last? Intertwining his fingers with Magnus's, Belle fell asleep smiling.

When his eyes fluttered open, it was still dark. He noticed his back felt cool, and when he reached out, so was the sheet behind him. He sat up. Where was Magnus? *He wouldn't leave—would he?*

Belle hopped out of bed and grabbed his robe from the back of the closet door. Quietly he padded into the living room. Magnus sat in the chair beside the fireplace, staring out into the soft light of the atrium. Through the open window, the sweet moisture and flower scents wafted in. Magnus half turned toward him. "Sorry I woke you. This view is just irresistible."

Belle sat on the arm of the chair. "Yes, it is, isn't it?"

For minutes they just stared. Magnus looked up. "I realized you never told me the name you want to give your women's centers."

"Oh. Well, I looked up your history online and learned that your mother's name was Beatrice."

Magnus's face went very still.

Should I keep talking? Belle felt like someone had thrown glass on the floor and he was barefooted. Sadly, the one who threw it might be him. "Uh, you told me she had cancer, and I was going to suggest the B. Strong Centers. It has two great meanings, and I thought it would inspire women. But we can certainly do a different name. Maybe you'd like them named for your father?" He realized he was babbling and shut up.

Magnus swallowed visibly. The look on his face screamed pain, fear, panic even. Belle wanted to grab him and hold him.

"Magnus, I'm sorry. I didn't mean to—"

"I killed her. How can I name a center for her?"

"What? What do you mean, you killed her?"

His eyes got wide and he stared at Belle but probably didn't see him. "I mean I killed her. If it weren't for me, she wouldn't have wrecked the car and died. I did it. I can't name a center for her as if I didn't do anything. As if I had the right to. I can't."

Belle grabbed Magnus hard, wrapped his arms tight like the bindings you put on people having panic attacks, then rocked and rocked and rocked. At first Magnus squirmed and tried to get free, but Belle wasn't letting go. Finally, rather than hurt Belle, Magnus calmed a little. His breath still sounded sketchy, but he stopped fighting.

Belle put his lips near Magnus's ear. "Tell me."

"No."

"Hey, baby, I'm a good listener, and I don't charge for a fifty-minute hour."

Magnus sighed. Maybe a good sign? Belle loosened his arms a little.

Magnus said, "She had cancer. I was fifteen, and her being sick made me angry. Mothers aren't supposed to get sick. They're supposed to take care of their kids. My father was always at work. She was my one parent, and she got sick." His voice sounded flat, like day-old champagne. "I was in the backseat of the car, sulking. She was driving, that scarf around her head to cover her baldness. I was yelling at her that she needed to go find a specialist. Someone who could cure her. I shrieked, 'You need to get over this.' She turned and looked in the backseat at me and ran a red light. The truck couldn't stop. Our car was totaled. So was she. I got off with cuts and bruises."

Belle's breath stopped in his lungs. Everything inside him felt cold. The answer to the often-asked question, "Why did Magnus Strong, billionaire, not have his face repaired with plastic surgery?" had just been answered. Magnus paid his penance every time he looked in the mirror.

Belle tightened his arms and pressed his cheek against Magnus's hair. "I know my saying you didn't kill your mother isn't going to count for much."

Magnus shook his head, a mix of anger and despair.

God, he knew that feeling. "Would you do it for me?"

"What?"

"Try to be a little happy? I have a very personal interest in you allowing yourself some joy… I kind of figure my own happiness depends on it. So will you consider cutting yourself a break? For me?"

"I don't know why you'd care." Magnus's voice sounded like that broken glass on the floor.

"You just have to trust that I do. Otherwise you'll piss me off. Okay?"

Long, painful pause.

"Okay."

CHAPTER 16

BELLE HELD Magnus's hand as they walked down the hospital hall toward Judy's room. As they got close to the door, Magnus let go.

Belle looked at him. "You don't want her to know we're together?"

"Uh, no, I thought you wouldn't want her to know."

Belle smiled and shook his head. With focus, he intertwined his fingers with Magnus's. "We're working on this lesson slowly." He laughed, and with their hands conspicuously clenched, he pushed into Judy's door, half dragging Magnus behind him.

She was sitting up in bed. Her face lit up when she saw them, her eyes dropped to their intertwined hands, her mouth flew open, and she shrieked and started clapping despite the IV still in her arm.

A nurse powered in behind Magnus. "What's wrong? Is everything okay?"

Belle laughed. "Just an excess of enthusiasm."

The nurse smiled. "So probably not fatal. Good." She exited, laughing. Lots of that going on.

They pulled two chairs over beside the bed and sat.

Belle took her hand. "How are you feeling?"

Judy smiled so big it looked like her cheeks might crack. "A lot better the last couple of minutes. I'm so glad you two came to your senses. The world's a better place."

Belle glanced at Magnus, wondering if he would look uncomfortable. No, he was blushing. "So, seriously, when can you go home?"

"I'm waiting for the doctor now. Maybe today."

"Yahoo. We're all prepared to whisk you out of here."

Magnus nodded. "I'll give Belle some extra time off so he can take care of you at home."

Belle snorted. "Are you kidding? Between Wanda and Mr. P, with occasional visits from Fatima and Ahmed, I'll be lucky to get close to her."

Judy smiled. "And Henry, of course."

"Henry? You mean Henry Kim? You've met the gardener."

Her turn to blush. "Oh yes. Lovely person. He speaks with this lilting Jamaican accent."

Magnus cocked his head. "I thought you said his name was Kim?"

"It is." She laughed and shrugged. "I guess he has an Asian ancestor, but he's mostly Jamaican as far as I can tell." Clearly she'd been doing some up-close observation.

Belle squeezed her hand. "I look forward to meeting the guy who made all that beauty happen."

"I know. Isn't it amazing? Gardening is actually his avocation. He's a stockbroker."

"You're kidding."

"Nope."

"Now I'm even crazier to meet him."

The doctor walked in and released Judy. Perfect timing. Belle called Leroy and asked him to bring the car around the front of the hospital. They completed some paperwork, most of which Magnus signed, and then the nurse did the required wheelchair push to the exit.

Leroy stood waiting, held the door, and helped Judy get in. She looked positively spry. As Magnus started to crawl in next, Belle gripped his shoulder. He looked back. Belle smiled. "I want you to get that you've not only made her well, you've made her happy. She gets to recover with people who care about her, not worrying about money. What a gift."

He shrugged, and that increasingly familiar blush stained his cheeks. "Anyone would have done it if they could."

"No. I can personally attest to the fact that many, maybe even most, people would not have done it. You're special that way."

Leroy nodded. "Count me in on that one."

Magnus cleared his throat. "Thanks, Leroy." He looked at Belle— deep in his eyes—and smiled. Funny how Magnus's smiles no longer looked scary. They looked beautiful.

A half hour later, the full residency of their apartment building crowded out on the curb to welcome Judy home—including the elusive Henry Kim. Henry proved to be a tall, handsome guy with flashing dark eyes. His face lit up when he saw Leroy helping Judy from the car. "Hey, *mi parri*. How you doin'?"

Judy blushed and stammered. Easy to understand why. "I'm doing good."

Wanda descended like Florence Nightingale. "We need to get you inside and into bed and get some good food in your stomach." She looked at Leroy. "Should she be walking?"

Belle replied for Leroy. "The doctor said walking is good. She can't lift anything heavy. Actually not much of anything at all for a while, so she gets to be a princess."

Leroy got on one side of Judy and Henry on the other. Mr. P. and Ahmed brought up the rear. Like the queen's guard, they escorted Judy slowly up the steps and into the building, then to her ground-floor apartment. When they threw open the door, Judy gasped. Streamers and banners announced "Welcome Home, Judy!" The table was laden with food, and delicious smells filled the space. Wanda at work.

Judy buried her face in her hands and cried.

Belle stepped up beside her and enclosed her in a hug. For a young woman who'd spent her whole life taking care of her family, having someone take care of her had to be overwhelming. He understood totally. "Happy tears?"

She looked up with a red nose. "The happiest."

"Good. Let's get you to bed, and then we'll deliver huge quantities of food you won't feel like eating, which we'll consume happily on your behalf."

"You're all heart."

"More like stomach."

He helped her to her bedroom—though Henry obviously would have enjoyed the duty—and pulled a clean set of very cute PJs out of her drawer. "Put these on and holler if you need any help. I'll send in Henry."

She giggled.

"Good choice in men, sweetheart."

She giggled harder.

He walked out and joined the throng gathered in her small living room—including Leroy, who he suspected had been invited to join them by Magnus. One more kindness Belle wished he'd thought of first. Everyone seemed to have consciously left a seat open next to Magnus.

Belle slipped into it and took Magnus's hand, then leaned back. "When do we eat?"

The bedroom door opened, and Judy stood there in her cat pajamas. "Not without me."

Belle stood. "Get in that bed, young lady. I turned it down for you."

Henry headed for the kitchen. "And I'm helpin' Wanda with the food, so it won't be long now. Come on, Ahmed."

Belle, Magnus, Mr. P, and Fatima all clustered around Judy's bed. As the food was served, Henry delivered the most digestible bits to Judy, complete with tray and huge towel to keep her pajamas clean. He then insinuated himself beside her on the bed and began feeding her— ignoring the fact that half the morsels ended up in his mouth.

When they all had their plates and managed to cram all their bodies in the bedroom, Mr. P. raised a glass. "To a perfect Sunday. Good friends. Good food. Good wine, which for the moment Judy must forgo."

She snuggled into her pillow and succeeded in leaning against Henry, who was reclining against her headboard. "But it's still perfect."

Belle squeezed Magnus's hand and dragged a quick palm over his eyes.

Magnus squeezed back. "Next weekend is the annual Spring Festival at Beauty, Inc. We entertain all the employees with their families and friends all over the world. Here in New York, we rent a large country club and have a day of fun, games, and too much to eat. I'm hoping Judy will feel up to coming for a little while—with some help from Henry and Leroy. And I'd love it if you'd all join us."

Wanda pressed a hand to her curvy chest. "What will I wear?"

"It's casual, but break out your spring colors for the celebration."

Fatima waved a hand. "Us girls will figure it out together. You too, Judy."

Magnus looked at Belle. "I'd be honored if you'd let me escort you."

Belle smiled. "We'll be coming out to the company."

"Yes."

Belle's smile widened. "I'd be honored to be escorted."

Everyone applauded, but a teeny worm crawled into Belle's warm glow. How would Beauty, Inc. feel about their boss dating an employee?

BELLE BRUSHED his pale hair to a glossy sheen, then flipped his head forward to give his floppy bangs more motion. He ran a hand down his lightweight pastel blue sweater and checked out the view of his ass in his black slacks. Looking good for the Beauty, Inc. Spring Festival? Check. Not trying too hard? Uh, well—

Was he nervous about showing up at a social occasion with the big boss? Hell, yes. But coming off one of the best weeks of his life, all the worries faded to a mist.

The door to the bathroom opened on a wave of steam—Magnus did like his water hot—and the big boss himself stepped out, dressed only in a towel and a smile.

Belle raised an eyebrow. "Are you trying to make us late for the Festival, sir, with that kind of blatant temptation?"

Magnus fell backward on the bed, his gaping towel revealing that massive cock of his perking up and saying howdy at the thought of more horizontal action. "God save me from horny twenty-two-year-old sex fiends."

Belle laughed. A few scars showed on Magnus's chest, but most of the damage had been done to his face when the glass on his side of the car shattered. The fact that he felt comfortable enough to prance around the apartment nearly naked amounted to a major victory. "Uh, excuse me. Who woke me from a sound sleep at 3:00 a.m. so he could shove his massive boner into my somnolent ass?"

"Hmm. I don't know. Who was that?" He rolled on his side and propped his head on his arm. "I didn't notice you having any trouble falling asleep after that screaming orgasm."

"Sleep fucking. I want to master the art."

Magnus raised his eyebrows. "By the way, I changed my mind about taking you to the Festival."

For a second Belle's heart skipped. Then he saw the slight twist to Magnus's lips under the scars. "Oh really?"

"Yep. You look so heavenly I can't bear to let mere mortals feast their eyes on you. I'm handcuffing you to the bed and making you my sex slave."

Considering that was exactly what Belle had been thinking when he first came to New York, he snorted volcanically. "I volunteer for the job." He turned slowly. "So I'm okay? Not too much?"

"Sweetheart, your existence on this earth is more of a good thing than any man has a right to expect, but the clothes are perfect."

Belle pressed a hand to his heart. "Thank you. I must have been doing good things in my sleep my whole life to deserve to be with you."

Magnus blushed and covered it by sitting up. He smiled at Belle. "So maybe I better give up on the handcuff idea and get dressed so I can show you off to the whole Beauty, Inc. family." He stood and the towel fell to the floor, uncovering his long legs, slim hips, and wide chest. "Help me pick out something to wear. I brought a few choices."

Belle took a deep breath and went into fashion consultant mode.

A half hour later, he and Magnus walked down the stairs from the apartment. Magnus had chosen, with Belle's help, some gray slacks, a dress-style shirt, but with a saucy stripe, and no tie. Over it he wore a light green leather jacket cut like a blazer. Totally cool.

Fatima stuck her head out the door. "Hey, Belle. Hey, Magnus. You guys look smokin'." Magnus had been at the apartment every night for a week, so all the residents were used to seeing him. One night he'd had dinner with the whole group, sex with Belle, and then went home because he had a 6:00 a.m. breakfast downtown. Otherwise he'd spent every night curled around Belle's body, waking him up for sex at all hours. Magnus might joke about Belle's libido, but his more than matched it.

Magnus gave a sweeping bow. "Thank you, my lady. So you and the crew will be at the country club by noon, right?"

"Yes, sir. Wouldn't miss a minute."

"Good. Leroy will come back for all of you once he's dropped me and Belle off."

A screech came from below, and Wanda waved up the stairs. "I get to ride in a limo?"

Magnus laughed and yelled down, "Yes, ma'am. But it's just a town car."

Wanda went flying into her door. "Carstairs! Did you hear? Limo."

Magnus fit right in here. Belle hadn't even seen Magnus's home. For all Belle knew, Magnus might have a wife and seven kids stashed in a brownstone somewhere, but he wasn't really worried. Magnus seemed to love Belle's apartment as much as he loved—uh, well, liked Belle.

At the bottom of the stairs, Magnus walked into the open door of Judy's apartment. She was sitting up in her living room, still wearing her robe, but her hair was styled and makeup on. He sat next to her on the couch and took her hand. "How are you feeling?"

"Rarin' to go. I'm stir-crazy, Magnus. I've studied New York law until my eyes cross. I need some frivolity."

Henry walked out of her kitchen with a tray. "Got some breakfast for you, mi Empress."

She glanced at Belle with a cute squinch of her nose. "Henry Kim, you're not feeding me another mouthful. I'm a fully functioning female, and I'm ready to boogey."

"Okay, baby. Let's boogey some food down dat throat."

She threw up her arms, and Belle saw the little wince. She lowered them slowly. "He's hopeless."

Henry sat beside her and placed the tray on her lap. "So eat by yourself if you don' want me feeding you."

"Okay, okay. But there's going to be a ton of food at the Festival, right, Magnus?"

Magnus pushed the plate of eggs and toast closer. "Yes, but you still need to eat now."

Henry pulled a plastic baggie from his pocket. "She needs serious calories to get down this hunk of vitamins and herbs, man." The bag contained maybe twenty or thirty pills of various sizes.

Belle leaned over and looked in her sulky, cute face. "Eat so you can finish getting beautiful for the Festival."

She glanced up and gave him the stink eye. "Manipulator." But she started eating and swallowing her pills.

Magnus slapped his leg and got up. "Okay, we'll see you all in a couple of hours." Grabbing Belle's hand, he headed for the limo.

Belle breathed in the city air as he climbed in the car. Funny how the chunky oxygen tasted sweet these days. *Here goes nothing.*

CHAPTER 17

SO FAR, so good. He and Magnus had arrived early and helped make last-minute decisions about some of the games, prizes, food displays, and even the decorations. So while most guests arrived, Belle just looked like one of the busy committee members who were running the event. The country club had a big pool, though it was too cool to swim, so they floated flowers and plastic boats with candles in them in the water. Huge flower arrangements on high stands so people could see under them decorated the buffet table and all the outside tables. Belle was in heaven. He flipped ribbons and positioned flowers until his head filled with their scent. The sun was warm and the sky blue. *Sigh.* Perfection.

Then all his friends arrived. Magnus had to circulate, and Belle hung with his pals and introduced them to people from his department. Mr. P. proved to be the wildest hit, having decked himself out in pastel plaid pants, a lavender shirt, and a brilliant green sport coat. Definitely an elf.

They picked a table under a big tree. As they settled in, a voice called, "Hey, boss."

Belle turned. Leroy came toward them with a lovely older woman beside him. She wore a flowered skirt and light denim jacket, which looked perfect for the day. "Hey, Leroy. Come join us."

"Boss, this is my mom, Erica. Mom. This is Dr. Belleterre, who I've told you about."

Belle smiled. "Just Belle. I'm so glad to meet you, Erica."

"And you, Belle. Leroy's told me so much about your new project, and I'm anxious to know more. If you're ready for volunteers, please count me in."

"I'd be so happy to have your help."

Leroy said, "I thought Judy might like to meet my mom."

"Great idea."

Chairs were pulled up, and Judy and Erica dove deep into conversation immediately. As soon as food was laid out on the buffet tables, Henry and

Leroy busied themselves making sure their respective females were fed, then took off with Ahmed to play a game of touch football organizing on the lawn. Belle sat quietly and basked while everyone talked. Yes, that's what it was like. He used to bask in the moisture and green of Oregon— alone. Now he basked in the warmth and glow of friends—something very much like a family. When had he ever felt so not alone?

There's the main reason why. Magnus walked toward Belle across the grass outside the country club dining room, where a continuous flow of food seemed to be manifesting at the huge buffet table. Belle sighed. The man did move like a rock star.

He smiled and got one in return. Magnus said, "You ready to eat?"

"Always. You done pressing flesh?"

"For the moment, and if I have to do more, you can join me."

Belle swallowed softly, nodded, and turned to Mr. P. and Wanda. Henry was busy feeding Judy, as usual, and Fatima and Ahmed seemed to have made friends with some of the people from the lab. "Are you guys ready to eat?"

Mr. P. smiled beatifically. "No, not yet. You two go ahead."

Belle gave Mr. P. a look. Did the canny senior citizen realize Belle was looking for some camouflage? Oh well.

Magnus extended a hand. Belle's heart did a wonky tango. He glanced at Magnus's offered hand. "You sure?"

"Isn't that my line?" Magnus grinned. "I'm sure if you are."

"Whew. Okay. Charge!" He took Magnus's hand, and they headed across the grass toward a whole passel of people in line for the buffet.

A couple of heads turned as they walked. When they got to the end of the line, the young guy who stood there looked at Magnus like he both wanted to run and wanted to hug him.

Magnus smiled. "Hi, Rory. Having a good time?"

Rory swallowed so hard it looked like he downed his own Adam's apple. "Yes, sir. It's a great party."

Magnus nodded at Belle. "Rory, I don't know if you've met our new Foundation executive, Dr. Belleterre. Belle, Rory is one of our mailroom experts."

Belle shook the young guy's hand. He couldn't be more than eighteen or so, and the fact that Magnus Strong knew his name clearly blew the kid's brains out of his skull. *Hell, it does the same to mine.*

A woman named Nancy came up beside them. "Mr. Strong, you don't have to wait in line. I'm sure someone will give you cuts." She grinned.

Magnus laughed. "Nope. With Belle's appetite, we might not leave enough food for everyone else. We better stay here."

She laughed but looked at Belle with intense curiosity.

Magnus chatted with the people who came by, and they all gave Belle more than a once-over. Magnus whispered, "Good thing you work in chemistry, since you're now officially under the microscope."

Belle snorted.

"Magnus?" The slightly nasal voice came from behind them. Magnus's expression got just an edge of tension, but he smiled and turned. "Hi, Christian. Having a good time?" He held tightly to Belle's hand.

The man called Christian gave Belle a hard stare but nodded. "A great party, as always." His head snapped toward Belle. "I'm Christian Archer, a member of Magnus's board."

Magnus squeezed Belle's hand. "Sorry, Christian. I thought you'd met Belle. May I present Dr. Robert Belleterre, who's heading our new cancer center project for the Foundation."

Christian smiled tightly. "Someone else to give the company's money away? Interesting to meet you, Dr. Belleterre." He didn't bother to extend his hand and turned pointedly to Magnus. "I thought you might join me and the special guests of the board, Magnus. Perhaps you'd come over after you get your food? Or better yet, why don't you have someone get food for you and join me now?"

"Oh, thanks, Christian, but no. I've already spoken to each of them. They're in good hands with you and the board. I'm having lunch with some friends Belle and I invited. Thanks anyway." He smiled—like a shark.

"I see. You—*and Belle*."

"Yes." Magnus's gaze never wavered. The man had balls.

"Very well." Christian turned abruptly and walked a few steps, then looked back. "Playing a little out of our league, aren't we, Magnus? Good luck."

Belle felt Magnus's whole body tense.

He squeezed Magnus's hand and whispered, "Want me to slap the bastard?" But Christian walked away. "Who shoved a stick up his ass?"

Magnus sighed. "My father put him on the board. He's been hitting on me since I was in prep school but never admits he's gay."

"What an asshole." Belle watched the stocky man march over to a group of older men, all overdressed for the party. Sadly, Belle had probably just made a powerful enemy.

They finally made it to the buffet, and Belle devised a game out of piling food on his plate and stealing it off Magnus's, but he didn't see the same relaxed happiness in Magnus he'd had before the asshole attack.

They ate with their friends and everyone laughed a lot, making sure Judy and Erica tasted a little of everything. Magnus joined in, leaning over to dangle grapes in front of their noses. It was so cool that he didn't mind being an obvious friend to a junior employee—and Belle's driver. Still, Magnus seemed distracted.

As sunshine turned to twilight, the parents started gathering up their kids. Magnus walked up to the porch of the club and picked up a microphone. "I want to thank you all for coming. As you've heard me say many times, the assets of this company walk out the door every night. I'm honored and grateful that each of you chooses to return the next morning. Beauty, Inc. sounds like such a frivolous company, doesn't it? And yet each of you makes an enormous difference in the lives of millions of people—with your commitment to quality, excellence, and sharing. We don't just make people more beautiful. We make them happier, healthier, and better. Thank you for sharing your gifts with us. I hope Beauty, Inc. will always be an enterprise you can be proud of. Have a wonderful Sunday, and I'll see many of you next week."

Belle wiped a hand across his eyes.

Mr. P. touched his arm. "Quite a man you found, my dear."

Belle nodded but couldn't quite talk around the lump in his throat. Would his father have ever made a speech like that? Not even when he was sober.

Leroy drove Mr. P. and the crew to take Judy and his mom home, but Magnus and Belle stayed on. Magnus said good-bye to everyone as they left, which took hours. Belle fell back into work mode and helped the committee supervise the teardown of all the décor.

When they finally crawled into the car with Leroy, who had insisted on returning at the wheel, they'd been there twelve hours. Belle slid over and snuggled against Magnus. Magnus kissed his hair. "Did you have fun?"

"A wonderful time. It was a perfect combination. I met a lot of new people and still got to hang out with my best friends." He laughed. "And I loved all the flowers."

"I hoped you would."

Belle looked up at Magnus's face. "You did that for me?"

"Well, I just suggested to the committee that flowers would be a wonderful addition to the décor, that's all."

He laughed. "All? I think that constituted a command."

He shrugged. "Perhaps." He squeezed Belle's hand. "I just learned I have to leave for the Midwest to visit some of our customers and suppliers. No chance you'd like to take an exciting tour of Cleveland and Kansas City, is there?"

Funny how that made his stomach flip. Nice to be wanted. "When do you leave?"

"Day after tomorrow."

Belle grinned. "You do live a thrilling life. I always say, if you can't do Paris in the spring, Cleveland is second best."

Magnus laughed.

"Actually, I'd come in a minute, but next week I'll be getting the contractors started on bidding the renovations of the building for the center."

Magnus sighed. "I don't want to slow that down. I'll miss you."

"Me too." Belle snuggled a little closer.

Magnus looked up at the rearview mirror. "Did you enjoy yourself, Leroy?"

"Yes, sir. My mom loved the whole event. She really loved meeting Judy. Nothing helps us as much as being able to help someone else."

"I think we should carve that on the building."

Leroy chuckled. "I'm really excited about her volunteering to help Belle too. I think that will give her a lot of purpose and take her mind off her worries."

Belle asked, "Does your mom work, Leroy?"

"She used to. She was an administrator for city government. Really good at her job. But when she got cancer, she was already past early retirement age, so she went ahead and hung it up."

Belle glanced at Magnus. "Maybe she wants another job?"

"Man, boss, that's one helluv'an idea. She'd be dope. I mean, that woman whips things into shape. Take me, for example."

He laughed, and Belle and Magnus joined in as Leroy pulled up in front of the apartment building. Funny how Leroy just assumed that Magnus would be staying with Belle. Happily, so did Magnus. He climbed out when Leroy opened the door. Belle slid after Magnus. "Don't tell your mom anything yet, Leroy. I need to think about what kind of jobs we'll actually have at the center."

"No worries, boss. I won't spill the beans. And if you decide you don't need her for a job, I know she'd still like to help out."

"Thanks for coming back for us. Get some rest. See you in the morning."

Belle walked up the outside stairs beside Magnus. "Sorry. I didn't mean to jump the gun. I'm not really responsible for hiring people for the center."

Magnus shook his head. "I think it's a great idea. I trust Leroy, and I liked Erica. I think you should speak to HR about defining a position for her. It could help us and her."

Belle stopped on the top step. Magnus started to open the door, then paused. "What?"

"I just wanted to say how proud I am to work for you."

A little catch of air seemed to suck into Magnus's throat. He cleared it. "I-I'm glad you like working for Beauty, Inc. I hoped maybe you would. I want it to be a place where you can thrive." He looked down at his shoes. Amazing. So confident and self-assured and yet so humble.

Belle leaned forward and kissed him gently. "You show me that power doesn't corrupt if it's in the right hands. You show me the kind of person I want to be."

Magnus frowned and shook his head. "Nonsense. You're the role model here."

No use making Magnus any more uncomfortable, though someday Belle wanted the man to be able to accept a compliment. Just once. Belle leaned in to Magnus's ear. "How about we work out this mutual admiration thing while fucking each other's asses?"

Magnus coughed. "You vixen."

"In the very best way."

"Right in my wheelhouse."

"Race you!" Belle tore open the door and powered to the stairs. Judy's door was closed and not a neighbor in sight. *Perfect.* Two stairs at a time, he raced past the second and third levels with Magnus chugging on his heels. He opened his door, ran across the living room, and started throwing clothes somewhere near the bedroom door. Hopping on one foot, he pulled off his deck shoes and tossed them toward the closet, ripped his sweater over his head, threw himself on the bed backward, and was shimmying out of his pants about the time Magnus pounced on him.

Magnus had lost his shoes and jacket somewhere, his shirt flopped out of his trousers, and his fly gaped open, but otherwise he wore far too many clothes. Crawling across the big bed like a lion, he speared Belle with his gaze. Belle giggled. Oops, had that sound really come out of him? "What are you going to do to me, you gorgeous beast?"

For a second Magnus's eyes widened; then he seemed to get the game and growled. "I may eat you." He sat back on his haunches, his erection distending the front of his briefs "Or I might fuck you. Take your pick." He grinned that distorted smile Belle had come to love.

Hmm. Love. "Well, I'd rather enjoy being eaten, but I think fucking sounds better—if I get to return the favor."

"Oh, you think you can hold off your orgasm through a whole fuck, my pretty sex fiend? Because otherwise your weapon will have faded from the field before you ever get it in my ass." Magnus raised an eyebrow.

Well, he had a point. "What if you go first? You're soooooo old, I mean being nearly thirty-one and all, you should have better control, right?"

"I can certainly try."

"Cool." Belle threw himself toward the nightstand and pulled out the condoms and lube. "Assume the position, old man, and prepare to get fucked."

"My pleasure." Magnus pulled off the rest of his clothes as Belle jacketed his overanxious cock and started lubing it enthusiastically, then shoved some lube in his own ass so he'd be ready for round two. Magnus extended a hand and Belle squirted lube in it, then drooled as Magnus poked a lubed finger into his own hole.

"Oh man, I want in there."

Magnus pulled his legs up, revealing his powerful ass and a beautifully gaping pucker. "Get in there and tame the beast, sweetheart."

"Oh yeah." He positioned his cock, gazing into Magnus's eyes. "Remember, don't come, 'cause I want some too."

"Your wish is my command, my beauty."

Belle pushed in. Hot, tight heaven. Magnus's eyes closed, and Belle's followed as he started to ride. It felt different trying to come fast rather than slow. Kind of fun for a change. Belle pounded his hips and let the white heat carry him. Every thrust lit up nerves all along his cock and sent lightning flashes into his balls. *Oh yeah. Oh boy.* Fucking Magnus was so damned great. So much fun.

He peeked open an eye and saw Magnus gritting his teeth, trying not to come. *Okay, get on with it, Belle.* He leaned forward on his arms and snapped his hips into Magnus's ass like a platinum blond jackhammer. *Crap.* Yes, that was wonderful. *So good. Oh man, too good. Good. Good. Yes!* Flash. The fire exploded in his balls and his brain at the same moment, lighting up his vision and releasing pleasure into every cell. "Oh God!" He tossed his head, his bangs flipping against his forehead, then collapsed, every particle of his being tingling and dissolving in a relaxed puddle of gooey joy.

For one second Magnus let Belle rest against his chest, then rose and flipped. Belle was piled on his back. Magnus had himself sheathed and lubed before Belle could muster the strength to pull up his legs to give Magnus access.

Belle giggled. "Mmm. Enjoy."

Magnus plowed inside, and his breath came like a Kentucky Derby winner as he pounded his big cock into Belle's totally tensionless ass. It felt wonderful, like a sexy dream—half exhilarated and half relaxed.

Magnus huffed, "Oh God, baby, you're so sexy. I love having you in me and I love being in you."

"Mmmmeeee too. Love. Love." His head lolled as his hole accommodated that incomparable cock, spreading waves of sweetness and heat through his groin. He half wanted to stay dreamy, but his dick, which clearly should never have been able to move again, was flexing like a wind sock in a growing breeze.

"Oh God, Belle. I love this so much." Magnus's abdomen rubbed against Belle's penis, creating just enough friction to raise the dead.

Guess who showed up.

Magnus laughed. "My beautiful sex fiend." He grabbed Belle's cock and started cranking as his hips thrust his dick against Belle's gland and shot bolts of pleasure through Belle's balls, up his spine, and into his head.

"Yes, Magnus. Right there. Like that. Oh God. Yes!"

"Just right for you, my beauty?"

"Perfect. You're perfect. Oh, Magnus!"

Magnus threw his head back and yelled as Belle's cum spurted into his hand. Amazing that such a small burst of jism could cause such a huge tidal wave of ecstasy.

Magnus froze and then started to shake as the orgasm washed over him. One, two, three spasms, and then he collapsed his full weight onto Belle's chest. So wonderful.

Belle's eyes closed. "Love. Love." That's all he remembered.

CHAPTER 18

QUIETLY MAGNUS padded down the stairs toward the atrium, the blackness of night showing through the glass ceiling. He'd thrown on some jeans he'd been keeping at Belle's and pulled on his bathrobe. If he kept this up, he'd have half his wardrobe in Belle's apartment soon. It was just so easy to be there. But really, it wasn't fair to Belle. He sighed. Belle drew energy from all this green. Maybe he would too.

As softly as he could, he opened the sliding door to the magical garden. Henry's transplanted Jamaica. Every kind of tropical tree, plant, and flower grew in here. Magnus didn't even know a lot of their names. Maybe some of them would be good botanicals for cosmetics. The moisture of the air and the heavy scents of soil and flowers surrounded him.

He slid the door closed, walked in the dim light to the teak glider, and sat. With a push, he set the glider in motion.

"Having trouble sleeping?"

Magnus jumped and looked behind him to where Mr. Pennymaker emerged from the jungle. Magnus pressed a hand to his chest. "You scared the shit out of me."

"Ah, sorry. One must keep one's shit, yes?" He chortled. "I often come here at night if I have trouble staying asleep. It's so comforting to be close to nature."

"I thought I'd try it out. Belle seems to like it."

"Yes. Belle likes many good things." Mr. P. sat in the garden chair opposite Magnus.

Magnus glanced up at Mr. P's steady gaze. "Any chance you're Superman?"

"I suppose it's possible. Why do you ask?"

Magnus snorted. "I think you can see through metal."

"Ah, and do you want to be seen through, Magnus?"

Excellent question. "Maybe."

"It's good for all of us to be gotten by someone, much as Belle gets you, I think."

"Hell no, he doesn't." He shook his head vehemently.

"Oh? How so?"

"I don't even know what a beautiful kid like that is doing messing around with me." He frowned. Christian's face flashed in his mind.

"Belle's a grown man with a lot of life experience. He can decide for himself what's good."

"Like hell. He's an angel descended from heaven, and he shouldn't be subjected to the likes of me."

Mr. P. crossed his arms. "So what are you doing with him if you're so bad for him? You're not the kind of man to do evil on purpose to hurt another."

Magnus dropped his head in his hands. "I know, but he's just so—"

"Perfect? Exactly what you want?"

He looked up. "He seems to be too much temptation for me to resist."

"Do you think he's tempting you on purpose?"

"No." He glanced at Mr. P. "Not exactly."

"Why do you think he wants to be with you?"

He shrugged.

"For your money?"

"God no. Belle doesn't seem to care about money."

"Out of gratitude?"

He blew out his breath. "Yes. He doesn't see it and he gets mad when I say it, but I think he's just grateful I helped Judy."

"Umm. I see."

Magnus looked up. "You do?"

"Well, if you say it's true. Myself, I can imagine how a person might be forced to have sex with someone they don't care for in order to feed themselves or their children, but it's hard to picture doing so because a person did a favor for a friend, especially when the favor is already accomplished." He smiled. "I've heard of being blinded by love, but never by gratitude."

"You don't understand."

"Don't I? What I see is a young man who arrived here lonely, suspicious, and lost. Now he glows with purpose and joy. That's not gratitude, Magnus. That's love." Mr. P. stood to his full five feet and a little. "Never try to pull the wool over Superman's eyes." He winked and walked out of the atrium.

Magnus stared after him. He didn't understand. Did he?

BELLE STRAIGHTENED Magnus's tie. "How long will you be gone? One day, I hope?"

Magnus stretched his neck to give Belle access. "I wish. No, it'll be several days at least."

"Damn. Cleveland is looking better and better."

"If it stretches out, I'll just fly you out, okay?"

Belle smiled. "Okay." He patted the tie. "Sorry I can't go to the airport with you. I would have rescheduled the contractors if I'd known earlier."

"I'm taking the private jet, so I won't be at the airport long. I'll call you from the air."

Belle wrapped his arms tight around Magnus. He'd always been happy alone. Well, if not happy, at least reasonably content. He'd never had anything in common with his brothers, so not sharing their activities never mattered to him that much. No guy ever really did it for him, so after some fast sex, he didn't miss them. Now he couldn't imagine being without Magnus for one night. "Be safe. I really will miss you."

Magnus held him at arm's length, seeming to fight mistiness in his eyes. "I can't imagine why." He smiled. "But I'm so glad."

Well, that was a step.

Belle followed Magnus down the stairs, where Wanda, Judy, and Mr. P. all joined in the bon voyage. Each gave him a hug, and then Belle got in one more. As Magnus walked down the steps, Leroy waved to Belle. "Be back in an hour, boss."

Belle nodded, fighting the desire to run down the steps and leap in the car with Magnus.

Judy put a hand on his shoulder. "You okay?"

He sighed. "Yes. I have tons to do. But I just have this uneasy feeling."

"You guys haven't been apart since you started seeing each other."

"Yeah. That's probably all it is."

Two hours later he stood in the shell of the building he'd arranged to lease. It was large, with the potential for both big and small rooms for group gatherings and intimate discussions. Above all it had light pouring into every corner from huge floor-to-ceiling windows. He didn't want to compromise that once it was renovated. Somehow light needed to reach even the interior of the building. He'd been through the details of the build-out with one contractor and was waiting for the second to arrive.

He looked up when the door opened. Judy walked in with a good half of her normal bounce, which represented a victory. "Hey, sweetie. What are you doing out and about?"

"I just had to see it. I'm so excited. I conned Leroy into bringing me with promises that I'd take a nap after."

"That man does get around. What do you think?" He turned in a circle, arms spread toward the unfinished walls.

"The light is amazing."

"Yes, that was my favorite thing. Now we just have to be sure the inner offices and meeting rooms don't become caves. I'm not sure how to do that, but glass comes to mind."

"Hmm." She glanced around. "Sometimes a cave is a good thing, or at least a powerful sense of privacy. So I think some of the rooms might have glass high in the walls to keep them bright but not too revealing."

"Great idea. Why don't you stay with me for the next contractor meeting—" His cell rang. "Oh. Maybe the guy's canceling." He pulled out his phone and frowned. "No. It's Rick. I haven't talked to him since I got here." He clicked to answer and smiled at Judy as he said, "Hello, Rick. How are you?"

"Not good, Belle. It's Dad. He's really not doing well. It could be it."

"What do you mean 'it'? You're not saying—"

"I just think you need to get here as soon as you can."

"Shit, Rick! How did this happen? Nobody told me he was sick."

"Hell, what did you expect? All the stress of dealing with your fucking product and not being able to make it work and you not helping."

"I couldn't." Damn, he was wasting time trying to justify himself. "Where is he? I'll get there as soon as I can."

"Just come home. I'll take it from there."

"Okay. Thanks." He clicked off and took deep breaths.

"What is it, Belle? Your father?"

He nodded, trying not to hyperventilate. "Rick says he's really bad. Sweetie, could you stay here a few minutes and tell the contractor I was

called away on an emergency? Tell him I'll reschedule as soon as I get back."
He hugged her. "And if he takes too long, don't worry. Just leave."

The door opened and a tall man walked in. Belle ran to him.
"Sorry. I've had an emergency. I'll call you as soon as I get back." He
turned to Judy. "You go home with Leroy. I'll take a cab back to the
office and talk to HR."

He ran out, waved off Leroy, and whistled for a cab. Fifteen minutes
later, he'd made it to HR at Beauty, Inc. and explained he had a family
emergency. They told him to take as much time as he needed. He ran to
Owen's office.

Owen looked up as Belle flew in his door. "What's wrong?"

"My father's ill. Will you keep tabs on the center for me? I'll e-mail
you all the details."

"Of course. Is there anything else I can do?"

"No, thanks. That will be huge."

By the time he reemerged on the sidewalk in front of the building,
Leroy had pulled up in front. He jumped out and held the door for Belle.
"Get in, boss. Judy told me. She's getting your clothes together at your
place. You call about flights while I drive."

"Yes, thank you so much." He slid in and had the phone to his ear
by the time Leroy closed the door. Reservations made, twenty minutes
later he jumped out and ran to his apartment with Leroy behind him.
The door to his place stood open, and Mr. P. and Wanda had obviously
enlisted themselves to pack in Judy's place. She sat on his bed giving
orders while they rummaged through his underwear drawer.

Despite the fact that Wanda giggled at his pink-and-white bikini
briefs he'd bought just for Magnus, he gave her a one-armed hug.
"Thanks so much for helping, you guys."

Mr. P. frowned. Not an expression you saw a lot on his face. "So
your father is ill?"

"Yes. My brother wasn't too specific, but he said he was serious.
I'm guessing the drinking has taken over. Rick and Rusty have never
been able to get him to do much for himself. Of course, I'm not much
better, but at least I can be there for him."

"Is he in the hospital?"

"I think so. My brother said to come to the house and he'd—" What had his words been? "—take it from there."

"Interesting."

Yes, it was an odd choice of words. Belle grabbed a suit and a couple of pairs of jeans from his closet to add to the toiletries already assembled. He pulled his laptop off the desk and snagged his phone charger. "I've got to hurry. I got a last-minute 'family illness' flight, but it's going to be close."

Leroy grabbed the closed suitcase. "I'll get you there."

If anyone could, it had to be Leroy.

Belle kissed Judy's cheek, hugged Mr. P. and Wanda, and took off like a bat. When he got in the car, he hit speed dial for Magnus.

"Belle?"

"Hi. I'm so sorry to bother you."

"No bother. A nice surprise. We're cruising toward Cleveland."

"I just need to tell you that—" He swallowed. "—my dad is sick and I need to go home. I got an emergency flight, and Leroy's taking me there now."

"Oh God, I'm so sorry. I can have the pilot turn around and take me back to New York. Pick you up. We'll go together."

"No, dear, wait. I'm not sure what the situation is, so I don't want you to change your plans." The fact that Magnus was ready to toss over his whole trip for Belle about made his heart burst. "I'll be on the plane before you'd get back. I'll call you from Oregon and tell you what's what, okay?"

"You're sure? Family illness is so tough."

"Thank you so much for wanting to be there." A grin crept across his lips for the first time in hours. "Besides, if you come with me, my brothers may end up in the hospital too from shock."

"There is that." Magnus chuckled, and the vibration seemed to transfer from the phone to Belle's balls.

"I miss you already."

"Me too. Call me as soon as you know the status, okay?"

"Will do." He hung there. The words *I love you* strained against his tongue. "Uh, have a good trip."

"Not without you. Talk soon."

Belle hung up and stared at the phone.

Leroy said, "You sure you don't want him to come to Oregon? It'd be great to have the support."

Belle nodded. "It really would." He sighed. He and Magnus were so new. Too new for family crap. "But that would be selfish, and I'm trying to be more like Magnus." A little frown crept across his forehead. "Besides, I need to know what's happening before I drag Magnus all the way across the country."

CHAPTER 19

BELLE YANKED up the handle on his suitcase and started pulling it behind him as he walked through the terminal. No Leroy to meet him. No brothers either. He hadn't really expected it. Just hoped.

Jesus, Belle, you're spoiled.

He'd already tried to get Rick once when he landed. No answer. He hit Redial.

One ring. Two.

"Hullo."

"Rick?"

"Yeah, bro. You're here. Good."

"Where shall I meet you? At the hospital? Which one?"

"Uh, no. Dad's here. But it's too late. Come tomorrow, okay?"

"So—what? You want me to take a cab all the way to my place and then back to the house tomorrow morning? I killed myself to get here tonight. It's only ten."

"Uber's cheaper."

"Rick, why can't I see Dad?" A woman rushing past him gave him a stare, so he lowered his voice. "What's going on?"

"Sleeping."

"Why can't I come there?"

"We're all sleeping. See you tomorrow, okay?" He hung up.

Shit! He was half tempted to go to his father's house anyway. But the truth was, he'd rather go to his place. He walked to the rental car desk. Sounded like he was going to need his own wheels.

BELLE DROVE into the upscale neighborhood outside Portland where he'd grown up. So many memories—almost all of them tinged with sadness. Being alone while his brothers played. Waiting at the door for his dad to come home and finally falling asleep on the rug like a German shepherd. Nursing his mom through her illness.

I feel weird.

Yes. Because that crazy-assed apartment in New York full of friends and wisdom and flowers—and Magnus—felt more like home than this ever had. *I want to go home.*

He pulled up in front of the Tudor-style home—so different from his taste. He hadn't called Magnus yet this morning. *As soon as I figure out what the hell is going on.*

After turning off the ignition on the barely adequate American car he'd rented, he hurried up the walkway. Both Rick and Rusty's cars were here. His dad's must be in the garage.

He'd forgotten his key, so he rang the bell. Like with the phone, it took two tries.

Rusty opened the door. He looked—odd. Kind of like he was holding back a smile. Or maybe he was trying not to cry. Belle grabbed Rusty's arms. "What's wrong? Where's Dad? What the fuck is going on?"

"No worries, baby brother." He grinned. "You're right on time. Come on in." He stepped aside and let Belle into the foyer.

"Time for what?" Belle looked around at the familiar baroque paintings and dark wood furnishings. His mom had liked a lighter traditional look, but this was luxury to his dad. Everything seemed a little—dusty, for lack of a better word. Not that it wasn't clean. It just looked unloved. "Where's Dad?"

Rusty pointed toward the hall that led to the family room.

What the hell was happening? Belle rushed toward the sound of voices. When he burst into the family room, his dad was lying on the couch, with Rick in a chair beside him. For a second Belle's heart stuttered. *Wait.* A glass of something that looked suspiciously like whiskey and ice sat on the coffee table beside him. The TV blared a football game. This could be any Sunday afternoon at the Belleterres'—except it wasn't Sunday and it sure as fuck wasn't afternoon. Belle stopped in the middle of the room and crossed his arms. "Will someone please tell me what's happening here?"

His dad waved a hand. "Great game. Grab a chair. Want some coffee?"

A black wave filled Belle's head. He wanted to scream, pass out, break something. He controlled his voice. "Why am I here?"

"Why, to see your dear old Dad, of course. Rick told you how badly I wanted to see you, right?"

"No. He told me you were sick."

Rick leaned back in his chair. "No I didn't, Belle. I said Dad was real bad. You must have assumed the rest."

"You knew what I assumed." The words squeezed out between his teeth.

"Whatever."

Rusty came in from the kitchen with a cup of coffee. It was black. No one in his family ever seemed to remember he liked cream. That tiny fact wormed into his brain until he wanted to collapse, crying. "So I can go back to New York, then?"

Rusty snorted. "Uh, maybe not."

"What do you—" His phone rang. Probably Magnus wondering what was happening. As if he knew. He clicked. "Hello. Sorry I didn't—"

"Dr. Belleterre."

"What? Oh, yes." He glanced at the phone, then looked up when he heard Rusty snicker.

"Dr. Belleterre, we've been informed that you have decided to return to work for your family's company. Since they're technically a competitor, we'll consider your resignation tendered as of now."

"What?"

"I believe your personal possessions are still in your office. I'll ask Leroy to pack them up for you. Since your residence is supplied by the company, I'll ask that you make other arrangements as quickly as possible. I hope you've left your projects in good order—"

"Wait! I didn't resign."

"Sir, I was informed by a member of the board, and it's been all over the trades this morning. I believe a press release was put on the wire with a rather deprecating quote from you regarding our company. If you haven't resigned, this is certainly an odd turn of events, and I suggest you work it out with a Beauty, Inc. executive. It's no longer a job for HR." She hung up.

Every cell in his body turned to ice. His job that he loved—his home—gone. Slowly, he raised his eyes to his father and brothers. "You did this."

Rick nodded. "We helped. Apparently you made a few enemies at that company you've been aiding and abetting. They did most of it."

"Why?"

His father sat up. "I made it very clear to you that we need you desperately or Bella Terra may go under. When a way to get you out of there presented itself, we jumped at it. You belong here."

Rusty nodded. "Yeah, we were just thinking of you, bro."

Belle let out a long stream of air. "You didn't ask me or let me know what you were planning. It made no difference to you what I wanted?"

Rick yelled, "Hell, Belle, make up your frickin' mind. You were pissed you had to go, and now you're pissed we brought you back."

I need to call Magnus now. He turned on his heel and ran down the hall and out the front door.

"Belle!" his father called after him, but he raced to the rental car and started it. Hitting speed dial, he clicked his phone on speaker and pulled away from the curb.

He tapped his fingers on the steering wheel. If Magnus heard the stories, what would he think? "Come on, pick up."

"Hello, this is Magnus. Sorry to have missed you. Leave me a message and I'll get back to you."

Tears spurted from Belle's eyes at the sound of that wonderful voice.

Beep.

"Magnus, it's Belle. I didn't quit. My family engineered this with someone in Beauty, Inc. Please believe me. I didn't know anything. I don't want to be here. I want to be with you. Wherever you are, I'm there. Please. I want to come home. Please." He dropped his head on the steering wheel. "Please."

Beep!

The driver of the car behind him leaned on the horn, and Belle took off from the now green light. It took forty-five minutes, but he made it to his house—he could no longer think of it as home.

He wandered through the small house and out to the backyard. He'd paid a neighbor boy to care for his plants, but the yard was still overgrown. The glider looked kind of inviting. With a flop he sat on the old cushion and started to rock, turning his face up to the misty air. *Nice. Not the same.* No rich soil or sweet scent of tropical flowers. Why didn't Magnus call him back? He looked at his phone. Only noon his time. That meant three in Cleveland. Must be in a meeting. Maybe he hadn't even read the trades. He sighed. This was Magnus. The man knew everything about everything. But would he believe it?

He sprang out of the glider. Oh hell, he *would* believe it. Magnus would believe that Belle was using him before he'd believe he loved him. Wait. Loved? Shit yes. Love. He loved Magnus Strong.

I have to tell him. I have to. Even if he doesn't love me back, I can't have him think that I'd betray him. He grabbed his phone and dialed.

"Hellooo, my boy."

"Mr. P, hi. Do you know what's happened?"

"I think so. I was contacted by HR at Beauty, Inc., saying you're no longer employed and therefore they will no longer require the apartment. But no worries, my dear. You know I'll keep it for you for as long as you need it."

"I need it forever."

"Oh?"

"Yes. I'm coming back, Mr. P. Even if Beauty, Inc. won't take me back, I'll find another job somewhere. I have to be near Magnus. I know he's going to believe this story, but it's not true."

"Why do you think he'll believe it?"

"Because he'll believe anything bad about himself, so he's going to figure that I just played along until I could get away. But I love him, Mr. P. And I can't let him think he's someone who doesn't deserve to be loved. I'll find some way to get through to him."

"Ah, bravo, Belle. But have you read the gossips today?"

"No. I don't usually read gossip blogs."

"Might want to check them out, my dear. Have you talked to Judy?"

"Not yet."

"She's worried sick, but I'll tell her you're fine and will be back soon. I'll let her know you have a few other important things to do first."

"I do?"

"Yes. I believe so."

MAGNUS SAT on the bed and stared at his laptop. Interesting that this e-mail came from Christian. According to him, Belle had used his father's health as an excuse to return to Bella Terra. Christian said Belle was back in Oregon and planning to stay there.

Magnus's heart hammered, and he took a couple of deep breaths to try to slow it down. He clicked on a few more links. The press release appeared in dozens of online media. Right down to the quote from Belle saying he'd paid his debt to Beauty, Inc. and now was returning to his true calling and his true home at Bella Terra. He planned to show Beauty, Inc. the ropes with his new resurfacing cream.

Magnus closed the laptop, got up, and crossed to the window. Outside, the sun shone brightly on the blue of the ocean. No Cleveland. There had never been a Cleveland trip. He'd planned to surprise Belle. Some surprise. Belle was back in Oregon.

What was the likelihood that Belle had anything to do with that news release? Almost zero. The timing just didn't work. The news must have come out seconds after Belle hit the ground in Portland. Plus Christian's part in the communication seemed damned suspicious.

He let out his breath in a long sigh and sank into a chair.

Was this actually a blessing? Belle was caught between his love for his family and the product he'd created, and his sense of obligation to Magnus and Beauty, Inc. He'd never go home as long as he felt he had a debt to pay. But now his leaving had been engineered for him—probably with no participation on his part. Wasn't it best to just leave it alone? *I was horribly selfish dragging him here. I deluded myself into thinking it was for his own good, but Belle was right. I really wanted to get into his pants.*

Magnus leaned his head back and let a few tears seep from his eyes.

Belle needed to go home. He loved Oregon and his family—worthless as they were. Belle couldn't stay in New York paying his so-called debts of gratitude to Magnus forever. Soon Magnus would send Judy home too, and then Belle would have his friend. He'd forget all about New York and Beauty, Inc. and Magnus soon enough.

Magnus wiped a big hand across his face. His ugly face.

The door opened. "Okay, Señor Strong, you must rest and prepare. Let me put the computer away with your phone. Big day tomorrow."

Should he check his phone? Hell, what would he say? *Leave it be.* He'd taken care of everything before he left. Now he could relax. He let out a breath between his teeth. Relax—bullshit. "Thanks, Maria. Here you go." He handed her the computer and went back to gazing at the ocean.

"No. No!" Belle stared at the screen.

Beauty industry billionaire Magnus Strong, famous for his ugly face, is rumored to finally be going under the knife to repair his scars stemming from a childhood accident. Why now, Mr. Strong? Could it have something to do with a beautiful young scientist who makes you want to be a prettier man? LOL, Mr. Strong. LOL.

Belle fell back on the bed and cried—for about two minutes. Then he sat up, gritted his teeth, and grabbed his phone.

An hour later his ear hurt from being pressed against the phone so hard, and he was hoarse from yelling and begging, but he had some answers—maybe. And he had a reservation. He ran to his safe, pulled out his passport, slammed the lid on the suitcase he'd brought, and started for the door. Then stopped.

Rusty and Rick stood in the middle of his living room.

Belle frowned. "Did I leave the door open?"

Rick nodded. "Ajar."

"I don't have time to deal with you now. I have an appointment."

Rick crossed his arms. His big arms. His oldest brother outweighed Belle by a hundred pounds. "An appointment to go back to your beloved new company? Fucking traitor. You won't be welcome back."

Rusty nodded and copied Rick by folding his arms. "Plus you have to stay here and get the product packaging working. The company's going to go under because of you."

Belle stared at his brothers—the brothers who'd let him spend his childhood alone and now didn't care if he spent his life alone. "That's bullshit. If the company goes under, it's because Dad drank and gambled it away and you two spent it away." He walked toward the door. "I have to go."

Rick stepped into his path. "We can't let you do that, Belle."

Belle paused. Would they really keep him from leaving?

CHAPTER 20

"READY TO go, Señor Strong? It's time." The nurse, Maria, smiled.

Magnus took one last long look out the window. Funny how the ocean changed so much from one minute to the other. From day to night to day. Black as hell to deep blue to aqua to almost white. Flat as ice to tossing and roiling. Like his guts.

He got up, wearing his hospital gown, and walked to the gurney the nurse held at his door. *Wish I could get peaceful.* He'd planned this as a gift to Belle. Now his reason was gone. *Oh well, shit. Why not? I can let go of the past. I can.* He crawled onto the moveable bed and lay down.

Maria fussed around him. "Are you comfortable?"

No. The answer was hell no. "I'm fine."

A young med tech started pushing the gurney down the hospital hall. A sign on the wall in Spanish and English said Surgery, with an arrow.

Magnus's stomach flipped.

His surgeon, Dr. Morales, stepped up beside the gurney and walked next to him. "How are you feeling, Magnus?"

"Okay." His fists clenched and unclenched.

"Remember, our current techniques will be able to erase most of the damage. You'll find the change to be remarkable."

"I'm kind of used to my ugly puss."

"And you'll enjoy the new face even more."

"What if—" He swallowed hard and his stomach heaved. "Wait."

Dr. Morales frowned. "What?"

"I need my phone. Stop and get me my phone."

Maria put her warm hand on his arm. "We'll get it for you as soon as you awaken."

He shook his head and sat up. Crap, he couldn't breathe. "No. I'm sorry, but I have to have it now."

She looked at Morales. "Doctor?"

The doc shrugged. "Get him the phone."

She took off running in her soft-soled shoes, which made little squeaks on the polished floors.

For minutes Magnus stared at his hands while the doctor and tech spoke to each other in Spanish. Magnus gathered the gist was how the American businessman didn't usually make any demands, so they were cutting him some slack.

Why now, idiot? You could have checked your phone last night or this morning.

Because I want—hell, I don't know what I want.

Maria ran back from the office where they'd stashed his phone and handed it to him. He nodded. "Thank you."

Everyone waited while he turned it on. It sorted through a lot of downloads, and the Wi-Fi was pretty bad considering they were outside the surgical suite in a hospital, but finally he could see his messages. The office. The office. Christian. HR. *Belle.*

He ran his finger over the name, then hit Play and pressed it to his ear. Belle's sweet voice filled his head. Tears gathered in Magnus's eyes and ran down his face, but he barely noticed. He might not have been able to say what he wanted, but he knew it when he heard it.

"I want to come home. Please. Please."

Dr. Morales asked, "Bad news, Mr. Strong?"

"No. Not exactly."

Magnus's head snapped up at the noise at the end of the hall.

Around the corner flew Belle, with three technicians and a nurse on his tail. He ran like Mercury chasing the sun until he saw Magnus, then stopped as if someone had nailed his sneakers to the floor. "Magnus. Don't!"

"Don't what, Belle?"

The techs and the nurse grabbed Belle's arms.

Magnus's voice filled the hall. "Let go of him, please. Now."

Their hands might as well have been on rubber strings, they moved so fast.

Belle took three steps forward. "This. Don't do this." He almost fell forward two more paces. "I mean, if you've realized you don't have to pay a debt to your mother and you want to do this, then fine. But Magnus, if even a tiny part of your reason is for—me, or-or others, please know that I love you just as you are. I look at your dear face and see the kindness and generosity and goodness, and you're beautiful and I want to look at your face just as it is forever." He swiped at his eyes. "And-and I'm sure this is true for all the people who love you."

He'd said "love." Magnus cocked his head. "Are you saying you love me like—my employees love me?" His heart lived somewhere just behind his soft palate.

Belle wiped his running nose on his sleeve. *Okay, adorable.* "Fuck no. If anyone on your staff loves you like I do, I'll cut out their heart and feed it to Henry's Venus flytrap."

Magnus wanted to laugh—and cry. Belle gazed at the floor, and Magnus saw a bruise forming on the side of his face. "Belle, what happened to you? Did someone hurt you?"

Belle's huge eyes glanced up. "Uh, I caught my brother's fist on the side of my face as I was slamming my suitcase into his belly."

"What?" Magnus leaped off the gurney. "I'll kill the bastard."

Belle cocked a smile. "You'll have to pick him up off the floor first."

Magnus felt a breeze on his butt and finally looked at Maria, Dr. Morales, and the tech, all smiling like they were watching a chick flick. "Uh, sorry. I guess that's the bottom line, doc. I can't get a new face, because the man I love loves this one."

The doctor nodded. "That seems like the best reason I ever heard for not getting plastic surgery."

Belle squeaked, "Did you say 'love'? The man—you love?"

"Of course. You don't think I'd go under the knife for my favorite chemist, do you?"

Belle squealed and ran full speed toward Magnus. A couple of steps away, he leaped, and Magnus caught him, effectively flashing the entire hospital corridor with a view of his ass.

Magnus laughed. "How about we get on the gurney and let these kind people give us a ride back to my room so I don't share any more of my anatomy with the hospital?"

Magnus crawled up, and Belle hopped up beside him. They entertained the patients as they kissed their way down the hall.

BELLE SNUGGLED against Magnus and watched the clouds roll by. "My family is so envious of this plane. We saw it in Las Vegas."

"Where we met."

Belle smiled. "Yes."

"I'm really sorry about your family. When I heard you'd gone back to Oregon, I thought you'd probably stay. After all, you didn't want to come to New York. I figured that even though your father has his issues, you'd rather help him with his company than come back to mine."

Belle let out a long breath. "I want to help my father, but I can't help as fast as he tears things apart. Mostly himself."

"I'm so sorry. Did you really hit your brother with a suitcase?"

Belle nodded and glanced up at Magnus. "He got between me and coming to find you. I guess I had an adrenaline rush. He sure did look surprised, lying there on the floor as I stepped over him."

"How on earth did you find me?"

Belle chuckled. "Promise she won't get in trouble?"

"Hmm. Are we talking Judy here?"

"How'd you guess?"

"Uh, charming birds from trees, etc."

"Yes. I called her, desperate. She managed to talk HR into telling her where you were. She said she had important legal issues she had to clear with you."

"I see. Who ever heard of a lawyer telling a lie?" He snorted.

"It wasn't a lie."

"No?"

"Nope. She figured you'd have to bail me out of jail if anyone tried to keep me from finding you."

Magnus laughed.

"Magnus?"

"Hmm?"

"Why were you going to do it, really?"

Magnus sighed against Belle's ear. "Originally I planned it as a surprise for you. Then when I heard about the press release, I thought I wouldn't see you again. I suppose I wanted a way to show you I had—let go of the past, at least a little. So you'd understand I could change. Not because I thought you'd come back, exactly. Just so you'd—know, I guess. Know how you'd impacted my life. How I'd never be the same for having known you and loved you. How you'd made me better." He shrugged.

"Oh, say it again."

Magnus smiled. "What?"

"That you love me."

"I do, Belle. I have, I guess, from the moment I saw you in that restaurant in Las Vegas."

He looked up and grinned. "Now say, 'I'm as better as I ever need to be.'"

"You don't want to make me over to suit yourself?" Magnus laughed. "You suit me fine."

"Will you forgive me if it doesn't sink in all the time?"

"What?"

"That I'm lucky enough to have you."

"We can remind each other." Belle sipped his champagne. "So you took care of everything with HR?"

"Oh yes. They were really upset when they found out they'd been duped by Christian. Your personal items are being returned to your office as we speak. Judy's been overseeing the build-out of the center, with a lot of help from Leroy's mom. Oh, and Christian's no longer a member of the board. I acquainted the chairman with his machinations, and they gladly replaced him with a woman executive the board had been wanting to bring on. Stupid to not have women on the board of a cosmetics company."

"Perfect. In fact, if you don't count my idiot family, everything feels pretty damned great."

Magnus gave him a little smile and held him closer.

A few hours later, Leroy drove them up in front of the apartment in Brooklyn. "Home." The word slid out of Belle's mouth on a long stream of breath.

Mr. P, Wanda, Judy, Henry, Fatima, and Ahmed all crowded out onto the narrow brownstone landing, holding a slightly rumpled sign that said Welcome Home, Belle and Magnus.

Judy started to run down the stairs, but Henry snatched her up and carried her as she protested with a look of love in her eyes. Henry transferred her to Belle's arms, and she embraced him wildly and gave him a huge kiss on the cheek. "Oh God, I'm so happy you're here. I couldn't bear to live without you, but I couldn't stand to leave everyone and everything I love here behind."

"I'd never leave you on purpose."

"I knew you'd never go permanently."

Belle looked at Magnus. "You should have told him."

"I would have if I'd known where he was."

Magnus laughed. "You certainly didn't have much trouble finding me."

She slapped a hand against her mouth. "You told him."

Belle nodded. "Yep. You're fired."

For a second her face fell; then she punched Belle's arm. "Liar. Magnus needs me to tell him about what's good—like you." She laughed, which prompted Belle to put her on her feet.

Mr. P. called, "Come in, my dears, so we can all feast and hear about your trials."

When all of them, including Leroy, settled into Wanda's living room with wineglasses in their hands and piles of fresh hummus and pita bread for snacks, Ahmed said, "So your family really hijacked you?"

Belle frowned. "Yes, with a lot of help from a disgruntled member of Magnus's board who doesn't like me. I guess it was his idea, and of course, my bizarre family jumped at it."

Fatima spread her hands. "Surely they want you to be happy? Don't they know you belong here?"

"Since my mom died, my dad's gotten worse and worse. My brothers have always been, shall we say, expedient. They just encourage him. But now they're stuck because they were all counting on the new product I developed to pull the company out of the hole. But they can't get the packaging to work properly, and my dad's burning through money with his addictions. It's a mess."

Wanda asked, "Can you make the packaging work?"

"I did before. But what's the use? My father will just gamble away any money the product brings in faster than it can earn it. It's a shame."

Judy nodded. "Your baby."

"Yes. But I can't force my dad to be successful or happy."

"This is where you belong."

He took Magnus's hand. "Yes, it is."

Well fed, Belle and Magnus walked slowly up the stairs to Belle's apartment. Magnus stopped him outside the door and gave him a gentle kiss. "I love being here with you." He pushed open the door so Belle could walk through.

Belle walked in and—stopped. In the middle of the coffee table was the beautiful Moroccan bowl he'd found in a tiny antique shop. On the end tables sat some of his favorite books, and a new bookshelf showed off the covers of more books and his favorite objects. "How—?"

Magnus smiled. "I thought since this was 'home,' you should have your favorite stuff. Judy guided us, and we arranged for things to be flown here while we were leaving Mexico."

Belle walked in and just stared, his heart beating like a drum. In among his favorite objects sat some more things—things that looked like Magnus. "Are those your books?"

"Uh, yes. I'm happy to take them away. I don't mean to presume—"

"Oh my God!" Belle threw his arms around Magnus's neck. "You're moving in with me? Oh, I love you!"

Magnus laughed. "Well, I think I should show you my house, but I'm guessing we're going to spend most of our time here, don't you? With our friends?"

Our time. Our friends. Tears sprang to Belle's eyes.

"What's wrong, dear?"

"I just realized for the first time in my life, I don't feel lonely."

Magnus hugged him tight. "You may wish you had some of that alone time back after everyone in this building gets finished with you."

Belle looked up and shook his head, wiping tears from his eyes. "No. I don't mind being alone, but being with you and Mr. P. and Judy and all our friends is like being alone but better."

"I tried to buy the apartment building, but it turns out Mr. P. owns it. Did you know that?"

"No. He's an enigma on top of a mystery."

"I guess he owns real estate all over the world. I have a suspicion he could buy and sell me."

They walked into the bedroom hand in hand until Belle starting clapping and bouncing when he saw a bunch of Magnus's clothes hanging in the big closet. "I believe it. You're really here."

Magnus laughed. "I barely believe it myself, but you've changed everything for me, Belle." He walked to the bed and sat on the edge. "I think I believed I didn't deserve to be happy. That if I wasn't happy, I didn't have to bear the guilt of my mother's death. You made me happy in spite of all my beliefs." He smiled. "You're a powerful engine for change."

Belle sat next to him. "When my mother was dying, I felt angry all the time. Angry at cancer, angry at God, and most of all angry at her. But it was too horrible to face that I was pissed because she was sick, so I blamed myself. I should have taken better care of her. I should have made her go to the doctor sooner. I was a kid, but I shouldered the whole burden."

"Did you change your mind?"

"Yes, thanks to Judy. I was really angry. My father was working all the time. My brothers were carousing, and no one was looking after my mom but me. I didn't realize that was their way of coping. Anyway, I rode home on my bike and was so upset I crashed it into a tree and broke my arm. Judy came running over. She took one look at me and pitched a fit. She screamed and yelled that it was her fault. She should have been watching out for me. She should have had my bike maintained. The girl practically foamed at the mouth, beating on cushions and throwing things. I actually got scared she'd hurt herself. I grabbed her and told her to stop being ridiculous. There was nothing she could have done to protect me. She stopped, just like that, looked me in the eyes, and said, 'Then why do you blame yourself for your mom?' It was like someone hit me with a brick. She was only a kid too. So smart. So much wisdom."

Magnus sighed. "I wish I hadn't distracted my mother."

"I know. I'd feel the same way. But how many times did you distract your mom while she was driving?"

Magnus shrugged. "Hundreds, probably."

"Do you regret those?"

Magnus fell back on the bed. "Hey, for a kid, you're pretty damned smart."

"I'm sure people have said things much wiser to you over the years. You're just ready to listen." Belle stretched out beside him. "We'll never forget our moms."

"No. We won't. What was your mom's name?"

"Analie."

"Pretty."

"Yes. So was she."

They lay quietly, thinking—separately and together.

CHAPTER 21

MAGNUS TURNED on his side and Belle looked at him. Magnus ran his hands through Belle's bangs. "I had this big apartment-christening ceremony in mind. I didn't plan to get so serious."

"I don't think our moms would mind if we did a little christening." He flipped onto his stomach and looked up at Magnus with big eyes. "What did you have in mind? Hmmmm?"

"Well, I bought us a housewarming present."

That got his attention. Belle leaped to his knees. "What? I want it!"

"Look up."

Belle glanced up. *Ceiling. Hmm.* He let his eyes wander. Uh— "Would those very large hooks in the ceiling have something to do with the surprise?" He looked down at Magnus and laughed. Just the hooks were inspiring a pretty awesome reaction in his pants. "Okay, I need to see the rest."

Magnus crawled off the bed and rummaged in the closet, emerging with a contraption of canvas, ropes, and hooks.

"It's a swing." Belle watched as Magnus pulled over a chair and hooked the swing to the ceiling. He stepped off the chair and positioned the swing so it was just the right height—at his groin! "Holy crap, it's a sex swing."

"Yep, I've always heard about them. Figured we had to try it for ourselves." He grinned.

Belle crossed his arms. "Adjustable, I trust?"

"Oh yes, fully adjustable."

"I'm in!" Belle scampered off the bed and started ripping off clothes.

"I gather you like this idea." Magnus started peeling clothes too.

"Are you kidding?" His pants made it into the closet—on the floor. "Are you sure it will hold me?"

"Leroy says it will hold double my weight."

"Leroy?" He swallowed.

"One never has any secrets from one's driver."

"That's for sure." He jumped up and down, and his cock slapped against his belly. "I'm so excited."

Magnus raised an eyebrow. "I can see that."

With a lot of maneuvering, they managed to get the straps of the swing around Belle's thighs, leaving him spread-eagle and wide open. "Whew. Good thing I trust you. This is a very compromising position."

Magnus walked toward him with lube in hand. "And I intend to compromise you fully."

"I can't wait." He bounded a little in the swing. Magnus stood in front of him, penis rampant. "That is one pretty picture." He dropped to his knees, pulled Belle's swinging ass toward him, and started rimming, pushing his tongue deep into Belle's hole.

"Holy crap! Oh God." Magnus had rimmed him before, but this was different. He felt helpless and powerful at the same time. Because he was spread so wide, Magnus's tongue reached new and amazing depths.

Magnus shoved two lubed fingers in and stroked Belle's prostate until rational thought left the building, and then went back to rimming.

"Oh man, oh man, oh man. Too good. Fuck. Fuck me fast."

The fingers kept stroking. Vaguely Belle saw Magnus stand. In one move he pulled out his fingers and inserted his sheathed cock. That big, huge, honkin' phenomenon of a cock plowed into Belle's ready and willing hole. Magnus grabbed his hips and started bouncing Belle off his dick like he was trying out for Olympic trampoline. Smooth as lube. "Shit, it's like fucking in spaaaaace."

Magnus set up a rhythm. Suddenly he pulled out, twisted the straps, and started ramming Belle from behind. New nerve bundles joined the symphony of pleasure, zinging bolts of ecstasy into Belle's balls. Time? Space? Long gone. All he had was joy. Even the orgasm that sent him into the lower reaches of the stratosphere couldn't compete with the river of love that poured from Belle's heart. "I love yoooooou." And the spurts of cum pouring out of his cock added their own punctuation marks.

THE REPORTER pointed at the building, all shiny and new, and the line that stretched to the corner of women waiting to get in. She smiled at

Belle and Magnus. "Mr. Strong, you must be very proud of your new project. It's going to be so important to the city of New York."

"Thank you, but it's actually Dr. Belleterre's project, from conception to reality. I'm just here basking in his glory."

She laughed. "But I notice it's named for you."

"No, it's actually named for my mother, Beatrice Strong. That was Belle's idea too. B. Strong Center. We hope it will resonate with women who are fighting cancer or those helping their friends and family in the battle."

"B. Strong." She smiled and blinked hard. "It's wonderful."

"Dr. Belleterre, why aren't you two in there greeting your guests?"

Belle smiled. "It's not our show. This center is for and about the needs of women. We have two wonderful cancer survivors greeting their sisters inside."

"I look forward to meeting them." She stepped a little closer with her mic. "So, now that you have this great program underway, what's next?"

Belle glanced at Magnus. "If this one is well received—"

She laughed. "I'd say it's already proving that."

"Yes, well, we hope to open B. Strong Centers in other cities around the country."

"Any new and exciting products to tell the world about?"

Magnus smiled. "I hope to have a major announcement for you very soon." He squeezed Belle's hand.

"Oh, I can't wait. Speaking personally, of course." She grinned. "Thank you both for your time today. I'm going inside for some champagne."

"Enjoy."

Mr. Pennymaker came out of the Center, carrying two glasses of champagne. "Here, my dears. I know we mustn't drink on the streets, but I'm sure the city will forgive you most anything today." He handed them each a glass. "Now, Magnus, I think you have something to tell Belle."

Belle looked up at the beautiful, ugly face of the man he loved. "You do?"

Magnus stared at his champagne. *Uh-oh.*

"Is everything okay?" Belle's pulse quickened.

"I hope so." Magnus glanced at Mr. P, then back at Belle. "I hope you won't think I'm being high-handed, but I—" He took a breath. "—bought your product line from your father."

"What?"

"I bought your baby from Ron. I offered to buy the whole company, but he said he wanted to have something for your brothers."

Mr. P. smiled. "Rumors are that you paid a rather substantially larger price than Mr. Belleterre had any right to expect."

"Well, not really, because I have the secret weapon. Belle. I know he can make the new product work just as he planned, so it's worth a lot to Beauty, Inc. More than it would ever be to Bella Terra."

Mr. P. nodded. "And I also believe there were stipulations."

Magnus turned to Belle. Belle just stared at him with his mouth open. "I put in the contract the condition that your father go to rehab. I know forcing someone into rehab isn't ideal, but I thought it might be worth a try. Plus I'm doling out the payments over time so he won't gamble away the money in one shot."

Belle wiped at his face. How was it possible he got to have all this? "I don't even know what to say. Except thank you. This means so much to me."

"I even have a name for the product."

"You do?"

"I thought we'd call it Analie."

Tears dripped down Belle's chin as he nodded. "I think that's a perfect name."

Magnus looked at him steadily. "Are you grateful?"

"Unimaginably grateful."

"Good. Because there's something you can do for me in return."

Belle cocked his head. "So you don't mind that I'm grateful to you?"

"Nope."

"Good. It's about time you asked for something for yourself. What can I do for you, my love?"

Magnus produced one perfect lavender rose from his pocket and handed it to Belle. "You can marry me."

Belle shrieked and leaped at Magnus, kissing him as he crawled up him like a tree—just in time for fifty news cameras to capture the photo.

TARA LAIN writes the Beautiful Boys of Romance in LGBT romance novels that star her unique, charismatic heroes. Her bestselling novels have garnered awards for Best Series, Best Contemporary Romance, Best Erotic Romance, Best Ménage, Best LGBT Romance, and Best Gay Characters, and Tara has been named Best Writer of the Year in the LRC Awards. Readers often call her books "sweet," even with all that hawt sex, because Tara believes in love and her books deliver on happy-ever-after. In her other job, Tara owns an advertising and public relations firm. Her love of creating book titles comes from years of manifesting ad headlines for everything from analytical instruments to semiconductors. She does workshops on both author promotion and writing craft. She lives with her soulmate husband and her soulmate dog (who's a little jealous of all those cat pictures Tara posts on FB) in Laguna Niguel, California, near the seaside towns where she sets a lot of her books. Passionate about diversity, justice, and new experiences, Tara says that on her tombstone, it will say "Yes!"

E-mail: tara@taralain.com
Website: www.taralain.com
Blog: www.taralain.com/blog
Goodreads: www.goodreads.com/author/show/4541791.Tara_Lain
Pinterest: pinterest.com/taralain
Twitter: @taralain
Facebook: www.facebook.com/taralain
Barnes & Noble: www.barnesandnoble.com/s/Tara-Lain?keyword=Tara
+Lain&store=book
ARe: www.allromanceebooks.com/storeSearch.
html?searchBy=author&qString=Tara+Lain

DRIVEN SNOW

TARA LAIN

A Pennymaker Tale

Young Snowden "Snow" Reynaldi is brilliant, beautiful, and alone. Though he's shy, weird, and tolerated by the NorCal University students because he's a renowned whiz at chess and helps put the school on the map, that doesn't keep him from dreaming of the object of his desires: Riley Prince, championship quarterback.

When Riley needs a physics tutor, Snow jumps at the chance, and their relationship heats up—but Riley has to come out of the jock closet to get anywhere. Meanwhile, Snow's one true friend and mentor, Professor Kingsley, marries a woman who secretly wants the chess tournament glory and money for herself. Soon after, the professor collapses and Snow finds himself underwater—literally. In a car!

Seven frat brothers from Grimm College rescue Snow just in time for his life to get even worse, and Snow discovers the one relationship he always wanted slipping away. With evil looming at every turn, Snow must survive if only to prove he's the fairest of them all and regain the trust of his handsome prince.

www.dreamspinnerpress.com

THE ALOYSIUS TALES

SPELL CAT

TARA LAIN

An Aloysius Tale

When Killian Barth, history professor, meets Blaine Genneau, quantum physicist, they ignite their own big bang. But Killian can't pursue a physics professor—or a human. As the most powerful male witch in ten generations, Killian must bolster his dying race by reproducing—despite the fact that he's gay.

Even a fling with Blaine is out of the question, because Killian has been told sex with humans drains his power. But if that's true, why can young human Jimmy Janx dissolve spoons with the power of his mind? If Killian can sort through the lies he's been fed, he'll still face his biggest obstacle—convincing rational scientist Blaine to believe in magic.

With his ancient and powerful cat familiar, Aloysius, on his shoulder, Killian brings the lightning against deceit and greed to save Blaine from danger and prove love is the greatest power of them all.

www.dreamspinnerpress.com

DREAMSPUN DESIRES

Tara Lain

TAYLOR MAID

He'll marry the maid to get $50 million but a secret could queer the deal.

He'll marry the maid to get $50 million but a secret could queer the deal.

Taylor Fitzgerald needs a last-minute bride.

On the eve of his twenty-fifth birthday, the billionaire's son discovers that despite being gay, he must marry a woman before midnight or lose a fifty-million-dollar inheritance. So he hightails it to Las Vegas… where he meets the beautiful maid Ally May.

There's just one rather significant problem: Ally is actually Alessandro Macias, son of a tough Brazilian hotel magnate. But if Ally keeps pretending to be a girl for a little while longer, is there a chance they might discover this marriage is tailor-made?

www.dreamspinnerpress.com

CPSIA information can be obtained
at www.ICGtesting.com
Printed in the USA
BVHW070923091218
534986BV00042B/430/P